Godfire Book 1

Other Five Star Titles
by Tim Waggoner:

Necropolis

Godfire Book 1

The Orchard of Dreams

Tim Waggoner

Five Star • Waterville, Maine

First Edition
First Printing: July 2006

Published in 2006 in conjunction with Tekno Books and Ed Gorman.

Set in 11 pt. Plantin.

Printed in the United States on permanent paper.

Library of Congress Cataloging-in-Publication Data

Waggoner, Tim.
    Godfire : the orchard of dreams / by Tim Waggoner.—1st ed.
      p. cm.
    ISBN 1-59414-445-1 (hc : alk. paper)
    I. Title.
    PS3623.A354G34 2006
    813'.6—dc22   2006002672

To Dennis L. McKiernan—bard, mentor, and friend.

CHAPTER ONE

Something happened.

It wasn't so much thought as instinct, an awareness beyond words that came to Tarian from somewhere within the darkness that swaddled him. He mulled the feeling over for a few moments, mentally poking and prodding it, picking it up and shaking it, like an impatient child trying to determine what was inside a Harvest Feast bundle. But the more he tried to understand it, the more the sensation dribbled away until it was gone, and he wasn't sure if he had ever truly felt it in the first place. Disappointed and confused—and unable to think of anything better to do—Tarian decided to open his eyes. The simple action was harder than he anticipated, however, and it took him several attempts.

Leaves swayed above, the sky beyond was overcast and gray. But that was only to be expected, wasn't it? The rains weren't as common in the Secondmonth of summer as in the first, but they had been frequent enough this year. The ground beneath him was still damp from last night's—

Tarian realized then that he was lying on his back looking up at tree cover, wet grass soaking his shirt and pants. Anghrist's eyes, what was he doing on the ground? The only answer Tarian received was the rustle of leaves in the afternoon breeze, which wasn't especially helpful. He tried to recall what he had been doing before . . . whatever had happened, happened. Something about mushrooms. Yes, Phelan, Lowri and he had gone into the forest in search of some clapperbell mushrooms. They always grew

7

well in summer, especially after a good rain, and Lowri used them to make the best venison stew . . .

Lowri. Phelan. If something had happened to him, what of his wife and son?

Soldier's training took over. He rolled to his right, pushed himself up—cursing for perhaps the ten thousandth time the loss of his right arm—and got to his feet. He looked around quickly, didn't see his wife or son in the forest gloom. That in and of itself wasn't cause for alarm. The southern edge of the Greenmark was safe enough, else he never would have built a cabin there, and both Lowri and Phelan could take care of themselves. Though his memory was still foggy, he suspected that the three of them had chosen to split up in their search for mushrooms, perhaps make a game of it, see who could find the most in the shortest time. That sounded right. Lowri loved to play games, Phelan too, though Tarian could take them or leave them.

He called their names, waited a five count, called again. No answer.

Panic began to scratch at the inside of his belly, but he ignored it. Panic did nothing except get you killed, as he'd seen too many times on too many battlefields. Besides, the fact his wife and son hadn't answered his calls didn't necessarily mean anything. Sound traveled in strange ways in the forest, especially when the air was hot and damp, as today. And really, what did he think might have happened, that they too had been rendered unconscious? Most likely he was just coming down with something, perhaps another bout of blackworm fever. He'd had it on and off for years, ever since the siege at Ebben Cor. Most likely Lowri and Phelan were fine. Still, he couldn't shake the suspicion that something . . . *more* had happened; something a great deal worse than blackworm fever. And that it hadn't happened just to him.

He needed to find his wife and son. Now. First, though, he took a moment to assess his physical condition. As one of his former commanders, Jolgeir Grayheart, had always said, a soldier's first and best weapon was his body. Tarian felt somewhat shaky, a trifle lightheaded, but that was all. Still, he examined his clothes for bloodstains, ran a hand over his skull, just to be certain. He didn't seem to be wounded. The small stump, all that remained of his right arm, itched like mad, but it did that sometimes. He didn't bother to scratch it. Itching was merely a sensation, and sensations could be ignored.

He had a long knife sheathed in his belt, but that was it for weaponry. He had a cloth sack for gathering mushrooms that lay on the ground where he had evidently dropped it. From the way it bulged, it looked as if he had been doing well at the game before he had passed out. Since he had no clear idea where he was, he picked a direction at random, trusting to soldier's luck, and set off. He didn't bother to retrieve the sack, even though he knew Lowri would get after him for leaving it behind. But he didn't want to have to deal with even so slight an encumbrance, should he have to fight, and he could always retrieve it later.

He shuffled along as fast as he was able. The battle that had cost him his arm had also left him with limited use of his right leg, and he was incapable of running. The best he could manage was a sort of shuffle-hop that was only a little faster than walking. He mentally cursed his broken, battered body. Some weapon. He was only forty-three, but he might as well have been a graybeard of ninety-nine right then.

He called to his wife and son once more, but again, no

response. As he galumphed along, he realized something: he could hear no birdsong. Usually the forest was alive with it, but not now. It was as if whatever awful event that occurred had also affected the animals. Something was seriously wrong, he was sure of it now, and he gritted his teeth and struggled to make his old soldier's body obey him. And it seemed to listen. With every lurching step forward he took, his bad leg seemed to loosen a bit, become more limber, until soon he was running—truly running!—for the first time in almost two years.

He told himself that it was fear and excitement that allowed him to push his body past its normal limits and not feel the resulting pain. Tarian had experienced the same thing in battle often enough. He would no doubt pay for this later, but he didn't care. Right now all he wanted was to reach Lowri and Phelan.

The itching of his stump increased until it felt as if a nest of ants were crawling on his skin and gouging his flesh with their pincers. Itching became fiery pain, but still Tarian ignored it, ran even faster.

"Lowri! Phelan!"

He wasn't sure, but he thought he heard laughter. Dark, mocking.

Faster and faster, he ran. Sweat poured off him, dripped into his eyes, soaked his clothes. The humid summer air felt heavy in his lungs, and it soon became an effort to breathe.

Tarian's shirt had no right sleeve. At his behest, Lowri had cut the sleeve off—as she did to all his shirts—and sewed the remaining flap to the shoulder. But now the cloth felt tight against his stump, the pressure making the fiery itch even more maddening. With a growl of frustration, Tarian stopped, grabbed his shirt at the waist, pulled it over his head and hurled it to the ground. Then he reached up to scratch his stump—and paused.

A tiny hand with five tiny fingers had sprouted from what had been a puckered nub of flesh and bone. The hand's skin was smooth and pink as the flesh of a newborn baby.

Tarian stared, unable to believe what he was seeing, let alone understand it. During the time he had served in the army of King Rufin—first as a simple foot soldier and later as a commander—he had seen many strange and wondrous sights, had witnessed enchantments both fair and foul. But nothing like this. He concentrated and the tiny fingers wiggled in response. Tentatively, as if he were afraid they might break, he touched them with his left hand. The skin was tender, like the white flesh revealed when a sunburn peeled away. But his new fingers possessed sensation; with them, he could feel the rough skin of his left hand.

"Gods of Light and Darkness," he whispered. Then he examined his chest and belly. The crosshatch pattern of scars that he had worn on his flesh for so long was smaller now, less pronounced. What was happening was undeniable: he was healing, and at an astonishingly rapid rate. Did this have something to do with whatever had happened to make him lose consciousness? He felt certain it did, but what precisely, he—

A woman's scream cut through the humid summer air. Lowri!

Tarian forgot about the miracle that had somehow been worked upon his body. He turned in the direction that he judged the scream came from and started running. Along the way, without thinking about it, he drew his long knife with his left hand and gripped it tight. His new fingers flexed and wiggled, as if they too hungered for a weapon to hold.

11

He broke into a clearing and there, facing each other across a distance of seven yards, stood Lowri and Phelan. But they too had been changed, and Tarian prayed to Rudra that he hadn't woken up after all, that this instead was nothing more than a terrible dream from which he might, by the grace of the Most Divine, awaken at any moment.

Lowri's face and long blonde hair remained unaltered for the most part, save for a mouthful of sharp teeth that she bared at their son. She had torn off her dress; only a shred of blue cloth remained about her waist. Her skin was covered with patches of greenish gray scales that resembled those of a lizard, only hers appeared harder, less flexible, more like the substance of a turtle's shell. Her fingers and toes had lengthened into long hooked talons, and a short tail protruded from the base of her spine. It was difficult to tell from the way the tail thrashed the air, but Tarian thought it was growing longer.

The most striking feature was the pair of glistening bat-like wings sprouting from her shoulders. They remained folded against her body, sticky-wet, like those of a butterfly that had just emerged from its chrysalis. They were too small to bear her aloft as yet, but it appeared to Tarian that, like the tail, they were growing before his eyes. It seemed that whatever horrible transformation his wife was undergoing wasn't finished yet. The thought gave him a flicker of hope. If the change wasn't complete, perhaps it could somehow be stopped or reversed. They could go to Pendara, find a mage there . . .

He stepped into the clearing and started across the greensward toward his wife.

"Lowri, beloved, are you—"

With a swift inhuman motion she swiveled her head and

fixed Tarian with feral yellow eyes that blazed with madness and fury. She hissed and spit, a venomous snake preparing to strike.

Tarian stopped, released his grip on the long knife and let it fall to the ground. He raised his left hand in a placating gesture, his new fingers—large, stronger, a hint of wrist now—mirroring the movement.

He spoke softly, soothingly. "It's me, love. Tarian. Something terrible has—" He broke off as he got his first good look at Phelan. The lad's face was twisted in agony and his hands clawed at his chest. A dark muzzle with ebon teeth was emerging from Phelan's body, tearing its way through his white shirt as it struggled to be born. Phelan seemed to be trying to push the apparition back inside, or at the very least halt its progress. But his hands passed through the shadowy substance of the creature—a wolf, Tarian thought—without effect.

Tarian stood, frozen, numb with shock, unable to decide what to do next. All of his soldier's training and experience couldn't help him deal with this nightmare. Should he go to his wife, talk to her, try to reach the woman he knew lay behind those animal eyes and wicked teeth? Or should he rush to his son and help him fight to contain the beast that struggled to free itself from his body?

A thought whispered through his mind, then, one spoken in the voice of a cold wind passing over a corpse-laden battlefield. *Pick up the knife.* It was a soldier's thought, not a husband's or a father's. A sensible, practical thought. Perfectly reasonable, given the circumstances. Tarian even started to kneel, began to reach for the blade. But he stopped. He couldn't bring himself to brandish a weapon at either Lowri or Phelan.

It was then that Lowri chose to attack.

She ran toward him, foot talons tearing up chunks of grass and earth, clawed hands raised, fanged mouth open to emit an ear-splitting shriek. Her wings, definitely larger now, spread open behind her, unfurling to cup the air as she ran. Strands of blonde hair detached from her head as she came, as if her body were working to shrug off the last vestiges of humanity as fast as it could. Tarian watched his wife's hair drift down to the grass. Somehow, of all of this, it was the sight of her beautiful, long hair falling dead to the ground that hurt the most.

And then she was on him, raking his face, neck, chest with her claws. He fell beneath her assault, and she straddled him, tearing, clawing, digging with her talons. The pain was beyond anything Tarian had ever experienced, beyond even the agony of losing his arm. But as excruciating as it was, it paled next to the agony in his soul when he saw the dark joy in Lowri's eyes and heard her wicked laughter.

As the pain began to grow distant and shadows crept into the edge of his vision, he wished that he could have his wife back whole and sane, if only for a moment, so that he might be able to say good-bye to her. As the darkness closed in, he thought he heard the wild howl of a wolf.

CHAPTER TWO

Tarian woke to the mingled smells of hearthfire and bedstraw. A flickering orange glowed through the doorway of his and Lowri's small bedroom. He was mildly surprised that the fire was still going so strong. Usually they let it burn down at night.

He reached for Lowri, but didn't find her. That wasn't uncommon. She was a light sleeper and often rose during the night. Likely it was she who had stoked the fire, perhaps so she could do some mending. He pushed back the heavy quilt that covered him and struggled to sit up. Gods, he felt weak as a half-dead kitten! Had he taken ill while he slept? His chest and neck itched—probably time to change the straw in the mattress—and he reached to scratch. With his right arm.

He stopped, stared at a hand he had lost two years ago, turned it around, slowly wiggled the fingers, made a fist. It was real. Sweet Lord of Light, it was real!

Then, all at once, his memory returned. The clearing. Lowri. Phelan.

He jumped out of bed, nearly losing his balance and falling to the dirt floor in the process. But he managed to steady himself and, dressed in only a breechcloth, hurried into the cabin's main room. Phelan sat cross-legged before the fire, gazing into the dancing flames. His chest and feet were bare; his boots rested by the door, alongside his father's.

Tarian was struck afresh by how handsome his boy was.

15

Boy? At seventeen, he was a man, or near enough to make no difference. Lowri said that the son resembled the father at that age, though Tarian didn't see it. Phelan was leaner, gentler of aspect, his face smooth and free of beard. True, he had the same thick black hair, though he wore it only to his shoulders, not halfway to the waist, as his father did; plus he didn't have a liberal salting of gray amidst the black. He looked to Tarian more like a scholar or merchant than a grizzled old soldier, and that was just the way Tarian liked it. Soldiering was a hard, bitter life, and he was glad his son wasn't suited for it by body or temperament.

"She's out there, Father." Phelan spoke softly, without taking his gaze off the fire. His face was expressionless; he might well have been chatting about the weather for all the emotion he displayed. "I've heard her laughing, sometimes far away, sometimes close."

Tarian reflexively glanced toward the door, saw Phelan had barred it. Good lad.

Tarian understood what had happened to his son: battleshock. He didn't blame the boy. How often does one see his mother transformed into a demon before his eyes? Tarian stepped over to the fireplace and knelt next to Phelan. He restrained the urge to reach out and place a hand on his son's shoulder. One had to tread carefully when dealing with battleshock.

Tarian kept his tone neutral. "What happened after she attacked me?"

Phelan didn't respond at first, just kept looking into the fire. But after a few moments, he said, "The wolf drove her off. The shadow wolf, the thing that came out of me." He pressed his hand to his chest. "Out of here."

Tarian nodded as if Phelan's answer were the most normal thing in the world. "And then what happened?"

16

"The wolf came running and leaped toward me. At first I thought it was going to go for my throat. I threw up my hands to cover my face, and then I felt a cold sensation in my chest, as if I had just been splashed with freezing-cold water. When I opened my eyes, the wolf was gone. I realized then that it had returned from where it came." He tapped his chest. "It's inside here, Father. I can feel it. It's . . . sleeping now."

Tarian wasn't quite certain what to say. He had lived his life as a man of action, and words didn't always come easily to him. "Did the wolf harm your mother?"

Phelan shook his head. "It pulled her off you and they fought for a few moments, but it didn't look as if it were really trying to hurt her. Then she flew off."

"Did she . . . was her transformation finished when she left?"

Phelan nodded. "She didn't look like Mother at all. She was just some . . . *thing*."

There was a good chance the reason the shadow wolf hadn't harmed Lowri was that its teeth couldn't penetrate her newly scaled flesh. Still, there was no reason to let the boy know that. "The wolf saved me and didn't harm your mother. Whatever the shadow creature is, it came from inside you, and you have a good heart. I don't believe it would do anything that you wouldn't do."

Tarian had no way of knowing whether the shadow wolf was dangerous or not, but right now he only wanted to reassure his son. Phelan turned away from the fire to look at his father.

"Do you really think so?" His desperate need for hope—even just a little—was evident in his face and voice.

Tarian didn't hesitate. "I do." Now he did lay his hand on Phelan's shoulder, gave a squeeze. "You're a good man,

Son. Evil doesn't come from good men."

Tarian knew better, of course. Sometimes the worst evils came from people who thought they were doing good. But they were words Phelan needed to hear right now, and the lad smiled gratefully.

"What happened next?"

Phelan told how he had examined his father, sure that he would be dead, only to find him already healing. Tarian was too heavy to carry, so Phelan had made a travois out of fallen tree limbs—just as his father had taught. He used strips torn from his and Tarian's tattered shirts to bind the wood together. Then he had rolled Tarian onto to the travois and pulled him back to the cabin.

"I had to rest several times, and night fell before we made it home. But we did make it."

There was a trace of pride in Phelan's voice. Tarian felt more than a trace. In his own way, his son was a warrior too. "You did well, Phelan."

Phelan inclined his head to acknowledge the praise. "You had completely healed by then, and your new arm had grown out almost all the way. Looks like it finished while you slept."

Tarian examined his restored arm in the fire light. There was little hair on it yet, and the muscles lacked tone, but exercise would take care of that. He ran his hand along his chest and neck. The flesh was smooth. Not only had his old battle scars had faded, but the wounds left by Lowri's attack were gone as well.

Phelan hesitantly reached out and touched his father's new fingers. Tarian gripped his son's hand and held it tight.

"It's a miracle," Phelan whispered.

Tarian pictured Lowri, her wild demon eyes and fang-filled mouth.

Or a curse, he thought.

Tarian was ravenously hungry. Whatever magic had brought about his healing, it seemed that his body needed more fuel, more sustenance to fully restore its strength. Salted meat, fruits, nuts—he ate whatever he could find, washing it down with water Lowri had collected from the nearby stream this morning. Phelan refused to join his father. Not only because it seemed his father had greater need of the food, he said, but also because he wasn't hungry.

Tarian felt somewhat ashamed. Instead of gorging himself, he should have been trying to determine what had happened, working to come up with some sort of plan for getting Lowri back and reversing her transformation. But all he could think about was food.

Finally Tarian, while not completely sated, felt full enough to turn his attention to other matters. He and Phelan sat at the table, each with a clay mug of hot cider.

"What do you think happened?" Phelan asked.

"Whatever fell enchantment changed us likely occurred when we were rendered unconscious." They had earlier established that both of them—and presumably Lowri too—had passed out at the same moment. Neither he nor Phelan were certain exactly how long they had remained unconscious, but they agreed it couldn't have been more than a candlemark or so.

"Perhaps a wandering mage cast a spell on us," Phelan suggested. "As part of some experiment."

Tarian smiled. "You've read too many of those adventure stories your mother bought in Pendara. I'm no wizard, but I've seen one or two at work in my time. Magic doesn't operate like that. Mages can't work transformations on

19

people, no matter what the tales may say. They can only affect the elements of the land—make trees fall down, cause avalanches, that sort of thing."

"That may be how magic works in Athymar, but the Rendish wizards can command the Volucar, the giant hawks that inhabit the mountains of their land. That's a different sort of magery, isn't it?"

Tarian allowed as to how it was.

"Then perhaps what happened to us is a new sort of enchantment. One the land has never seen before."

Tarian nodded. He couldn't argue with that. "Whatever happened, it's beyond either of us. We need the help of a mage, and the only mages nearby are to be found in Pendara. Come dawn, we start out for the city."

Phelan cupped his cider in his hands, looked down into the mug as if it were some manner of scrying pool wherein answers to the most difficult of questions might be found. "We can't."

Tarian frowned. "Why not?"

"We can't leave Mother. We have to try to find her, talk to her, bring her back to her senses . . ."

"Magic changed her, Son," Tarian said gently. "Only magic can restore her."

"The enchantment changed her body, but her mind—"

"Has been changed too. Else why would she have attacked me?" And at the time, it had looked to Tarian as if she had been about to go after Phelan before he arrived at the clearing. But he didn't mention this. Why make the lad think any worse of his mother?

Phelan looked up from his mug, eyes narrowed, jaw tight. It was what Tarian had always thought of as the boy's "stubborn face." Tarian had seen it quite often over the last seventeen years.

"Maybe she was confused by her change. Once she's had time to get used to it—"

"She's had nearly half a day by this point. If her mind had cleared, she'd have returned by now."

They had heard eerie laughter once or twice since Tarian woke, but there hadn't been any now for some time.

"Then she's ashamed of what she's become, is afraid to show herself to us."

"Lowri knows we love her, Phelan, and she knows our love has nothing to do with the way she looks. If she were sane, she would be here now."

Phelan's grip tightened on his clay mug, and Tarian thought it might crack in the boy's hands. "What do you know about how Mother feels?" he accused. "How often have you been home in the last ten years? Before you lost your arm, that is. If we tried to reckon the amount of time you were here instead of off fighting in the King's latest campaign, I'd doubt the days would add up to more than a year altogether."

Tarian gritted his teeth and held his tongue. He told himself the lad was frightened by what had happened to them, that was all. But deep down, he knew it was more than that. Much more.

"We can't just leave her, Father. We can't!"

Tarian was silent for several moments before responding. "When I was only a bit older than you are now, my company tracked a band of Lukashen to the edge of the Twrch."

Phelan sneered, his lip curling in a manner that put Tarian in mind of a wolf's snarl. "This isn't time for one of your war stories, Father."

Tarian ignored him. "It was the Firstmonth of autumn, but it felt more like the height of summer. The air was so hot and humid, it sapped the life out of you. The Lukashen took refuge in the great swamp rather than fight us, and we—foolish youths that we were—followed.

"The going was difficult, but we eventually caught up to the Lukashen and engaged them in battle. The Twrch is a very difficult place to fight. The trees are thick, the ground uncertain, the air distorted by heat and clouded by mist. Two of us—myself and a man named Vladik—became separated from the rest of our company. We dispatched our foes, though not without some difficulty, and then attempted to rejoin our companions. We dared not call out to them for fear of alerting any surviving Lukashen, so we made our way as silently as we could. Bloodflies and leeches made a banquet out of us, and our flesh became scored by numerous encounters with sharp branches and thorns.

"And then it happened: I took a step and instead of my foot connecting with solid ground, it sank, pulling the rest of me with it."

Despite himself, Phelan seemed caught up in his father's tale. "Quicksand?"

"Perhaps. Or just mud. I was wearing mail armor and carrying a sword—which I immediately lost when I slipped—and I quickly sank up to my chest. Then my descent slowed, though I didn't stop sinking altogether. I assumed the muck now beneath my feet was somewhat thicker than that above, but I knew it would only slow my death, not prevent it.

"Vladik had been fortunate enough to tread on more solid ground, and now he bent down to try to pull me free, but the muck held me fast. Worse, our efforts seemed only to make me sink faster. After a few more moments attempting to pull me out, Vladik released me and rushed off without a word.

"I cursed him for deserting me, shouted that I hoped Anghrist would devour his soul. But soon I could shout no more, for it became difficult to breathe. I sank up to my neck, chin, mouth . . . finally the muck was lapping at the base of my nose when Vladik returned with the rest of the company. Working together, they were able to pull me free. When I could breathe normally again, I apologized to Vladik for doubting him. He shrugged it off, said he'd have probably shouted the same things in my place, and that was the end of it." Tarian sighed. "Vladik died six months later, helping stop the Lukashen and the Rendish from seizing control of the Golden Coast."

Tarian gazed into the embers of the dying fire for a bit. Then he asked, "Do you know why I told you that story?"

Phelan shook his head.

"Because I learned something from Vladik. I learned that sometimes you have to abandon someone before you can save them. I love your mother, Phelan, more than you'll ever know. The only thing that kept me going, that kept me alive all those years I wielded my sword for the King was the knowledge that she—and you—were here waiting for me. I love her so much that I am willing to leave her in the forest, no matter how hard it might be for me to do so, in order that I might go find help for her. Do you understand?"

Phelan considered, then nodded.

"Good." Tarian downed the rest of his cider, then took Phelan's and finished it off as well. He wiped his mouth with his fingers, then stood. "We should try to get what sleep we can before we leave."

"Father, do you think she's going to be all right out there?"

"Whatever your mother has become, she's very strong now. Frankly, I doubt there's anything in the Greenmark that could hurt her. So in a sense, she's quite safe. Whatever she is now will protect the woman she used to be, until such time as we can find a way to reverse what's happened to the three of us."

"Reverse what's happened to Mother and me," Phelan pointed out. "Your enchantment is a positive one."

"Perhaps." But Tarian knew enough of magic to know that a spell that might seem benign at first could easily turn out to be otherwise. "Come now, to bed with both of us. You should sleep next to me, just in case anything might happen."

Tarian wished he kept his sword and armor within the cabin instead of buried in a cloth-wrapped bundle out back. He was tempted to go dig it up right now, but the forest wasn't always the safest place at night. And now, with Lowri—or rather the wild demoness she had become—out there, it was even less so. Still, he had the long knife that Phelan had thought to retrieve before putting Tarian on the travois, so that was something. He would excavate his sword in the morning.

"No, Father, I think I should sleep in my own bed tonight." Phelan nodded toward his mattress on the dirt floor in a corner of the main room. "Just in case anything should happen."

Tarian understood; Phelan was worried the shadow wolf might appear again while he slept. A distance of a dozen feet wouldn't protect Tarian from the wolf should it emerge and choose to attack, but he saw no reason to tell Phelan that. Why worry him any more?

Tarian nodded and started toward the bedroom that he had shared with Lowri for nearly twenty years and which,

Rudra willing, he would soon share again.

"Father?"

Tarian paused.

"What if we aren't the only ones who changed?"

Tarian didn't know what to say to that. "Go to sleep, Son."

CHAPTER THREE

"Phelan, honey, can you hear me?"

Phelan struggled to open his eyes, but the lids were so heavy, and the darkness that called for him was so warm . . .

"Phelan—look at me!" The voice was harsher now, and accompanying it was a slapping sound. At first he didn't know what it was, but then he realized that whoever was speaking was also smacking his cheek, and none too gently, either. Irritated—and sensing that the speaker wouldn't leave him alone until he did what she said—he opened his eyes.

Dimly lit by the glow of candlelight, but illuminated clearly enough for the worry in her eyes to be visible— Phelan saw his mother looking down at him.

"How are you feeling?" The harshness was gone from her tone now; her voice held only love and concern.

Phelan frowned. He wasn't sure where he was or what was happening. His mother's face seemed different than the last time he'd seen her, younger and . . . *human*—the word whispered through his mind before drifting away like so much dandelion fluff in the wind.

"I'm . . . hot. Thirsty." His voice came out rough and dry, as if he hadn't spoken for some time.

Lowri's smile seemed strained, but she said, "I'll get you a drink." She stood and walked away from his bed then passed through the doorway.

Bed. He was lying down, with a woolen blanket pulled up to his chin, despite how hot he felt. He wanted to kick the blanket off but was too weak and weary to try. There was a small table next to his bed—he remembered helping his father build it—and atop it sat a small tallow candle. The candle was nearly burnt down to a nub, which meant he'd been lying here a long time. He wondered if Lowri had been kneeling at his bedside all the while the candle had been burning. Probably, he decided. He didn't wonder where his father was. Tarian was no doubt off somewhere, playing soldier for the King.

No, that's not right. He's sleeping in his room—his and Mother's. Tomorrow we're going to set out for Pendara and . . . and . . .

And what? He tried to keep hold of the thought and finish it, but it vanished like dew beneath a hot morning sun.

Lowri came back into the room, carrying a cup made from a gourd. She knelt next to him and brought the cup to his lips and slowly tilted it so he could drink. The water that passed over his dried, cracked lips was tepid, but Phelan didn't care. It tasted as fresh and cold as springwater to him. He began gulping the water, and before long Lowri pulled the cup away from him.

"That's enough for now. Drink too much too fast, and it'll just come right back up." She set the cup on the table next to the candle, then turned back to Phelan and lay her hand on his forehead.

"The fever hasn't broken yet, but I don't think it's as bad as it was," Lowri whispered softly, as if speaking to herself. She sometimes spoke like this when Tarian was away, as if she needed another adult to talk to, even if it was just herself.

"Fever?" Phelan didn't recall getting sick. He'd felt fine when he'd lain down to go to sleep. Physically fine, that is.

Lowri reached up and brushed her fingers through his sweat-matted hair. "You stumbled across a nest of spine-borers when you were out playing. You suffered a dozen or so stings, but I think the worst is over now."

Spine-borers? He'd been six the last time he'd been stung by the insects. He'd lain unconscious for four days and nearly died before slowly beginning to recover. The next time Tarian had returned home, he'd made a careful search of the woods surrounding their cabin and burned out every spine-borer nest he'd found. Since then Phelan hadn't seen any sign of the insects in this part of the Greenmark.

The memories came tumbling back in a rush then. Phelan remembered losing consciousness the same time as his father and mother had. Remembered what had happened to them . . . how they'd all been *changed.*

Lowri smiled at him, displaying a mouthful of sharp teeth.

"Still thirsty?" Her voice was guttural now. Inhuman. With fingers that were now scale-covered talons, she reached for the gourd-cup and brought it to his lips once more. Only now instead of water, the cup was filled with blood.

"No . . ." Phelan shook his head and tried to scoot away from the cup, but he was too weak to move.

"Not interested?" Lowri no longer resembled the mother he knew. She'd become the monstrous creature he remembered from earlier that day. "That's all right. I know someone who is."

She moved the cup until it was directly above his chest, then turned it over. Thick dark fluid poured out of the cup, but before it could splatter onto the blanket, there was a loud ripping sound and a black wolf's snout shoved through the tear in the fabric. The wolf opened its mouth and greedily lapped at the blood dribbling onto its muzzle.

And as the shadow wolf drank, Lowri cackled in dark glee.

Phelan sat up in bed. He was covered in sweat and shivering, but not from any fever.

God of Light, what an awful dream!

He feared that he might have cried out as he awakened, but if he had, Tarian must not have heard. The cabin was silent.

Phelan knew he should lie back down and try to get some sleep. He'd need his rest for the journey ahead, for Phelan intended to get to Pendara as swiftly as possible, so his father and he could find a wizard to help make Lowri human again. But he was wide awake now, and though he knew what he'd experienced had been only a nightmare— and it was only natural that he'd have bad dreams after what had happened this day—Phelan was disturbed nevertheless.

He got out of bed, used the chamber pot, and then quietly walked out of his room so as not to wake his father. Tarian needed his rest just as much as Phelan, but that wasn't the main reason the boy didn't want to rouse his father. He just felt like being alone right now.

He went outside and gently closed the door behind him. Though he was wearing only his breechcloth, he didn't feel self-conscious. He'd grown up in near isolation here in the Greenmark. What use was modesty when there was never anyone else but family around to see you?

The night air was cool on his bare flesh, and the breeze began drying his sweat. The moons were bright enough tonight to paint the clearing around the cabin with soft silver-white light, and insects and birds called to one another, seeking mates or prey, depending on their needs. Phelan felt no fear being outside alone at night. He'd spent his entire life in the Greenmark. Day or night, light or dark, this was his home.

He walked several yards from the cabin and sat down on the ground. He hugged his knees to his chest and looked up at the ebon sky above. There were no clouds to block his view of the stars, and not for the first time he gazed up at them and wondered what they were. Were they even now looking back down at him, and if so, what did they think of the change that had taken place in him since last they'd showed their faces in the night sky? Maybe they were too far away to care, Phelan thought. After all, how could mere worldly matters concern them as removed as they were up there in the heavens? Phelan envied them. How much simpler life would be if you were above it all, looking down, untouchable, safe.

He heard a rustling from the branches of a nearby tree, as if something were shifting its weight to get more comfortable. Something large.

He quickly turned to look in the direction of the sound and saw the silhouette of his mother framed by moonlight. Though he couldn't make out the expression on her face, he knew she was gazing down at him. He thought of his dream then, and a wave of sadness washed over him. He doubted Lowri now looked at him with the same love and concern he'd seen in her eyes when he'd been a child sick with spine-borer fever.

Phelan tensed, waiting to see if Lowri would attack. But all she did was chuckle.

"You have nothing to fear from me, Phelan. At least, not at this moment."

He wanted to believe her. After all, despite the hideous

transformation that had afflicted her, she was still his mother. But he felt a deep suspicion of her, so strong that it quickly edged over into rage. The fury took hold of him and he stepped forward, hands balled into fists, a low rumbling sound in his throat.

Lowri cackled. "It appears that your new friend doesn't like me, Phelan."

He stopped, confused. He felt the anger burning inside him, and yet at the same time, it seemed muted—as if it wasn't truly his but rather an echo of someone else's emotion.

The wolf's, he realized. The shadowy creature that now dwelled inside him didn't trust Lowri, was wary of her in the way that only one predator could be of another. And it was preparing to come forth and attack her if need be.

It's all right, it's just Mother. Phelan had no idea if he could communicate with the beast inside him, but the fury receded, though it didn't leave him entirely.

"You don't belong with your father," Lowri said. "Not anymore, not after what you've become. Leave with me, Phelan, right now. We'll run wild through the Greenmark, hunting and killing as we wish. We'll rule the forest, just the two of us. Mother and son."

There was a pleading note in her voice, and for a moment Lowri sounded like her former self, the mother that had loved and cared for Phelan since before his birth, who'd knelt at his beside for four days, seeing him through his bout of spine-borer fever.

But this creature wasn't his mother. Not only didn't she appear human, her earlier actions had made it abundantly clear that she no longer thought like one. She was an animal now, a monster, and a vicious one at that.

"I can't go with you, Mother." His voice came out

stronger than he expected, firm and resolute. "But I promise that I'll do everything I can to help you become your true self again."

Lowri stared at him for several moments, eyes gleaming in the moonlight. Then her scaled lips pulled back from pointed teeth in a sickening parody of a human smile.

"This *is* my truest self, Phelan. Just as the shadow wolf is yours."

With that, she launched herself from the tree, spread her wings, and came gliding straight at Phelan. He threw himself to the ground and felt the rushing wind of Lowri's passage as she flew over him. He rolled onto his side and looked up to watch the ebon shape that had once been his mother shrink as it soared away. And then Lowri was gone, as if the darkness had swallowed her.

Though she was lost to Phelan's sight, still he lay there for some time, gazing up at the night sky, as the stars looked back down at him, mute, distant, and uncaring.

CHAPTER FOUR

Tarian woke the next morning feeling physically better than he had in years. He hadn't realized how accustomed he had become to rising with a multitude of aches and pains until that dawn when he rolled out of bed, limbs lithe and limber, back silent and uncomplaining, neck and shoulder muscles loose and relaxed. He actually found himself humming an old marching tune as he walked into the main room of the cabin to check on Phelan. As soon as he realized what he was doing, however, he stopped humming. This was no time for such foolishness, not with Lowri changed and lost to them, perhaps forever unless they could find help.

Tarian stepped into the main room and found it empty, the door unbarred.

He felt a rush of fear. What if Phelan's battleshock had been worse than Tarian had first thought, and the boy had wandered off in a daze? Or what if, like Lowri, Phelan had lost his senses, overwhelmed by the enchantment that had transformed them?

He opened the door and stepped outside. He was wearing only a breechcloth, and he shivered when the morning air touched his flesh, though the sensation wasn't altogether unpleasant. The ground beneath his bare feet was dry, which was odd for this time of year. Come to think of it, they hadn't heard any rain at all last night. Tarian briefly wondered if the magic that had changed Lowri, Phelan and himself had done something to the weather as

well. A spell that powerful . . . . He decided he didn't want to think about that, not right now. First things first: he had to find Phelan.

He called his son's name.

"I'm down by the stream, Father!" came Phelan's reply. "Rinsing out the chamber pot!"

Tarian released a breath he hadn't realized he'd been holding. He considered going down to the stream and lecturing Phelan on leaving the cabin by himself when Lowri was still presumably somewhere in the vicinity. Not to mention Rudra only knew what other dangers might have been created by the spell that had altered them. He decided not to bother. Phelan wasn't particularly fond of being lectured to. Besides, the chore would be good for the lad, restore a sense of normalcy to him, even if only in a small way. Still, he waited outside until Phelan came walking up, clay chamberpot held upside down so it could drip-dry.

He gave his father a wan smile. It wasn't much, but any smile after last night was a good sign, Tarian thought.

"How did you sleep?" he asked.

Phelan shrugged. "Not too well. I had dreams . . ."

Tarian didn't have to ask what they'd been about.

"You should get dressed," Phelan said. He had on a new shirt and clean pair of trousers. "The sooner we get started, the sooner we'll reach Pendara." And, although he didn't say it, the implication was clear: and the sooner we'll get help for Lowri.

Tarian nodded. "Let me go wash up in the stream first." Though Phelan had done his best to clean his father after bringing him home yesterday, some dried blood still clung to his skin.

"I'll get the horse and wagon ready, then," Phelan offered.

Tarian knew he could make better time if he went alone. He would have no need of the wagon, could ride the horse himself. But that would mean leaving Phelan behind to deal with the thing his mother had become—not to mention whatever other dangers might now lurk within the Greenmark. Besides, the boy resented him enough as it was. Tarian knew Phelan would never forgive him if he kept the lad from coming along to seek help for his mother.

"Very well," Tarian said, "but keep the long knife with you. Just in case."

"What about you? Perhaps you should dig up your sword before you bathe."

Tarian smiled. "Spoken like a soldier. All right—sword first, bath second."

They walked around to the back of the cabin. They headed for the small barn—it was too crude to be called a stable—where they kept the only animal they owned: a scrawny piebald mare named Anci. Tarian was glad to see she was unharmed. He had been afraid that Lowri might attack the horse in the night out of hunger, sheer malice, or both. But the mare seemed fine.

While Phelan fed Anci her morning oats, Tarian went to the shelves where their gardening and woodworking tools were kept, and found a short-handled shovel that was a souvenir of his soldiering days. He then stepped outside the barn, walked six strides north, turned east, walked three strides, turned south, took two strides, and then bent down and began to dig.

There were many ways for a retired soldier to store weaponry. Tarian's own father, who had fought as a mercenary in the north for many years, had kept his sword above the mantle of their home for all to admire. Tarian had once received the thrashing of his life for taking the sword down

35

to play with when he was a child and accidentally nicking the blade on the stone hearth. Now, decades later, his buttocks still stung when he thought about it.

Others might conceal their weapons within a secret compartment in a wall or the floor, and some might simply keep their sword scabbarded and stored beneath the mattress for easy access. But Lowri wouldn't have any of this. She refused to have an "instrument of death," as she put it, anywhere inside their cabin.

So Tarian had oiled his sword well and wrapped it and his mail armor tightly within burlap and buried the bundle behind their home. Lowri had made it quite clear that she would have been happy if he had taken his gear to Pendara and sold it, but he refused. Not that he had wanted to save it for Phelan. He knew the boy would never be a soldier, and that was all right. Everyone had his own path in life to follow. No, Tarian had kept his gear because getting rid of it would've been like, well, like losing an arm. It was part of who he was.

As he worked, he became aware of birdsong filtering through the forest. Somewhat hushed and tentative, but it was present. *Good,* he thought, *at least some things are returning to normal.* His new arm had its full growth of hair now, and though it was thinner and weaker than his left, it moved easily and surely, and it grew stronger with each shovelful of earth he dug. Soon a light sheen of sweat covered Tarian's body; it felt good to be working with two whole arms again. Very good.

When Tarian judged he had dug far enough down, he set the shovel aside and began uncovering the remaining earth with his hands so as not to damage his gear. When he had removed enough soil, he was able to grasp two handfuls of burlap and pull the bundle free. It was heavier than he remembered, and his lower back gave a twinge of protest, but the pain vanished so quickly that Tarian wasn't certain he had truly felt it in the first place. He lay the bundle gently on the ground and began to undo the knots of twine that held it closed.

He had loosed the first knot when he became aware of a tingling on the back of his neck—a sensation he had felt far too many times as a soldier. Someone was watching him, a someone who most definitely wasn't Phelan. Tarian continued working on the knots, faster now. The birds had stopped singing.

"Father?" Phelan's voice sounded hollow, afraid.

Tarian assumed his son had come out of the barn, but he didn't glance back to confirm this. Instead, he looked up and there, crouching on a branch of a large oak tree, was Lowri.

Clawed toes gripped the tree limb, leathery wings were folded against her back. Her long tail hung down past the branch, swaying gently, as if it were a serpent possessed of life independent of its mistress. Her head was bald now, completely covered by lizard-scale, and she no longer had ears, just two tiny holes set into her skull. In her talons she gripped the wet, ragged remains of a gray squirrel. Her mouth was crimson with its blood.

"Don't let me stop you, Tarian. Go on with your work." Her voice was thick, guttural, more animal than human. But even so changed, it was still unmistakably Lowri's voice. Colder, crueler, mocking—but hers.

Tarian heard the soft rustle of grass as Phelan stepped closer. "Mother, are you—are you all right?"

Tarian wanted to warn his son to stay back, but he was afraid of doing anything that might spur Lowri to attack. He continued working on the knots, keeping one eye on Lowri as he did.

She brought the squirrel to her muzzle and tore a chunk of meat from its carcass. She threw back her head and gulped the morsel down, as if she were a bird. Then she looked down at them and licked her blood-flecked lips with a long black tongue.

"You always were such a considerate child, Phelan. I'm fine, thank you for asking. In fact, I'm better than I ever have been. Certainly I'm more beautiful, wouldn't you say?" She laughed, a harsh, raspy sound that set Anci to whickering nervously in the barn.

Tarian had loosed enough knots by then that he was able to open the bundle. He drew back a flap of cloth and exposed to the air—for the first time in two years—his sword Cathal, which meant battle-strong in the tongue of the hill people who had forged it.

"Go ahead, Tarian darling, pick it up," Lowri purred. "I'd love to see that new arm of yours in action."

Phelan's hand fell on his shoulder. "Don't, Father! It's—it's Mother!"

"It *was* your mother." Tarian reached for Cathal's hilt with fingers he had not possessed yesterday, wrapped them around the metal. And screamed.

A rush of images flashed through his mind. Faces of men and women—human, Lukashen, Dretchen—grimacing in pain, shrieking in agony as Cathal bit into their flesh, jarred against bone, slid through vital organs, set their blood free to rain upon the ground in endless crimson torrents. Hundreds of faces, hundreds upon hundreds. Tarian felt their pain as if it were his own, felt every wound he had ever visited upon a foe as if it had been inflicted upon his own body.

Phelan gripped Tarian's forearm and pulled his hand away from Cathal. The images ceased, and Tarian fell back onto the grass, breathing hard, body slick with sweat.

Lowri laughed. "What a shame, Tarian. You get your arm back, and now you can't stand to touch your sword. Tell me, what good is a warrior who can't grasp a weapon?"

Phelan helped his father to sit up. The pain—or rather, the memory of others' pain—was fading now, becoming a distant echo. He scowled up at the thing that his wife had become. "You speak as if you understand what just happened to me."

Lowri grinned, displaying bloodstained fangs. A small tuft of gray squirrel fur was stuck in her teeth. "I understand a great many things, Husband. My instincts have become much sharper since I was reborn."

"Then tell us, why have these changes occurred and what can we do to reverse them?" Tarian disliked the pleading tone of his voice, but he couldn't help it.

Lowri laughed again. "Why, it's very simple. The world has changed, as has our place within it. There is no going back. Hitch Anci to the wagon, ride to Pendara, seek out a mage if you wish. It will do you no good. No magic wrought by Man can undo what has been done. Even if it could, I would not return to the way I was. I am strong now, and free. I can do what I wish, when I wish. Why in Anghrist's dark name would I wish to return to being the weak, fettered woman that I was?"

"You were not weak," Tarian said, his voice hardly more than a whisper. "You were stronger than a legion of soldiers, and more beautiful than all the sunrises since the dawn of time. And inside, somewhere, you still are."

Lowri cocked her head like a bird, blinked several times. Finally she threw the squirrel's carcass at them. It landed with a wet thud at Tarian's feet.

"Words!" she spat. "Might as well be a pig's grunting for

all they mean to me now!"

She launched herself from the tree branch, spread her leathery wings, and sailed over Tarian and Phelan, reaching out with one claw to nick Tarian's cheek as she passed. Then Lowri arced upward and soared above the treetops until she was lost to sight.

Tarian wiped away the thin line of blood that trickled down his cheek. The small cut was already healed.

"What can we do, Father?" Phelan said, sounding like a lost little boy instead of the young man he was.

Tarian knew just how his son felt, but he also knew he had to be strong, not only for Phelan and himself, but also for Lowri. He rose to his feet, took a deep breath, and fought back tears. When he spoke, his voice was strong and sure.

"The only thing we can do: we go to Pendara."

Tarian bathed and dressed in a dark green tunic and brown leggings, while Phelan decided to keep wearing his more simple outfit of shirt and trousers. They packed an extra set of clothes apiece, and brought bedrolls and raincloaks, though the latter seemed unnecessary, as the sky was unseasonably clear that day. They brought bread, cheese, nuts, several apples and full waterskins. Tarian would've preferred wine, but they didn't have any. Perhaps they could obtain some at an inn along the way. Not that they could afford to indulge much. The bag of coins Tarian had secreted beneath the wagon's seat held more copper than silver or gold.

Tarian couldn't bring himself to touch his weapons, so Phelan had to pack Cathal and the long knife. Tarian decided to leave his armor behind. Anci had enough weight to pull as it was, and what was the point in bringing armor if he couldn't bear contact with his sword?

By noon, they were ready to depart.

As they settled into the wagon, Tarian asked Phelan, "Do you need to relieve yourself before we go?"

Phelan laughed. "Father, I'm not a child anymore. I can take care of such necessities without reminders, thank you very much."

Tarian smiled. "Yes, I suppose you can." And then he realized: he himself hadn't needed to make water or pass soil this morning, and he still didn't. He felt a sudden chill. Perhaps Lowri wasn't the only one in the family who was no longer quite human.

Tarian grasped the reins and gave them a gentle shake. "Let's go, Anci."

The mare began to pull and with a creak of turning wheels, they were off. As the wagon rolled forward, Phelan asked, "Father, what do you think Mother meant when she said that the world had changed, along with our place within it?"

"I don't know. I suppose we'll find out soon enough." But Tarian had a strong suspicion that whatever change had overtaken the land, it was not, to put it mildly, a change for the better.

CHAPTER FIVE

Normally, the journey from their cabin in the Greenmark to the city of Pendara took five days by wagon on the Southern Road. But Phelan insisted they push Anci harder, give her rest less often, force her to continue pulling the wagon even after sundown. Tarian guessed that such efforts would only save them a day, if that, but Phelan said if they could get help to Lowri even an hour earlier than they might have otherwise, it was worth it.

So they pushed poor Anci, who valiantly tried her best to accede to her masters' wishes, but by the end of the third day, she was so weary that Tarian called a halt well before sundown.

"Father, we must keep going!" Phelan protested.

Tarian climbed down from the wagon and began undoing Anci's harness. He could feel the mare's pain as if it were his own. "Look at her, Son. If we force her to work any more this day, she'll drop from exhaustion, and there's a chance her old heart will give out."

Phelan didn't look happy, but he didn't say anything more.

Tarian finished freeing Anci and the mare clopped slowly forward and began nibbling grass. They had stopped on the edge of a field, near a copse of trees. Not the best place to make camp for the night; it was a bit too exposed for Tarian's tastes, but he supposed it would have to do.

"Father," Phelan said, "if Anci can't keep up the pace, then perhaps we should get another horse."

Tarian turned to Phelan. "And where would we purchase this horse?"

"The village of Emlyn. It's only ten miles or so from this point. Surely someone there would be willing to sell us a horse."

"Perhaps. But what if Anci dies before we reach the village? By the time we walk there, buy a new steed and return to where we left the wagon, we'll have lost all the time we've saved so far, perhaps more."

Phelan scowled, but he didn't say anything.

Tarian suppressed a smile. It hadn't been that long ago when he was a young soldier with such lessons to learn. And he hadn't been any happier about learning them, either. "Come down and help me push the wagon away from the road."

Phelan disembarked and did as his father asked, although he was obviously unhappy about it. Together, they moved the wagon closer to the trees.

"This should do it," Tarian said. "If we cut some underbrush for cover and drape it about the wagon, I doubt anyone passing along the road tonight will notice it."

"Do we really need to take such precautions?" Phelan asked.

"How many riders have we seen since we left home?"

Phelan thought. "About a half dozen, four riding north, two south. But some were clearly the King's riders. They pose no threat."

"Perhaps. But the other riders weren't so clearly identifiable. They could just as easily have been bandits as anything else."

"If they were bandits, then why didn't they stop to rob us?" Phelan pointed out.

"I said they *might* have been bandits. It's best not to take any chances. It won't take long to conceal our wagon, and the effort could save our lives."

Phelan considered. "Why don't we move the wagon even closer to the trees then?"

Tarian shook his head. "Until we know more about what the Change has done to the land, I'd rather not camp too close to woods."

None of the riders they had seen—King's men or not—had stopped to exchange news with them. Tarian took this as a bad sign. It meant that the current situation in the kingdom was so serious that no one had time to stop and gossip. But Phelan and he had managed to glean some scraps of information since leaving the Greenmark.

They now knew that the enchantment that had befallen them and Lowri—which they had come to refer to as the Change—had also overtaken others. Toward the end of their first day on the road, they came across an old man wandering aimlessly in a field. When Tarian called out to him, the old man looked at them and opened his mouth as if to reply. But instead of sound, out poured a rainbow of color that drifted on the air for a few moments before dispersing like mist.

Tarian stopped the wagon, intending to go talk to the old man, but when the graybeard saw what Tarian had in mind, he fled in terror. Perhaps, Tarian assumed, because he feared whatever the Change might have done to them.

On the second morning, they encountered their first rider. It was a young woman, in her early twenties, Tarian judged, though it was difficult to tell since she rode past them at a full gallop. She wore a white tabard upon which was sewn a stylized yellow sunburst, the symbol of Rudra, God of Light. Below the sunburst was a golden crown. Together, the two symbols marked the woman as a servant of

44

King Rufin. Tarian recognized the emblem well; he had worn a similar one during his time in the King's army.

"Ho, the rider!" he called out as she drew near, an old soldier's hail. But she didn't slow down, didn't even so much as look at them. As she thundered past, they saw that instead of hair, tendrils of crimson flame trailed from her skull. Her eyes burned the same color.

And then she was gone.

Some riders that passed them appeared completely normal, but others had obviously been affected by the Change. One rider, a youth not much older than Phelan, had been covered with short brown fur, while a second man sported what looked like gray feathers. A woman had an extra arm jutting from between her shoulder blades. The limb was tied down to keep it from flopping awkwardly as she rode.

They had encountered the most disturbing evidence of the Change just before noon of this day, when Tarian and Phelan reached the village of Gudrun. It was a small settlement, consisting mostly of shopkeepers who sold the wares of nearby farmers to traders bound for Pendara. On the few trips they had made to the city as a family, Lowri always insisted they stop at Gudrun to buy lush red apples and a wheel of crumbly cheese, the latter far too sharp for Tarian's taste.

But when Tarian and Phelan entered the village, they found it deserted. Not a man, woman, child or animal remained. There were no signs of foul play or struggle—all that had lived in the village were simply gone.

Tarian and Phelan didn't tarry long in the empty village.

Phelan got a small hatchet from the wagon and went into the copse of trees—"Not too far," Tarian warned—to gather some brush to conceal the wagon. Tarian would've

45

have done it, though his stomach turned whenever he held the hatchet. Still, it wasn't as bad as his reaction to touching Cathal or, to a lesser degree, the long knife. He had tried to handle both several times during their journey, and each time he experienced the same horrifying result as he had in Lowri's presence. Whatever the Change had done to Tarian to allow him to heal so swiftly, it had also instilled within him a strong aversion to physical contact with instruments of death.

So as Phelan scrounged for camouflage, Tarian rubbed down Anci and gave her some water, but not too much, since their supply was running low. Normally, he would have refilled their waterskins from Gudrun's well, but after finding the village deserted, Tarian didn't trust the water to be safe, so they had made do with what they had. If he remembered right, there was a stream not too many miles down the road. They could resupply there tomorrow.

Phelan brought back an armful of tree limbs with the leaves still on them, and two small bushes. Tarian had him set them down on the far side of the wagon. There was no point in trying to hide the wagon before sunset. Without the cloak of darkness, their efforts at disguise would just look foolish and draw even more attention.

Tarian drove a stick into the ground on the other side of the wagon, and then tethered Anci to the makeshift stake. Hopefully, the camouflaged wagon would help conceal her during the night. Then Phelan and he sat down to a supper of bread, cheese, dried fruit, and water. Tarian's stomach felt like a vast, empty pit before they began, and if anything, it felt even emptier when they finished. He was glad he hadn't needed to do any healing since they set out, else he would likely have been ravenous.

Tarian tried to draw Phelan into conversation about the

strange weather—they hadn't felt so much as a drop of rain since setting out—but Phelan only grunted in response to his father's attempts, and eventually Tarian gave up. The lad had become increasingly illtempered and withdrawn the farther away they traveled from home. Tarian reckoned it was a mixture of concern for Lowri and brooding over the shadow wolf that presumably still dwelled within Phelan's breast, though thankfully the beast hadn't made another appearance since the day of the Change.

Once, years ago, Tarian had led a squadron against a group of desert Reavers who had captured the city of Halima. After they had driven the Reavers off into the shifting sands of the Kjartan, they stayed on in the city for several weeks until order could be restored. Halima was an ancient city, full of wonders, not the least of which was its menagerie, said to be the finest in all of Athymar, perhaps even in all the Nine Known Lands.

Tarian had spent many an off-duty hour observing the strange and wonderful creatures in the menagerie. One of his favorites had been the sandtiger, a tan-furred beast of unworldly grace and power that had constantly paced back and forth behind the bars of its cage, as if endlessly searching for a way out.

That's what Phelan put him in the mind of now: a restless, barely contained sandtiger. Or perhaps it wasn't Phelan he was seeing so much as the ebon beast within him, a wild dark thing which paced irritably within the cage of flesh that imprisoned it.

After supper, Phelan continued to brood while Tarian did a series of push-ups to help strengthen his right arm—a poor substitute for the sword drills he was incapable of performing. Tarian was just finishing his second set of fifty when they heard the sound of approaching horses.

He stood and wiped a light sheen of sweat from his fore-head. Phelan stepped to his side, and together they looked south, the direction the riders—for Tarian judged there were at least two—came from.

"Should I get Cathal, Father?"

Tarian knew Phelan wasn't offering to bring him the sword, since he couldn't bear to touch it. The boy was instead asking if he should arm himself. While Phelan was no warrior, Tarian had instructed him from time to time on the basics of swordcraft when he was younger, during Tarian's rare visits home. But the lad hadn't handled a sword in at least five years. He'd be just as likely to injure himself as he would an opponent.

"No, but why don't you get the long knife?"

Phelan looked as if he might argue, but then he nodded curtly and hurried to the wagon to retrieve the blade. By the time he returned to his father's side, the long knife gripped in his right hand, a pair of riders hove into view.

Tarian knew from experience that first impressions could sometimes make all the difference in whether or not a soldier had to fight. If a warrior looked dangerous enough, a potential opponent might think twice about engaging in battle. Tarian drew himself straighter, placed his feet farther apart, held his arms away from his body, hands relaxed—not quite a fighting stance, but close. He furrowed his brow, narrowed his eyes, tightened his lips, and concentrated on projecting an image of a man who would just as soon slide a blade between someone's ribs as look at them.

"Perhaps they'll pass on by like the others," Phelan whispered.

But the riders slowed as they drew near.

Tarian sized them up with a practiced eye. Two men, both in their late twenties, both sporting curly black hair

and beards—brothers, or perhaps cousins—one a bit shorter
and heavier than the other, though not by much. Both wore
rapiers at their sides and daggers sheathed at their thighs.
By the way they wore their weapons, Tarian knew the heavy
one was left-handed, the other right-handed. They wore ill-
fitting jackets trimmed with elaborate gold brocade: the
heavy one's jacket was purple, the other's yellow, and both
were clean and new-looking. The jackets struck Tarian as
the sort of foppery a Pendaran merchant might wear. But
the riders' trousers, which fit them much better than their
jackets, were of a simple style, cut from brown cloth, and
their boots were worn and scuffed.

Their horses—a black mare and a tan gelding, Tarian
guessed—seemed fresh and in good health, the saddles they
wore polished and quite expensive. Tarian himself had
never sat upon anything so fine.

Merchant-style jackets that were too new and which
didn't fit; saddles and horses which hadn't seen much use
and which undoubtedly cost more than these men could afford. It all added up to one unmistakable conclusion: bandits.

Tarian's right hand itched for a sword, but the thought
made his stomach churn, so he focused instead on examining the bandits for signs of the Change. Physically, they
appeared perfectly normal, but Tarian knew that meant
nothing. After all, neither he nor Phelan displayed any outward signs of the changes they had undergone.

The two men reined their horses to a stop, and the
slightly thinner one smiled.

"Good day to you, travelers. Or perhaps I should good
evening, for dusk will soon be upon us, eh?"

The man's accent, though mild, was unmistakably that
of the Black Coast. A wild, lawless part of the land, fre-

quented by bandits and pirates, both Athymarian and Rendish.

Tarian inclined his head, but said nothing.

"Father and son be you?" the thin one asked. "I note a resemblance."

Tarian nodded again. "And the two of you are cousins, or perhaps brothers."

Both riders grinned. "You have the right of it," the stockier one said. "I'm Brak and this is my brother, Drem. We're free traders, just come from Pendara."

Free traders. It was possible, Tarian mused. He glanced at their saddlebags, which were full to bulging. Perhaps with wares, but also, perhaps, with booty.

"Traders of what?" Tarian asked evenly.

The thinner one—Drem—shrugged. "Oh, a little of this, a little of that."

Brak nodded. "Last season it was luster shells. They're common enough in Pendara, but quite a novelty elsewhere in the land. Fetch a good price, too."

Drem scowled. "But that was before this winter's hurricane. The storm stirred up the ocean floor so much that the light crabs—skittish creatures that they are—retreated to the deeps for safety. Who knows when they'll return?"

"Or if they'll return," Brak added gloomily.

"In the meantime, we've been forced to seek, ah, alternative methods of making a living."

Tarian was about to reply, when Phelan stepped forward and brandished the long knife. "Enough of this talk! Are you bandits or are you not?"

Tarian was shocked. Phelan was normally a quiet, gentle lad, not rash and combative. This was completely out of character for him. Perhaps his aggression was merely a cover for the fear he felt. Whatever Phelan's reason for confronting Drem and Brak, Tarian had wished the boy had held his tongue. As long as the two men were talking, they weren't a threat. And if they talked long enough, perhaps they would provide some information on the current situation in Pendara. But Phelan's provocation had ruined the chances of that.

The two brothers looked at each other, as if conferring silently. They seemed to reach a conclusion and dismounted.

"'Bandit' is such an unpleasant term," Drem said as he drew his rapier.

"We prefer to think of ourselves as gentlemen who are making the best of a bad situation," Brak added as he took his own weapon in hand.

Together, they walked into the field, heading for Tarian and Phelan.

Drem's eyes seemed to flash with an inner light. "I'd appreciate it very much if you both would remain completely still."

Tarian suddenly felt as if iron bands bound his body. He couldn't move his arms or his legs, couldn't turn his head, couldn't even open his mouth. All he could do was blink his eyes and breathe through his nose. He tried to glance at Phelan to see if he was similarly affected, but he couldn't move his eyes. He could only assume that his son had also been rendered motionless.

"Be grateful that my brother has had a few days to practice his newfound ability," Brak said. "The first person he tried it on stopped breathing. For good."

"An unfortunate part of my learning process, I'll admit," Drem said. "But I've gotten much better, as you can see." When they reached Tarian and Phelan, the brothers sheathed their rapiers and patted down their captives. He

51

turned to his brother. "Anything?"

Brak shook his head. Then he peered intently at them, first Phelan, then Tarian. "What do you think the Great Enchantment has done to these two?"

Drem shrugged. "Who can tell? For that matter, who cares? If either of them could break my spell, he'd have done so by now. They'll remain immobile while we go about our work, and afterward we'll question them. Perhaps they'll be able to point us in the direction of more booty. But if not . . ." He trailed off, grinning. "Come, let's check the wagon."

The brothers walked out of Tarian's line of sight, and he listened as they reached the wagon and began rummaging through it. It was clear that once Drem and Brak had gotten what they wanted, they would slay Phelan and him, either by Drem commanding them to die or simply by slitting their throats as they stood motionless, unable to defend themselves.

"Here, now! Take a look at this sword!" Brak said. "This should fetch a pretty copper or two."

"Take it. And look what I've found." The sound of jingling coin. Drem had discovered their money.

Brak sniffed. "Doesn't look like much."

"So? Coin is coin, isn't it?"

"True enough, I suppose. Let's see what else they have."

Tarian was filled with helpless fury as he listened to the two bandits go about their work. He struggled to throw off the spell that bound his muscles, concentrated on mustering his healing magic in the hope that it would somehow nullify Drem's enchantment, but nothing happened. He was still unable to move.

As a soldier, Tarian had experienced his share of losses, though thankfully never the ultimate defeat of death. But to be taken without even a struggle, without even a chance to put up a fight . . . it was infuriating!

"That's it, I think," Brak said. "Just the sword and the money. Their horse certainly isn't worth anything."

"Don't sound so disappointed. It's not a bad haul for a few moments' work, is it?"

"I guess not. Let's go take care of those two and be on our way. Might as well take their food, too. Wouldn't want it going to waste, would we?"

Tarian wished he could speak to Phelan one last time, tell his son that he loved him. Even to be able to look in the lad's eyes would be enough. He fought with all his will to turn his head, but he couldn't move even the merest fraction of an inch. They would die side by side, but in a sense, alone, for they would not be able to say farewell.

The sound of boots shsshing through grass indicated Drem and Brak's approach.

The two brothers stepped in front of Tarian and Phelan. They set down the cloth-wrapped sword, the bag of money, and bundle of food they'd liberated from the wagon. They then drew their daggers.

"We really were free traders," Drem said, almost apologetically. "If the light crabs hadn't gone away, perhaps we still would be."

"Then again, perhaps not," Brak said, grinning. "The Great Enchantment has changed everything. Besides, this is much easier work."

"True," Drem said, grinning as well. "And much more profitable, too. Which one first, do you think? The father or the son?"

"Oh, I don't know. Why don't we just do them both at the same time?"

"All right. On the count of three. One, two—"

But before Drem could reach three, an ebon shape slammed into his brother and knocked him to the ground. Brak shrieked as the shadow wolf clamped its jaws around his throat. Whether from pain, surprise, or both, Brak released his grip on the dagger and the weapon fell to the grass. Tendrils of greenish mist burst forth from Brak's fingertips and began to encircle the wolf's shadowy form. But whether they would've had any effect on the creature was destined to remain forever unknown, for with a quick twist of its head, the wolf tore out Brak's throat in a spray of blood. With their creator mortally wounded, the tendrils simply vanished.

If Tarian hadn't been bound by Drem's spell, he would have cried out in agony. His own throat felt as if it had been savaged by the shadow wolf's night-black fangs. As if his own blood were gushing forth from the ragged ruin of his neck. He experienced an overwhelming urge to go to Brak, to kneel at the bandit's side and take his hand. It was a need more powerful than any Tarian had ever experienced before: stronger than hunger or thirst, more maddening than lust or battle fever. But Drem's enchantment held him fast where he stood, and all he could do was watch as Brak died.

Drem's face was ashen. His mouth worked, as if he were trying to speak, perhaps issue a command such as that which had bound Tarian and Phelan. But nothing came out. The shadow wolf turned toward Drem, his brother's blood dripping from the beast's black muzzle. The wolf started forward, growling low in its throat.

Drem found his voice at last and shouted, "Stop, wolf! I command you!"

The animal kept coming.

Drem took a step back, too another. "S-stop, damn you! STOP!"

The wolf continued forward.

With a cry of fear, Drem hurled his dagger at the lupine apparition, but the bandit was either too afraid to throw straight or else he lacked training, for the blade went wild. Tarian couldn't turn his head to follow the dagger's trajectory, but he heard it strike flesh, heard Phelan take in a sharp breath, heard the dagger fall to the ground with a metallic thud.

As with Brak, Tarian experienced Phelan's pain as his own. Fire blossomed in his left shoulder, and he could feel blood welling forth from a phantom wound. Now, more than anything, he needed to go to Phelan, to grasp his son's hand. But he still could not move.

Drem could, though. He turned and ran as if every demon in Damaranth were in pursuit, which in a way, Tarian thought, wasn't that far from the truth.

The shadow wolf brought the bandit down before he had taken five steps. Tarian felt the man's pain, but it didn't last long. And with Drem's death, Tarian and Phelan were freed.

Phelan gasped and fell to the ground. Tarian rushed to his son and took his hand. A jolt ran through Tarian's entire body, a tingling sensation as if vast power surged through his veins. Phelan stiffened, gripped Tarian's hand tight, clenched his teeth.

And then the sensation faded. But still Tarian held on to his son's hand.

Sweat rolled down Phelan's face, but his breathing was relaxed, even. "The pain is gone, Father." He pulled his hand free from Tarian's, reached over to touch his bloody shoulder. Then he reached under his collar to touch the flesh itself.

His eyes widened. "I feel blood but . . . there's no wound!"

Tarian didn't have to check for himself. He knew Phelan was healed. Knew it to the very depths of his soul. He smiled. It seemed his powers were good for more than just regrowing his lost arm; they could be extended to heal others as well.

Phelan looked past Tarian, an expression of wonder and puzzlement on his face. Tarian turned just in time to see a fist-sized ball of white light rise upward from Brak's chest. It hovered over his body for a moment, then winked out of existence.

Father and son looked to Drem. The dead bandit lay face down in the grass, the shadow wolf standing off to one side. A second orb rose from Drem's corpse, but where his brother's had glowed white, his was a glossy black, as if made of highly polished obsidian. It too hovered for an instant before disappearing.

"Did we just . . . see their spirits leave their bodies?" Phelan asked in a hushed voice.

"I doubt it. I've seen many men die, but this is the first time I've witnessed anything like this. My guess is that those whatever-they-were have something to do with the Change, but what, I don't know."

Tarian helped Phelan to stand. They then turned to the shadow wolf, which remained standing near Drem's remains. The wolf regarded them impassively for a moment, then began loping toward Phelan. Tarian stepped in front of his son to protect him, though he wasn't certain what, if anything, he could do to stop the ebon beast.

Phelan pushed Tarian aside. "It's all right, Father." Phelan's voice was dreamy, as if he were in shock. "It just wants to come home."

The wolf continued toward Phelan, picking up speed. As it neared, the creature leaped into the air and struck the lad's chest. But instead of knocking Phelan back, the wolf sank into his chest, merging with its host once more. When it was gone, Phelan touched his chest, an expression of mingled awe and fear on his face. Then he looked up, saw the corpses of the two bandits, and suddenly went pale at the sight of what the monster within him had done.

"We should hitch up Anci and move a ways down the road," Tarian said. What was left of the bodies would soon draw predators, though he wasn't about to tell Phelan that, not right now. Without another word, he took Phelan by the elbow and led him toward the wagon.

CHAPTER SIX

"What is the Church's position on this—foul—enchantment?"

The Queen's head lolled forward and for a moment, Cynric thought she might fall out of the large oak chair. Alarmed, he rose from his own chair and reached for her, but Cambria gripped the armrests with thin, pale fingers and through what looked like an act of sheer will, kept her seat.

She smiled thinly at Cynric from the other side of a highly polished mahogany desk, her eyes half lidded, as if she struggled against sleep. "Our thanks, Master Wizard, for your concern. Perhaps we should be bound to the chair like a senile old woman so that we might stay aright."

Cynric sat back down. He wasn't certain whether Cambria was joking or not. The Queen could display a morbid sense of humor upon occasion, and Rudra knew there had been ample reason for her to fall back upon it these last few days.

He glanced at Saeth, who sat beside him. She was younger than Cynric by several decades, in her late thirties, perhaps early forties. Her shaven head and lack of eyebrows—a sign of devotion to Rudra—made judging her true age difficult. She gave him a sideways glance and an almost imperceptible shrug, as if to say, I don't know how much longer she can hold on.

Cambria smiled dreamily, the result, Cynric feared, of the various herbals that coursed through her veins. Who knew how many drugs and in what combination the Royal Physic had prescribed for her?

"You needn't bother with trying to hide your thoughts, you know. I can hear them as clearly as a trumpet blast."

Saeth reddened and smoothed the front of her ivory robe of office, a gesture Cynric had come to recognize as one of embarrassment.

"My apologies, Majesty." Saeth's voice was tight, her words clipped. Whenever she spoke, it sounded to Cynric as if the sound had to struggle to squeeze its way through her perpetually pursed lips. "We have yet to become accustomed to your . . . new gift."

"Gift?" Cambria turned and gazed into the flickering flames in the fireplace. The burning logs washed the royal map room in warm orange light, casting liquid, shifting shadows upon the shelves full of scrolls and rolled parchment which covered the walls from floor to ceiling. "I suppose some might use that word. I, for one, would not."

Three days. Ever since the moment of what people in the street had come to call the Change, Cambria's mind had been opened to the thoughts of those around her. At first, she could only read the minds of those nearby, but as time passed, her range increased until now she could sense thoughts as far away as a quarter mile in any direction. And she was unable to shut them out.

Gift? No, a curse was more like it. The mystical training Cynric had received from the Eyslken that allowed him to Shape hadn't included instruction in telepathy. As far as Cynric had been concerned, such mental abilities, while perhaps possible, were primarily claimed by fakers and confidence men and were in truth nothing but parlor tricks designed to separate gullible people from their coin.

But that was before the Change. Cynric tried to imagine

what it must be like for Cambria to constantly hear the thoughts of those around her, as if she were in the midst of a conversation consisting of hundreds of people all talking at once in their loudest voices.

The Queen looked at the wizard. "It's like trying to hold the ocean inside my head."

Saeth frowned, confused, but she didn't ask for clarification. They were all becoming used to their Queen speaking what sounded like non sequiturs to those who couldn't read minds.

"It's been better since you suggested we have the palace cleared of all but the most essential staff," Cambria said. "And even better still since you had the city guard cordon off several blocks around the palace and ask our subjects to vacate the area. What was before a near deafening assault upon my mind has become mere whispers that tickle at the edge of my awareness. Our thanks to you, Wizard."

Cynric inclined his head. "I wish, though, that your Majesty would reconsider taking the Royal Physic's potions. The medicines he has prescribed are obviously quite strong and cause serious strain to your system."

"Be thankful we didn't allow the old leech to bleed us as he wished. We need his potions, though, else we would not able to withstand close contact with anyone." Her voice grew hushed. "Your thoughts are like screams in my ears."

Cambria shuddered and hugged herself, looking more like a lost little girl than a woman in her prime, wife of a King and mother to a Prince and Princess. And was she losing weight? Cynric thought so. Her light blue gown—tailored as all her clothes were—hung loose upon her. The skin beneath her eyes was dark and puffy, the eyes themselves bloodshot. Her blonde hair, usually so lustrous, seemed limp and dull as straw. Had she slept at all in the last three days? Cynric feared not. How long could she go on like this before her newfound curse, along with the Physic's noxious brews, took their toll?

"How long indeed?" Cambria whispered. She closed her eyes and for a moment, Cynric thought she had drifted off to sleep but then, without opening her eyes, she said, "Now, Priestess, to return to our earlier question, for which we still await an answer. What does the Church have to say about this enchantment which has befallen us?"

Saeth sat up straighter and cleared her throat. She was an assistant to a High Priest, a mid-level functionary in the Church hierarchy who normally would never have been consulted by the Queen. But since her superiors had accompanied King Rufin on his journey to Heart's Wound, she was the highest official remaining. "I and other priests have pored over the sacred texts, Majesty. All the holy prophecies, proverbs and commentaries collected since the beginning of the world." She shifted in her seat, looking suddenly uncomfortable. "And, at the Royal Wizard's urging, we have also consulted texts which are somewhat . . . suspect in nature. Dark and forbidden works that the Church captured over the millennia and kept locked away for the good of all. We've even looked into some Rendish writings that—"

Cambria opened her eyes and waved Saeth to silence. "And you have found no mention of anything that might relate in even the remotest fashion to the Change."

Saeth placed her hands in her lap, looked down at them. "No, your Majesty."

"Tell us, then, what do your instincts say upon the matter?" the Queen asked Saeth.

The priestess looked first to the Queen, then to Cynric,

clearly confused. "I . . . am uncertain how to answer, your Majesty."

Cynric felt sorry for Saeth. She was a bureaucrat, used to consulting the opinions of others before forming any of her own. She lacked the imagination to even understand the Queen's question, must less respond to it.

Cambria sighed. "Never mind, then." She turned to Cynric. "And what have you to report, Wizard?"

Cynric drew back the fur-trimmed sleeves of his purple robe. He hated the way the cuffs constantly fell over his hands. A mage's hands were his most important tools, and they should always be free to work a casting. But as Royal Wizard, he didn't have much choice in what he wore. The robe—irritating sleeves and all—came with the office.

"Though I have only my memory to consult, I cannot recall anything in Eyslken lore which hints at an enchantment like the one which has befallen us. I have examined dozens of people—members of the palace staff, guards in the City Watch, citizens brought in off the street. Whatever new-found power resides within them, it is not Chaos-based, as Eyslken and Lukashen magery is."

"Could it be related to Rendish magic?" the Queen asked.

Cynric shook his head. "Rendish wizards can bond with animal familiars. That's the sole extent of their powers over other living creatures."

"Then what of the ancient magic?" Cambria asked.

"You refer to the thaumaturgy of the Dragon Mages, I assume? Their spells derived from substances and materials harvested from dragons—scale, teeth, bone, blood and so on. There hasn't been a dragon in Athymar for over five hundred years, not since the time of the Blood Wars and the Reunification."

The Queen scowled, perhaps because of Cynric's attempt to obscure his thoughts. "Than what in Rudra's holy name can you tell us?" she snapped.

Cynric had barely slept in the last three days, had spent most of his time examining people who had been affected by the Change and poring over musty tomes of history and legend, as well as going through his own voluminous notebooks that he had kept faithfully over the last several decades. He was weary, he was frustrated, and he was more than a little scared.

His first impulse was to snap back at the Queen, but then he reached up and touched one of his Honor Braids—the right one—and ran his fingers slowly down the intricate arrangement of knots and beadwork which told of his exploits and accomplishments. The wearing of Honor Braids was an Eyslken custom. An individual Eyslk might have as many as ten by the time he or she reached three hundred, the age at which each member of their race died. At sixty-three, Cynric had two Honor Braids, the most any human had ever earned.

The ritual of touching an Honor Braid before speaking was intended to make one pause before voicing thoughts, to remind one of whom he or she was so they might comport themselves in an appropriate fashion and avoid bringing dishonor to their clan name. In human culture, it was the equivalent of taking a deep breath and counting to ten before speaking.

If the Queen were aware of his inner struggle, as surely she must be, she gave no sign.

When Cynric finally spoke, he was able to keep his words calm and measured. "Riders have brought word that the Change affected more of the land than just Pendara. How much more isn't clear yet, but I have heard tell of changes from as far north as the Golden Coast and as far west as the edge of the Kjartan. It also appears that one had to be literally standing within the boundaries of Athymar to be affected. Sailors at sea, fishermen in their boats, even children simply wading along the shore in search of shells— all were spared the effects of the Change."

"Does this mean the other eight known lands were not affected?" Cambria asked.

"It is far too early to say with any certainty, Majesty, but my guess is that only Athymar has been touched by this enchantment."

Cambria gave a sigh of relief. "Thank Rudra. I had visions of a Rendish invasion fleet bearing hordes of soldiers possessing vast mystical powers."

Cynric hadn't even considered such a possibility. He was glad it hadn't occurred to him, else he would have been able to think of little else. "The Change seems to have altered people at random. Some, like yourself, were granted great power, while others gained only trifling abilities, such as being able to alter the color of a flower's petals by breathing on them." One of the palace cooks possessed that particular talent. "But so far I have seen no one who has more than one newfound magical ability. And whatever the Change was, it would seem to be more than a singular event. In the last three days, a number of babes have been born in Pendara, and some of them clearly display signs of the Change. Unfortunate signs, at that." He thought of one girl who had been born with gills and who had died before her parents could think to immerse her in water.

The Queen was quiet for a moment as she considered Cynric's last statement. "Does this mean Athymar has been changed for all time? Are we now to be a land populated entirely by . . . what? What have we become? Mages?

Demons? Or something altogether different?"

Neither Cynric nor Saeth could answer that.

Cambria's eyes narrowed. "Neither of you appear to have been affected by the Change, yet you both were within the land's borders when it took place."

Cynric didn't have to ask how the Queen knew. She had surely read their thoughts. "I cannot speak for the Priestess, but it's possible my training in Chaos magic has kept the Change from me. It's also equally possible that, if I have been affected, my new abilities might take some time to manifest. Or perhaps they have merely not had the opportunity. If I now possess, say, the power to make a stream run backwards, how would I know until I actually go near one?" He turned to Saeth to see what she might say on the subject.

The priestess looked uncomfortable. "Other priests have been affected. Perhaps it is as the Royal Wizard says, and I will learn of my new talent in time. Though, to be honest, I do not look forward to it."

Cynric's stomach suddenly gurgled loudly. "My pardon. It appears something I ate may have decided to enter into a disagreement with my stomach."

Cambria smiled. "I imagine quite a few people have had similar 'disagreements' these last few days, if they've been able to eat at all. What else, Wizard?"

"The weather appears to have been affected. The summer rains have ceased, at least for the time being. There are rumors of cows producing curdled milk, of cats having litters of deformed kittens, that sort of thing. I haven't been able to verify any of these tales yet, and they well be nothing more than people's imaginations and fears getting the better of them. There is one other thing . . ."

"Yes?" the Queen urged, though surely she could hear it in his thoughts.

He stroked his neatly trimmed white beard. "I am not a particularly devout man." The Eyslken who had trained him to Shape had long ago turned their backs on the Gods, and while he did not subscribe completely to their beliefs, he was uncomfortable discussing matters of religion. "Perhaps the Priestess would be more suited to address this issue than I."

"You speak of the manifestations which have occurred upon death?" Saeth asked.

Cynric nodded.

"Though I have not witnessed them myself, others of my order have. There have been dozens of deaths within the city these last three days. Some were due to natural causes, others the result of accidents or crimes. Some occurred due to individuals being unable to control their new powers."

Saeth looked a bit queasy as she said this, and Cynric didn't blame her. He had heard tell of some truly hideous deaths that had resulted from such misadventures.

"But in every case, once someone has died, a small globe of energy has risen from the body. Some seem to be made of light, others of a dark shadowy substance. The globes hover in the air for a moment, then vanish."

"Might they be the souls of the dead, departing the body before traveling on to the afterlife?" the Queen mused. "Perhaps something about the Change has rendered these spirits visible to the human eye."

"That is one line of thought," Saeth conceded. "Some of my order believe the light globes are souls bound for Girasa, and the dark globes souls destined for Damaranth."

"But you do not."

"No. My . . . a niece of mine died two days ago. Her mother's left hand now causes fever in anyone she touches. She didn't know, and she touched my niece . . ."

"I am truly sorry, Priestess," Cambria said.

Saeth nodded her thanks for the Queen's words. "Dia was four. Such a sweet little girl. Her smile . . ." Saeth swallowed, as if fighting back tears.

Cynric's gut churned again, painfully this time. A sympathetic reaction, perhaps.

Saeth continued, speaking more forcibly than she had since entering the Queen's study. "When Dia passed on, the globe that emerged from her body was black as night. There is no way that child's soul could be condemned to Damaranth. Dia was a good girl; she rarely misbehaved, let alone committed any evil deeds. Besides, the Word of Rudra is clear on this point: only adults can choose evil; therefore, only adults can pass through the Gate of Skulls and enter Damaranth. Children always go to Girasa. And that's where Dia is now."

Cynric's faith in the Word of Rudra wasn't nearly so certain, but he was glad for the priestess' sake that hers was. Even if such beliefs were in the end only delusions, at least this particular one provided comfort for her now.

"Perhaps this phenomenon is somehow more directly related to the Change," Cynric offered. "In a manner we have yet to determine."

"Perhaps," the Queen said. "But if —"

A high-pitched shriek came from the hall outside the study.

Without thinking, Cynric leaped from his chair and rushed to the closed oaken door. He threw it open and raced into the hallway, his mind casting outward, searching the stone walls, ceiling and floors for Chaos fragments—called *Paytah* in the Eyslken tongue—which he might use to work a spell.

The hall was lit by a single torch set in an iron sconce.

By its guttering light, Cynric saw a robed figure bent over and frantically rubbing her head as she screamed. Black spiders covered her robe, and more dropped from the ceiling above her, the gray of the stone completely obscured by the dark mass of arachnids which clung to it. There must have been hundreds, thousands . . .

At the end of the hall, a chubby black-haired boy dressed in a tunic of royal blue stood laughing at the plight of the robed girl.

"Get-them-off-get-them-off-get-them-off!" the girl cried as she slapped at the spiders covering her head and body.

Cynric found a Chaos fragment in the wall to his right. It was small, but it would do. He reached out to touch the stone, closed his eyes, pictured the fragment as water trapped within the wall. Under his breath, he chanted a song of Minor Shaping, and imagined the water flowing forth from the stone and into his fingers.

Then he stretched his hand forth and spoke the Eyslken word for wind.

"Ventim!"

The power of Chaos, the residue left over from the Shaping of the world itself, shot forth from his fingers and whipped the air in the hallway into a sudden gale. Winds blasted the ceiling, rushed past the girl, and the spiders were blown away.

The girl was still shrieking when the wind died down. Cynric stepped toward her and put his hands on her shoulders.

"It's all right, Olesia. They're gone now."

The girl looked up at him, and Cynric struggled to keep his face impassive. Up until the moment of the Change, the queen's daughter had been a pretty girl of twelve, with strawberry-blonde hair and a light dusting of freckles on her face. But now her skin was completely transparent, her hair like strands of spun glass. The poor girl was perfectly healthy, but she looked as if she had been skinned alive. A network of blue veins covered raw, red bands of muscle. Her eyes seemed wide and staring, for though she blinked, her eyelids were not visible. Her teeth appeared to be constantly bared and grinning, though her lips might well be pressed tightly together.

She quickly turned away from Cynric and drew her hood over her face. She then whirled to face her younger brother, Enar, who continued to chuckle. The spiders he had commanded to drop on his sister were now gathered on the walls near him, as if awaiting further instructions.

"I am going to pound you for that!" she shouted and ran toward him. With a yelp, Enar turned and dashed off, his sister in hot pursuit. The army of spiders scuttled along the walls behind them, trailing their young master.

When the children had gone, their shouting naught but distant echoes, Cynric became aware of Cambria and Saeth standing behind him.

"Would you like me to go after them, your Majesty?" Saeth asked.

Cambria sighed. "No, the Change has been hard on them both—Olesia especially. I'll speak with them later."

Cynric didn't have to ask what Olesia had been doing outside the study. Doubtless, she had hoped to learn about what had happened to her, to them all. Cynric wished they had an explanation to offer her.

"As do I, Wizard." Cambria turned to Saeth. "Tell me, Priestess, are there members of your order praying within the Dawn Cathedral at this moment?"

"Yes, your Majesty. Some of them have been praying without let since the Change occurred."

Cambria gazed down the hallway, into the gloom where her children had gone.

"Tell them to pray harder."

CHAPTER SEVEN

The night was free of clouds, leaving the Dragon moon and its eternal quarry, the smaller Wolf moon, a clear sky across which to conduct their nightly chase. The two celestial orbs were close to full and provided more than enough light to see by. Danya didn't like it, though. This time of year, the sky should have been overcast and at the very least a light drizzle should have been falling. It wasn't natural. But then again, what was these days?

A gentle breeze blew in from across the bay, wafting the cool, comforting saltwater scent of the Shashida through the city. At least the air smelled right. It was the kind of night to curl up in bed with the shutters open while the sweet sea air and the soft shsshing of waves breaking against the shore in the distance lulled you to sleep. Too bad she'd pulled a double shift and had to work this night. But she couldn't complain too much. She'd managed to sneak in a few hours of rest in the last three days. Some of her fellow Watchers hadn't even gotten that much.

She walked down Cerulean Street, in the Merchant's Quarter. Most of the streets in Pendara were unpaved, meaning you kicked up clouds of dust when you walked or had to slog through mud—or worse. But not here in the Merchant's Quarter. These streets were made of cobblestone, and no matter how tough your boot leather, walking over them for any length of time made your feet ache. Danya would've rather dealt with mud.

Despite the unnaturalness of the moonslight, she was

grateful for the illumination it provided. She and her comrades in the City Watch sorely needed any advantage they could get. The last three days had been a nightmare, and she doubted this night would prove any different. She almost wished she were on duty guarding the Palace. Quite a few Watchers had been assigned to help the Royal Guard keep Pendara's citizens at a distance from the Queen, though no one had a clear understanding of why. It would be boring, but safe. At least, safer than this.

She passed manor houses with well-landscaped yards surrounded by high iron fences topped with wicked needle-sharp points. Often, Merchants would set hounds loose at night to patrol their grounds, and as a Watcher walked by, the dogs would run alongside the fence, barking. But not tonight. Save for the songs of crickets and the faint cries of gulls down by the Merchants' private docks, the Quarter was silent. Fireflies dotted the grounds, winking on and off in their attempts to attract a mate. But their light, instead of bright cheery yellow, was a dim sour green. It appeared even the animals and insects had been affected by the Change.

Danya herself had seemed to escape the effects of the Change, at least so far. She was grateful that she hadn't taken a husband yet, had no children. She didn't think she could stand it if a child of hers had been deformed or driven mad by the Change, as so many had. Her brother Liuz, a baker who lived in Wharfside, had gotten off lightly. The Change had given him the ability to spit a small stream of fire. He had nearly burned down his bakery at first, but he was an intelligent man and had adjusted to his new condition quickly. As long as he was careful, he would be safe enough. Liuz's wife had died in childbirth, and the baby hadn't survived long. He'd never remarried, so he had no one in the city—besides Danya, of course—to worry about. Thus, he had departed two days ago to travel to the small village where they both had been born in order to check on their parents. Danya hadn't heard from Liuz yet, but she knew it might be days, even weeks before he could get word to her. In the meantime, she tried not to worry about the three of them. She had enough to worry about right here in Pendara.

Her last musing proved prophetic as a noise cut through the night, a dog's yelp followed closely by the unmistakable sound of snapping bone.

Danya stopped, listened, tried to judge from which direction the sound came. She heard a soft rustling, as of someone moving quickly across grass. To her left. She trotted over to a fence enclosing a medium-sized manor house. It belonged to Merchant Anwir, if she remembered correctly. A rotund little man with foul breath who traded in spices that smelled far sweeter than he did.

She peered between the bars, scanned the grounds, searching for signs of movement. There! A shadowy figure moving quickly across the grass toward the house. She didn't yell for the intruder to stop, for she knew it wouldn't do any good. Instead, she began climbing the fence. Reaching the top, she negotiated her way past the sharp points carefully, and dropped lightly to the other side. She drew a dagger; her short sword would be too cumbersome to run with. Crouching low to make herself less visible—which wasn't hard given that she was barely five feet tall—she started running toward the manor house.

Despite the chain mail she wore beneath her red Watcher's tunic, she moved gracefully, breathed easily. Some Watchers were content to merely amble along their rounds, availing themselves of "complimentary" sweets from street vendors, growing fat and lazy in the process. Not Danya. She believed her body was a much a part of her weaponry as her blades and armor, and she kept herself in good condition by jogging through the streets during her off hours and taking long swims in the Shashida.

She came upon a black form lying upon the ground. It was the body of a huge mastiff, its head twisted at a sickening angle. Such dogs were bred for size and ferocity, and trained to be deadly killers. Even assuming that the beast had been listless due to the aftereffects of the Change, it would still take great strength to break the neck of such a large animal.

Danya barely slowed. The hound was dead; there was nothing she could do for it. She leaped over the mastiff and continued toward the house.

She wondered who the intruder might be. A thief emboldened by a magic power granted by the Change? Or a professional assassin hired by a rival Merchant who wished to take advantage of the confusion of these past few days and kill off a competitor? She thought the latter was the most likely possibility. There had been a number of such assassinations lately, the latest round in the endless trade wars waged by the Merchant class. Danya cared naught for their petty conflicts. As far as she was concerned, Anghrist could drag the lot of them down to Damaranth. But as a Watcher, she had sworn an oath before Rudra to protect Pendara and all who lived within its walls, and she would fulfill her pledge, regardless of her personal feelings.

She heard the sound of metal scratching glass, saw the shadowy form of the intruder standing outside a window at the side of the manor. No simple sneak thief here; a glass cutter meant this was a professional. Danya drew near, and the figure turned toward her, its head seeming to swivel 180 degrees to face her.

Even in the moonslight, she could barely make out the woman's features—though Danya was relatively certain of the intruder's gender. She had close-cropped black hair, cut much the way Danya wore her own blonde, and she had smeared her face with soot. She was dressed completely in black: black shirt, black trousers, black boots. Even the blades of the daggers thrust through her belt had been coated with lampblack. An assassin, no doubt about it.

Watcher protocol was to announce one's presence and demand surrender, but Danya wasn't about to give the assassin the chance to attack first. Without slowing, Danya flipped her dagger into a throwing position, and hurled it at a point between the woman's shoulder blades. All the while, her eyes kept telling her that the assassin's head couldn't possibly be turned all the way around like that, that it had to be some trick of the moonslight. But deep down, Danya knew it wasn't. The assassin had been Changed.

The dagger hit its target, but instead of burying itself in the assassin's back with a satisfying *thunk*, it merely bounced off and fell to the grass.

Once she was within striking distance, Danya came to a halt. She reached for her sword, wondering what good it would do her if a dagger couldn't penetrate the assassin's flesh. But before she could draw her blade, the woman in black's left arm flew over her shoulder and whipped through the air like an ebon lash.

Danya saw the blow coming and tried to duck, but a gloved fist smacked into the side of her head, sending her reeling. She fell to one knee, hand still grasping her swordhilt, bright sparkles of light flashing behind her eyes. She shook her head to clear it, and through blurred vision saw the assassin's body turn around beneath her head until both were facing the same direction. Danya thought there was something wrong with the way the woman moved. It was too fluid, as if she were made of liquid instead of flesh.

Danya struggled to rise, and the assassin brought her right foot around in a sweeping kick aimed at the Watcher's jaw. Just as the arm had, the leg moved bonelessly, more like a thick-bodied serpent than a human limb. But when the assassin's boot connected with Danya's jaw, it certainly felt as if the foot inside were solid. Danya saw another, brighter flash of light this time, followed swiftly by darkness.

When Danya came to, she was surprised to find herself lying face down in grass instead of standing between the Pillars of Judgment, the warm air of Girasa wafting gently around her. The assassin was gone. The woman must have assumed that either she had been killed by the last kick, or at the very least was going to be unconscious for some time. But Danya had managed to roll with the blow enough so that she had escaped the worst of the impact, though her jaw and head still hurt like blazes.

Danya was surprised—though hardly ungrateful—that the assassin hadn't taken a moment to slit her throat, as a precaution, if nothing else. Perhaps the woman was afraid to spare the time. Their encounter, however brief it may have been, might well have alerted the residents of Anwir Manor. Given the protections a Merchant could afford, stealth and surprise were everything to an assassin. If the woman believed there was a chance Anwir was aware of her presence and intent, she would do one of two things: either she would run like hell, or she would continue into the manor and hurry to fulfill her contract.

Either way, Danya needed to get off her rump and start moving.

She staggered to her feet and did her best to ignore the throbbing in her head and jaw. She drew her sword, gratified to hear the soft rasp as the blade left the scabbard, then she stepped closer to the window.

Window glass was rare enough in Athymar, let alone clear glass like this, which one could actually *see* through. The artisans of Thais were the sole suppliers of clear glass in the Nine Known Lands, and importing it to Athymar took quite a bit of gold. Only the royal family, the Land Barons, and the richest of the Merchant class could afford such a luxury. It almost broke Danya's heart to see that a circle a bit larger than the size of a human head had been cut in this fine glass.

Danya tried to open the window, found it still locked. She glanced down at the ground, saw the discarded circle of glass with a bit of honey-and-paste stickum affixed to it. The assassin had used the glop to hold the glass so it wouldn't fall inward when she was finished cutting.

By all appearances, the assassin had managed to cut the hole before Danya had reached her, but had chosen retreat rather than try her skills against Anwir's security. Nothing to do now but walk around to the front and pound on the door until someone answered who could verify that everyone inside was safe.

Except something wasn't right. Danya supposed the assassin could have locked the window once more after gaining entrance. But what bothered Danya the most was that the hole the assassin had cut was much larger than it should be. Normally, a thief or assassin would create a space just wide enough to reach a hand through so they could unlock a window. Why would this particular killer make a hole so much larger?

Danya thought of the fluid way the assassin moved, of

how her head had seemed to turn all the way around while her body remained motionless, of how her limbs had appeared almost boneless when she attacked. Perhaps the assassin had made a hole in the glass large enough for her purpose, which hadn't been to open the window, but rather to provide a space wide enough for her malleable body to squeeze through.

The assassin was inside the manor.

Danya cursed the Merchants for being so foolhardy as to not have bars over their windows. The idiots considered such a simple precaution to be garish and common; besides, it would cover the fine clear glass they paid so much for. Nevermind that bars might actually keep out one or two of the hired killers they constantly sent after one another.

Danya quickly sheathed her sword and reached through the hole in the window. She found the lock, turned it, then pulled her hand free and threw open the window. She crawled inside, and once both feet were on the floor, drew her sword again.

The curtains were open, providing sufficient moonlight for Danya to see. She stood in what she assumed was a drawing room. She could make out the dark shapes of chairs, a love seat, end tables, what looked like a small octagonal harp in one corner. But no assassin—though considering that the woman was dressed completely in black, she could be standing pressed against a wall and Danya might not detect her. Common sense dictated that Danya proceed with caution, but common sense wouldn't keep Merchant Anwir alive.

The air held an exotic scent that Danya couldn't place, but which she assumed was a mixture of spices Anwir traded in. Danya found this a trifle odd. Merchants tended to hire others to see to the day-to-day operation of their businesses. Perhaps Anwir took more of a personal interest than some Merchants. Or perhaps he had a son or daughter who oversaw the family holdings. Danya sincerely hoped Anwir had no children—or grandchildren—of any age, at least not any on the premises. While professional assassins weren't blood-mad butchers, they wouldn't hesitate to kill anyone who came between them and their target.

As Danya started across the drawing room, she heard a harsh *mrrreeeooow!* from deeper inside the manor, followed by snarling and spitting, and then the sound of a scuffle. The assassin had encountered another of Anwir's guardians, this one of the feline variety. Big one, too, from the sound of things.

Danya made her way across the room as fast as she could without tripping over any of the furniture. She reached the doorway, passed through, and entered a dark hallway, keeping her free hand on the wall to guide her as she hurried along. Danya didn't expect the cat to stop the assassin any more than the mastiff outside had, but she hoped it might prove enough of a distraction to give Danya an advantage over the woman.

But before she could reach the assassin, Danya heard the sound of cracking bone followed quickly by the cat's final shriek of pain, and a thump as the body was dumped to the floor. When she got to the body, the assassin, of course, had moved on. Danya knelt and touched the warm corpse of the beast. It was big, larger than the mastiff, and covered with coarse, bristly fur. The tusk-like teeth jutting from the upper jaw confirmed it: the creature was a lesser direcat, from the northern climes of Athymar, bred for high intelligence, deep loyalty to its owners, and utter hatred of everything else under the sun. Direcats—even the smaller variety, such as this one—were extremely rare, unbelievably expensive and unimaginably deadly.

And the assassin had dispatched it in mere moments.

Danya couldn't tell in the dark how the cat had died—perhaps from a dagger thrust, or else by a blow from one of the assassin's whip-like limbs. In the end, what did it matter? Either way, the animal was dead.

Danya stepped over the direcat and found herself at the foot of a wide staircase. She reached down, brushed her fingers over the first two steps. No blood. As difficult as it was to believe, it seemed the assassin hadn't been so much as scratched during her brief battle with the direcat. And if a direcat couldn't injure the woman, let alone stop her, what chance did Danya have?

Still, she continued. She was a Watcher; it was what she did.

Danya set her foot on the first step and heard a soft *snik!* She froze, thinking that she had activated a trap of some sort. But when no blades sliced into her flesh, no swinging hammer smashed into her skull, she realized the sound had come from the *top* of the stairs. She hadn't tripped the trap; the assassin had.

Danya listened. She heard no cry of pain, no harsh breathing, no thud of a falling body. Too bad. She headed up the stairs, knowing the assassin could be waiting for her anywhere in the darkness.

As she neared the top of the stairs, Danya smelled a bitter tang that cut through the miasma of spices that hung in the air. She stopped and used her sword to probe the step ahead of her. The tip of her blade pinged against metal. A spike, from the feel of it, no doubt honed to an exceedingly fine point and, from the smell, coated with poison. She sniffed again. Krakenfish toxin, a perennial favorite of the Merchant class. A few drops beneath the skin caused instant paralysis and death from asphyxiation. Nasty stuff.

Obviously the assassin had avoided the trap, or else her stiffened body would be lying here waiting for Danya to summon a deathwagon—unless the Change had somehow given the woman the ability to resist poison in addition to her other talents. But Danya doubted it. From what she'd seen so far of the Change's effects, however powerful they might be, they were limited to one aspect—such as just spitting flame, as in her brother's case. If the assassin now possessed a serpent's flexibility, then that would be the sum total of unearthly power at her command. Or so Danya hoped.

Danya slid her sword against a spike, hoping some of the poison would rub off onto her blade. In her younger days, she wouldn't have lowered herself to use such a base weapon. But although she'd been a Watcher for only four years, in her time patrolling the streets of Pendara, she'd learned two very important lessons: ultimately, there was no such thing as a fair fight, and a smart Watcher used whatever weapons were available to ensure that the King's justice was done—and that she survived the doing of it.

Danya stepped over the row of spikes and onto the second-floor hallway. She heard sibilant whispering, saw flashes of baleful green light from the far end of the hall. The assassin had encountered some manner of spellward—probably on the door of Anwir's bedchamber—and from the sound of things, the woman was trying to neutralize it.

Danya hesitated. Was the assassin a wizard in addition to her other abilities? Green light was a sign of Lukashen magery, which could be wild and dangerous. Such spells were unstable and could well explode in the caster's face midway through an enchantment, if he or she were unlucky. No, Danya decided. If the assassin were a wizard, she'd have used her powers before now. More likely she'd acquired, or been given, a mystical object to counter the protective spells on the door to Anwir's bedchamber. The only magic inherent in the assassin was that granted to her by the Change.

But Danya still hesitated. Should she attack while the woman was busy, or should she wait a moment, and hope the assassin was unskilled enough at using a magical device that the spell would backfire, doing Danya's work for her?

Balefire sparked from where the assassin pressed a runestone against the wooden door. The release of mystic energies illuminated the woman's face, the concentration in her eyes; the calm, sure movement of her lips as she whispered the incantation. This was not a woman likely to make mistakes.

Attack, Danya decided. Now.

She crept quietly down the hall, sword held at the ready, hoping to take the assassin by surprise. The woman continued whispering and the balefire increased in intensity, until it looked as if the assassin held a blazing green torch against the door. The assassin's voice rose in volume to a final shout as she completed the incantation, then she closed her eyes and looked away.

Danya sensed what was coming, but she didn't have time to avert her gaze before the runestone erupted in a last blinding flash of mystic energy. Spots danced before Danya's eyes, and she was forced to stagger to a stop, lest she veer off course and slam into a wall. She blinked furiously, tears streaming from her aching eyes, and she rubbed them with her free hand, as if she thought she could massage her sight back.

Danya heard the now useless runestone clatter to the floor as the assassin discarded it. Heard the woman thumb the doorlatch, heard it click open.

Danya was dumbfounded. Not even an overconfident Merchant would rely on a single spellward as the sole defense of his bedchamber. And by Chaos, he would at least *lock the stupid door!*

Danya's vision began to clear, and she saw the assassin framed in the soft glow of candlelight emitting from the crack of the open door. No further traps sprang, no more guardians—animal or human—rushed into the hall to attack. It didn't make sense. The defenses of Anwir Manor, while formidable enough when taken separately, were mediocre when considered collectively. They simply weren't enough, not for a Merchant who feared assassination.

Evidently, the serpent-limbed woman was thinking along similar lines, for she paused at the entrance to Anwir's bedchamber, as if she couldn't quite believe how easy it had been to get here.

And then a weary voice issued from within the room. "Come in, child. I've been expecting you. Or someone very much like you, at any rate."

The scent Danya had been smelling ever since she entered the manor grew thicker now, cloying, and sickly sweet. The odor was so oppressive that it quickly became an effort to breathe. She knew then that something was wrong here. Seriously wrong.

But the assassin had been only temporarily deterred. The killer slid an ebon dagger free from her belt, opened the door all the way, and stepped into Anwir's bedchamber.

Her vision almost completely clear now, the Watcher ran the rest of the way to the bedchamber and entered the room, prepared to engage the assassin in combat and save Merchant Anwir's life if she could.

But as soon as Danya crossed the threshold, and saw what lay within Anwir's bedchamber, she froze in shock.

CHAPTER EIGHT

The assassin stood just inside the doorway of a bedchamber larger than Danya's quarters in the Watchers' barracks, gaping at the being that lay sprawled across Anwir's luxurious bed. Danya stepped forward and stood next to the woman, their enmity for the moment forgotten as together they stared at the thing Anwir had become.

The light of a lone flickering candle sitting on a cherry wood dresser revealed what transformation the Change had wrought upon Anwir. He was unclothed save for a dingy breechcloth. His entire body had turned dark green and small black thorns thrust forth from his flesh—or what had once been flesh. He no longer possessed fingers or toes. Now long, curling tendrils which looked more like roots than digits sprouted from the ends of his arms and legs. The tendrils covered the fine silken sheets in tangles, spilled over the edge of the bed and piled in clumps upon the floor. They didn't so much as twitch, and Danya wondered if Anwir could move them at all.

The Merchant's face was the worst. Save for the verdant skin tone, it still appeared human, the features recognizably Anwir's. But instead of hair, a crown of bright orange fronds, each three feet long, extended from his skull. The fronds were wilted, tinged brown at the edges. Danya noticed similar patches of brown covering Anwir's new body.

The Merchant sat propped up against a mound of puffy silk pillows that Danya imagined were stuffed with goose down. Any one of those pillows likely cost more than she

84

made in a month. Anwir regarded the Watcher and the assassin with sad, watery eyes whose whites were tinted green.

"Horrible, isn't it?" Anwir said in a conversational tone of voice which sounded incongruous given the situation. "One of the first things I did after the Change was order my servants to remove the full-length mirror I kept next to my dresser. It was a beautiful thing, the frame inlaid with gold filigree." He sighed, as if the loss of his mirror were one of the saddest things he could imagine. "But I have no desire to look upon my current countenance, as I'm sure you both can understand."

His lips moved, and his eyes blinked, but no other part of his body stirred. Danya wondered if he had truly become as a plant and had lost the ability to move.

The cloying scent Danya had smelled since entering the manor was far stronger in here, and she realized that what she had at first taken for the smell of mingled spices was instead the aroma given off by the plant-thing that Anwir now was. If the Merchant's condition hadn't been so pitiful, she might have found it ironic that a man whose breath once could have felled a Kjartan dungbeast now smelled so sickeningly sweet.

The assassin spoke, her voice soft and low. "That's why there's no one else in the house. No guards, no servants, no family. You sent them all away, didn't you?"

Anwir nodded slightly, his head fronds bobbing. "Even my wife. I couldn't stand to have any of them look at me, couldn't bear to see the disgust in their eyes. I have one servant who has faithfully taken care of me since I was a child. I allow her alone to tend to my needs, such as they are, once or twice a day. It was she who lit the candle earlier this evening, else I would be forced to lie here in darkness. I . . . no longer seem to require sleep."

Danya's gaze was drawn to Anwir's nightstand, upon which rested a jewel-encrusted goblet and a fine pewter bowl with intricately etched designs. The goblet was full of wine, the bowl of broth. Both appeared to have been untouched.

Anwir must have realized where Danya was looking, for he said, "My servant tried to feed me today, but I no longer have the stomach for food. The smell alone nauseates me. I would've had the woman take it away, if it wasn't for my little friend there."

Danya noticed movement and saw a small gray mouse peek from behind the safety of the bowl.

"All I can do is turn my head, and even that simple action takes a great deal of effort," Anwir said. "With nothing else to occupy me for the last three days, I've amused myself by watching my little friend go about his mousy business—exploring the room, sneaking sips of broth and such." He spoke fondly, as if of a favorite pet.

The mouse, seeming almost to sense that it was being talked about, came out from behind the bowl, crawled forward to the edge of the nightstand and sat on its haunches, looking at them.

No, Danya thought, *looking at me.*

She felt as if the world had suddenly tilted sideways. Hot, dizzy, fluttery in the stomach. She forgot about the assassin, forgot about Anwir. Everything fell away from her consciousness: the Watch, Pendara, the Change, even her own name. All she could think about was that mouse.

The rodent reached up with its front paws and scratched its nose. It then lowered its head and scratched behind both ears, first the right, then the left.

"You want to die." Danya spoke to Anwir, but she didn't take her gaze from the mouse. "You paid one of your people to leak word on the street of what had happened to you, so that other Merchants would be tempted to seize the opportunity to make an attempt upon your life."

The mouse rolled over onto its back.

Danya continued, eyes still fixed upon the tiny animal. "Then you reduced the Manor's defenses to a bare minimum so any killers would be assured of reaching you. You intended to commit suicide by assassination."

The mouse rolled onto its feet again and stepped back half an inch.

"However, you knew once whichever assassin arrived finally got a look at you, he or she might be tempted to leave you as you are. After all, the other Merchants would rather see you incapacitated and unable to run your business effectively than have you dead and a competent successor take your place."

The mouse shivered, as if in a draft.

"So you have a satchel of gold beneath your bed, an offering to help overcome any possible reluctance an assassin might have to doing you in."

Danya blinked. She felt as if she were waking from a dream. The mouse stood, put its front paws on the edge of the bowl, and leaned forward to take a few delicate sips of broth, as if its performance had made it hungry.

"How can you possibly know that?" the assassin hissed. She sounded half-skeptical, half-frightened.

"The Watcher is correct," Anwir said. "Either she is an extremely good guesser, or the Change has given her certain . . . insights. Not that it matters to me which is the case. My only wish is to die. Can you ladies accommodate me?"

Danya reluctantly turned away from the mouse to face Anwir. "What do you mean 'accommodate?'"

"My dear Watcher, obviously you detected my other guest—" He nodded to the assassin. "—and followed her into the Manor with the intent of preserving my life. But as gratifying as it may be to see that the taxes I render unto the city treasurer have paid for such diligent civil servants such as yourself, I do not wish my life preserved. Thus, there is no need to stop Milady Assassin, is there? Why don't you depart and let the lovely woman go about her work?"

Danya shook her head. "I can't do that."

Anwir sighed. "Don't be tiresome. If it's coin you want, I have money secreted in various locations about the Manor. You're more than welcome to some of it. Take as much as you can carry. Just leave."

"She's right," the assassin said. "We can't do that. She's seen me, seen how I work. I can't allow her to leave here alive."

"Come now," Anwir said, sounding as if he were starting to lose his patience. "Surely we can reach some sort of an agreement."

Merchants, Danya thought, *always trying to make a deal.* "Sorry. No sale, Anwir. I took an oath to protect the citizens of Pendara—even from themselves. And I intend to keep it."

"Idealistic rot," Anwir spat. "You really should come down out of the clouds for a moment and join the rest of us here in the real world. Surely, you—"

The mouse let out a high-pitched squeak and Danya ducked to the left just as the assassin aimed a kick at her throat. The blow missed, and Danya moved forward and swung her sword at the assassin's stomach, hoping her blade might be able to penetrate the woman's soft belly. If Danya could manage to even scratch the assassin's supernaturally pliable skin, the poison smeared on her sword would do the rest.

The assassin reached out with her right hand—to block the swordblow, Danya thought. But the woman's arm wrapped around Danya's wrist like a serpent and squeezed.

The pain was instantaneous and excruciating, and Danya knew then how the assassin had dispatched the mastiff and direcat. The woman had wrapped her boneless limbs around the animals and constricted them, squeezing tighter and tighter until the creatures' necks snapped.

Danya felt the bones in her wrist grind together, and as hard as she tried to maintain her grip on her sword, her fingers were forced open and the blade dropped to the floor.

The assassin grinned as she unraveled her arm from around Danya's wrist and lunged forward.

Danya heard the mouse scratch a quick rhythm on the nightstand—*skkrrtch, skkrrtch, skritcha-skritch!*—and she raised her arms just in time to avoid having them pinned to her sides as the assassin wrapped her own arms around Danya's midsection. And began to squeeze.

The air whooshed out of Danya's lungs as the iron bands that were the assassin's arms tightened around her chest. Danya boxed the assassin's ears as hard as she could, but it did no good. The woman's skull was as pliable as the rest of her. It felt as if Danya were punching a pillow.

"Really, now," Anwir said, "is all this fuss necessary?"

"It'll only take the Watcher a few moments to die, and then I'll tend to you," the assassin said. Bloodlust blazed in her eyes, and Danya knew the woman was enjoying this.

"Oh, very well," Anwir said, "but be quick about it. I abhor violence."

You abhor it! Danya thought. *I'm not particularly fond of it myself at the moment!* She continued wildly slamming her fists into the assassin's head, but nothing she did seemed to have any effect on the woman. Danya struggled to breathe, but couldn't pull any air into her lungs. Her vision was starting to gray around the edges, and she could hear a dull roaring in her ears. It sounded like the ocean. Not a bad sound to hear before one died, she thought, though she rather would have heard the Shashida itself one last time, listened to the waves breaking against the shore, the gulls crying out to one another as they drifted lazily on the warm sea air . . .

A clatter cut through the roar, and Danya turned her head toward it. The mouse had tipped over the goblet. Red wine ran over the edge of the nightstand and splattered to the floor. The mouse, standing in a puddle of wine, began spinning round and round frantically, as if trying to catch its own tail.

Danya understood. She gripped the assassin's head with both hands and began to twist. She turned the woman's head all the way around, and then started to turn it again.

"What are—" The assassin's voice cut off with a gurgle as Danya continued twisting, twisting, twisting, closing off the woman's airway. Four turns, five, six, seven . . . . The assassin's face turned red, then purple, then blue. Her arms began to loosen around Danya's chest, and the Watcher was able to draw in a most welcome breath of air. Even though it was thick with Anwir's floral stench, it was the sweetest breath she had ever taken.

Eight turns, nine. The assassin's arms fell away from Danya, and hung limply at the woman's side, restored to their normal shape. The woman swayed, and then Danya released her. The woman's head spun wildly around, like a child's top, as she fell. By the time the assassin hit the floor, her head had returned to its usual position, but it was too late. She was quite dead.

Danya stepped back as the woman's chest began to glow white. A sphere of bright energy rose from the assassin's body, hovered in the air for a moment, and then vanished. Danya had heard other Watchers speak of this strange effect that occurred in the presence of the newly dead—yet another wrinkle of the Change—but this was the first time she had witnessed it herself.

"What in the Realms of Man was that?" Anwir asked.

Danya could only shrug. She looked over at the mouse, but it ignored her as it happily lapped up some wine. If the events of the last few moments had disturbed the animal in any way, it gave no sign.

"If I could move my hands, I would applaud your performance, Watcher," Anwir said. His shaken tone belied his words, however. "I don't suppose there's any chance you killed her because you want all the money for yourself?"

"None." Danya picked up her sword and wiped the poison off on the assassin's trousers.

Anwir sighed. "I didn't think so. You haven't really saved my life, you know. Other assassins will come. And if they don't, I'll hire one myself."

Danya sheathed her sword. "If you're so determined to die, why not just ask someone in your family to do the deed? I'm sure you have any number of relatives who would like to see you out of the way so their own standing in your House would increase."

Anwir was silent for a moment. "Honestly? Pride. I don't want to give any of them the satisfaction. Especially not when killing me would be so easy given my current condition."

Danya smiled. "Seems to me like you still have some fight left in you. These last few days have been hard on everyone in the city, Anwir. Granted, you have a more extreme change to adjust to than some, but you might well get used to your new . . . situation, given some time. You still have your mind, and to be frank, that's a good deal more than some of Pendara's citizens have."

"But *look* at me! Not only am I hideous, I can't move!"

"I am looking at you. Your fronds are drooping and you have brown patches all across your body. Tell me, have you tried taking any water and getting some sun? I mean, you are a plant now, at least partially."

Anwir stared at her. "I—I hadn't thought of that."

"Perhaps the reason you can't move and your spirits are so low is because you're undernourished. Have that servant of yours bring you some water and draw open the curtains." She glanced at the tendrils where Anwir's fingers and toes used to be. "And perhaps you should get some rich soil to sink those roots in as well."

"I . . . shall consider it."

"Good." Danya nodded toward the assassin's corpse. "I'll drag her downstairs and out onto the lawn. When I get back to Watcher barracks, I'll make sure someone sends a deathwagon round to collect the body. They might not get here till morning, though. They've been awfully busy of late."

Danya turned to go, then stopped. She stepped over to the nightstand and held out her hand. The mouse took one last lap of wine, then scurried onto her palm.

"And if you don't mind, I think I'd like to take this little fellow with me." Danya tucked the mouse into her tunic pocket, and she felt it curl up. *He's probably in need of a nap after that wine,* she thought.

"Whatever do you need that mouse for?" Anwir asked, clearly unhappy to lose a creature he had considered something of a pet.

Danya thought for a moment. "He's a witness." Then she bent down, grabbed the assassin by the ankles and began dragging the woman downstairs.

CHAPTER NINE

Ashur Dal sat cross-legged at the thick base of a huge elm tree that was nearly as old as he. The Eyslk leaned his back against the trunk so that he might connect to the tree's lifeforce, and through it, to that of the entire forest. Eyes closed, he listened with small but sensitive ears to the night sounds of *Selyv Nahele*, which the humans called the Greenmark. Crickets chirped, owls hooted, raccoons crawled through the underbrush, treegliders drifted from branch to branch making soft *click-click-click* sounds with their mandibles. To a casual listener, everything would have sounded normal. But Ashur Dal had lived in this great forest for the better part of his 293 years, and he knew its rhythms as intimately as he did those of his own body. Something wasn't quite right, but he couldn't put his finger on precisely what.

True, the summer rains had ended early, but though this was a rare event, it wasn't entirely unheard of. He doubted the premature cessation of the rains alone would have caused the forest creatures to become so . . . tentative, as if they were afraid to move too loudly, too suddenly.

There had been a time when Ashur Dal might have cast his awareness about the forest, searching for a fragment of *Paytah*, the power of primal Chaos itself. He could have used this *Paytah*, shaped it to form a spell that would have permitted him a deeper link with the land, a link he might use to gain insight into what was wrong with *Selyv Nahele*. Unbidden, his breathing deepened and his lips began to form the first syllables of the necessary chant. As soon as he realized what he was doing, though, he stopped. He had not gathered *Paytah* in the last twenty years, and he would not do so now.

He was irritated with himself for even beginning a Shaping, but then old habits died hard, he supposed—if they died at all.

"Preceptor?"

His eyes snapped open to behold a young Eyslka. He realized that while he had heard her coming, he had been so deep in thought that her approach hadn't registered. There was more than enough moonslight for his Eyslken eyes to see by, and he judged the girl to be a young adult, less than a century old. He couldn't recall her name, but from her aspect, he guessed that she belonged to the Leyati clan, a humble folk given to serving others.

Ashur Dal stood and adjusted his mottled green tunic with an irritated tug. He thought of correcting the girl—he had forsworn the title *Preceptor* at the same time he had given up Shaping—but when he gazed upon her face and saw how nervous she was, he decided not to make an issue of it.

"I trust you have good reason for disturbing me?" he asked.

She bowed her head, her fine white hair spilling forward to display her Honor Braids. Ashur Dal noted that she possessed three. Not bad for someone so young. He himself had once had eight, but he had cut them off long ago. He had worn his alabaster hair long and loose ever since.

The Eyslka kept her head respectfully lowered as she spoke. "My apologies, Preceptor. I was sent by Entoria Taj. She says you have been . . . Summoned."

Ashur Dal realized then that the girl was garbed in the

diaphanous white robes worn by those who tended *Aiyana*, the Orchard of Dreams.

"Summoned?" He couldn't quite believe his ears. No one had been Summoned in his lifetime. "Why me?" he mused to himself.

Mistaking it for a direct question, the Leyati Eyslka answered. "I do not know, Preceptor. I suppose only the Timeless Ones themselves know for certain."

He barely kept from rolling his eyes at such an obvious statement. "Indeed. Well, lead the way, then." Ashur Dal knew the path to *Aiyana*, of course, but it was the Eyslka's responsibility to escort him there. And while he wasn't much on protocol, he saw no reason to prevent the girl from doing her duty.

She bowed deeply, then turned and headed down a forest path that was only visible to Eyslken eyes. Not even animals could sense it. And if any of the forest's denizens should happen to stumble across an Eyslken path, they would become disoriented and flee in terror. It was this magic—an enchantment woven by fifty Master Shapers working for ten days without let—that had kept Vallanora, the Eyslken settlement within *Selyv Nahele*, hidden from the outside world for close to two thousand years. Not that the concealment and aversion spells didn't need shoring up from time to time. Ashur Dal himself had helped to maintain them before he had forsworn Shaping.

Soon the path led them to the heart of Vallanora, past simple wooden structures designed to blend in with the forest as much as possible. Most windows of the homes they walked by were dark, but a few still had lanterns burning within. Wooden windchimes clattered softly in the night breeze, and despite the fact he was being led to *Aiyana*, Ashur Dal experienced a powerful feeling of peace, the kind one can only know when he is truly in a place he belongs, a place he loves with all his heart and soul.

The path branched off to the right, and they left the homes behind as they headed back into the forest. Fireflies flickered among the trees here, and cicadas thrummed lazily. They continued walking for a while until they reached the white ash tree that marked the entrance to *Aiyana*.

The Eyslka stopped. "This is as far as I may go. Entoria Taj awaits you within." She bowed, then turned and walked away.

Ashur Dal hesitated at the entrance to the Orchard of Dreams. In his long life, he had risen to many challenges, faced many dangers. He had fought battles with both steel and magic, more than once risking not only his life, but his very soul. But never had he done anything like this.

Never had he spoken with the dead.

As he stepped past the white ash tree and into *Aiyana*, he wondered what the Timeless Ones wanted with him. Whatever it was, he didn't think he was going to like it.

Chapter Ten

"It won't be much longer now," Tarian said. It was mid afternoon of the fourth day since they left their forest cabin, and Anci pulled their wagon up Ocean's Rise, the last hill before the Southern Road sloped downward to Pendara. The air was cooler here, and held the tang of saltwater. Gulls drifted on the breeze, several of the curious birds dipping down to see if they had any food to offer.

Sitting next to him, staring straight ahead as he had done since their encounter with the bandits, Phelan merely grunted.

Tarian gave the reins a gentle shake, more to have something to do than because he wanted Anci to hurry. When Phelan had been younger, he'd always been excited about going to Pendara, but not now. Of course, this was hardly a pleasure trip. Still, Tarian took Phelan's apathy as a bad sign. The lad had barely said five words since Drem and Brak had attempted to rob them. Tarian had tried raising the subject, tried to get the boy to talk about it. But Phelan had refused to acknowledge his father's efforts, let alone respond to him.

The shadow wolf hadn't emerged since rejoining Phelan. Tarian thought he could sense the beast, though, lurking just below the surface of his son's awareness, watching, waiting for its next chance to be free. Tarian hadn't been able to prevent the Change from warping Lowri's mind, and despite the fact they had traveled all this way in hope of finding a mage who might help restore her, Tarian secretly feared there was nothing the magics of man could do to reverse the effects of the Change. He still intended to do everything in his power to try to save her, but he had to at least prepare himself for the possibility that she might be lost to him forever. This made him even more determined not to lose his son as well.

"Did I ever tell you about my first time in battle?" Tarian didn't wait for a response; he knew none was forthcoming. "I was fifteen, two years younger than you. My father, your grandfather, had decided it was time I learned to fight. Oh, he had spent much time schooling me in the art of swordplay—when he wasn't off fighting other people's wars, that is. And he had taken me on many a deerhunt, and by this time I could acquit myself with a bow well enough. But he wanted me to experience what it was like to engage an opponent that could fight back. Not a sparring partner who ultimately was just helping me hone my skills, but someone who wanted to take my life, and who wanted to preserve his own in the process.

"We lived on the Northern Steppes then, in a cabin not much different than the one I built for you and Lowri. One morning, Father and I donned leather armor, said good-bye to my mother and two sisters, and we headed out onto the plain, traveling on foot. As we jogged along, I asked Father where we were bound, hoping to gain some insight into what he had in store for me, but every time I asked, he merely shook his head grimly, and soon I stopped asking. We ran until noon, pausing only to rest twice.

"'This is it,' my father said. I looked around, unable to discern any features that made this part of the plain different from any other.

"'Here.' He drew his sword and pushed aside a clump of tall yellow steppe grass, revealing a hole large enough for a man to crawl through. There was a cold wind blowing across the Steppes that day, but it had nothing to do with the chill that ran along my spine. I knew very well what that hole meant."

"Dretchen?" Phelan asked without taking his gaze from the road before them.

Tarian nodded. "It was the den of a solitary male, and not a warren, thank Rudra. My father said, 'I am going to move off a dozen yards while you lure the creature out and dispatch it. Mark my words well: whatever occurs, I shall not interfere. You are my son, and I love you dearly, but this is your test and you must take it alone. Do you understand?'

"I swallowed nervously and nodded. I was terrified, but I very much wanted to make my father proud of me, wanted to do honor to his training. He sheathed his sword, then reached into his rucksack and removed a cloth-wrapped bundle. He handed it to me. It felt damp, and I could smell that it had been soaked in lilac water.

"'Inside is a hunk of rotten venison,' Father said. 'Your mother sprinkled lilac water on it to cover the stink. Once I have stepped away, unwrap the meat and drop it on the ground, no more than three feet from the hole. Then unsheathe your sword and make ready. If the dretch is hungry enough—and out here, it most likely will be—it will go for the bait quickly. Once it sees you, it will attack without hesitation, for you offer a much more substantial meal than a small hunk of deermeat.' Father glanced up at the sky. 'It's a somewhat cloudy day, but there should be enough light to confuse the dretch, at least at first. It won't take long for its eyes to adjust, so make sure to press your advantage. Stand over here—' He pulled me over to where he stood. '—where you'll be downwind of the hole.'

"He placed his hands on my shoulders then. 'Remember all that I have taught you, and you'll be fine, Son.' I nodded. I was frightened, but excited as well. I was looking forward to trying my skill against a real opponent for the first time, and to proving my fitness as a warrior to my father—and to myself.

"Father trotted off, and when he had gone a dozen yards, he stopped, turned and waved. I waved back, then unwrapped the deermeat, tossed it on the ground before the dretch's lair, discarded the cloth, and quickly unsheathed my sword.

"I expected the dretch to come charging out of its hole instantly, but for long moments nothing happened. Despite the coolness of the air, sweat trickled down the sides of my face; my swordhand trembled, the point of my blade wavering in response. My stomach roiled, as if a restless, thrashing serpent had taken up residence within, and at that moment, I fully expected to die.

"The scutter-scratch of claws on dirt issued from the hole, and I could hear harsh breathing as the dretch worked its nose, pulling in the scent of rotten meat. I saw its hands first: long tapering fingers with prominent joints and sharp black nails. I had never seen a crab at that point in my life, had never even been close to the ocean, but that's what those fingers put me in mind of now: crab's legs. Then came the head, a gray, misshapen thing covered with a thick leathery hide like a lizard. The dretch's eyes were small black dots, like those of a mole, and it blinked as it emerged into the light. Its mouth was huge, twice as wide as a human's, and filled with two rows of tiny pointed teeth. Those teeth didn't look like much in and of themselves, but I knew that working together with the dretch's powerful jaw muscles, they could tear flesh and snap bone as easily as my sword could slice through a blade of steppe grass.

"The dretch hesitated before coming all the way out of its hole, and sniffed the air warily. Large ears unfolded from the side of its head like leathery sails that had caught the wind. I stood completely still and held my breath, lest the foul thing hear me above the sound of the breeze and the rustling steppe grass. I was surprised by how cautiously the creature was proceeding. I'd expected it to immediately lunge toward me, eyes wild, jaws wide, slavering for a taste a man-meat. But instead it was taking its time, trying to determine whether it was safe to emerge all the way.

"The dretch decided it was, and pushed the rest of its body out of the hole. I was taken aback by how lean the creature was. My father had told me that dretchen possessed the strength of three men, sometimes more, but now that I stood face to face with one of the things, I found it hard to credit, and wondered if what my father had told me was naught by a warrior's exaggeration. The dretch was smaller than an adult human male. Its limbs were spiderleg-thin, and its ribs and pelvis jutted out so much, the creature almost looked like a walking skeleton. This was what I had been afraid of? I grinned in relief, certain I could cut the pathetic beast in two with a single blow.

"But when I grinned, without realizing it, I released the air I had been holding. The dretch's body tensed and it swiveled its head to face me. The creature opened its mouth wide and hissed like a snake, its breath far fouler than the stink of rotting venison; it was like a draft blowing from the lowest depths of Damaranth.

"And then it came at me."

Tarian paused in his story, then, and waited to see if Phelan was paying attention.

After a moment, the lad said, "So? What happened?"

Tarian kept the smile he felt from showing. "Your grandfather's training took over, and I managed to lower my sword in time to meet the dretch's charge. The creature impaled itself, but its momentum knocked me to the ground."

"So you killed it. End of story."

"Not quite. Dretchen are far tougher than they look. According to legend, Anghrist created them millennia ago from a cannibalistic tribe of humans that was shunned by all other men, and invested them with some of His own dark power." Tarian shrugged. "Whether this is true or not, I can't say. But I can tell you that it took me seven good blows to fell the dretch, and even then, it was some time in dying.

"I had taken a number of wounds myself, none of them serious, fortunately. I wiped my sword on the grass to remove as much of the dretch's grayish-black blood as I could, then I sheathed the blade. My father came running over, and he cleaned and dressed my wounds with supplies from his rucksack while I stood and watched the dretch die. Neither of us spoke a word.

"When the dretch finally breathed its last, Father said, 'Do you wish to take a trophy?'

"I looked down at the beast's corpse for a moment and then I burst into tears.

"Father put his hand on my shoulder and steered me away from the scene of my first battle. 'That's all right,' he said. 'When I stood where you stand now, I didn't want one either.'

"I cried on and off the entire time as we walked home. My father said nothing, just kept his arm around my shoulder as he walked next to me. Night had fallen by the time our cabin hove into view, and I stopped and looked at my father.

"I am sorry that I cried, Father." I lowered my gaze to the grass. "Sorry that I shamed you."

"Father cuffed me across the face, not hard, just enough to get my attention. 'You have not shamed me. You have done much credit to yourself and the name of Ambrus.'

"'But I *cried!*'

"'You cried because you killed. It is one thing to slay an animal for food or sport, but quite another to kill a man, even a creature such as a dretch, who is only distantly related to Humankind. Remember this as long as you carry a sword, Tarian: the taking of life is just as sacred as the giving of life. It is the power of the Gods themselves, and a man must learn to use it responsibly. When you must kill, do it as quickly and cleanly as possible. And while a warrior can't afford to cry on the outside—for opponents and allies alike might mistake this for weakness—know that a true warrior, one who honors the power of life and death that he wields, always cries on the inside, at least a little, every time that he takes a life.'"

Tarian fell silent, his tale finished. He waited to see how Phelan would react, if at all.

"Why did you tell me this story?" Phelan continued watching the road in front of them.

"Yesterday, you took a life—two lives—for the first time. I . . . wanted to tell you I know how it feels."

Phelan considered this for a moment before giving his father a tentative smile. "Thanks. It was a good story."

And that was the last either of them said on the matter before their wagon crested Ocean's Rise and there, spread out before them at last, the mighty Shashida sparkling beyond, lay the city of Pendara.

The wall that enclosed the city was surrounded by an

outer canal twenty feet wide which also served as a moat. Though the canal stank of the city's sewage, the seawater was still the same rich, deep blue as the ocean from which it was drawn. Tarian pulled the wagon up to the edge of the moat before Bloodgate, the main entrance. He drew back on the reins and Anci stopped, gratefully, it seemed to him. Tarian didn't blame the old girl. It had been a long haul for her, and frankly, he hadn't expected her to make it the entire way.

He was surprised to find the drawbridge up and the portcullis down. Not only that, but Phelan and he were the only ones there. Normally, there was quite a bit of traffic going in and out of the city from sunrise to sunset. Farmers, traders, travelers—most on foot, some on horses or in wagons, a very few riding in fine carriages. But there was no one now save the two of them. Tarian supposed he should have expected it, since they hadn't seen much traffic on the road; and what they had seen was mostly heading away from Pendara, not going toward it. *I guess I had other things on my mind,* he thought wryly.

Pendara's wall rose fifty feet into the air, and was constructed of the finest granite, mined from the Grimkell Mountains in northern Athymar and brought south by ship to Pendara a thousand years ago, during the Lands War. The stone was then hewn into blocks by Eyslken artisans, for this was back when the First Folk still took an occasional interest in the affairs of Man. Once the blocks were finished, Dragon Mages used blood spells to strengthen the stone and make it resistant to time and the elements, giving the granite a dark brownish-red cast. The wall had taken nearly four years to complete, but in the end, it proved Pendara's salvation, not just in the Lands War, but again, six hundred years later, during the third Rendish invasion.

Over the top of the wall, the spires of the Southern Palace were visible. From the highest flew the flag of the sun and crown, which meant the royal family—or at least some of them, at any rate—were in residence. Also visible was the golden dome of the Dawn Cathedral, the great temple of Rudra. Sunlight reflected off the dome in a dazzling shimmer, almost as if a portion of the sun's fire had descended to earth and taken up residence within the temple.

Behind Bloodgate—so named because the reddish iron bars of the portcullis had long ago been treated with dragon's blood so that they might never rust or break—was the great wooden drawbridge, which was only raised in time of war or great distress. In all Tarian's visits to Pendara, this was the first he had seen the bridge up.

Tarian waited a moment for someone to come out of the gatehouse, a small wooden shack on the other side of the moat to the left of Bloodgate. When no one did, he cupped his hands to his mouth and shouted, "Ho, the keeper!"

The door remained closed.

"What do you want?"

The voice came not from the gatehouse, but from above. Tarian and Phelan looked up. On the wall above Bloodgate stood a man dressed in a mail shirt and wearing a metal helm. He appeared to be in his mid-fifties, had a drooping salt and pepper mustache, and sported a brown patch over his left eye.

Tarian cursed himself for a fool. Of course no one would be in the gatehouse if the bridge was up and the portcullis down. Tarian drew himself up on the wagon seat and said loudly, "We request admittance to Pendara, greatest city in the Nine Known Lands!"

"Not so great these days, I'm afraid." the gatekeeper

called. "Don't bother stating your business. If you know what's best for you and your boy, you'll turn that rickety wagon of yours around and head back to wherever it is you came from."

The gatekeeper started to walk away.

"We can't do that!" Tarian said quickly. "We've come on an errand of vital importance!"

The man stopped and turned back around to face them. "Oh?" He sounded almost amused. "Vital to whom? Not to me, I'll tell you that!"

Tarian was about to answer when Phelan cut in.

"Vital to my mother," the lad said. "She . . . changed. We hope to find a mage who might be able to help her."

The gatekeeper regarded them for a few moments. After a time, he said, "Poor boy," quietly, almost as if he were speaking to himself. Then he went on, more loudly. "I meant it when I said you might as well turn around. There's no help for you in this city. Everyone's too busy trying to help themselves, and doing a piss-poor job of it, if you ask me. Only reason I'm on gate duty is because it's safer up here than down on the street."

"Then the Change has struck Pendara too?" Tarian had expected as much.

The gatekeeper nodded. "As well as a good part of the Golden Coast, from what I hear, and Rudra only knows where else." He shook his head. "These are dark times, my friends. Dark times indeed."

Tarian couldn't argue with that. "Please—may we enter?"

The gatekeeper considered. Finally, he said, "I'm not permitted to raise the portcullis or lower the drawbridge. Couldn't even if I wanted to, as I'm the only one on duty. But wait there."

The man left, and Tarian and Phelan waited as he had asked. It wasn't as if they had a choice. Several moments later they heard the sound of grinding stone, and a door opened in the wall next to the gatehouse. Tarian was impressed; there had been no obvious seams to mark the door's edges.

The gatekeeper walked out, dragging a long wooden plank behind him. On one end of the plank was tied a rope, and the man gathered it in a loop and stepped to the edge of the moat.

"Catch!" He heaved the rope across the moat. The throw was a bit short of the opposite side, but Tarian managed to lean out over the water and snatch hold of the rope without falling in. He and Phelan then reeled in the rope, pulling the plank toward them. The gatekeeper fed the board to them and helped keep it from dipping into the water. When the end of the plank was within reach, Phelan set it on the ground and stepped down on the wood to press it firmly into the earth.

Tarian dropped the rope and called to the gatekeeper. "What about our horse and wagon?"

The man shook his head. "There's no help for it; they won't fit through the doorway. Best get what you need from the wagon and leave the rest."

Tarian didn't like leaving Anci, but it seemed they would have to if they wished to gain entrance into Pendara. Phelan didn't seem to care. He merely walked over to the wagon and began unhooking Anci's harness. Tarian helped, removing bit and bridle, and storing the gear in the wagon. Better to let poor Anci forage for herself than keep her bound to the wagon for however long they'd be in the city. She was a meek animal, and would likely not roam far from Bloodgate. With any luck, they'd find her when they had finished their business in the city. And if not, losing Anci would be a small price to pay for a chance to help Lowri.

Phelan got the purse containing their money, but Tarian took it from him and asked the lad to carry Cathal instead. Tarian could touch the sword as long as it remained wrapped in cloth, but it still made him uneasy to carry it.

Then one at a time, son and father walked across the crude, narrow bridge the plank made. When they reached the other side, Tarian and Phelan helped the gatekeeper pull back the plank and then store it within the empty chamber hidden inside the wall. The rope got wet and rather aromatic in the process, but the man didn't care. "It'll dry soon enough," he said. "And no one will be down here to smell it."

Tarian offered his hand to the gatekeeper. "My thanks for allowing us entrance."

The man refused to shake. "I don't know that you'll feel like thanking me once you've seen what it's like inside. Pendara's in a terrible state; that's why the drawbridge is up. The Queen has declared martial law—no one in or out save those who have been sent to discover the nature of the enchantment which has befallen us."

"Then you're taking a risk by letting us in." Tarian withdrew his hand and reached for his purse. "Allow me to give you something for your trouble."

"Keep your money. I gave you entrance because I had to." The gatekeeper looked at Phelan. "I know what it's like to have someone you love affected by the Change. I was one of the lucky ones. All that happened to me is that my good eye changes color every candlemark or so. Goes from blue to brown to green, then back to blue again. But not everyone in my family was so fortunate. My youngest grandbaby—" The man took a deep breath and continued

109

in a tremulous voice. "Well, let's just say that if there's any chance you two might find help for your loved one inside the city, I won't be the man to stop you." He rubbed a tear from his good eye, then said, "All right, let's go."

The gatekeeper lifted a lantern off the ground, lit it, and pressed his palm against a stone on the inside wall. The door slid smoothly shut in response.

"I don't have any use for Eyslken," the gatekeeper said, "but I surely do appreciate their craftsmanship. C'mon now."

He led them out of the chamber and down a narrow corridor, then up a flight of stairs to an open trap door. He blew out the lantern, hung it from a peg on the wall, and motioned for Tarian and Phelan to precede him. When they were all outside, the gatekeeper stomped three times on a certain stone, and the trap door swung closed.

"When you have a fifty foot high wall around your city, it helps to have a few extra ways in and out," the gatekeeper said with a smile. "That was just one of them."

"Such a door would be quite effective during a siege," Tarian said. "Spies and saboteurs could use it to steal out among enemy forces under cloak of darkness and do more than a bit of mischief."

Phelan rolled his eyes. "Father, don't you ever stop thinking like a warrior?"

Tarian considered for a moment. "Not really," he answered.

"You a soldier?" the gatekeeper asked Tarian.

"Used to be. Had to retire to due to certain . . . injuries." He didn't want to be more specific, else he'd be forced to explain how his arm had grown back.

The man nodded. "I know what you mean. I used to fight in the King's army myself. See this?" He pointed to his patch. "I lost my eye fighting a Rendish warrior when I wasn't much older than your boy, here." He rolled up the sleeve of his right tunic to reveal a wicked scar on his forearm. "Bastard cut me up good before I managed to kill him. I recovered from my wounds, but my hand never had enough strength or nimbleness to wield a sword again. I ended up settling here in the city and becoming a candlemaker."

"Then what are you doing on guard duty?" Phelan asked.

The gatekeeper laughed. "I ask myself that same question every day, lad! Truth is, save for the Queen's personal guard and the City Watch—both of whom stayed behind under orders from Cambria herself—most able-bodied men and women who could lift a sword left months ago to travel north and join King Rufin's army. That left duffers like me to fill in until they come back. If they come back. I pray to Rudra they do; I have a son who marched with them."

"Where were the King's forces bound?" Tarian had a terrible feeling he knew what the gatekeeper was going to say.

"To Heart's Wound, there to engage the legions of Anghrist in final battle."

Tarian felt as if someone had punched him in the stomach. During his years as a solider, he'd heard rumors of prophecies and visions foretelling a great final conflict between the forces of Light and Darkness on the ancient battlefield of Heart's Wound. He'd always discounted the tales as mere superstition, but now, after what had happened these last several days, he wasn't so sure.

What if the Change was somehow connected to the Final Battle? What if it meant the battle had already been fought, and the forces of Light had lost?

CHAPTER ELEVEN

Before Tarian and Phelan took their leave of the gate-keeper, Tarian reached out and grasped the man's shoulders with both hands. Confused, the gatekeeper tried to pull away, but Tarian held him fast. The man stiffened and took in a sharp hiss of air. When Tarian released him, the gatekeeper reached up and tore his eye patch away from his face.

He now had two perfectly good eyes: one brown, one blue, though they'd both likely change color within the next candlemark.

The man gingerly probed his restored eye with trembling fingers, and Tarian smiled.

"A token of our thanks," he said.

Tears of gratitude in his eyes, the gatekeeper shook both their hands—first Tarian's, then Phelan's, then Tarian's again for good measure—and told them he'd keep watch on their horse and wagon from his post atop the wall, even see they were both brought in if the Bloodgate were opened for any reason.

Tarian and Phelan thanked him once more, said their good-byes and left, walking down a set of stairs carved into the wall. When they gained street level, Phelan said, "Why did you do that?"

"Hmmm?" Tarian was looking around, trying to get a feel for how Pendara was weathering the Change. They stood on the edge of Traders' Walk, the largest open-air market in Athymar. Usually, the jam-packed collection of stalls, tents and shops was a riot of noise and motion. But not this day. Only a few die-hard vendors were open for business, but even fewer folk were out browsing. Those that were moved slowly, their faces expressionless, as if they were in shock.

"I said, why did you do that? Heal the gatekeeper, I mean. You didn't have to; he'd already let us in."

Tarian turned to Phelan and fixed the lad with a steely gaze. "There's only one thing in this world I *have* to do, Son, and that's die. Everything else, I do because I choose to."

And it had been a choice: Tarian hadn't experienced the same compulsion to heal the gatekeeper as he had when Phelan was wounded during their encounter with the bandits. Perhaps that was because Phelan's injuries had been fresh, while the gatekeeper's was an old wound.

"Then why did you *choose* to?" Phelan asked.

"My first commander, a grizzled old war-dog named Lorant, used to say that a sword isn't much good if it's kept in the scabbard."

Phelan frowned. "And what does that mean?"

Tarian smiled. "That's exactly what I asked him the first time he said it to me."

"And what did he tell you?"

"He said, 'Let me know when you figure it out.'"

Phelan sighed. "I don't suppose you have a different answer for me."

Tarian just grinned. He put his hand on his son's shoulder and said, "Let's go. We've a blacksmith to see."

Phelan tucked the cloth-wrapped sword under his arm and together he and Tarian headed through the nearly empty streets of Traders' Walk.

After a bit, Phelan asked, "How come the Change did so

little to the gatekeeper and so much to us—and to Mother?"

Tarian thought of how Lowri looked the last time he saw her, crouching in the tree and gnawing on a bloody squirrel like some animal.

"I don't know," he said softly. "You know the expression that life is but a game of cards, and we must all play the hand we're dealt?"

Phelan nodded.

"I think, for some reason I can't even begin to guess, we've all been dealt a new set of cards, and now we have to play them, whether we like it or not."

Phelan smiled.

"I thought you said the only thing you *had* to do is die."

"That's right. In the end, every player has to give up his cards. It's how you play while you have them that matters."

Phelan looked thoughtful after that, and Tarian didn't like the way the boy ran his fingers over his sternum—the spot from which the shadow wolf emerged. He couldn't help thinking of the times Lowri, Phelan and he had visited Traders' Walk over the years. Lowri would stop and look at anything that caught her eye, whether she had any intention of buying it or not—and when she did wish to buy, she could haggle as well or better than any trader ever born. Phelan, especially when he had been younger, would constantly sniff the air and beg for every sweet treat his nose detected.

Happy times, good memories. Tarian prayed that somehow the three of them would have the chance to make even better memories in the future.

"What's the name of this smith we're going to see?" Phelan asked. "Kol-something."

"Kolgrim."

"Was he a soldier too?"

"No, as far as I'm aware, he's always been a smith. He and I have talked a few times over the years as he's shoed Anci, repaired a broken ax head, that sort of thing. The man loves to gossip. He'll not only be able to fill us in on what's been happening in the city since the Change, he'll likely have some information on how things have been going for King Rufin and his army."

If Tarian hadn't lost his arm two years ago, he would have been marching under the King's banner right then. Fighting—and quite possibly dying—at Heart's Wound. Tarian expected to feel something: shame, anger, disappointment, relief. . . . But he didn't feel much of anything. Perhaps, like the few people they'd seen in Traders' Walk so far, Tarian had been more numbed by the Change than he'd thought. Or perhaps, he'd been retired from soldiering for so long that the idea of fighting in the final battle of Good versus Evil held little meaning for him anymore.

Tarian continued. "Plus, while Kolgrim's not a swordmaker, he knows a great deal about the art. He'll make us a fair offer on Cathal, or know who will."

"An offer?" Phelan gaped, incredulous. "You mean, you want to sell your sword?"

Tarian laughed. "You act as if I just said I want to cut out my heart and trade it for a handful of pebbles."

"Near enough. This is Cathal we're talking about, Father. The finest sword you've ever owned."

"And right now, the most useless. I can't touch the damned thing, Phelan, let alone wield it. Besides, we don't need a sword; we need money. Wizards don't work cheap. Not good ones, at any rate. If we're going to hire a mage powerful enough to restore your mother to her previous self, we need all the gold we can get."

"What if we don't find Kolgrim at his forge? From the

look of things, a number of folk have chosen to stay at home today."

Tarian shrugged. "Then we see if we can find where he lives. If not, we keep looking until we find someone who's willing to buy Cathal."

Phelan considered for a moment, then nodded.

Pendara was an old, rich city, and more buildings than not had slate roofs instead of thatch. The streets in this section of town might have been unpaved and too narrow, but they weren't choked with filth, as in some cities Tarian had visited. Most people tossed their waste into the canals instead of the streets, and horses and cattle were only permitted in certain areas of the city.

But where the air was usually filled with the hum of people going about their daily business, this afternoon the atmosphere in Pendara was silent and oppressive. The few folk they saw were obviously having trouble dealing with the effects of the Change. One woman sat in the middle of the street, hands limp in her lap, crystalline tears streaming from her eyes only to float away as if they were dandelion fluff. A man stood arguing with a wall, occasionally smacking the brick with the flat of his palm. Every time his flesh struck the wall, a sonorous tone like that of a large, heavy bell rang out. One being—it was impossible to tell the gender, for he/she appeared to be an amalgam of both sexes—hovered three feet above the ground, eyes closed, slowly turning round and round in the breeze.

The sight of these people shook Tarian more than anything that he had witnessed in the last few days—including seeing what the Change had done to his poor wife. He had suspected the Change had affected more than just him and his family and had his suspicion confirmed by their encounter with the bandits. But to see these people and know

116

there were thousands more like them huddled within their homes, frightened, trying desperately to make sense of it all . . . it was almost more than he could bear. It was as if Pendara had been transformed into a hell to rival Damaranth itself.

They passed a little girl whose face possessed no features to speak of, only a covering of smooth skin with dips and rises to indicate where eyes, nose and mouth had once been. Tarian stopped to help her, though he had no clear notion of what he might be able to do. But the girl, despite her apparent lack of sensory organs, was somehow aware of them, and when they drew too close, she fled into a nearby alley.

Phelan watched her go, his face ashen. "You know, I've been feeling sorry for myself these last few days—and resentful of you, to be honest. The Change gave you a great gift, while it made Mother and me into monsters. But now—" He broke off and shook his head. "Let's go find that blacksmith."

Tarian wanted to tell his son that everything was going to be all right, that they would all be returned to normal somehow. But he couldn't; he wasn't certain he believed it himself. They continued walking in silence.

They left Traders' Walk, crossed over a small stone bridge that spanned a canal, and entered the Artisans' Quarter. Here blacksmiths, wagonwrights, stoneworkers, tanners and all manner of skilled artisans plied their trade. It wasn't as showy as Traders' Walk, but then this wasn't a place to attract the custom of visitors—this was a place where work got done. Normally the air was filled with the smell of smoke and the sound of hammers ringing on metal or pounding on wood. But today the air held no hint of woodsmoke, no sound of tools being used by skilled hands.

The Quarter wasn't completely silent, though. From around the next the corner came the sound of angry voices, cursing and shouting.

Tarian started forward, but Phelan grabbed his arm to stop him.

"Whatever's going on is none of our concern, Father. And given what we've seen since entering the city, it might very well prove to be dangerous."

"I appreciate your concern, lad, but I've faced danger often enough in my time."

"Perhaps so," Phelan countered, "but how often without a sword in your hand?"

"There are many ways to fight. Wielding a sword is just one of them. Besides, we need to find somebody to talk to, and whatever else is going on, at least from the sound of things, those people aren't too battle-shocked by the Change to speak their minds. Stay behind me, now."

Phelan didn't look happy, but he did as his father bade, and they headed around the corner.

A small crowd had gathered around a man in a leather jerkin who stood with his back against the wall of a tin-smith's shop. He had the darker skin and thicker features of the Rendish, though his hair was curly and brown, not straight and black. Tarian quickly sized up the crowd—five men, three women, none of them armed with anything more deadly than a dagger, and some of them likely not armed at all.

"It's yer bloody fault!" shouted a pig-faced man with a stubbly beard. Tarian wondered if he had always looked like that, or if it had been a result of the Change. "You and yer Anghrist-worshippin' brethren!"

"Aye!" agreed a fat woman with shiny red cheeks. "You Rendish have been trying to take over Athymar for nearly three thousand years! Now you've resorted to demon-sorcery to put a spell on all of us!"

The man—who Tarian judged to be an Athymarian with some Rendish blood in his ancestry—put up his hands in what he likely hoped was a placating gesture.

Pig-Face drew a dagger and leveled the point at the man's chest. "Don't you be tryin' to work any o' yer black arts on us! I'll slice ya from stem to stern, I will, and be happy t' do it!"

Tarian felt a cold twisting in his gut at the sight of the dagger's steel.

"Didja see that?" said a lanky man with bright green hair. "He tried to put the evil eye on me!"

"No! I didn't!" protested the target of the crowd's ire. "I don't know anything about magic! I'm a simple dockhand."

Rosy-Cheeks scowled. "Then why ain't you down on Wharfside?"

"My baby daughter has the colic, and I was just going to the herbwife's for some tonic to settle her stomach."

"A likely story!" Pig-Face said. "Yer out spyin' for your Rendish masters, that's what yer up to! Findin' out just how much damage yer evil enchantment's done t'the poor folk o' Pendara!"

"No, no!" But the man's words were drowned out by hoots of derision.

Tarian had seen and heard enough. He had no love for the Rendish—he'd matched steel against too many of their mercenaries over the years—but he'd also learned during his time as a soldier that you judged a man by how he acted, not by what he looked like.

Tarian stepped forward. "Why don't you people leave the poor sod alone?"

The crowd turned as one to look at him and Phelan, who

trailed reluctantly behind.

"'Ere, now, what's this?" Green-Hair said. "We got ourselves another spy?"

Tarian stopped when he was six feet from the closest member of the mob, to give himself some room to maneuver. "What you have is a man with two good eyes and enough sense to tell him this fellow's no more a Rendish spy than any of you are. He just has a trace of Rendish blood in his veins, that's all. If that were a crime, near a quarter of the city would be locked up in Knaves' Keep— along with a few of you, I suspect."

Pig-Face, Green-Hair, and Rosy-Cheeks glared at Tarian, while the rest of the crowd merely grumbled. A few even had the decency to look ashamed.

Tarian went on before any of the mob leaders could speak. "You're scared, and you want to know who's responsible for the enchantment that has befallen your city, and for all we know, the rest of the Nine Known Lands as well. But you can't go around waving daggers at everyone who strikes you the least bit odd. Anghrist's balls, thanks to the Change, just about everyone's at least a little odd these days."

A few of the crowd were beginning to nod. He was getting through to them. If he could just—

Pig-Face stepped forward far faster than Tarian would have thought the stout man capable of. He thrust his dagger under Tarian's nose, the point just barely dimpling the flesh.

"You speak like yer a learned man," Pig-Face said in a low, dangerous voice. "Maybe yer a wizard."

Tarian's insides twisted at being in contact with the blade's metal, but he did his best not to let his discomfort show. "I'm not a learned man; I'm a thoughtful one.

There's a difference. And as to my being a wizard, if I were, I'd have used my magic to flay the flab from your sorry bones by now."

Pig-Face blinked in confusion, obviously unable to understand how a man with a knife to his nose could talk so tough.

Pig-Face wasn't a man to be swayed by words, it seemed. That was all right with Tarian. He was quite familiar with other, more physical methods of persuasion. He balled his hands into fists, getting ready to box Pig-Face's ears. But before Tarian could raise his hands, his gut cramped up so painfully, it felt as if someone had jammed a boot in his belly. He immediately relaxed his hands, and the cramping eased. Not only couldn't he wield a weapon of steel anymore, it appeared he was no longer capable of inflicting violence of any sort upon another being. *This is a fine time to find out,* Tarian thought sourly.

CHAPTER TWELVE

Tarian felt cold fingers grip his heart as he heard the sound of rustling cloth and then a hiss of steel as a sword was drawn from its scabbard.

He didn't have to turn his head—couldn't turn it, unless he wanted to risk goading Pig-Face into slicing his nose in two—in order to know what was happening.

"Release my Father," Phelan said, "or I'll be forced to use this."

This, of course, meant Cathal. Tarian wanted to curse his son for a fool for making such a bluff, though he had to admit the boy's voice was remarkably steady. Perhaps he could pull it off. After all, he knew how to hold a sword, even if he didn't possess the strength or training to wield it effectively, and he knew how to fall into a battle stance.

Still, Phelan could likely use a little help.

"I'd listen to him, if I were you," Tarian said. "The Change has made my son a trifle . . . unstable. He's been itching to stick that blade of his in someone for four days now."

A few of the mob eyed Phelan warily as they backed off. They'd no doubt seen some bizarre happenings since the Change had occurred, and they had little desire to see another—not this close, anyway.

Pig-Face didn't seem worried, though. He looked at Phelan and smiled, displaying yellowed, rotten teeth. "Y'know how to use that thing, boy?"

"You know how to bleed?" Phelan replied.

Tarian had to choke back a laugh. That was a line from one of those dreadful romances Phelan liked to read, one Tarian had thumbed through once on a rainy day: *The Lay of Borysko the Bloodletter*. Borysko was a supernaturally skilled swordsman who constantly fought hordes of Rendish and Lukashen raiders single-handedly. Tarian wasn't as skilled a reader as his wife and son, but what lines he could decipher made him laugh until he cried.

Pig-Face didn't find the line amusing, however. His eyes narrowed dangerously. "I know how t'do a lot o' things, boy. Especially since the Change."

Pig-Face wasn't a fat man, but he didn't look like he had missed too many meals in his life, either. He was of medium height, with thick, stumpy arms and legs. But one moment he stood holding a dagger to Tarian's nose, and the next he was gone, moving so quickly and gracefully that Tarian's eyes couldn't track him.

Tarian turned, saw that Pig-Face now stood with the edge of his dagger pressed against Phelan's neck. A tiny bead of blood formed above Phelan's throat apple. Tarian felt an instant urge to step forward and heal the wound, but he knew he couldn't, not yet.

Phelan had been so surprised by Pig-Face's sudden attack that he'd dropped Cathal's scabbard, though he'd managed to maintain a grip on the blade itself, for all the good it would do him now.

Pig-Face grinned. "Looks t'me like yer the one as knows how t'bleed, boy. And yer goin' to be doin' a lot more bleedin' afore we're through."

"You're pretty slick with that dagger," came a voice from the street. "How about trying it on me?"

Everyone turned to face the newcomer. It was a Watcher, a woman, who couldn't have been more than twenty-five, Tarian guessed, though she might have been a bit younger. She was on the petite side and wore her blonde hair shorter than some men. She was on the plain side of pretty, but not altogether unattractive. Not that Tarian cared about that right then. As long as she could swing the sword she held at her side, she could look like the southern end of a northbound dretch as far as he was concerned.

The appearance of a member of Pendara's illustrious City Watch was enough to scatter the rest of the mob, including the "Rendish spy." Tarian hoped the man would be able to get that tonic for his baby now, though it might just be safer for him if he went home and stayed there awhile.

The Watcher paid no attention to those who fled. She kept her gaze fixed on Pig-Face. No, not quite, Tarian realized. She was actually looking slightly to his left. That was odd.

"You Watchers think yer so tough, don't ya? But you weren't able to do anythin' to stop the Change, and you haven't been able to keep good people from dyin' since, have ya?"

The Watcher sighed, and Tarian noted the dark puffy patches of skin beneath her eyes. He wondered if she'd gotten any rest at all since the Change occurred.

"It's been a long hard four days for all of us, friend," the woman said. "Why don't you do me a favor and just put the dagger away and go home?"

"You should do as she says," Phelan said quietly. "Since the Change, I have a . . . creature living inside me. A shadow wolf. It's only emerged twice so far, but both times were during situations when I was in danger. The last time, it killed two bandits. I can feel it inside me right now, pushing to get out."

Pig-Face paled. "Yer lyin'," he said, as if he were trying

to reassure himself. "People can claim t'do anythin' since the Change. I met one fella in a tavern who said he could turn pebbles to diamonds just by touchin' 'em. When I told him to prove it, he said he couldn't do it less'n he were drunk, and would I mind buyin' the first round?"

"Did you ever consider that the man might have told you the truth?" the Watcher asked. "If I've learned anything in the last few days, it's that the Change works in its own strange ways."

"I am not lying," Phelan said, his voice louder this time, an edge of fear to it now. "The wolf is going to come out any moment unless you let me go."

"Then maybe I should just go ahead and slit yer throat right now. That might stop yer so-called 'shadow wolf.'"

"That might work," Phelan allowed. "But without a cage to return to, you might just set him free forever."

Pig-Face pondered that while a line of sweat formed on his upper lip.

"I'd listen to him, if I were you," the Watcher said. "I think he's telling the truth."

She still wasn't looking at either Pig-Face or Phelan, though. She was looking past him, at a spot toward the base of the tinsmith's wall, but Tarian didn't see anything there save a mouse nibbling on an old apple core which someone had been too lazy to chuck into a canal.

"I'm pretty light on m'feet now," Pig-Face muttered to himself. "Even if there was a wolf, I could probably dodge the mangy thing." Pig-Face's eyes glazed over as he thought.

Tarian watched as the mouse turned away from the apple and did a somersault. The Watcher nodded, then stepped quickly forward, grabbed Phelan's collar, and yanked him away from Pig-Face's dagger. Phelan stumbled and fell onto his backside, losing his grip on Cathal. The sword tumbled to the dirt, less than three feet away from Tarian. He actually started toward Cathal until he remembered that he wouldn't be able to bring himself to touch it.

Pig-Face blinked, startled by the Watcher's sudden move. Tarian guessed that while the man's body was abnormally fast and graceful, his mind was still slow as pudding on a cold morning.

The Watcher glanced at the mouse again, jumped to the left, and raised her sword, blade pointing back over her right shoulder, pommel facing forward.

At the same instant, Pig-Face became a momentary blur as he sped forward—only to slam his forehead against the Watcher's sword handle. He took two stagger-steps back, dropped his dagger, then collapsed to the ground, unconscious.

Tarian went to Phelan and helped the lad to stand. He then touched the first two fingers of his right hand to Phelan's throat and healed the small cut left by Pig-Face's dagger.

"That was a damn fool chance you took, boy," Tarian said gruffly.

Phelan shrugged. "Someone once told me a sword isn't much good if it's kept in the scabbard."

Tarian couldn't help it; he burst out laughing, as much from relief as anything else.

"The wolf?" he asked.

"Quieting down," Phelan said. He too, sounded relieved. "I tried to hold him back, and I think I was able to, at least a little."

"A little was all you needed this time. Who knows? Perhaps one day you'll be able to control the shadow wolf completely."

"Perhaps." Phelan sounded doubtful, but he was obviously cheered by his success, however minor it might be.

Tarian heard the Watcher sheathe her sword. He looked over and saw the woman had stepped to the wall where the mouse was. She crouched down, her back to them, so Tarian couldn't quite see what she did, if anything. After a moment, she stood and walked over to them, smiling. Tarian thought she had a nice smile. As nice as Lowri's, in its own way.

She spoke to Phelan first. "My apologies for pulling you away from the man's dagger so abruptly. I didn't mean for you to take a tumble."

Phelan's faced reddened and he self-consciously brushed dirt off his rear. "That's all right," he mumbled, gaze focused somewhere in the vicinity of his feet.

Tarian was amused by how his son had come over shy in the Watcher's presence, not that he would have reacted any differently at seventeen. He inclined his head to the woman. "Our thanks. It seems Pendara's become a bit more hazardous since the last time we visited. I'm Tarian Ambrus, and this is my son, Phelan."

The Watcher nodded to each of them. "I'm Danya Arden, of the Pendaran City Watch." She plucked at the red fabric of her tunic. "Not that you didn't already know that." Then she frowned. "Did you say you were visitors? Both Bloodgate and Seagate have been closed since the Change occurred. No one in, no one out, by orders of the Queen herself."

"The gatekeeper took pity on us when he heard our tale," Tarian explained. "I'd appreciate it if you didn't report him, though. I'd hate for the man to suffer for doing us a good turn."

Danya smiled once more. "Why don't you tell me why

127

you're here, and I'll decide whether the gatekeeper made a legitimate exception or not?"

"Very well, but first there's something I must attend to." Tarian stepped over to Pig-Face and laid a hand on the man's shoulder. He sensed that if he healed Pig-Face too thoroughly, the man would awaken soon, so he stopped short, doing just enough to take care of a minor injury to the man's brain and heal the bruised and swollen skin on his forehead. He then withdrew his hand, stood, and returned to Phelan and the Watcher.

"What was that all about?" she asked.

Phelan shrugged. "Since the Change, he can heal. If someone's hurt, he has to help them. He can't stop himself."

"It's true," Tarian confirmed.

Danya smiled. "That has to be one of the more useful changes I've heard of, though I can't say I'm happy you wasted your newfound power on the likes of him." She nodded toward Pig-Face. "Now you were about to tell me what you and your boy are doing here?"

Tarian noticed Phelan's face redden at the Watcher's use of the word *boy*. Phelan turned away from them and bent down to pick up Cathal, the scabbard and the cloth that had covered them. He wiped dirt from the blade with the cloth while Tarian told the Watcher their story.

By the time Tarian was finished, Phelan had cleaned the sword, replaced it in its scabbard, and wrapped both up in the cloth once more.

"I can't say as I blame the man," Danya said. "That's one of the rougher tales I've heard in the last few days. I'm afraid you may have wasted a trip, though."

"Why's that?" Tarian asked.

"Even if you could find a wizard, hundreds of citizens

would already be lined up begging for him to reverse what the Change has done to them or their families. But all the truly powerful mages in the city are gone. They left weeks ago, accompanying the forces of King Rufin on their march to Heart's Wound."

Tarian smacked his forehead with his palm. "I should have realized once the gatekeeper told us that the Final Battle was in the offing. Of course the wizards rode with the King!"

"Those few mages who remain in the city possess no real power to speak of," Danya said. "And most of those are charlatans who use parlor tricks to separate the gullible from their coin." She thought for a moment. "I've heard rumors that Cynric Fenfallow stayed behind at the King's request to look after the Queen and her children. I don't know if it's true, though."

Tarian understood now why the Queen had taken residence in the Southern Palace instead of remaining at Garanhon, the ancient keep of the kings of Aythmar. Rufin wanted her and the children as far removed from the Final Battle as possible. Heart's Wound lay far to the north, and Pendara was situated on the southernmost point in the land.

Phelan's eyes widened at Danya's words. "*The* Cynric Fenfallow? The wizard who stopped a Rendish invasion fleet single-handed?"

Danya grinned. "Unless you know another wizard by that name."

Phelan turned to Tarian. "I've read all about him, Father! He's the greatest mage who ever lived! Surely he can help us!" He faced Danya. "Do you think we could see him?"

The woman laughed. "I'm just a simple street Watcher. I don't have any pull with the Palace. Nothing against either of you or your situation, but I doubt Cynric would have the time to see you, should he have a mind to do so. He's most likely trying to figure out what caused the Change and how it may be reversed." More softly, she added, "At least, that's what we all hope."

Tarian knew of Cynric's exploits as well as Phelan did. He'd even seen the wizard once, ten years ago, when Tarian had been in command of a small regiment of men who'd uncovered a Thaisian deathmage trafficking in undead slaves on the Black Coast. They'd sent word of the situation to Garanhon, made camp and waited. Several weeks later Cynric Fenfallow rode into their camp. Tarian and his men led him to the deathmage's lair, then stayed out of the way while the wizards fought. Cynric won, though it had seemed to Tarian to be a near thing at the time.

Still, as mighty as Cynric was reputed to be, Tarian didn't see how a single man—no matter how skilled in the mystic arts—could hope to undo the Change.

"The Queen has been of ill health lately," Danya said, "possibly due to whatever effect the Change has had on her. But criers have been circulating throughout the city today, announcing that Cambria intends to a give short address to her subjects in the Palace courtyard before dusk. You should go. Rumor has it that the Queen has information on how King Rufin and the forces of Light fare at Heart's Wound. She might well have something to say about the Change also."

"Will you be there?" Phelan asked, a little too quickly.

Danya smiled. "The entire Watch will be in attendance, as well as the Queen's Royal Guard. Somebody has to keep an eye on troublemakers like you two, right?" She gave Tarian a wink.

Tarian smiled back. "Thanks for letting us know about the Queen's address. We shall do our best to attend." He paused.

"I hate to ask, but could you help us with one more thing?"

"Of course. What is it?"

Tarian gestured at the cloth-wrapped bundle under Phelan's arm. "Do you know anyone who would like to buy a sword?"

Danya waved as Tarian and Phelan continued on their way down the street. The father waved, while the son turned away, stole a glance back—*Probably hoping I'm not looking,* Danya thought—then turned quickly away once more, face crimson. Danya grinned. *That boy sure blushes a lot.* Then the two turned the corner and were gone.

They reminded Danya of the folk in the village where she grew up. Friendly and plain-spoken. She'd found them a refreshing change from the usual brusqueness and sometimes outright rudeness of Pendarans. Plus, Tarian wasn't exactly hard on the eyes, was he?

She'd given them the names of a couple swordsmiths, and a wizard who wasn't as big a fake as some others. That sword of theirs was a fine piece of work. She might have offered to purchase it herself, except it was made for a man and was too long and heavy for her to wield effectively.

She offered up a quick prayer to Rudra that He might help them succeed in their quest to cure Lowri. Deep down, though, she feared there was nothing any of them could do about the effects of the Change except somehow learn to live with them, as difficult as that might be.

The dagger-wielding idiot groaned as he began to wake. Danya was tempted to haul his carcass to Knaves' Keep, but she knew it would be an exercise in futility. The city had seen a significant increase in crime over the last few days, and every cell in the Keep was full, and then some. This morning, the Watch Commander had ordered his people not to bring in anyone else unless they had committed "about a half dozen or so" murders. Otherwise, the Watchers were told merely to do their best to prevent what trouble they could. And if that meant a few bodies had to end up facedown in the canals, then so be it.

Danya didn't think this fool posed enough of a threat to bother cutting his throat. She picked up his dagger and tucked it in her belt, then patted him down to make certain he wasn't carrying any other weapons. He wasn't. Then, just for fun, she removed all his clothes and left him lying naked in the street, groaning as he struggled to return to full consciousness.

She hoped he could run fast enough to keep anyone from getting an eyeful of his natural glory. Not for his sake, but for anyone who might be unfortunate enough to be looking in his direction as he passed.

Several blocks later, she rolled up the man's clothes and tossed them in an alley. Then she decided to head for a little cheese shop she was familiar with on the other side of town. She gently patted her tunic pocket and felt the mouse—whom she had named Jessex after a rat-faced boy she had known growing up—wriggle in response.

"How about a treat, Jessex? I'd say you earned it."

The mouse gave a little *eeeek* which Danya interpreted as a sound of approval, although she supposed it probably didn't mean anything, really. As she walked, she found her thoughts drifting back toward Tarian Ambrus. Perhaps she would look for him in the crowd after the Queen's address. Just to check up on him and his son, of course, see how they had fared with the swordsmiths and the wizard.

Jessex made a snuffling sound. Danya knew better, but she could have sworn it sounded as if the little beast were chuckling to itself.

CHAPTER THIRTEEN

"You can't do this, your Majesty!"

Cambria, wearing a flowing green grown covered with emeralds, stood while a lone handmaid—all that she could bear to have near her—pinned up her hair in preparation for donning a wig. "Of course we can, Saeth. And for your future reference, we don't take kindly to being told what we can and cannot do by anyone other than the King." Cambria smiled. "And we're not particularly fond of it even then."

The priestess blushed furiously and lowered her gaze to the stone floor of the Queen's dressing chamber. Up until a few days ago, Saeth had never been in Cambria's presence, and she was still struggling to learn the proper protocol. She stood—not sat—six feet away from the Queen. Was that too far? Too close? Was standing presumptuous? Should she sit instead? Saeth had tried kneeling after she'd first entered, but Cambria had immediately snapped at her to stand before she got a crick in her back.

"I beg your pardon, Majesty."

Cambria accepted the woman's apology with a feeble wave. "We're all doing the best we can, Saeth. A Queen can ask no more of her people."

Saeth suppressed a shudder. She still wasn't used to the way Cambria could hear the thoughts of those around her, and she doubted she ever would be.

Cambria swayed then, and the handmaid grasped the Queen's elbow to steady her. Cambria nodded her thanks to the woman, then touched her hand to her forehead.

"Is it hot in here?" Cambria asked. "It feels so to us."

There was no fire lit in the small hearth, and the shutters were open, allowing a gentle salt-scented breeze to waft in through the window.

"Perhaps it's the gown, Majesty," Saeth offered. "It is rather . . . elaborate."

Cambria chuckled. "It is at that. Which of course, is the point. There are going to be quite a few people attending our address today. We need to make sure we look like a queen. Or rather, what they expect a queen to look like."

The handmaid finished pinning up the Queen's hair and Cambria checked the woman's work by glancing into the full-length standing mirror to her right. She nodded, and the woman walked over to a mahogany cabinet and opened its doors to reveal several shelves full of wigs. The handmaid stepped to the side so Cambria could select.

The Queen examined the wigs for a few moments. "Oh, I don't know," Cambria said at last, forgetting to use the royal plural. "What do you think, Saeth?"

"Ah . . ." The wigs came in every color and style—from short, straight and black to beehive-shaped alabaster mounds. More than a few had jewels pinned to the hair. Saeth rubbed her shorn scalp. "To be honest, Majesty, I'm a terrible one to be asking. I haven't had a full head of hair since I was twelve."

Cambria laughed. "We'll take that one." The Queen pointed to a wig of fiery red curls. "That reminds us of the King's hair color. Perhaps it will remind the people as well."

The handmaid nodded, and gently removed the wig from its stand.

As the woman began putting the wig on Cambria, Saeth

decided to continue her earlier line of argument. Not that she thought it would do any good in the end, but with every higher-ranking Church official gone with King Rufin to Heart's Wound, Saeth was by default the spiritual advisor to the royal family, and thus it was her duty to at least try.

"Majesty, I'll admit that you've made progress in adjusting to your new, ah, condition, but the truth of the matter is that you still have difficulty blocking out the thoughts of others. To address a crowd of hundreds could at best prove overwhelming for you, and at worst, it might damage your mind."

The handmaid finished settling the wig and began pinning it in place.

"Cynric has been kind enough to teach us some basic Eyslken meditation techniques which have helped tremendously. He has also convinced us to forgo the Royal Physic's potions, which has also helped much. We realize now that we need a sharp, clear mind in order to resist the tide of thought which constantly assails us."

"Even so, giving the address will still be difficult for you, to say the least. Is it so important that it's worth risking your health and perhaps your mind itself?"

Cambria fixed Saeth with a steely look. "The people of Pendara are frightened and confused. They need to see their Queen, to be reassured by her. They need to know that whatever else has occurred, the monarchy is still strong and we are still here to protect them." She paused, then added more softly. "Even if ultimately there's nothing we can do."

The handmaid completed her task and stepped back. Cambria looked in the mirror, tilted her head first to the right, then to the left, then smiled. "Very good, Jaleh. You may leave us now."

The handmaid curtsied to the Queen, then to Saeth, before departing the chamber. Saeth was taken aback by the woman's show of respect. She was used to acolytes bowing to her, but not to gestures of deference from anyone outside the Church's hierarchy.

The Queen looked grim. "You'd best become accustomed to it, Saeth. If things go badly for your fellow priests at Heart's Wound, you could very well end up as a High Priestess or even Radiant."

Saeth was horrified at the notion of her brothers and sisters in Light falling in battle, but a small part of her thrilled at the idea of being a High Priestess. But to become Radiant—absolute head of the Church, second only to Rudra and His daughter Lodura—was unthinkable. Wasn't it?

If the Queen were aware of Saeth's thoughts, as she surely must be, she chose not to comment on them.

"Let's go, Saeth. The people await their Queen." Cambria gathered up her voluminous skirts and headed for the door. Saeth hurried after, praying that her monarch wasn't making a terrible mistake.

The courtyard of the Southern Palace was packed wall to wall with people, and the streets outside were jammed with even more. A line of the Queen's Royal Guard kept the citizens from coming too close to the balcony from which Cambria planned to address her subjects, but only because they were each armed with wicked-looking poleaxes and expressions which said they weren't in the least afraid to use them. Normally, there would have been a hum of excitement in the air—people joking, laughing, singing bawdy songs, hollering for the boys selling apples and nuts to "Git on over 'ere, lad!" But not this day. The Pendarans in attendance—many of whom looked rather more exotic than they had four days ago—spoke quietly, almost reverently amongst themselves, as if they had come to participate in a religious service of the utmost solemnity instead of hear their Queen speak.

Tarian and Phelan stood well toward the rear of the crowd. There were so many people jammed into the courtyard that Tarian half expected the walls to give way and burst outward any moment. As a soldier in the King's army, he had been present during Rufin's coronation at Garanhon eighteen years ago, and then again at his marriage to Cambria, two years after that. The people gathered for each event numbered more than this, he judged, but not by much. He took in a sharp breath as an even sharper elbow dug into his ribs. No, not by much at all.

The main keep of the Southern Palace rose before them, and though Tarian had seen it before on numerous occasions, he never failed to be impressed by it. It was constructed entirely of white stone with one long tower in the center flanked by two smaller ones. The towertops were covered with white tile, and the royal standard flew from the tip of each needle-like spire, though at the moment the flags hung limply in the still, humid air. The courtyard was paved with white flagstones, and the inside of its walls was lined with cherry trees. In the center of the courtyard rose a large marble fountain topped by a sculpture of a Glory, one of the demigods who served Rudra. The Glory's feathered wings were extended to their full length, and its slim, graceful hands stretched upward as if they might touch the heavens. Water streamed forth from the Glory's eyes, running down its polished naked body to trickle into the basin below. According to legend, the Glories cried for one hundred years after the Sundering, when the First Land was split into what eventually became the Nine Known Lands, and their tears flowed together to form all the oceans of the world. Whenever it rained in Athymar, parents told their children that somewhere a Glory was crying.

Garanhon was unquestionably the more effective fortress of the two, but to Tarian's mind, the Southern Palace was the more beautiful, not in the least due to that fountain and the wonderfully sad sculpture which topped it.

Tarian mopped his sweaty brow. The close presence of so many people in the courtyard made the summer air all the more stifling. He felt as if his body were bound in strips of warm, wet cloth. Each breath was a struggle to suck air through a mouthful of moist cotton.

Tarian turned his head—the only part of his body he could turn at the moment—to ask Phelan how he was handling this heat, but the boy wasn't looking his way. Instead, he was scanning the crowd, head darting back and forth, an expression of mingled hope and worry on his face.

"You'll have a hard time picking her out in this chaos, boy," Tarian said. "Red tunic or no." They'd seen a number of Watchers in the crowd so far, but no Danya.

Phelan didn't turn to meet Tarian's gaze. "I'm not looking for anybody in particular; I'm just . . . looking."

Tarian grinned. "Sure you are."

Phelan ignored him and kept searching.

Tarian was amused by his son's obvious attraction to Danya Arden. Not that he blamed the boy. She was comely enough in her own way, and from what they had seen, she was a damn fine Watcher. But he was also saddened to see the boy so pathetically eager to catch a glimpse of her. Phelan had spent most of his seventeen years living on the edge of the Greenmark with only Lowri for company. Tarian had come home whenever he could, but it hadn't been often enough. Lowri would sometimes take Phelan to a small village a day's ride away from their cabin, where they would stay with friends. There, Phelan could play with other children his own age and live like a normal boy for a time before they had to return home. Lowri never took Phelan to Pendara by herself. Southern Athymar was more civilized than much of the rest of the land, but the region was still far too dangerous for a woman and a little boy to travel alone.

Several times over the years, Lowri asked Tarian why they couldn't move to a village—any village—instead of living in such an isolated spot. Tarian always told her the same thing. As a soldier in the King's army, he had seen many things, heard many rumors. The increase in Lukashen and Dretchen attacks on human settlements, the stream of Rendish mercenaries flowing into the northern lands, the influx of foreign sorcerers who practiced dark and forbidden magics—all of these things pointed to one inescapable conclusion: the Final Battle between Rudra and Anghrist, prophesied by Lodura just before her execution at the hands of the Bloodlord Kalle two thousand years ago, was coming. And when it came, Tarian was determined that his wife and child would be safe.

But now, seeing his son acting like any other young man obsessed with a woman he had met only hours ago, Tarian wondered if in his desire to protect Lowri and Phelan he hadn't made a mistake. Would it have been so terrible if they had lived in a village? Yes, there was a chance of attack by Lukashen or Dretchen, but there were so many other ways to die. An innocuous wound that became infected, a simple cold that worsened into a far deadlier sickness. . . . At least if they had lived in a village, Phelan would've had a chance to make friends, court girls. He might even have taken a wife by now.

What was the point of preparing for the future, Tarian realized, if it robbed you of the present?

"There she is!"

Tarian looked in the direction Phelan pointed and saw Danya waving. She was only a hundred feet or so away, but in this crowd, that might as well have been several miles. Still her red Watcher's tunic, along with a liberal dose of attitude, enabled her to make her way toward them through the mass of Pendaran citizenry without too much difficulty.

"Good to see you two made it," she said. She nodded toward the cloth-bound bundle Phelan held. "I take it you weren't able to locate any of the swordsmiths I recommended?"

"Their shops were closed," Tarian said. "As was that of the wizard you told us about. Like as not, they've all come to hear the Queen. We'll try again tomorrow."

Danya nodded, then turned to scan the crowd. *Still on duty,* Tarian thought approvingly. He glanced sideways at Phelan. The lad watched Danya intently, his mouth opening and closing several times like a fish too long out of water. Probably trying desperately to think of something to say. Tarian had been the same way when he'd courted Lowri. He had wanted to hear her voice, have her look into his eyes as she spoke. But try as he might, he could never come up with anything to say which wouldn't make him sound like an idiot.

"How much longer do you think it will be?" Tarian asked. "I'm not overfond of crowds." He grunted as a heavy-set man with an extra eye set into his forehead stepped on his foot. He scowled at the man, eliciting a shrugged apology. "Especially when they seem determined to squash me to jelly."

Danya grinned and looked to the west. The sky was

splashed with orange and the sun was no longer visible. "Not long now. The Queen will want to finish the address before nightfall, if she can, to make it easier for the crowd to disperse. She—"

Danya broke off as a trio of Royal Heralds dressed in tabards emblazoned with the crown and sun insignia stepped onto the balcony. They walked to the edge, thirty feet above the flagstone floor of the courtyard, and lifted polished brass horns to their lips. They each took a deep breath, and in perfect unison sounded a series of notes announcing the arrival of Queen Cambria. They lowered their instruments and stepped back as Cynric Fenfallow, garbed in a fine robe of deepest purple, came forward, accompanied by a priestess of Rudra wearing the plainer white robe of her order.

The crowd fell silent. No one spoke, no one moved; they seemed to scarcely breathe. It was so quiet, gulls could be heard crying faintly in the distance.

Cynric looked older than Tarian remembered him, which was only to be expected. The wizard's face was thinner and he moved slowly, as if it pained him. He gestured to the heralds, and they bowed their heads and filed back into the Palace. Cynric and the priestess then took up positions on either side of the doorway and waited. A few moments later, she appeared—Cambria, Queen of Athymar and Mistress of the White Isles. She wore an elaborate verdant gown studded with emeralds and instead of its usual blonde, today her hair was fiery red. A wig, Tarian decided. The colors she had chosen formed a dramatic contrast against the backdrop of the Palace's ivory stone, Tarian thought.

As the Queen moved to the edge of the balcony, Tarian saw that she wasn't wearing her crown or carrying either

141

scepter or crystal orb. Such accouterments were normally employed only on the most important and sacred of occasions. By leaving the devices of her office behind, Cambria was signaling to the crowd that this address was to be an informal one. That suited Tarian fine. He wasn't one for pomp and ceremony.

Danya leaned over and whispered in his ear. "She doesn't look good. She's so pale—and see how she moves, as if she might fall any moment."

Cambria did look a trifle unsteady, and when she reached the stone railing, she gripped it with both hands as if she desperately needed support. She closed her eyes and stood a moment, seeming to gather her strength. She swayed, and the priestess started forward, but Cynric stopped her with a sharp gesture. Cambria steadied, then opened her eyes. When she spoke, there was no sign of weakness in her voice. It rang through the courtyard, strong, clear and confident.

"We greet you, our subjects, with admiration for how well you have borne the hardships of the last few days. Your courage does all of Athymar proud, and we stand humbled before it." She inclined her head in a gesture of respect, then straightened and swept her gaze across the assemblage, her expression growing more serious. "We have come before you this day to speak of the mysterious and troubling enchantment that has fallen upon Pendara."

She paused and slumped forward, and for a horrible instant, it appeared as if the might fall over the railing. The crowd gasped and Cynric and the priestess rushed forward. But then Cambria regained her strength and waved the wizard and priestess off. Cynric hesitated, then he and the priestess returned to their positions flanking the doorway.

"Please forgive us," she said so softly that Tarian had to

strain to hear it. "We too have been affected by the Change and are struggling to learn to deal with our new . . . condition." She continued, louder now. "But learn we will, as shall all of you. Make no mistake, we shall do everything in our power to see this enchantment is lifted from our land, but in the meantime, I charge you all with the task of learning everything you can about your newfound abilities. Explore them, master them. Ignorance leads only to fear and weakness, but knowledge is the road to strength."

The crowd seemed to draw reassurance from Cambria's words, but not Tarian. He didn't miss the hidden message behind what the Queen said. She had no more idea what had caused the Change than did any of those listening to her.

"We have heard many rumors over the last few days: That the Change is but a prelude to a new Rendish invasion, that a cabal of foreign sorcerers has invaded the South, that Baron Cavillor and his forces are outside Pendara's walls at this very moment, laying siege to the city. All of this have we heard, and much more besides. We are here to tell you that none of these tales are true. Our navy has reported no Rendish ships in southern waters. The Royal Wizard—" she gestured to Cynric "—has detected no invading mages, and as for the dark Baron Cavillor . . ." She paused and drew a deep breath. "Your King sent word a month ago that the Baron's forces were assembling in the North, in preparation to engage the army of Light at Heart's Wound. Cavillor and his foul allies could hardly be outside Pendara's walls and fighting at Heart's Wound at the same time, could they?"

From somewhere in the midst of the crowd, a man shouted, "How goes the battle, your Majesty?"

Cambria lowered her gaze and gripped the stone railing

even harder. "Alas, we have had no word since the King's last message. The battle may still be in the offing, or it may be over and done with. We dispatched riders to Heart's Wound immediately after the Change took place; however, it shall be some time before they return. But remember Lodura's promise and take heart. Two thousand years ago, the daughter of Rudra spoke of the Great Battle to come. She told that while the struggle would be long and hard, in the end Light would prevail. And so it shall."

Several feeble cheers went up, but the rest of the crowd didn't catch their fellows' enthusiasm. The Queen continued as if she didn't notice.

"Cynric Fenfallow—perhaps the greatest wizard our land has ever known—is currently making plans to leave Pendara on a journey to determine the true nature of the Change and to discover whether . . . that is, *how* it may be reversed."

Bit of a slip, there, Tarian thought. The Queen's obvious weariness was catching up with her.

"If anyone can . . . solve the great mystery—" Cambria reached up with trembling hands to rub her temples "—of the Change, it is . . . Cynric." The Queen grimaced as if struck by a sudden wave of great pain. The wizard and the priestess started for her, but they were too late. Cambria's eyes rolled back in her head, and she pitched over the railing, falling thirty feet to the flagstones below.

CHAPTER FOURTEEN

The crowd's mingled cries of shock and horror failed to drown out the terrible meaty thud of the Queen's impact.

Tarian experienced a jolt and the breath whooshed out of his lungs, as if he too had just taken a fall. This sensation was followed by a rush of agony that spread through his body like wildfire. It felt as if his bones had shattered and turned to dust, as if his skull had split open and his brains poured onto the ground. But all that was nothing compared to the overpowering need to reach the Queen's side—now!

He pushed at the man ahead of him—a beefy fellow in a leather jerkin—but the man wouldn't, or perhaps couldn't, budge.

"Let me through!" he shouted. "I can heal her!"

A number of citizens at he front of the crowd surged forward, perhaps to render aid, more likely out of a terrified need to see how badly their Queen was injured. The Queen's Guard quickly closed ranks around her body and crossed their poleaxes to form a barricade. The maneuver convinced the onrushers to keep their distance—for now at least.

Cynric and the priestess stood at the railing looking down. The wizard shouted orders to the Guards below, but precisely what he said, Tarian couldn't make out over the wailing and weeping of the crowd. Even from this distance, he could sense Cambria's pain as if it were his own, and he knew instinctively that her injuries were severe. If something wasn't done in the next few moments, she would die.

He looked at Danya. Could the Watcher clear a path for him? No, he decided, not in all this confusion. No one would listen to her. There was only one person who could help him get to the Queen.

"Danya, Phelan! I need you both to lift me up!"

They looked at him, uncomprehending, barely hearing him through their own shock. He grabbed each by the front of their tunic and gave them a quick shake to clear their heads.

"Both of you, kneel down so that I might stand upon your shoulders! I need Cynric to see me!"

Understanding dawned in Danya's eyes and she gave Phelan a backhanded swat on his shoulder. The lad started and blinked, as if waking from a nightmare, and then he nodded. Danya and Phelan bent down, and Tarian stepped onto their shoulders—Danya's right, Phelan's left. He crouched and placed his hands upon their heads to steady himself as they stood. When they were upright, he straightened, and they each grasped one of his legs to help brace him.

He cupped his hands to his mouth, drew in a deep breath, and called out in a voice that had once shouted battle orders through the din of neighing horses and ringing steel.

"Cynric Fenfallow!"

The wizard, who had turned away from the railing and was heading back into the palace stopped. When he saw Tarian, he frowned and hobbled back to the railing.

"I can heal her!" Tarian shouted.

The wizard hesitated.

"Damn your eyes, man, she's dying!"

Cynric paused a moment longer, and Tarian had the sense that the wizard was trying to decide whether to trust him or not. Finally, Cynric gave a curt nod, then began running his fingers rapidly across the railing, as if he were searching for something. He shook his head, then knelt and brushed his hands over the balcony floor. He stopped, then closed his eyes and began moving his lips.

Tarian didn't know much about wizardry, but he knew that Cynric was working some manner of spell. Whatever it was, Tarian hoped the man would be quick about it. The sympathetic pain he felt was beginning to diminish, and he knew this meant the Queen didn't have much time left.

Cynric stood once more, thrust both hands into the air and shouted a word in a language Tarian didn't recognize. Then he lowered his hands and began speaking, and his voice echoed throughout the courtyard, seeming to come from everywhere at once.

"CITIZENS OF PENDARA, LISTEN TO ME!"

The crowd fell instantly silent.

"YOUR QUEEN IS BADLY HURT. THERE IS A MAN AMONGST YOU WHO CAN HELP HER." Cynric pointed and everyone turned to look at Tarian.

"IF YOU LOVE YOUR QUEEN, YOU WILL CALMLY AND QUIETLY STEP ASIDE TO MAKE A PATH FOR THIS MAN. HURRY, NOW! CAMBRIA MAY NOT HAVE MUCH LONGER!"

The people hesitated for a moment, and then the beefy fellow in the leather jerkin in front of Tarian pushed to the left as the woman next to him moved to the right. Tarian didn't wait for the path to finish forming. He jumped down from Danya and Phelan's shoulders and began charging forward as fast as he could, distantly aware that the Watcher and his son followed. People moved quickly aside as he ran at them, some barely in time to avoid a collision. It seemed as if he ran for miles, though Tarian knew it was at the most a few dozen yards. But with every step he took, he could feel Cambria's lifeforce weaken, and he feared he wasn't going to reach her in time.

The last of the crowd parted and Tarian found himself approaching the Queen's guard. Several of the men lowered their poleaxes and stepped aside to permit Tarian to enter the protective circle they had formed. Tarian rushed to the Queen's side and knelt next to her unconscious form. Cambria lay on her back, legs folded beneath her, left arm bent at the wrong angle, right wrist clearly shattered. Blood trickled from her left ear and both nostrils. He couldn't tell whether she was still breathing. The impact had dislodged a scattering of emeralds from her dress, and they lay strewn across the white flagstones. Her fine red wig had come partially unpinned and sat askew on her head.

Tarian reached out to take Cambria's limp right hand, but stopped when his fingers were mere inches from hers. It was foolish, but he was suddenly aware that this was the Queen of Athymar that he, a commoner, was about to touch. To actually lay his hand upon her person—

"What are you waiting for?" Danya snapped from behind him. "Get a move on!"

Despite the situation, Tarian almost found himself grinning. It was just the sort of verbal kick in the seat he might have once administered to an inexperienced warrior who froze in battle. He took Cambria's small, delicate hand in his, closed his eyes, and waited to experience the feeling of vast healing energy welling within him.

Nothing happened.

Surprised, he opened his eyes, fearing that his power had somehow deserted him when he needed it the most. The Queen's chest blazed brightly as an orb of glowing white light slowly began to emerge from her body. Cambria had died.

Tarian refused to accept it. He squeezed his eyes shut, tightened his grip on the Queen's hand, and concentrated. Cambria still had to have a spark of life left within her somewhere, and Tarian was determined to reach it and fan it back into full flame. He felt his awareness plunging deep into Cambria's body, searching, searching, until he found what he was looking for: a tiny flicker of life, like that last guttering flame of a candle that was about to burn itself out.

Now that it had something to work with, the power within him responded, surging forward through his fingers and flooding Cambria's body, seeking out her injuries from the gravest to the most minor with unerring accuracy and repairing every one. Tarian felt more than heard the soft crackle of bones setting themselves and fusing together, the gentle relieved sigh of contused and swollen flesh returning to its former state.

Finally, the sea of power within Tarian grew calm, and he opened his eyes to behold the Queen of Athymar looking up at him. The globe of light was no longer visible. Since the Queen still lived, Tarian assumed the sphere—whatever it was—had settled back into her body.

Cambria frowned slightly. "Who are you?"

Tarian smiled.

The Queen's Guard were the first to break out in cheers, but they were far from the last.

Afterward the Queen suggested—no, *insisted* to the point of royal command—that Tarian, Phelan and Danya be her guests for the evening within the Palace. They were escorted inside by the Queen's Guard and led to the Great Hall, while Cambria herself retired to her bedchamber to recover from her ordeal. The three of them were fed full to bursting on beef, trenchers of bread, fruits, cheeses and nuts, and while it was quite odd being the only ones dining in the otherwise empty Hall, they didn't let it hamper their enjoyment of the meal.

Then a servant showed them to their bedchambers. In the corner of Tarian's room rested an overstuffed canopy bed with silken sheets, more luxurious than anything he had ever slept on in his entire life. He was half-afraid to go near it, let alone actually sleep on the damn thing. What if he kept slip-sliding around on those sheets? Finely woven tapestries lined the walls, depicting scenes of armored knights on dragonback clashing with Lukashen warriors who sat astride coiling werms. Not exactly the most soothing of subject matter for a bedchamber's decor, Tarian thought.

But the room's greatest wonder was the tiny closet which contained a small latrine. Tarian was fascinated by it, and unashamedly asked the servant a number of questions about its operation and design before the man departed.

After a brief interval, the servant reappeared to inform Tarian that Cynric Fenfallow requested their presence in his quarters. Now he, Phelan and Danya sat at a polished cedar table before a stone hearth and a cheerful, cozy fire.

"Wine?" Cynric asked.

Tarian couldn't get used to the notion that he was being served by one of the most powerful wizards who'd ever lived.

"Just a bit, thank you. I'm still quite full from dinner." He held up his goblet and Cynric, despite Tarian's request, reached across the table and filled it to the brim from a crystal decanter. The vintage was from one of the royal family's own wineries, and the dark red wine tasted as if the grapes had been grown on the eternally green slopes of Girasa itself.

Cynric nodded to Phelan. "How about you, son?"

Phelan had already downed a goblet's worth of wine and then some at dinner and was looking drowsy. Sitting so close to the fire probably didn't help, Tarian thought. He almost spoke up to suggest that perhaps the lad had drunk enough for one evening, but then he held his tongue. Phelan was a man, or near enough, and he didn't need his father making decisions for him.

Phelan looked at the empty goblet on the table before him as if he expected to find an answer to the wizard's question within it. He looked up and smiled sleepily. "Thank you, sir, but no."

"Madame Watcher?"

Danya thought for a moment, then lifted her goblet. "A little." She gave Cynric a warning scowl. "And I mean a little."

Cynric chuckled and, if he poured more than Danya wanted, at least he didn't fill her goblet near to overflowing, as he had Tarian's. The wizard then put the carafe down without, Tarian noticed, filling his own goblet.

"I take it this is your study," Tarian said. The walls were lined with shelves crammed with books, scrolls, and loose sheets of vellum which, Tarian presumed, the wizard used for note-taking.

"One of them. I have three here in the Southern Palace. In Garahnon, I have five." He shrugged, almost as if he were a trifle embarrassed by this admission. "I'm afraid one tends to gather a great deal of research material in a lifetime devoted to the mystic arts. Normally, I don't entertain in this room, but I had one of the servants bring some extra chairs in. We could have talked in the Great Hall, but I prefer a more intimate atmosphere. Besides, the Hall tends to be a bit on the drafty side for me. Also, it's farther away from Cambria's bedchamber. Hopefully, our distance will help her rest easier."

Danya frowned in puzzlement. "I don't understand, Sir Wizard."

"Please, just call me Cynric. I was trained by the Eyslken, you know, practically raised by them. The only title they use is Preceptor, and that honorific is reserved for their oldest and wisest. And while I might be old enough by the standards of human culture, I'm certainly not wise enough to deserve the honor of being referred to as Preceptor. I expect I never will be." He stared into the fire for a bit, seemingly lost in thought. Then he gave his head a quick shake and continued.

"But there's no reason you should understand my previous comment, Madame Watcher, since the Palace staff and I have worked very hard to keep Cambria's condition a secret. Though after tonight, I imagine it won't be secret much longer." He paused, as if considering how much, if anything to tell them. Finally, he sighed. "The Change has turned the Queen into a powerful telepath who is unable to shut out the thoughts of those around her. She insisted on delivering tonight's address even though I feared that close proximity to so many people would prove overwhelming to her. Which it unfortunately did."

"How awful!" Danya said.

Tarian nodded in agreement. To be constantly privy to the thoughts of those around you, unable to shut them out, even when you tried to sleep, would be a nightmare. Once again, he thought of how lucky he had been that the Change hadn't dealt with him as harshly as it had some.

There was a knock at the chamber door.

"Come," Cynric said.

The priestess—whom Tarian had learned was named Saeth—entered.

"How is she?" Cynric asked.

Saeth shrugged. She closed the door and crossed to the table to take a seat next to the wizard. He lifted the carafe but she declined his offer with a slight wave of her hand. "The Queen sleeps, though fitfully. It seems whatever potion the Royal Physic gave her was only partially effective."

"Damn leech," Cynric spat. "I suppose we should be grateful the fool didn't poison her."

"Otherwise, she seems perfectly healthy." Saeth looked across the table to Tarian and inclined her head. "Thanks to you."

"Don't thank me, Priestess. Thank whatever gave me the power to heal."

"You're too modest," Danya said. "It wasn't your power alone that saved the Queen. It was your quick thinking as much as any magic that did it."

"Quite true," Cynric agreed.

"A soldier's training," Tarian demurred, "nothing more."

"Before the Change," Saeth said, "what you did would have been hailed as a miracle. Now . . ."

Cynric smiled. "Having a crisis of faith, are we?"

Saeth looked shocked. "Absolutely not!" She paused and ran an index finger along the rim of her empty goblet. "But I must confess to a certain amount of confusion these days."

Cynric let out a barking laugh. "Believe me, my dear, you're not alone in that." He turned to Tarian. "Tell us a bit about yourself, Tarian Ambrus. I take it from the trail dust on you and your son's clothing that you traveled a bit to come to Pendara."

Tarian and Phelan looked down at their outfits, both suddenly self-conscious.

Cynric chuckled. "Don't worry. You'll all have a chance at a warm bath tonight, if you want it, and the Palace servants will see that your clothes are laundered. But tell us, what brings you to the city? From what I've been able to glean, the Change hasn't exactly made traveling any safer."

Tarian looked at Phelan, took a deep breath, and began. When he was finished, both Cynric and Saeth regarded them with sympathy.

"I wish I could say that's the most tragic tale I've heard since the Change," Cynric said grimly. "But while Lowri's transformation was certainly extreme, I've heard tell of others that were just as horrible, in their own ways." He held up a hand before either Tarian or Phelan could speak. "Do not mistake my words. In no way do I wish to seem as if I am unmoved by your loved one's plight. It's just, there have been so many . . ."

"We came to Pendara hoping to find a mage who might be able to restore Lowri to her true self," Tarian said.

"You can do it, can't you, Cynric?" Phelan asked. The hope in the boy's voice, the sheer *need*, was awful for Tarian to hear, because he knew how the wizard would answer.

"In truth, I do not know, son," Cynric said softly.

Phelan looked as if someone had just told him that Harvest Festival sprites were only a story parents told their children. "But . . . you're *Cynric Fenfallow!* You stopped a Rendish invasion fleet single-handedly! You can do *anything!*" This last word was practically a wail of anguish.

Cynric sighed wearily. "Phelan, I practice Eyslken magic, which is based on the Shaping of fragments of Chaos left over from the creation of the world. I can use those fragments to affect the physical domain, such as in the courtyard earlier. I employed a Chaos fragment I found in one of the Palace's stones to enchant the air to carry my voice clearly to all within the courtyard. But Eyslken magery in and of itself cannot work transformations upon living creatures."

"You mean there's nothing you can do?" Phelan asked. "That Mother is going to stay like she is forever?" The lad's eyes teared up, and he rubbed at them vigorously.

Tarian reached out to put a hand on his son's shoulder, but Phelan drew away.

Cynric gave a small smile. "I didn't say that, now, did I? While I may practice Eyslken magic, I know something about other schools of wizardry too: Rendish, Thailasian . . . even Lukashen."

Saeth gasped, Danya's eyes widened, and Phelan's mouth dropped open. The Lukashen worshipped Anghrist, the Howling One, and their magic flowed from the power of His absolute evil. Tarian, however, wasn't as surprised as the others. During his time in the King's army, he had heard rumors that while Cynric Fenfallow only practiced Light magic, he had at least a nodding acquaintance with that of the Dark.

Cynric ignored their reactions. "If I can discover what precipitated the Change, perhaps there's a chance I can find a way to undo its effects."

To Tarian's ears, the wizard didn't sound all that confident.

Cynric looked into Phelan's eyes, his gaze intense, his jaw set in a stubborn line. At that moment, he looked every inch the legendary wizard he was purported to be. "I promise you this, lad. If there's any way in Girasa or Damaranth to restore your mother's humanity, I shall find

155

it. It is the very least I can do after your father saved Cambria's life."

Phelan sat back. He looked relieved, as if he had just set down an enormous weight he had been carrying for far too long. "Thank you," he whispered.

Tarian wanted to warn the boy not to get his hopes up too high, that not all the world's problems could be solved by magic, no matter how powerful. But when he saw the hope in Phelan's eyes—the first he had seen there since the Change—Tarian decided to keep his mouth shut. Let the boy hope for now. If nothing else, perhaps it would enable him to get his first decent night's sleep in four days.

Danya let out a sudden squawk and everyone turned to look at her.

The Watcher's face reddened. "Sorry, I, uh . . ." She grimaced, then scowled. "What in the world has gotten your tail in such a twist?" She reached into her tunic pocket and brought forth a small gray mouse.

Tarian couldn't swear to it, not being much of an expert on rodents, but he was willing to bet that was the same mouse Danya had been keeping her eye on when she had come to Phelan's and his aid in the Artisans' Quarter this afternoon.

"This is Jessex. For some reason the naughty thing took it into his fuzz-covered brain to give me a nip through my pocket." She held the mouse up to her face. "What was that all about now?"

Saeth looked as if she had just bitten into a rotten lemon. "I wasn't aware members of the City Watch were now being issued vermin as standard equipment."

"Jessex isn't *vermin*," Danya said indignantly. "He's a mouse. He . . . helped me out the other night."

Saeth scooted her chair close to Cynric—and away from

Danya and Jessex. "That still doesn't explain why you allow the filthy thing to nest on your person."

Tarian experienced a sudden urge to urinate. It was so powerful that for a moment he feared he might wet himself like a child. But thankfully the need diminished as quickly as it had come upon him, though it didn't subside altogether. *Too much wine,* he decided.

"Control yourself, Saeth," Cynric said. "It's only a mouse. The worst it can do is deposit a few droppings."

"Ugh," Danya said. "I didn't think about that." She put Jessex down on the table and peered into her pocket.

Jessex started scuttling toward Saeth. The priestess jumped out of her seat, exclaiming, "Lodura have mercy!"

Phelan let out a thunderous belch.

Tarian couldn't help it; he burst out laughing. Cynric joined him, and a few moments later, so did Danya and Phelan. Saeth, however, stood back from the table and continued to scowl.

When the laughter had finally died down, Phelan manage to gasp out, "P-Pardon me," and that set them all off again.

"I'm glad you're all enjoying yourselves so bloody much," Saeth snapped. "But would someone please do something about that cursed rat?"

The "rat" in question was busy lapping up a bit of spilled wine off the table.

Cynric wiped tears of merriment from his eyes. "Danya, you said this fine specimen of mousehood helped you out the other night? How so?"

Danya told them of her encounter with the assassin at Anwir Manor, and how Jessex had helped her defeat the serpent-limbed woman. Then she recounted how he had helped her stop the dagger-wielding idiot who had been

157

threatening Tarian and Phelan.

"Sometimes Jessex will just start to move a certain way," Danya explained. "I mean, there's nothing special about what he does, exactly. At least nothing I can put my finger on. But when it happens, I find myself compelled to watch him. And from his movements, I can tell what's going to happen next and what I should do about it."

"You mean he tells you the future?" Phelan asked. He reached out to gently pet Jessex on the head with the tip of his forefinger. The little mouse didn't flinch from the boy's touch, though he didn't seem overly fond of the attention, either.

"I suppose," Danya said. "But only the immediate future, what's going to happen in the next several moments."

Cynric grinned. "Do you know what the Change has made you, Danya Arden? You've become a myomancer."

"A what?" she asked. She took a piece of dried bread out of a second pocket and set it on the table for Jessex, who fell to eagerly.

"A myomancer," Cynric repeated. "One who can interpret omens made from the sounds and signs of mice. Nothing but a bit of folklore, really, with no basis in reality. At least, not until the Change touched you, Danya."

Saeth let out a disgusted sigh. "Of all the ridiculous. . . . If you'll excuse me, I've had quite enough for one evening. Good night." She started toward the door.

Jessex eeeped! and let go of the bread to nibble on the tip of his tail.

"Someone's at the door," Danya said.

Saeth didn't bother to look back. "Please, if you think I'm going to—"

There was a knock at the door—three sharp, short raps.

Cynric laughed. "What are you waiting for, Saeth? Open

it and see who it is. Unless you want Danya to ask Jessex for you, that is."

Saeth hesitated a moment, then she reached out and opened the door.

Tarian expected it to be a servant come to check on them, or perhaps even a rider with word from King Rufin. What he didn't expect was an Eyslken warrior.

Saeth let out a soft sound of surprise which didn't sound much different from the noise Jessex had made a moment ago. She retreated backward into the room, nearly tripping over the hem of her robe in the process.

The Eyslk stood six and a half feet tall, and like all his folk possessed skin so pale it was nearly alabaster. His hair was equally white and hung loose well past his shoulders. The hair concealed his ears, but Tarian knew they were smaller than a human's and tapered to tiny points. He had large ice-blue eyes that seemed to stare at them, but that was because Eyslken blinked less often than humans, only once every twenty heartbeats. His body and limbs were deceptively lean, but Tarian knew from battling their relatives, the Lukashen, that they were far stronger than humans. Twice, maybe three times as strong. He had a thin long nose and arching eyebrows which gave him a patrician air, but the mottled green tunic he wore made him look more like a simple woodsman. The only weapon he bore was a simple dagger sheathed on his belt.

Despite the fact the Eyslk was virtually unarmed, Tarian found himself reaching for a sword he no longer wore. It had been a Lukash that had taken off his arm, but Lukashen had once been Eyslken who had chosen to follow Anghrist and who had been tainted by His dark influence. Tarian hated Lukashen, and as a byproduct, he had no love for Eyslken either.

"Rudra's eyes," Cynric whispered. He rose to his feet, his face almost as white as the Eyslk's. "Everyone, I'd like you to meet someone I thought I'd never see again in this world. This is Ashur Dal, the Preceptor who taught me everything I know about Shaping. My mentor, and in many ways, my second father."

Cynric introduced the others one by one, then said with forced casualness, "So, what brings you to Pendara, Ashur?"

"Actually," the Eyslk said in a voice that sounded like wind whispering through the branches of ancient trees, "he does."

Ashur Dal pointed to Tarian.

CHAPTER FIFTEEN

Saeth stepped into the courtyard. The Queen's Guard and the City Watch had long ago cleared out the citizens who had attended Cambria's address and closed the Palace gates. The priestess's sandaled footsteps echoed hollowly in the night air, and the courtyard was awash in moonlight provided by the Wolf and Dragon above. Both moons were one day shy of being full, and the white stone of the Palace glowed with their reflected glory. In ancient times, priests used to believe that the will of Rudra was written in the movements of celestial bodies, and all one had to do was interpret the signs. Superstitious nonsense, of course. But now Saeth stopped a dozen yards from the trickling fountain, and looked up into the sky. She wished that it was that simple, that all the answers really were contained in the heavens for anyone with the wit to read them.

She had remained in Cynric's study for only a short time after the Eyslk's arrival. As the highest-ranking Church official currently in the city, she felt it her duty to stay and hear what the godless creature had to say, but when he started talking about how the spirits of his ancestors had told him to come to Pendara to fetch the healer and bring him to the Eyslken settlement deep within the Greenmark, Saeth excused herself and departed. She could no longer tolerate being in the Eyslk's heretical presence.

At the dawn of time, Rudra and Anghrist had worked together to bring forth life. First, they raised a vast lone continent from the sea. Then they filled the world with the

161

beasts of land, air and water. The greatest of these beasts were the mighty dragons, and for a time they held dominion over all. But then Rudra decided the two brothers should create beings that more closely resembled themselves, beings who would be their children in the truest and most profound sense. Anghrist, who was quite fond of the dragons, disagreed, but in the end, Rudra changed His brother's mind and the Eyslken were born. They were a people of great grace and beauty, and over the millennia they developed a culture of vast intellectual, artistic and magical achievement.

But over time Anghrist became angry at the Eyslken, for they favored Rudra over Him and eventually came to worship Him alone, excluding Anghrist entirely. In His jealousy, Anghrist turned against His brother, and they quarreled. Anghrist no longer wished to work in partnership with His twin. He wanted to shape the destiny of the world and its peoples by himself. And He wished to begin by destroying the Eyslken and creating a new race—one that would adore Him and Him alone.

Rudra refused to let the Eyslken be destroyed, and thus the twin deities fell to battle. The force of their godly might was too much for the physical world to bear, and the lone continent shattered, splitting apart into untold fragments. This event became known forever after as the Sundering, and the spot upon which it happened came to be called Heart's Wound.

The devastation caused by the Sundering destroyed the Eyslken civilization, leaving only a handful of the First Folk as survivors. The Eyslken blamed both Gods for the destruction of their people, and turned their backs upon them, refusing to worship either ever again.

Saeth shook her head. As far as she was concerned, the

Eyslken were fools. Rudra had been trying to *protect* them *from* Anghrist. It was clear that only one god was in the wrong, so why turn away from both?

Because they were hurt and scared.

Saeth jumped. The soft, quiet voice had seemed to come from right next to her ear. She looked around the courtyard, but saw no one.

How would you feel if your parents fought, and as a result of their argument, your house burned to the ground, killing your brothers and sisters and leaving you as the lone survivor? And when you crawled forth from the ashes, you found your parents still bickering, seemingly unconcerned by what their conflict had wrought? I'd wager you would feel as betrayed as the Eyslken did.

Saeth realized the voice wasn't one she heard with her ears. Rather, it seemed to come from within her own head. She then heard a true sound, a grinding, as of stone sliding against stone. She detected movement out of the corner of her eye, and looked up at the marble statue of the Glory atop the fountain. The Glory was no longer gazing upward at the heavens, but rather looking down at her, streams of tears coursing over its polished white cheeks.

Before the Change, Saeth would have taken this to be a miracle and immediately dropped to her knees. But she had seen so many strange things since the Change, and had heard tell of so many more, that she found herself doubting.

You suspect this manifestation to be a trick. The Glory's mouth did not move as it "spoke." *You wonder if someone you cannot see is using a power granted by the Change to make this statue move, to make you seem to hear this thought-voice. You even wonder if perhaps you are doing it yourself without being aware of it, if your own personal change is finally making itself known.*

The Glory paused, and Saeth found herself replying, "Yes." She experienced a wave of shame for doubting the miracle before her, but she couldn't help herself, not after the events of the last few days.

Do not chide yourself. After the Change, you would be a fool to accept this manifestation without question—and the Light has no use for fools. Believe me, Saeth Fama, I am what I appear to be: a Glory in the service of the most high god Rudra.

Saeth was startled to hear herself called by her family name. She hadn't used her last name since she renounced all familial ties upon entering the priesthood at the age of twelve. But employing the patronymic didn't prove this manifestation was real. If she were somehow making the statue move and providing its mental voice, then of course it would know her family's name.

Have a care, Priestess, the Glory thought-spoke, sounding a trifle irritated. *A certain amount of skepticism is a useful quality. But too much can grow tiresome rather quickly. Behold.*

The Glory lowered its arms and cupped its marble hands beneath its chin to catch its tears. When its hands were full, the Glory flung the water into the air. The droplets splashed to the flagstones below, then pooled together. They solidified, took on form and color. When the process was finished, the water had become a silver dagger which gleamed in the moonlight.

Pick it up.

Saeth hesitated, for she had never held a weapon before. But finally, she did as the Glory commanded. She found the metal smooth and cool to the touch, and the blade seemed to quiver gently in her hand as if it were somehow alive.

Listen well, Priestess. The latest clash between the forces of Light and Darkness began seven days ago. It lasted three days.

"That's . . . when the Change happened."

The statue nodded. *The campaign at Heart's Wound did not . . . turn out as expected. Despite your people's insistence on referring to it as the 'Final Battle,' the outcome was inconclusive, and the ancient war between Light and Darkness continues unabated. Tomorrow, the Eyslk will depart with the healer on a journey to Vallanora, the Eyslken Hidden Place within the Greenmark. Cynric Fenfallow will accompany them, as will the Watcher and the healer's son. You must go, too.*

"Me?" Saeth had lived her entire life in Pendara. She had only been outside its walls once or twice, and even then she had never gone far. The thought of traveling any distance—especially to an Eyslken settlement!—filled her with dread.

And wherever they may go after Vallanora, you must remain with them. For when the time is right, you must take the dagger I have given you, and use it.

Saeth looked at the blade glimmering in her hand and began to tremble. "Use it how?"

A foolish question. A dagger serves only one purpose: to slay.

Saeth didn't think she could do it. She had never so much as struck another human being, let alone stabbed one.

The Glory's thought-voice grew stern. *You are an unimaginative, timid woman, Saeth Fama, who is prone to irritability when afraid or confused. But despite these shortcomings, your faith in Rudra has always been strong, and you have never wavered in your duty to the Most High. Will you do so now?*

Saeth thought for several long moments. "How will I know when it's time to . . . *use* the dagger?" she asked softly. She wasn't certain when or even why she had come to accept the Glory as genuine, but she had.

The demigod smiled, and even though its face was

sculpted from cold marble, the smile filled Saeth with a reassuring warmth.

*The dagger will tell you when. And when it does, strike
swiftly, for you will not get a second chance. Hold strong to your
faith, Priestess, for it will shield and sustain you during the ar-
duous journey to come. Farewell.*

The Glory stretched its hands to the heavens, tilted its
head skyward, and became a statue once more.

Saeth looked at the dagger for a long time before at last
tucking it into a pocket of her robe. "Rudra help me," she
whispered, and then hurried off toward her quarters in the
Dawn Cathedral where she intended to pray for guidance
until sunrise.

Ashur Dal stood before the table, arms folded across his
chest. He had declined Cynric's invitation to sit, not because he was adverse to sharing a table with humans, but
because he needed to stand after the Long Run he had just
completed, else his legs would cramp most painfully.

"Well, healer? What do you say?"

The human turned to Cynric, a question in his eyes, one
he was too polite—or perhaps merely too prudent—to ask
aloud.

"I believe the Silent Ones have indeed sent Ashur for
you, else he would not be here. Nor would he have gone to
such measures to reach Pendara so quickly."

The healer's son—Phelan, Ashur recalled—frowned.
"What do you mean?"

"It took us three days to travel from our cabin to the
city," the healer said. "According to the Eyslk's story, he
left his home, which is located somewhere deep within the
Greenmark, late last night. That means it took him less
than a full day to get here."

The youth looked at Ashur with a mixture of awe and fear. Although the Eyslk hadn't had contact with many humans in his 293 years, it was a look he was familiar with.

"Your horse must have wings," the female—called Danya, Ashur reminded himself; he was terrible with human names—remarked with a smile. Ashur was mildly surprised at how calmly she was taking his presence. True, she was a Watcher, and living in Pendara doubtless had made her more cosmopolitan than most humans, but she most probably had never seen an Eyslk before. Still, after the initial surprise of his arrival had worn off, she had acted as if he were no more exotic than a common fishseller in the market. Interesting.

"The only steed Ashur rode was shank's mare," Cynric said. "Eyslken Shapers can draw on Chaos fragments as they run to make the earth more . . . accepting of their footsteps, to create a strong wind at their backs, and make the air they breathe richer and more nourishing, so that their lungs and heart work to their highest capacity. Along with their natural speed and endurance, such an enchantment can allow an Eyslken to cover great distances in a short amount of time."

The other humans looked at Ashur with awe, but in Cynric's gaze, the Eyslk read only concern. What Cynric had failed to mention to his companions was that the Long Run came with a high price. It took a great toll on the body, and there was a chance that illness or even death could result. But that wasn't all: the Long Run shaved weeks, even months off one's life.

Which was undoubtedly why Cynric looked so upset. Barring accidents and illness, all Eyslken lived precisely three hundred years. One of the gifts the Gods had given to Ashur's people was the ability to know the exact moment of their natural deaths, as if they had a clock in their heads which continually counted down the time remaining to them in the mortal world. At 293, Ashur Dal had little time to spend on Long Running. His journey to Pendara had brought him one month, three weeks, two days, and fifteen hours closer to his death. And while Cynric couldn't possibly know the precise amount of time lost to Ashur, he was well aware of the price his former mentor had paid to reach the city this quickly.

Cynric looked at Ashur a moment longer, a sad wistfulness in his eyes. Then he shook his head and turned his attention to the healer. "Well, Tarian? Will you go?"

The healer considered for several moments before saying, "I need some time to think about it."

"I understand," Ashur said. "However, the Silent Ones made clear to me the need for urgency. Might you be able to reach a decision by morning?"

The healer hesitated, then nodded.

"Good." Ashur turned to Cynric. "Would it be possible to have a servant begin the preparations—ready horses, supplies and such? That way, we will lose no time in departing, should Tarian choose to accompany me."

"You never were one to let dust settle on you, Ashur," Cynric said with a smile. "I'll see to it. Would you do me the honor of taking your rest in my quarters this night?"

Ashur had known this invitation was coming and he had been dreading it. The Eyslken people considered it a great insult not to accept an offer of hospitality, but Ashur could not accept this one.

"My thanks, but I must spend some time in meditation to counter the aftereffects of the Long Run. I believe such meditation would be more effectively conducted outside the city walls, where I could be in closer proximity to nature."

Cynric nodded, his expression impassive, but the hurt was there if one knew how to read the wizard's face, and Ashur Dal knew better than anyone alive. "I understand completely. Until the morning then."

Ashur nodded to his former pupil, then turned and made a half bow to the humans. "It was an honor to meet you. Good night." And then he took his leave.

As he walked down the dark corridors of the Southern Palace, Ashur Dal hoped the healer would choose to go with him, despite the man's obvious distaste for Eyslken. The Silent Ones hadn't told Ashur why they needed to see the healer, only that the future of Athymar itself—and perhaps the entire world—depended on it.

It was too bad his people had forsaken the Gods so long ago, Ashur thought, else he might have whispered a prayer just then.

"Well, *that* was interesting," Danya said. She scooped Jessex up, brought him to her face and nuzzled his nose before putting the tiny mouse into her tunic pocket.

Tarian was too busy thinking over the Eyslken's words to respond.

"How did he get into the city?" Phelan asked. "I thought Bloodgate was closed." he frowned. "For that matter, how did he get into the Palace?"

Cynric smiled. "Ashur's an Eyslk, lad. He can easily scale Pendara's walls, and as for getting into the Palace, even if the staff were at full strength, Ashur would have little trouble. He can move so swiftly and silently when he wishes that he becomes practically invisible to human perception."

Danya grinned. "I thought Saeth was going to start foaming at the mouth when she first saw Ashur in the doorway."

"Rudra's priests and priestesses aren't known for their love of Eyslken," Cynric said. "Quite frankly, I was surprised she stayed as long as she did."

"Why wasn't he wearing a sword?" Phelan asked. He sounded almost disappointed. Tarian knew why. In the chronicles Phelan read, the Eyslken were always portrayed as mighty warriors.

"It's not easy to run with a sword belted at your waist," Danya said, "or slung across your back, for that matter. Especially not as far and fast as Ashur ran."

Cynric nodded. "And as swiftly as he was traveling, little could threaten him. A sword wasn't necessary."

"What bothers me," Tarian said slowly, "is how the Eyslk knew exactly where to find me. I know these 'Silent Ones' of his supposedly told him where I would be and when I would be here, but I find it hard to believe anyone can predict the future so accurately."

"The Silent Ones are the spirits of the Eyslken dead," Cynric said. "When Ashur Dal's people turned away from the Gods after the Sundering, entrance to both Girasa and Damaranth was denied to them, and their spirits were forced to remain earthbound. Rather than allow their departed loved ones to wander the world aimlessly, the living Eyslk decided to create their own afterlife. In Vallanora, that place is called the Orchard of Dreams. I know little about it. Few living Eyslken are permitted within, and then only when the Silent Ones summon them." He looked at Tarian with a newfound respect. "I have never heard tell of them ever summoning a human before."

"I suppose I should be honored," Tarian said in a tone that indicated he was anything but.

"As spirits, the Silent Ones are not bound by time and space the way the living are," Cynric said. "I am not surprised they were able to tell Ashur where to locate you, just as I am not surprised that they seem to be aware of the Change, and are evidently disturbed enough by it to send for you." He chuckled. "It's ironic, really. Do you recall when Cambria spoke of the journey I planned to take to discover the true nature of the Change?"

They all nodded.

"I intended to go to Vallanora and ask Ashur Dal if he or his people might know anything which could help us." He shook his head, grinning. "Ashur always was at least one step ahead of me."

"So you think Father should go," Phelan said.

"Yes," Cynric replied. "The Silent Ones are reputed to possess great power and insight. If anyone can help us—and ultimately perhaps aid the two of you in restoring Lowri—it is them."

Tarian grunted. As a soldier, he was used to dealing with problems that could be faced with strength and wit. He was uncomfortable, to say the very least, at having to deal with enchantments and summons from dead folk.

"Why bother going through the motions of deciding?" Danya said. "Come morning, you'll leave with Ashur Dal, as will Phelan and Cynric."

"How do—" Tarian broke off. "I suppose your mouse told you."

Danya smiled. "Yes, while Ashur Dal was talking."

If it wasn't for his healing powers, Tarian knew he'd have a headache by now. "And did Jessex tell you anything else?"

"Just one more thing: I'm going too."

Tarian, Phelan and Danya left not long after that to get what sleep they could before morning. Cynric wasn't certain what time it was, but he judged it to be well past midnight. As tired as he was himself, he still had work to do, though. He summoned one of the servants on night duty and instructed him to prepare horses and travel gear for five. Ashur Dal would also need a mount for his return trip to Vallanora. Even if the Eyslk could perform another Long Run so soon after the last, they'd never be able to keep up with him, so he would be forced to travel at their speed. Not that it would concern him overmuch. Cynric was certain Ashur would endure the slower pace as stoically as he did everything else.

Cynric then gathered quill, ink, blotter and vellum, and began composing a letter to the commander of the City Watch, requesting that Danya Arden be granted leave from her duties so that she might accompany him on a mission of the "most vital importance." It wasn't one of the better missives he'd ever written, but with his signature and seal on it, he supposed it would serve its purpose well enough.

As he wrote, he marveled at the Watcher's newfound power of myomancy. Before the Change, he would've found the very notion of such a magical talent ridiculous. Now it struck him as rather charming, and certainly far more benign then many transformations that had occurred.

Cynric could understand why Tarian and Phelan might want to accompany Ashur Dal to Vallanora, but the Watcher's motives were unclear to him. Perhaps it seemed like a grand adventure to her. In his younger days, Cynric would've gone on any number of foolhardy and dangerous quests for less reason—and often had. More likely, Danya's reason for wishing to join their party had something to do with the way she looked at Tarian. Or rather, the way she looked at him when she thought he wasn't looking at her. Which wasn't much different from the way Phelan looked at her when she was looking at his father.

Cynric sighed. A burgeoning romantic triangle wasn't exactly the firmest of foundations upon which to build an expedition. If nothing else, though, he supposed it would make the journey interesting.

He finished the letter, read it over, made a few corrections, blotted them, then set the letter aside to dry. He would see it was delivered in the morning. The fire was little more than embers now, but Cynric didn't bother stoking it, nor did he get up and head for his own bedchamber. Instead, he sat at the table and stared at the dying fire, left hand idly toying with his empty goblet.

He'd had no desire to fill it earlier, and he had none now. He had been steadily losing his appetite for food and drink over the last few days. In fact, he couldn't clearly recall the last time he had taken nourishment of any sort. He had told himself that it was merely due to stress, but now he feared it was something more. Much more. He feared the Change was finally manifesting in him.

Cynric turned his mind to other thoughts. It had been awkward seeing Ashur Dal after all this time—twenty years. When Cynric was just a boy, one night the small fishing village where he lived was set upon by Lukashen riders, and every man, woman and child was either killed or taken captive so they might serve as sustenance. For that was how the Lukashen managed to defy the 300-year limit on lifespan which bound their Eyslken cousins: they extended their own lives by devouring the flesh and blood of other sentient beings.

Somehow, they had missed Cynric, who had hidden underneath a large upside-down basket used for carrying fish. He pressed his hands hard against his ears to shut out the screams of the villagers and the wicked laugher of the

Lukashen, but it didn't help. Even when the last hoofbeat of departing horses had sounded, Cynric sat like that, hands jammed against his ears, and it was in that position that Ashur Dal found him the next morning. A band of Eyslken warriors had been tracking the Lukashen raiding party for weeks, and Cynric was the first survivor they had come across.

Cynric never knew why Ashur decided right then to make him his *filmarr*, which roughly translated meant a combination adopted son and apprentice. Cynric had asked several times over the next few years, but Ashur always gave the same answer: "One day, you will tell me." Cynric had hated that answer, though as a wizard, he had a tendency to be cryptic himself. He supposed it came with the territory.

Ashur Dal took Cynric along on the search for the Lukashen raiders, and when the Eyslken finally caught up with them several weeks later, he let the boy watch as the Eyslken slew the raiders with brutal, merciless efficiency, using a combination of steel and Chaos magic. They didn't bother searching for survivors of Cynric's village. They had long since been . . . used by the Lukashen.

Ashur took Cynric back to Vallanora and began to teach him, and not merely Shaping, although that was a big part of it. An Eyslken wasn't permitted to teach until he or she had reached their two-hundredth birthday and had in addition through deeds of honor and service earned the rank of Preceptor. Preceptors didn't merely instruct their pupils in a given subject—Preceptors taught their students how to *live*. From Ashur Dal, Cynric learned not only magic, but swordcraft, woodslore, history, mathematics, logic, medicine, strategy, philosophy, and a host of other disciplines, some of which the human tongue hadn't a name for. In time, the frightened young survivor of a Lukashen raid became Cynric Fenfallow, Master Wizard, as much Eyslken as he was human.

Ashur Dal had been his father, his teacher, his mentor, and his friend. But all that ended twenty years ago, when Cynric used a huge Chaos fragment located off the Black Coast to swamp the Rendish invasion fleet. The Eyslken believed strongly in honorable combat, and in their eyes—and most importantly, in Ashur's—there was nothing honorable about drowning men who didn't have a chance to defend themselves. But Ashur might have forgiven Cynric, in time, if he hadn't then committed the most serious sin of which a Shaper was capable. He began to teach Eyslken magic to others without the permission of his own teacher.

Cynric had felt he hadn't a choice. The strain of casting the spell which had destroyed the Rendish invasion fleet had taken a severe toll on his health. What's more, it had damaged his mind in some fashion, so that he was no longer able to work major Shapings, only minor ones. Athymar needed a strong protector—the Rendish invasion fleet had made that clear enough—and what was more, there were signs that the Final Battle between the forces of Light and Darkness, prophesied so long ago by Lodura, was fast approaching.

So Cynric began teaching, and by the time he was finished, twelve new wizards walked the land. The oldest, Lopahin, was in his late forties now, while the youngest, Velika, was only in her mid-twenties. Singly, none of them were as adept as Cynric had been in his prime, for try as he might, Cynric was nowhere near the teacher Ashur Dal was. Still, Cynric's pupils were powerful enough in their own ways, and working together they were a force to be reckoned with.

He wondered about them now. They had ridden with

King Rufin's forces to Heart's Wound, leaving Cynric to "watch over" the Queen and Rufin's children for, as the King had put it, "I trust you more than any other man in this world or the next." While Rufin was doubtless sincere, Cynric knew that he had been left behind because of his fragile health and his relatively weak powers. And it galled—gods, how it galled! Especially because he knew that he would have done the same as Rufin if their positions had been reversed.

He feared for his students. If the battle at Heart's Wound was over—and his gut said it was—then there was a good chance some of them hadn't survived. Perhaps none of them had. And if that were the case, then by choosing to teach them, in a way, Cynric had set them on a path that in the end had led only to their destruction.

He wished he still had a taste for wine; he could've used a drink right then.

Ashur hadn't been wearing his Honor Braids tonight. He'd cut half of them off when Cynric destroyed the Rendish fleet, and he'd cut the rest when Cynric took his first student. In accordance with Eyslken custom, Ashur Dal would never braid his hair again for as long as he lived. The sight of Ashur's unbound hair had been like a knife in Cynric's heart. But everything the wizard had done to betray Ashur's teachings had seemed perfectly logical at the time. Indeed, Cynric hadn't been able to see any other recourse. Now, he wondered if that was because he just hadn't looked hard enough.

Sudden, tiny movement caught his eye, and he saw a black spider scuttling across the surface of the table. One of Enar's, no doubt. The army of spiders the Queen's son had summoned obeyed him only when he was awake. When the boy slept, the spiders' autonomy returned and they roamed the Palace freely.

As Cynric watched, the arachnid came nearer, and the wizard felt something cold and dark move deep within him, like a huge sea creature stirring in the frigid depths of a black ocean. Of its own volition, his hand stabbed out and snatched up the spider. Cynric could feel the small creature struggling in his grip, its tiny legs brushing feather-light against his palm. Then he felt a warmth where the spider touched his flesh, a satisfying tingling, and the spider's struggles grew weaker and soon ceased altogether.

Cynric opened his hand and the spider fell to the table-top, legs curled tight against its body. It was dead.

The wizard experienced a sense of satisfaction then, almost of refreshment, as if he had just taken a gulp of cool springwater on a hot day, and he knew why he hadn't been hungry or thirsty for so long. More, he knew for certain that the Change had finally caught up with him at last. But one spider wasn't enough. Not nearly.

He got up to go look for more.

CHAPTER SIXTEEN

Come dawn, Ashur Dal was waiting for them in the courtyard, along with a groom, three mares and four geldings from the Palace stables. Five of the horses bore saddles, while the other two were to serve as pack animals. The latter were already loaded with supplies—food, water, bedrolls, oats and the like.

Danya hadn't slept well. She'd been too excited by the prospect of the journey to come, though truth to tell she wasn't precisely certain why she was going, beyond Jessex's prophecy that she would, of course. A chance for adventure was part of it, she supposed, but more important was the chance to do something about the Change. She had taken an oath to protect the citizens of Pendara, and if there was anything she could do to help reverse the Change, she had to do it.

She felt a pang at the thought, for if the Change were nullified, that meant she would lose Jessex, or at least lose whatever mystical bond they shared. Still, given what terrible effects the Change had had on so many others, losing Jessex would be a small price to pay to return Athymar to the way it had been.

She glanced at Tarian. If she were being completely honest with herself, she would admit that another reason she wanted to go was to be near him. She knew he was married—though unless they found a way to return Lowri to her human form, that situation would rectify itself. Still, she wanted to be close to him, to be his friend and traveling companion, and if deep in her heart she hoped for more, what of it? A girl could hope, couldn't she?

Tarian and Phelan wore the same tunics and breeches they had had on yesterday, though as Cynric promised, the Palace servants had laundered their outfits. As he had when she first met them, Phelan bore Tarian's sword, called Cathal. Danya had sent her own Watcher's tunic back to the barracks—she didn't feel right wearing it outside the city—though she had kept her chain mail vest, sword and dagger. The Palace servants had supplied her with a powder blue tunic and black leggings which, while not exactly her style, would serve well enough.

Cynric had exchanged his purple robe for a tan jerkin, brown breeches and black boots more suitable to a common tradesman than to the Royal Wizard. Cynric was an old hand at traveling and obviously placed comfort above all other considerations. Danya didn't blame him. While his mage's robe might likely impress anyone they encountered along the way, it certainly wouldn't have made for the most comfortable outfit to wear while riding in the summer heat.

In addition to their outfits, they all had wide-brimmed hats to keep off the sun, and raincloaks which were stored away with their supplies. Not that they would likely need the latter, as if hadn't rained a drop since the Change.

Ashur Dal was dressed the same as he had been last night. He stood, so motionless he might have been kin to the statue of the Glory that adorned the fountain, his face expressionless. Danya found the Eyslk fascinating. Not only because he was the first nonhuman she had ever met, but also because he had been Cynric's teacher. She found the Eyslk hard to read, but she thought she'd detected a certain amount of tension between Ashur Dal and Cynric last night, and she wondered what had transpired in their shared past to account for it.

"Good morning, Ashur," Cynric greeted his old mentor. "Your meditations were fruitful, I trust?"

"They were. I am completely recovered from the effects of the Long Run."

Cynric nodded, though something in the wizard's expression told Danya that he didn't believe the Eyslk was as restored as all that. Still, neither of them said anything more about it, and Cynric turned his attention to the horses. "These look like they'll do well enough. Thank you, Groom."

The man bowed. "My pleasure, Sir Wizard."

Tarian stepped forward. "Might you do me a service, Groom? Yesterday, my son and I were forced to leave our horse and wagon outside Bloodgate when we entered the city. The gatekeeper on duty at the time was kind enough to offer to look after them for us. Could you let him know that he's welcome to keep both or sell them, as he will?" Tarian described the gatekeeper then, and the groom nodded.

"That's old Barra you're speaking of. He's a kind-hearted man, right enough. I'll be glad to take your message to him. What's your horse's name?"

"Anci," Tarian said. "She's a good horse, for all her years. She pulled her load and then some without so much as a complaint."

The groom smiled, and Danya found herself wondering what the Change had done to the man. Whatever it was, it didn't show. He was lucky; there were too many folk in Pendara who couldn't say the same. "If Barra doesn't want her, then I'll take care of her myself, and I'll see to it she's waiting for you when you return."

"My thanks," Tarian said, looking relieved.

Danya found it endearing that Tarian—a man who had

once been a warrior in the King's army—would be so concerned about the welfare of an old draft horse.

Tarian looked at Phelan to see how the boy felt about giving Anci away, but he merely shrugged. Danya tried not to smile. It hadn't been so long ago that she had been in the habit of answering her own Ma and Pa with the same all-purpose gesture.

"I'm glad you decided to come with me, Tarian," Ashur Dal said. He glanced at Danya and Phelan, and if he had any feelings about their coming along, he decided to keep them to himself. He seemed to take Cynric's presence as a given.

Tarian's only reply was a curt nod. Danya had noticed that he didn't seem particularly comfortable in the Eyslk's presence, though he hadn't made an issue of it. Though she didn't share his feelings, she couldn't blame him. For many centuries, Eyslken and humans had been, if not exactly friends, then at least allies. But that all changed five hundred years ago, when the Blood Wars ended with the restoration of the one true King of Athymar to the throne in Garahnon, and the resultant Reunification of the Northern and Southern kingdoms. The Eyslken had aided the Southern King against the Northern usurper willingly enough, but less than a dozen years after the Reunification, the Eyslken, for reasons known only to themselves, withdrew from the affairs of men and thereafter were only rarely seen by humans. The fact that the Eyslken withheld their aid, especially during the last ten years as Baron Cavillor rose to power, didn't sit well with many folks, Tarian included, it seemed.

If Ashur Dal noted Tarian's attitude toward him—and Danya was certain he did—the Eyslk gave no sign. "Then let us be off. We have a seven-day ride ahead of us, and the

sooner we get started, the sooner we'll reach Vallanora."
Ashur Dal picked a chestnut mare, seemingly at random,
and began to mount.

"Hold for a moment, if you would, Ashur," Cynric said.
"I spoke with Cambria not long ago. She wished to bid you
all farewell in person, but she is still weak, and I managed
to convince her that it wouldn't be prudent to exert herself
so soon after what happened last night. She asked me to
thank you again, Tarian, and to tell the rest of you that this
expedition has her official sanction and blessing. She also
asked me to tell you that we carry with us not only her
hopes, but those of her children and her subjects as well.
She also gave me this."

Cynric reached into his shirt pocket and brought out a
medallion. Upon it was the sigil of the crown and sun.

"The royal seal," Phelan said with awe.

Cynric smiled. "One of them, at any rate, lad. It
wouldn't be very smart for the Queen to be giving away the
only one she had, would it?"

Phelan's cheeks flushed, but Cynric gave the boy a wink
to take the sting out of his words. "In truth, the seal may
not do us much good. Most folk will probably think it's an
especially clever forgery, like as not. Still, it may come in
handy." Cynric tucked the medallion back into his pocket,
and gave it a pat for good measure.

Danya thought the wizard seemed to be in especially fine
spirits today. He certainly looked better than he had last
night. His eyes were no longer red, and his cheeks had more
color to them. Perhaps unlike herself, Cynric had managed
to get a decent night's sleep.

The wizard grew serious. "I also have something for you,
Ashur, if you will do me the honor of accepting it."

The Eyslk cocked his head in a manner that put Danya

in mind of a bird. Cynric stepped over to one of the pack-horses and from between bundles removed a swordbelt, scabbard and blade. As he brought them over to Ashur Dal, Danya could see that the scabbard was far thinner than she was used to—far thinner than hers, certainly—almost but not quite narrow enough to hold an epee.

Cynric held the sword out to Ashur, and the Eyslk hesitated for a moment before reaching out to take it. He drew the weapon with a soft hiss, then handed the empty scabbard back to Cynric. The blade was foil-thin and translucent, as if it were made of crystal instead of steel. The rounded guard and pommel were also made from the same substance.

Ashur Dal stepped back and made a few experimental passes with the sword. The blade cleaved the air without making so much as a whisper of sound, and despite the morning sun, its crystalline substance reflected no sparkling glitter of light. As Ashur maneuvered the sword with economical movements of his supple wrist, the blade seemed almost to disappear, so difficult was it to track with the eye.

Ashur finished, took the scabbard and belt from Cynric and housed the blade. A ghost of a smile passed over the Eyslk's lips. "You've taken good care of it."

Cynric bowed his head, as if accepting a great compliment. "It would do me much honor were you to wear it, Ashur. And to be honest, I'm not as fast as I used to be before . . . my health worsened. It would be far more effective in your hands than mine."

Phelan broke in. "And you need a sword, since you had to leave yours behind to perform the Long Run."

Tarian looked as if he might scold the boy for interrupting, but Ashur managed a full-fledged smile this time. "A most practical argument." He nodded to Phelan. "From both of you." He then bowed slightly toward Cynric. "The honor is mine, *Filmarr g'tanu.*"

Whatever Eyslken phrase Ashur had used, it seemed to hit Cynric like a slap to the face, but then he composed himself and made his expression as neutral as that of his former mentor. He held out the sword, and Ashur took it and buckled it on.

Phelan opened his mouth again, no doubt to ask what *filmarr g'tanu* meant, but this time Tarian stepped lightly on the boy's foot to get his attention, and when Phelan turned to him, his father shook his head slightly. Phelan looked from Ashur to Cynric, then nodded, a trifle sullenly, Danya thought.

Phelan turned to Cynric and held out the cloth-wrapped sword he carried. "You could always carry Cathal." He shot Tarian a look. "Since Father can't."

Tarian bristled, but remained silent. As Tarian had explained to them last night in the wizard's study, as a side effect of his healing powers, he could no longer stand to touch weaponry of any sort. This had even extended to the knife given to him at dinner yesterday. He had been forced to tear off pieces of bread and use them to scoop food into his mouth.

"That's a kind offer, lad," Cynric said, "but if I can't effectively wield something as light as an Eyslken mistblade, I certainly couldn't handle a sword as heavy as that." The wizard looked at Danya.

The Watcher reached up to pat her own sword, which she now wore strapped to her back for easier riding. "I like my blade just fine, thank you."

Ashur Dal frowned. "Why not let the boy wear it?"

Tarian hesitated.

"Well?" Ashur's voice was soft and even, but there was

an edge of demand to it nevertheless.

"He hasn't been properly trained in its use," Tarian said. "The fault is mine. I . . . was away campaigning quite a bit when Phelan was growing up, and I hadn't the time to instruct him as well as I should have."

Danya saw the look of anger and pain that flashed across Phelan's face, and she knew this was a sore point between father and son.

Ashur looked Phelan up and down. "I admit to not being the best judge of human age, but your son is a man, or near enough, is he not?"

Tarian nodded.

"Then it's high time he learned how to handle a blade," Ashur said decisively. He turned to Phelan. "Does the sword have a proper belt?"

Phelan shook his head.

"Then hang the scabbard from the one you're wearing; it'll serve well enough."

Phelan looked to his father, and after a moment, Tarian nodded. Phelan handed Danya the sword, and she unwrapped it as the boy removed his belt. She threaded the belt through the scabbard's metal loop, then handed it back to him. Phelan rebuckled the belt around his waist with fumbling fingers, then looked down at the sword that now was his. It hung a little low on him, and they'd have to show him how to position it when he was on horseback so it wouldn't keep smacking into his mount's side, but all in all, she thought it suited him.

Phelan's grin said he thought so too, but Tarian's face held an expression that was hard to read. A mixture of pride and sadness, Danya decided, with perhaps a little guilt thrown in for good measure.

Ashur Dal nodded, satisfied. "Now we may depart." He

put his boot in the chestnut mare's stirrup, but before he could haul himself into her saddle, they heard a woman shout, "Wait!"

Ashur sighed—it was the most human thing Danya had seen him do yet—and removed his foot from the stirrup. They all turned to see Saeth hurrying across the courtyard. Or rather, hurrying as fast as she could, burdened as she was by a highly polished armored breastplate emblazoned with the sunburst of Rudra, and a helmet that sported a large white kethrek plume. She wore the breastplate over her robe of office, though from the noise she made as she walked, it sounded as if the priestess had wisely exchanged her sandals for boots. A simple rucksack worn on her back completed her outfit.

The huge feather bobbed comically as Saeth drew near, and Danya had to nearly bite her tongue to suppress a giggle. Tarian had suddenly become extremely interested in a passing cloud formation, and Phelan inspected the tops of his boots, jaw clenched tight. Cynric didn't bother to disguise the merriment in his eyes, and Ashur Dal gaped at the priestess as if she had suddenly gone insane. For his part, the groom fiddled with a bridle that wasn't in any particular need of adjustment.

Saeth reached them and stopped, breathing heavily. "Thank Rudra I got here in time. It took me forever to figure out how to get this armored whatever-it-is on by myself."

Tarian, still engrossed in his study of clouds, let out a cough that sounded suspiciously like a laugh.

"I take it you're not here to merely say a blessing before we leave," Cynric said.

Saeth drew herself up with as much dignity as a woman with a two-foot feather on her head could muster. "I'm going with you, of course. This mission is too important to exclude a representative of the Church."

"Strange," Cynric said, casting a sideways glance in Ashur's direction. "You didn't seem to feel that way last night when you departed my study so abruptly."

"After I left you all, I spent a great deal of time in prayer," Saeth said. She looked at the fountain in the center of the courtyard, or rather at the statue of the Glory atop it. "My devotions served to clarify my thoughts."

Ashur Dal spoke then. "Where in the Nine Known Lands did you get that breastplate and helmet?"

"I found them at the Dawn Cathedral, on a statue of Radiant Jolanta, she who was known as Wermslayer." Saeth gazed down at the breastplate's sun design. "I thought they were quite nice."

"What they are is ceremonial," Ashur said. "Not only do they look ridiculous, they are only a little stronger than tin. A sword would slice through them as if they were butter."

"Forget the sword," Tarian said. "A stiff breeze would be enough to penetrate that metal."

"And you really shouldn't wear that robe," Cynric added. "Not for a long journey on horseback. Your legs'll be rubbed raw before we make our first camp. If you truly insist on accompanying us . . ."

"I do," Saeth said, her mouth set in a determined line.

Cynric sighed and turned to the groom. The man nodded. "I'll see if I can't rustle up a more . . . suitable outfit and some travel gear for the priestess. Not to mention a horse. I won't be long." The groom made sure each of them held the reins of one of the mounts before he headed off toward the stables. The man's shadow stretched out behind him in the morning sun, and as he walked, it danced and capered behind him. The sight made Danya shudder.

187

Tarian extended his hand toward Saeth. "I'll be glad to hold your rucksack while you remove your breastplate."

She jerked away from him. "No! Uh, I mean, thank you, Tarian, but that won't be necessary." She turned her back on them, as if she were seeking to preserve her modesty. Then she removed her rucksack, and set it on the ground between her legs. Danya noticed she held the sack tight between her feet, almost as if she were afraid one of them might try to snatch it up and make off with it. She wondered what the priestess had in there that was so all-fired important. Maybe some sort of religious artifact that served as a ward against evil. Then again, considering the armor and helmet she had chosen, perhaps whatever she had in her sack was equally as showy and useless, and she wanted to keep the others from discovering it in order to prevent any further embarrassment to herself. That was probably it, Danya decided, and thought no more upon the matter.

Before too long, the groom returned, leading a piebald mare and carrying a travel pack. Draped over the horse's saddle were a light green tunic, brown belt and green hose. Saeth wrinkled her nose at the outfit, but she took it—leaving the groom her armor and helmet to return to the Dawn Cathedral—and went inside the Palace to change, taking her rucksack with her. After what seemed a longer time than the groom had taken, Saeth returned, tugging on the tunic.

"It doesn't fit as well as it could, but it shall have to serve, I suppose," she said.

Danya's throat felt suddenly dry, and she was tempted to take a drink from the waterskin which lay within her mount's saddlebag, but Ashur Dal had already swung into the saddle of his own horse and was starting toward the courtyard gate. Danya decided she'd wait until they were underway before getting a drink, and mounted her own steed.

The others climbed into their saddles—Saeth with the aid of a boost from the groom—and they were finally off, bound for Vallanora and Tarian's appointment with the spirits of the Eyslken dead.

CHAPTER SEVENTEEN

"Rudra preserve me!"

Saeth, returning from a call of nature, hobbled over to the small campfire like she was well into her dotage instead of merely her fifties. She still wore her rucksack on her back, refusing to let anyone take it for her while she attended to business.

"Why bother building a fire at all?" the priestess asked as she made her way slowly over to her traveling companions. "Rudra knows we don't need it for heat, not in summertime. And we have trail rations to eat, so we don't need it to cook."

"You won't be saying that after you've had a taste of them," Tarian said with a grin.

Ashur Dal stood next to the fire. "Have you ever spent a night out of doors?"

Saeth shook her head.

"Even in summer, it can get colder than you think, Priestess. But the main reason I built the fire is this." The Eyslk tossed a handful of herbs into the flames. As they began to blacken and curl, they produced coils of putrid black smoke.

Saeth reached up with a hand to cover her nose and mouth. "Gods of Light and Darkness, what a stench! Is this some sort of barbaric Eyslken rite which up to this point in my life I've been blessedly unfamiliar with?"

Ashur Dal actually smiled. "This particular combination of herbs helps repel insects. Mosquitoes and biting flies do

190

not seem to have much of a taste for my people, but they dearly love to nibble on you human folk."

Saeth looked at Ashur for a moment. "In the Dawn Cathedral, we use a special incense for the same purpose. Although we tell the acolytes it's an aid to help them concentrate while they pray."

Tarian grinned, Cynric and Danya laughed, while Phelan looked a trifle angry—probably on behalf of the misled acolytes, Tarian guessed.

Saeth finally reached one of the small logs Tarian and Ashur Dal had collected and arranged around the fire, and did her best to sit. It was a slow, painful process to watch, and the priestess let out several less than pious comments as she settled onto the log. She slipped off her rucksack, and placed it on the ground between her feet. She pressed her legs against the sack, as if afraid one of them might try to snatch it away from her any moment. What did she have in there that was so damn important? Tarian wondered. Some manner of religious artifact that she'd brought along? If that was the case, though, why be so secretive about it?

"Feeling a bit sore, are we, Saeth?" asked Danya, who sat on the opposite side of the fire, next to Tarian. "Some deep knee bends will help."

Saeth made a face. "I'm not getting up again until it's time to crawl into my bedroll." The priestess sighed. "Now I understand why Rudra created horses." She looked over to where their mounts—free of tack and rubbed down— grazed. The steeds were tethered to stakes to prevent them from wandering off in the night. "It was to give His children a taste of Damaranth's eternal punishment."

Cynric, who sat next to the priestess, laughed. To the wizard's right, sat Phelan, who ineffectively hid a grin. On the other side of Tarian, Ashur Dal crouched down and sat

191

back on his heels rather than on a log with the rest of them. Tarian had at first taken this way of resting as a sign that the Eyslk wished to keep himself apart from the rest of them, until Cynric explained that it was the way of Ashur's people to sit in that fashion, for they could do so for hours on end without moving or cramping.

Ashur Dal said, "The Eyslken do not believe souls are tormented in Damaranth. We believe that Anghrist uses the spirits of those who follow Him—whether knowingly or not—in order to increase the ranks of his demonic armies."

Phelan, who had been staring at Danya, Tarian noticed, turned to the Eyslk. "You mean Anghrist turns the spirits of the dead *into* demons?"

"Demons have to come from somewhere, lad," Cynric said.

"Does that mean that Glories—" Phelan began.

Saeth cut him off firmly. "No. The holy texts are unequivocal on the matter. Rudra created the Glories from a tiny portion of His own essence. However, the texts are less clear on the origin of demons. Some contain references which support the Eyslken view."

Tarian was surprised to hear the priestess agreeing with Ashur Dal on anything, however obliquely.

Saeth shifted on the log and hissed in pain. "I don't suppose anyone thought to pack any salve?" she said through gritted teeth.

"There's no need for that, Priestess." Tarian stood and walked around the fire until he stood behind Saeth. "You've brought a healer along, remember? Just sit still now." He placed his hands on her shoulders, and Saeth stiffened, obviously uncomfortable at his touch. While the priests and priestesses who served Rudra weren't officially forced to practice celibacy, they normally did, as a sign of complete devotion to their god. There was a good possibility that Saeth had never experienced a man's touch before.

"Take care, Tarian," Danya said. "If you heal her completely, her body will never adjust to spending time in the saddle. And while you could heal her whenever we make camp for the night, every day will be as her first upon a horse."

Cynric nodded. "An excellent point, Madame Watcher." He turned to Tarian. "Can you heal her partially, take away only the worst of the pain, just enough so she can sleep for the night?"

"I think so." Tarian had been able to heal the dagger-wielding idiot who'd tried to take a slice out of Phelan and him without returning the man to consciousness. Theoretically, he should be able to do something similar with Saeth.

He tightened his grip on her shoulders slightly. "Just—" He broke off as his guts suddenly twisted in a knot. It felt like the worst case of indigestion he had ever experience, even though they had yet to break out the rations.

Danya stood. "Tarian, are you all right?"

"It's nothing, just a little—" The pain intensified, and Tarian stepped back and placed his hands on his belly. And just like that, the sensation was gone, extinguished as quickly as a candleflame in a strong breeze.

Danya had taken several steps toward him, but Tarian waved her off. "I'm fine now. That was odd, though. I'm not usually one to fall prey to a weak stomach."

Cynric frowned. "Especially now. I would think your healing capacity would deal with such minor discomforts as a matter or course. You most likely wouldn't experience them in the first place."

It was true. Tarian wasn't the slightest bit stiff from riding all day, and while the others had picked up a touch of sunburn on the backs of their hands—Ashur Dal excluded; despite the Eyslk's fair skin, he seemed immune to the sun's rays—Tarian's hands hadn't so much as tanned, let alone burned.

Cynric gave Saeth an appraising look. "You know, I believe we may have just discovered our priestess's change."

Saeth sniffed dismissively. "Nonsense. I somehow managed to avoid the Change, as have you, Wizard."

Tarian saw something flicker in Cynric's gaze, then, though he couldn't quite put a name to it. Then it was gone, and Tarian wasn't certain it had ever truly been there in the first place.

Cynric went on. "I've noticed over the last few days that my own stomach tends to be somewhat more unsettled when I'm in your presence. I've seen others—servants, even the Queen herself—respond in similar fashion. They became flushed or experienced a sudden urge to relieve themselves. I believe you possess the ability to affect the body's natural processes, Saeth Fama. So far, this ability has only manifested itself randomly, when you became irritable or—" He glanced at Tarian and smiled. "—uncomfortable."

"Madness," Saeth said, but she didn't sound so certain.

"It's simple enough to test," Cynric said. "Look at me, and concentrate on making me experience a sensation akin to those I mentioned before. Don't tell me which one, though."

"This is ridiculous," Saeth muttered. But she looked at the wizard and furrowed her brow, as in intense thought.

Cynric suddenly began choking. His eyes bulged in panic and his face grew red. He gestured frantically for Saeth to stop whatever it was she was doing. Phelan pounded the wizard on the back, but the lad's actions didn't help any. Tarian felt Cynric's distress as dry tightening in his own throat, and he took a step toward the mage, but then stopped. He sensed that his healing ability would be of no use here. Cynric wasn't actually wounded or ill; he was in the grip of an enchantment.

The priestess looked horrified. "What should I do?"

Ashur Dal spoke to Saeth, but he kept his gaze trained on Cynric. "Your concentration brought his attack on; simply concentrate on making it stop." The Eyslk's voice was steady and calm, but Tarian had been around him long enough to recognize the subtle signs of concern—eyes slightly narrowed, lips pressed together more tightly than usual, the way he leaned toward Cynric the tiniest bit.

Saeth looked too flustered to gather her thoughts effectively, but she stared at Cynric for a moment, and soon the wizard's breathing eased.

"I'll—" Cynric broke off and coughed several times before again trying to speak. "I'll be all right," he managed to get out. His voice was raspy, but he seemed to be breathing normally now. He gave Saeth a lopsided grin. "I apologize if our little experiment caused you any distress."

Ashur Dal shook his head. "You always were too impulsive for your own good, Cynric. I sometimes wonder how you ever survived your *divisha*." The Eyslk glanced at the rest of them. "That means *apprenticeship,* more or less."

"What happened?" Danya asked the wizard.

"Saeth made me thirsty," Cynric said.

"That's all?" Phelan asked.

Cynric turned to the lad. "You misunderstand, son. She made me *thirsty*. I felt as if I had swallowed half the Kjartan. Every fiber of my being screamed for water. It was one of the most . . . interesting sensations I have ever experienced."

Tarian shook his head. "Only you would deem it such, Wizard."

Cynric laughed, still hoarse. "You're probably right."

Danya stood. "I'll go get some cold water from the stream."

As difficult as it was for Tarian to believe, during Ashur Dal's Long Run, the Eyslk had made mental note of all the potential campsites between Vallanora and Pendara as he sped past. This spot, a small clearing in a grove of trees about a quarter mile off the road, was near a cool, rushing stream.

Cynric gestured for her to sit. "Don't bother, Madam Watcher. The effect was only temporary. I wasn't truly in need of water; Saeth's power only made me feel as if I were. I'm fine now."

Danya eyed Cynric skeptically, but she sat back down.

Tarian found the wizard's dismissal of Danya's offer to be a bit odd. Even if he only felt as if he needed a drink, wouldn't one help? If it had happened to him, Tarian knew he'd want to drain a whole waterskin at the very least. And what about the raspiness that still lingered in Cynric's voice? It certainly didn't sound like an illusion. Come to think of it, Tarian couldn't recall seeing Cynric drink at all during the day, despite the fact that he had sweated in the summer sun like the rest of them—Ashur Dal excluded, of course. Tarian gave a mental shrug. He probably just hadn't noticed when the wizard took some water, that's all.

"You are in possession of a great power, Priestess," Ashur Dal said. "You must learn to control it, lest it control you."

Ashur's words were nominally for Saeth, but Tarian had

the sense the Eyslk was addressing them all. When they had taken a break for lunch around noon, Ashur had asked them about the Change. The Eyslken hadn't been affected, but the Silent Ones—or at least the individual spirit Ashur had spoken with—had informed him about the basics of the Change, though if the Eyslken dead had any notion of exactly what it was and why it had happened, they had kept such information to themselves. They told Ashur about their own experiences and the specific changes which had occurred in them. The Eyslk actually seemed somewhat taken with Danya's friend Jessex and had spent a few moments holding the little gray mouse. Thanks to the Silent One he'd spoken with, Ashur was already familiar with Tarian's change, but when Phelan spoke of the shadow wolf that lay hidden within him, the Eyslk's expression became grim and thoughtful, though he didn't say anything at the time.

"I do not wish in any way to seem presumptuous," Ashur continued, "but I've learned a thing or two about magic in my time. If I can train a thick-headed human child such as *he* was—" The Eyslk nodded at Cynric, who smiled. "—to Shape, then I might be able to help you deal more effectively with your newfound abilities." Ashur paused before adding, "And Cynric might be able to offer a word or two of advice as well."

The wizard's eyes widened in surprise, but then he nodded to his old teacher.

Although Ashur Dal's offer was clearly intended for them all—save Cynric, Tarian supposed, who had yet to manifest any signs of the Change, perhaps due to his time among the Eyslken—Tarian guessed it was more for Saeth's, and especially Phelan's benefit. So far, Danya and he seemed to be handling their changes fine, but then nei-

197

ther of theirs had demonstrated any potentially harmful effects to others. Not yet, at any rate. But if what Saeth had done to Cynric was any indication, the priestess's power could possibly be life-threatening. Could she speed up a person's heartbeat, make the organ work so hard that it exploded? Perhaps. And Tarian had seen Phelan's shadow wolf in action against the two bandits who had waylaid them. He had no doubt the beast was deadly dangerous.

Tarian still didn't like the Eyslken as a race, though after traveling with Ashur Dal for a day, he had come to feel a certain amount of respect for him as an individual. Tarian was less than elated by the idea of his son becoming the Eyslk's pupil, but if Ashur Dal could help Phelan learn to control the shadow wolf, Tarian would be forever grateful to him.

Tarian watched his son, saw the boy nod his head to Ashur Dal ever so slightly, saw the Eyslk nod back. He was glad, mostly. But he couldn't help feeling a certain amount of jealousy and resentment as well.

"My thanks, Eyslk," Saeth said, "but I have my faith in Rudra and my prayers to guide me. With the help of the Most High, I shall learn to suppress whatever foul magic now resides within me."

"As you wish," Ashur said evenly. "But if you change your mind, you have only to let me know."

"Now how about letting Tarian use some of his 'foul magic' to heal you, Saeth," Danya said. "For if you think you hurt now, just imagine what you'll feel like in the morning when your muscles have had all night to tighten up."

Saeth's face went white at the thought, and Ashur Dal explosively broke wind.

They were all silent for a long moment, and while Tarian

didn't know Eyslken well enough to tell, he thought he detected a slight reddish tinge to Ashur's ivory cheeks.

"Sorry," Saeth said sheepishly. "I'll work harder on controlling my power."

The rest of the humans laughed, and this time Tarian was certain the Eyslk blushed.

Tarian healed Saeth after that, though not completely. He eased the worst of her pain, softened the stiffness in her muscles, reduced her blisters, but he didn't take them away.

They ate then, and Tarian was right—Saeth didn't enjoy the rations of jerky, dried fruit and biscuit. When Cynric pointed out that priests and priestesses of Rudra were supposed to be ascetics, and thus rations should be akin to a banquet for her, she threatened to give him a crippling case of indigestion if he didn't shut up.

Tarian noted that while the wizard took his share of rations, he didn't actually eat any.

The Palace servants had packed a short bow and a quiver of arrows. Tarian considered going out while there was still a bit of light left to see if he couldn't bring down a rabbit for their breakfast, but then his gut twisted at the thought, and then he remembered, he could no longer kill. No loss; he'd never been more than adequate with a bow anyway.

The servants had also packed some hooks and twine for fishing. Tarian didn't know if hooks counted as weapons, but he'd a mind to take them and head to the stream and see if he couldn't set up a few lines. If they couldn't have rabbit for breakfast, maybe they could have fish.

He asked Phelan if he'd like to go along. Not only because Tarian might need help if it turned out he was unable to set the hooks, but because he wanted to get his son alone for a few minutes so they could talk. He wanted to check in with the boy, see how he was doing. But Phelan was engrossed in a story Cynric was telling about his first successful—or rather semi-successful—Shaping, and so the boy declined. Tarian tried not to feel miffed by the rejection, but he wished that Phelan would act that interested in one of *his* stories sometime.

Danya stood. "I'll go."

Tarian accepted her offer with a nod and together they walked to the stream. It wasn't far from their camp, and while there were elm trees on the opposite bank, there were none on this side, and they had a clear line of sight of the camp, though they were out of earshot. Tarian was able to tie the twine on the hooks, he was able to lift up rocks at the stream's edge and retrieve worms, but he couldn't push the barbed hooks through their wriggling flesh. He had to leave that to Danya. When she baited the first hook, Tarian felt a small twinge of pain, and he automatically reached out and touched an index finger to the writhing worm to heal it. But nothing happened.

He tried again, but without success.

"Perhaps it can't heal while it's still on the hook," Danya said. They removed the worm and Tarian tried again, but the creature's wound refused to heal.

"It looks like your power only works on people." Danya replaced the worm on the hook, and held the lines out to him. "Do you want to try casting them into the water?"

He shook his head. He could sense that he wouldn't be able to do that, either. Frustrated, he busied himself with gathering three makeshift stakes and sticking them into the bank while Danya tied small rocks to each of the three lines for weight. She then cast the lines into the water and tied them to the stakes. She then sat down on the bank and patted the grass next to her, indicating that he should sit as well.

200

Tarian glanced back to the camp, heard the others—including Ashur Dal—laugh at something Cynric had said. He felt uncomfortable being alone with Danya like this, almost as if it were wrong, somehow, though he couldn't have said exactly why. In the end, with no good reason not to, he sat.

They watched the lines be dragged southward by the stream's current, listened to the sound of crickets warming up for the night's symphony to come.

"It just struck me," Danya said. "You can't kill, not even a worm, but you can eat meat. So even though you can't slay an animal yourself, you can still reap the benefits of its death."

Tarian nodded. "I'd come to realize the same thing. I guess it's the causing of an injury that bothers me. I feel the pain and distress of a wounded creature as if it were my own, and that sensation spurs me to try to heal it. But once something is dead . . ." Tarian shrugged. "It's just meat."

Danya removed her boots and dangled her feet in the water. Tarian noticed she had small, delicate feet, not so very different from Lowri's.

"That feels good," she said. "I'm tempted to jump all the way in, let the stream wash the day's travel off me."

Tarian smiled. "Right now, you'd probably end up catching a hook in your backside and scaring away all the fish in the process."

Danya grinned. "If I did get punctured by a hook, at least I'd have a healer with me." They returned their attention to the stream then, and watched the lines for several more moments. Danya took Jessex out of her pocket and let the little mouse nose around through the grass.

"Aren't you worried he might run off?" Tarian asked.

"No. I can't explain it, but I know Jessex isn't going anywhere. We're bound, he and I, one to the other. Till death do us part." She reached down to lovingly stroke the mouse with a forefinger, then turned back to Tarian. "So what do you think of our little group?"

"Saeth is more of a pain than a whole rear full of fish hooks. Especially with that power of hers. None of us possess magic which spills over onto others when we're not thinking."

"Maybe she'll relent and accept Ashur's offer to teach her to control her power," Danya said.

"Perhaps. But she strikes me as an extremely stubborn woman, so I wouldn't hold my breath if I were you."

"Have you noticed the way she keeps a death grip on that rucksack of hers?" Danya asked.

"I have. My guess is she has some sort of holy object in it that she doesn't want the likes of you and me defiling with our touch."

"Maybe she has some of that insect-repelling incense." They laughed.

"Cynric's a good man," Tarian went on. "He's a very experienced traveler, probably more so than I am, and I've been up and down the length of Athymar in my time in the King's service. I'm not sure exactly what's going on between him and Ashur Dal, though. Oh, they're polite enough, even given to bantering just a bit, but there's a tension, a distance between them, as if they had a falling out somewhere along the way, and neither of them wish to speak of it around others."

Danya nodded. "I've noticed the same thing." She swished her feet around in the water. "What do you think about Ashur Dal?"

"He's an Eyslk," Tarian said too quickly. "What is there to think?"

Danya frowned at him, then looked away.

Tarian knew it had been a stupid thing to say, but he hadn't been able to help himself. He decided to change the subject. "What are your impressions of Phelan?"

"He's a nice boy. He has a chip on his shoulder, but then I did too when I was his age."

"He's got a bit of a crush on you, you know."

"Nonsense," Danya said. This time it was her turn to speak too quickly.

"He does," Tarian insisted. "I can't say as I blame him. You're a very capable, intelligent, attractive woman."

Danya smiled. "Careful, Tarian Ambrus. Flattery will definitely get you somewhere." Then, as if embarrassed by her words, she looked back out at the water once more.

Tarian told himself not to make too much of the comment. After all, Danya had a wry sense of humor, and she wasn't shy about sharing it with others. She hadn't shown any overt signs of attraction toward him, and even if she had, he was a married man. For Rudra's sake, he had come on this mission primarily to find a way to restore Lowri to her human form. Besides, there were at least fifteen years between Danya and him. A few more, and Tarian would've been old enough to be her father. No, a woman like Danya wouldn't see anything in an old soldier like him.

"Do you miss her?" Danya asked in a soft voice.

"Hmmm?"

"Your wife. Do you miss her?"

What kind of question was that? Of course he missed her! "It's easier for me than for Phelan. I'm used to being away from Lowri, out campaigning somewhere—hunting for Lukashen in the Wastes of Nelek, clearing out an infestation of Dretchen in the fruit groves of Casimir. I just try to pretend that I'm back in harness again, and Lowri's home, waiting."

"It must have been hard for her," Danya said.

Tarian frowned. "How so?"

"Your cabin is on the southern edge of the Greenmark, right?"

Tarian nodded.

"It must have been difficult being alone, taking care of a little boy, not knowing when or if your husband is going to return. I don't think I could do it."

"I . . . never thought of it quite like that before." Tarian's only concern had been for Lowri and Phelan's safety, that the darkness he fought against never came near to threatening them. But in all the years he was out wielding his sword for Rudra and King, it had never occurred to him to consider what Lowri's life was like. At the time, he thought he was being a good husband and father. Now he wasn't so certain.

Danya picked up Jessex and tucked him into her pocket. Then she withdrew her feet from the water, picked her boots, and stood. "If there are any fish in this stream, it looks as if they're not going to bite as long as they have an audience. Let's get back to the others."

Tarian nodded and stood. Together they walked back to camp, each lost in his or her own thoughts.

Neither of them heard the rustling of leaves, as if something hid within the branches of one of the elms on the opposite side of the stream. Something large and winged, which watched Tarian and that little snip of a girl with baleful, jealous eyes.

CHAPTER EIGHTEEN

Ashur Dal insisted they set watches for the night. Tarian thought it a wise precaution. Even though this part of Southern Athymar didn't have a reputation for being particularly dangerous, since the Change there was no guarantee that anywhere in the land was truly safe. They decided on four watches, each lasting two hours. Ashur would take first watch, for although his people rarely slept, after the Long Run of the previous day, he needed to spend most of the night in deep meditation to restore his strength. Danya volunteered to take the second watch, and Cynric the third. Tarian would take the fourth and last.

Saeth looked relieved that she didn't have to keep watch, but Phelan wasn't happy.

"I can take a turn at watch; I'm old enough," he said sullenly.

Tarian opened his mouth to speak, but before he could say anything, Ashur Dal said, "Yes, you are. But come morning I plan to put the mistblade Cynric was gracious enough to loan me through its paces. I'll need a sparring partner who's well rested."

Phelan's eyes widened and his mouth slowly worked its way into a grin. "You mean me?"

"If you would do me the honor."

Tarian thought if Phelan's grin got any wider, the edges of his mouth would split. "Sure!"

Ashur Dal nodded. "Excellent. Then it's to bed with you all, and I'll wake you, Danya, when two hours have passed."

Part of Tarian wasn't happy with the way the Eyslk had become de facto leader of their party. True, he knew the way to Vallanora, and he had two-and-a-half centuries more experience than the rest of them. But Tarian had been a commander in the King's Army when he had been forced to retire due to his injuries, and it wasn't easy for him to get back to the mindset of having to *follow* orders—though, to be fair, Ashur Dal merely made strong suggestions—instead of *giving* them. Still, even if the Eyslk had a high-handed way about him, Tarian couldn't fault any of his *suggestions* so far. And so he crawled into his bedroll without complaint and, lulled by the song of crickets and the gentle blinking of fireflies in the darkness, he soon fell asleep.

Tarian woke with a start. Something wasn't right. He sat up and looked around the campsite, saw that the fire— which they had left burning to keep away insects—was almost out. The others were all asleep, save Ashur Dal, who sat cross-legged, hands resting on his knees, eyes closed, breathing so slowly he could easily have been mistaken for a statue of an Eyslk rather than the genuine article.

"Ashur?" he said softly. But the Eyslk didn't stir. He'd said the meditative state he needed to reach was deeper than sleep, and that it would be difficult, if not impossible, to rouse him before dawn. At the time, Tarian had thought the Eyslk had been exaggerating, but not now.

He crawled out of his bedroll and looked up at the moons' positions to try to gain a sense of what time it was. Well past midnight, he judged, though morning was still several hours off. Toward the end of Cynric's watch, then. Tarian looked around. The twin moons of the Wolf and the Dragon, both swollen and bright, provided more than enough illumination to see by, but the wizard was nowhere in the vicinity. Perhaps, Tarian allowed, he had gone off to see to a call of nature. Though since Cynric hadn't touched food or drink all evening—at least not that Tarian had seen—the man would seem to have no need to relieve himself. It was foolish to go any distance from the camp for such a reason anyway, but Tarian wasn't especially worried about someone of Cynric Fenfallow's abilities being able to take care of himself. But it was irresponsible to leave without waking someone to keep watch while he was gone. The wizard didn't seem to Tarian to be the kind of man who would do such a thing.

He heard several of the horses whicker nervously. He was about to go over to check on them, when he heard a voice, little more than a whisper, really, come from the branches of a nearby tree.

"Wondering where the wizard went?"

Tarian looked up and saw a dark shape perched among the leaves, feral eyes glowing yellow in the moons' light. Lowri.

Tarian wondered if he should wake the others. If Lowri chose to attack, there was nothing he could do to defend them.

Lowri's chuckle was a snuffling, animal sound. "I always could read your face like a book. Don't worry, I won't attack your friends—not even the little blonde slut—unless they give me cause."

Tarian bristled at her description of Danya, but he knew better than to let her get to him. He decided he had no choice but to take Lowri at her word. If he woke the others, there was an excellent chance that one of them—most likely Danya, or Ashur Dal, if he came out of his trance—would provoke Lowri into attacking merely by drawing their weapons.

"Why are you here?" Tarian kept his voice barely above a whisper.

"To talk to you, *dear husband*. You really are dense, you know. Every last one of you. Going on a quest to learn the nature of the Change." She shook her head, as if it were the most ridiculous notion she had ever heard of. "You have all the answers inside of you, but none of you know how to listen."

"How do you know what we're doing?" he challenged.

"I've been keeping my eye on you, Tarian. And our son. I've learned to fly quite silently when I wish, and there are many trees along the road to conceal me. My hearing, too, has improved a great deal since I became the glorious creature you see before you." Another snuffling laugh. "I don't need to get all that close to listen in on you and your new friends."

"I had a hunch you might be following us," Tarian admitted. "I even thought I caught a glimpse of you a time or two, but I was never certain." He stared into the lizardish face of the thing crouching in the tree and tried to find some trace of the woman he loved therein, but he saw none. "You say you know more about the Change than we do. What do you know?"

"I spent a great deal of my time alone while you were off playing soldier. Once Phelan was in bed, I would sit up for hours. I'd open a shutter and listen to the sounds of the forest at night, hear my own heart beating in time with the ancient rhythms of the Greenmark. I became quite skilled at listening, Tarian. After all, there wasn't much else for me to do, was there?

"Because of this, I can hear the darkness whispering inside me, telling me what I've become, what I'm supposed to do." She laughed again, a bit more loudly this time, and

Phelan stirred in his sleep, though he didn't wake. "It doesn't really matter that you can't hear the Voice inside you, Tarian, for you're doing exactly as it commands, whether you realize it or not." She gestured to the others tucked away in their bedrolls. "All of you are. Save the Eyslk, of course." She spat in Ashur Dal's direction. "He doesn't have a Voice inside him."

"You're not making any sense, Lowri. Tell me plain and simple: what is the Change, why did it happen, and how can it be reversed?"

She grinned, displaying a mouthful of razor-sharp teeth. "You wouldn't want me to spoil your fun now, would you? You'll find out soon enough. Besides, I didn't come to talk about the Change."

"Then what do you want to talk about?"

Lowri hesitated, and her grin fell away. When she spoke, her voice almost sounded human again. "Us."

Tarian felt as if a hand of ice closed around his heart.

"I know there is nothing I can say that will dissuade you from this quest you're on—and a quest it is, or will become soon enough. But you have to abandon any hope that you can *save* me. Even if you could find a way to transform me back into the human woman I once was—the woman you took as your wife—I wouldn't let you. I like what I've become, Tarian, and I intend to stay this way."

Tarian shook his head in disbelief. "You don't mean that. The Change has driven you mad."

"No, the Change has driven me *sane*. I see things far more clearly now, more clearly than I ever imagined possible. I don't love you anymore, Tarian. I don't know if I ever did. I married you because you asked me, because I was a stupid village girl who thought that when a brave, strong soldier asked you to be his wife, you were a fool to say no. I stayed with you because I thought it was a wife's duty to obey and support her husband. I moved to the Greenmark because you wished it, lived in isolation with the son I bore you because you wished it. I did everything for you and for him, never anything for *me!*"

This last word came out high-pitched and shrill. Saeth's eyes flew open, and Tarian feared the priestess would see Lowri and give forth a terrified shriek, but Saeth's eyes drooped almost immediately, and she fell back into slumber.

Tarian didn't know what to say to Lowri. He'd thought he'd been taking care of Phelan and her all these years, but he'd come to see that he had been wrong, that what he had thought was a sanctuary on the edge of the Greenmark, was instead to his wife and son a prison.

"In all honesty, I did do a few things for myself," Lowri said, her voice now resembling a cat's purr. "Whenever it got too lonely in our cabin, I would pack Phelan up and visit the nearest village, remember? During those nights, I didn't have to sleep alone. There were many men who desired my company for an evening, and I had my pick."

Tarian felt as if he had just received a blow to the stomach. A soldier's life held many temptations, but even though he had had ample opportunity, Tarian had never betrayed the pledge he'd made to Lowri on the day they were joined as man and wife. Not once.

"You lie," he hissed.

"Why would I? To hurt your feelings? I don't give a fig for your feelings, Tarian Ambrus. All I care about is myself now, and the Voice that whispers within me."

"Then why tell me these hurtful things? Why bother talking to me at all? Why don't you just fly away and never look back? Is it because despite what you say, you still care for me—and for Phelan?"

Lowri paused, as if she were giving Tarian's question serious thought. "Perhaps I do have some residual feelings," she admitted. "Especially for the boy." She nodded toward Phelan's sleeping form. "So, for the sake of what we once shared, hear me now: give up, Tarian. Go home. I do not wish you to come riding to my rescue like some idiotic knight out of a child's bedtime tale. I am strong now; I have my wings, and I have the Voice within to guide me. I don't need you to protect me anymore. I don't need anyone."

"I have fought for the Light my entire adult life, Lowri. I can't stop now."

"Then you're a bigger fool that I thought, Tarian. If you were smart, you'd break off with the others and take that strumpet you've hooked up with back to the cabin and set up house with her. She may not be much to look at, but she'd be willing enough to have you, I wager."

Tarian wanted to defend Danya against Lowri's insults, but he knew his wife was merely trying to goad him, although it seemed that, in her own way, she was trying to protect him. From what, he wasn't certain. But just the fact that she was gave him hope that the woman she had been hadn't been completely subsumed by the creature she had become.

"Danya isn't interested in me as anything more than a traveling companion."

Lowri laughed. "Not only are you stupid, you're blind, too! The signs are easy enough to read, if you have the wit to see them." She shrugged her scaly shoulders. "Take up with her or don't. What do I care? But know this, Tarian. If you continue walking down the path you've chosen, it will lead only to your death, and likely to Phelan's too. Is that what you want for the son you worked so hard to protect?

To die on a fool's quest?"

Tarian heard a soft rustle, as of someone moving stealthily through grass.

Lowri's head jerked in the direction of the sound, and she scented the air. "The wizard returns from his little walk. Cynric Fenfallow has just begun to start listening to the Voice within him. Tonight, it told him to feed. Who knows what it will tell him tomorrow?"

Lowri grinned, then launched herself off the tree limb and ascended almost soundlessly into the night sky. Tarian watched her go, the moons illuminating her progress until she climbed too high for him to see.

He turned as Cynric walked into camp. The wizard was carrying a limp bundle of gray fur. A hare, Tarian realized, a good-sized one, too.

Cynric stopped when he saw Tarian was awake. He smiled awkwardly. "You're up early. You still have—" He glanced at the sky. "—another half hour until your watch starts."

Tarian realized that the wizard hadn't heard or seen Lowri. So much the better. He didn't want to have to discuss what they'd talked about, and right now he was too upset to come up with a good lie. "Where did you go?" he asked.

"Thought I'd heard something suspicious, and I went to investigate. Turned out to be my friend here." He held up the hare by its long ears. "He's a beauty, isn't he? I thought he'd make a good breakfast, so I cast a trifling spell to freeze him in his tracks. After that, it was a simple matter to wring his neck. Hardly sporting, I know, but Saeth isn't the only one who dislikes trail rations."

Tarian had to give the wizard this: he told a good story. Although it was still a foolish move, Tarian could believe that a mage as powerful as Cynric might not think twice about going off by himself to check out a suspicious noise. But Tarian knew better than to accept that bit about using a spell to render the hare motionless. Cynric didn't likely expect a simple soldier to know much about thaumaturgy, but Tarian knew that Eyslken magic could affect only nonliving things. Cynric couldn't have cast such an enchantment because it didn't exist.

Perhaps the wizard had used a new power granted him by the Change to freeze the hare. But if that were the case, why didn't he just say so? Cynric had no reason to be ashamed. Aside from Ashur Dal and his people, they'd all been affected by the Change. Then Tarian remembered what Lowri had said.

Cynric Fenfallow has just begun to start listening to the Voice within him. Tonight, it told him to feed.

Tarian looked at the lifeless hare dangling from Cynric's hand. The animal appeared intact. If Lowri had been telling the truth—and given the state of her mind since the Change, that was a mighty big if—then what, precisely had Cynric fed on?

"We only have a couple hours or so until daylight, and I'm still quite awake," Cynric said. "Why don't you go back to sleep while I dress this cony and start cooking it? That way, it'll be ready in time for breakfast. I'm sure you know how to do it, but with your aversion to knives . . ."

Cynric's reasoning on this last point was sound. Even though the animal was dead, the thought of using a knife to skin and gut it set Tarian to shivering. "My thanks, Wizard. See you in the morning." He resisted looking up into the sky once more to see if he could catch a glimpse of Lowri, and returned to his bedroll, though he had no intention of sleeping. He was still going to serve his watch, only now

Cynric would be the focus of it. He closed his eyes partially, and observed the wizard through the slits of his eyelids. It would be difficult staying awake like this, but Tarian had done it before in his military career, and he could do it again if he had to. Especially after the things Lowri had said to him. He didn't think he could sleep if he tried.

Cynric started in on the hare, while Tarian began to mentally relive his conversation with Lowri. He would do so many more times before sunrise.

In the bedroll to Tarian's right, Danya, though her eyes were shut, wasn't sleeping either. She had awakened when Lowri first spoke, though neither the demoness nor Tarian had noticed at the time. When she had felt relatively confident Lowri wouldn't attack, Danya closed her eyes and listened as they spoke. She knew it was wrong to eavesdrop, but there wasn't a great deal she could have done about it in this case.

Like Tarian, she was concerned about Cynric's strange behavior in abandoning their camp during his watch, but mostly she thought on what Lowri had said. The woman claimed to no longer love Tarian and that she wanted nothing more to do with him. If that were true . . . then maybe she had a chance with Tarian after all.

She lay there thinking until morning.

CHAPTER NINETEEN

Come dawn, the smell of cooking hare filled the campsite and roused the others. Tarian stretched and yawned, doing his best to seem as if he were just coming awake. Cynric had used deadwood to make a crude spit over the fire, and he'd tended the cony well, carefully turning it so it would cook evenly. He looked quite cheerful this morning, well rested and full of energy, despite the double watch he'd served.

"Good morning, everyone! Breakfast shall be ready before long."

Saeth looked at the roasting hare with undisguised hunger, then went off to see to her morning ablutions—toting her ever-present rucksack with her, of course. Danya, after giving Tarian a good morning smile, followed along close behind. Tarian thought of what Lowri had said last night. Did Danya favor him? He supposed it was possible, but he hadn't seen any signs of affection from her so far. Perhaps Lowri was right, and he was too dense to notice them.

The Queen's servants had added tea to their provisions, and Tarian decided to brew some. He was about to wake Phelan and ask the lad to fetch some water from the stream, when Ashur Dal's eyes snapped open. The Eyslk sat for a moment, looking around, as if he didn't quite remember where he was or who these humans surrounding him were. Then he rose gracefully to his feet, moving without the slightest trace of stiffness, though he hadn't moved a muscle all night.

"Good morrow to you, Tarian," Ashur said. Tarian nodded as the Eyslk walked past him and knelt next to Phelan. Ashur shook the boy by the shoulder, none too gently.

"Wake, Phelan. The sun is up and you should be too."

Phelan opened his eyes and made some inarticulate sound which might have been "Good morning," but was just as equally likely to have been "Go away."

Ashur Dal reached beneath Tarian and lifted the boy as if he weighed nothing at all. Phelan squawked as the Eyslk set him on his feet still cocooned in his bedroll.

"Last night, you indicated a willingness to be my sparring partner," Ashur Dal said. "Fetch your sword and let's be at it."

Phelan looked dazedly at the Eyslk. "What time is it?"

Ashur yanked the bedroll down to Phelan's feet. "Time to get moving. If you wish to go relieve yourself, do so quickly. I'll be limbering up." Ashur turned and walked away.

Phelan cast an aggrieved glance at his father, but Tarian just shrugged and headed over to where they had left the saddlebags last night after removing them from the horses. Despite his dislike of Eyslken in general, Tarian had to admit he liked Ashur Dal's style. He'd have made a good commander.

By the time Tarian had gotten the tea, a pot and some water and set it all close to the fire to boil, Danya and Saeth had returned, and Ashur and Phelan were ready to begin. The women stopped to watch, but Tarian remained by the fire with Cynric.

"Don't you want to go watch your son?" Cynric asked.

"Yes, but I think he'd prefer I didn't. I'd probably just make him uneasy." Tarian smiled. "Besides, having Danya watch him is going to make him nervous enough as it is."

Ashur Dal bowed to Phelan, and the lad bowed awkwardly back, and then they began. Phelan swung Cathal clumsily at first—the boy didn't have the muscle mass to wield the sword effectively yet—and despite the narrowness of the Eyslken blade, Ashur easily blocked his blow. Cathal made no sound as it struck the mistblade.

Tarian looked at Cynric questioningly, and the wizard said, "Mistblades are made from raw *Paytah*. The discipline of turning Chaos fragments into physical objects is extremely rare, even among the Eyslken, and mistblades are the pinnacle of that art. They weigh next to nothing, are unbreakable, have a deadly cutting edge which never loses its sharpness, and they actually absorb the energy of an opponent's blows." Cynric paused and they watched Phelan and Ashur spar for a while. The boy's motions became smoother as they went on, and Tarian was surprised at how comfortable Phelan looked with a blade in his hand. He remembered the lad as being awkward with a sword, but then he hadn't given Phelan a lesson in several years. The boy had grown some since then.

"Ashur Dal gave me that blade on the day my training ended and I left Vallanora to enter the King's service," Cynric said. 'It seemed only right to return it to him." He gave the hare another turn. "Almost done. It'll be ready to eat by the time those two are finished."

"I don't mean to pry, but I couldn't help noticing that the relationship between Ashur and you is somewhat . . ."

"Strained?" Cynric said with a thin smile.

Tarian nodded.

Cynric said nothing for a few moments, and Tarian watched Phelan and Ashur Dal exchange blows. The Eyslk was obviously a master swordsman, especially with that mistblade in his hand, but Phelan wasn't doing half bad, and Tarian experienced a surge of pride.

"Yesterday morning, Ashur called me *g'tanu fillmar*. In the Eyslken tongue, *fillmar* means something like 'son and apprentice.' *Tanu* means 'one who was,' while the prefix adds a tone of regret. So Ashur called me 'the son and apprentice who regretfully once was.' That can be taken two ways. Either Ashur expressed regret for our falling out, or he was saying that he wished he had never taken me on as *fillmar* in the first place."

Tarian wondered what had led to the two parting ways, but he decided not to pursue that just now. "Why don't you just ask him which he meant?"

Cynric chuckled. "Eyslken don't discuss such things openly. Especially Ashur Dal. With him, everything is a test. I have no doubt that he used the term the way he did to purposefully make me wonder." He shook his head. "The man can be most infuriating at times."

"You care for him a great deal, don't you?"

Cynric looked over to Ashur and Phelan. They had paused and the Eyslk was telling the lad something, and Phelan, breathing hard and trying not to show it, was nodding in response.

"Yes, I do." He turned to Tarian and changed the subject. "Tell me, do you miss it?"

"Swordplay?"

The wizard nodded.

"I don't honestly know. Before the Change, I hadn't been able to wield a sword for two years." Tarian explained how he had lost his swordarm in battle to a Lukashen warrior. "I suppose I got used to not being able to wield a blade. Now that I have my arm back, I can't bring myself to touch a weapon. I occasionally find myself reaching for a sword without thinking, but otherwise, I haven't felt much longing to hold a blade again."

"I don't know as I would be able to accept such a loss as easily as you, Tarian. After I stopped the Rendish invasion fleet, I was close to death. The Shaping took a great deal of strength out of me, and I was months recovering. When I finally did, I discovered that I could no longer cast spells of any significance. Oh, I got by well enough, but I'd never be stopping any invasions again. Even though I can still do magic, I find myself longing for the days when I possessed my full strength." He smiled. "Listen to me go on. I sound like an old man, don't I?"

"I've noticed that you move a bit stiffly and seem to favor your right leg. Is this also due to the strain of stopping the Rendish fleet?"

Cynric nodded.

"I can help you, you know. My power isn't just effective at healing fresh wounds; it can take care of old ones as well. Such as my arm, for example." He held out his left hand, palm up. "And this hand used to be scarred and callused from a lifetime of swordplay. Since the Change, it's become as smooth as if I hadn't done a day's work in my life."

Cynric looked shocked. "Sweet Rudra," he whispered. "It never occurred to me."

"It would be no trouble." Tarian reached out to touch the wizard's arm, but Cynric held up a hand to forestall him.

"This may not make much sense, but I've gotten used to my body the way it is. My stiffness and limp are reminders of the price I paid to defend my land. I'm not certain I wish to give them up so readily." He smiled. "Perhaps I'm just an old man set in his ways. Thank you for your offer, though. I promise to think hard upon it."

Tarian nodded. Now that he had gotten the wizard talking, he decided it was time to ask how he had really snared the cony. But before Tarian could say anything, Saeth came over to the fire and inhaled deeply.

"That smells wonderful, Wizard. When do we eat?"

Cynric cast an appraising eye on the hare. "Now, I'd say. Why don't you go tell the others?"

Saeth hurried off, obviously eager to get breakfast underway.

Tarian had missed his chance. While he could raise the subject of what Cynric had been up to last night in front of the others, he preferred not to. He didn't want to arouse suspicion in the rest of the party, not unless it was absolutely necessary. And this was Cynric Fenfallow—a wizard who had wielded his magic on behalf of Athymar and its people for close to forty years. If it hadn't been for him, the rest of them might well be subjects of the Rendish empire right now. The man had built up more than enough goodwill for Tarian to abandon the subject of his nocturnal activities, at least for the moment. But he would wait for another opportunity to speak with Cynric alone, for if the Change had taken a dark turn in Cynric Fenfallow, the wizard might well become a greater threat to the land than even Baron Cavillor himself.

Tarian decided to go check on the fishing lines Danya and he had set up last night. He found the lines gone, and three mutilated fish covered in excrement lying on the bank. He knew it was his imagination, for the only sound in the vicinity was the burbling of the stream, but he could have sworn he heard Lowri laughing somewhere off in the distance.

Though it was yet morning, the air had already begun to

grow warm by the time they set out upon the Southern Road once more. Despite the heat, the sky was overcast, and it looked as if it might actually rain. Tarian took this as a sign that perhaps the land was beginning to recover from the shock of the Change. The most encouraging sign, though, was the sight of farmers out in their fields, harvesting wheat with hand scythes. Despite the enchantment which had befallen the people of Athymar, there was still work to be done, and these good folk weren't about to let their harvest fail just because a little magic had touched their lives. On the contrary, some had obviously embraced what the Change had done to them, and were using their new abilities to aid in the harvest. Most striking to Tarian was the small girl who stood alone in the middle of a field, eyes closed, while a dozen scythes moved by themselves around her, cutting wheat faster than any human possibly could.

That girl, more than anything else, gave him hope that even if the Change couldn't be reversed, the folk of Athymar would adapt to their altered circumstances, and life—however different it might be from here on out—would go on.

Ashur Dal was on the road up front, Cynric on his right, Phelan on his left. Before they had mounted up, Tarian had heard the Eyslk tell Phelan that he wanted to talk about the shadow wolf the boy carried inside him, that he had some ideas how it might be better controlled. Tarian knew that he should be grateful Phelan was receiving the Eyslk's council—after all, hadn't Tarian and he traveled to Pendara in the first place to find a mage to help Lowri? Now Phelan was talking with two wizards: the great Cynric Fenfallow and his teacher. If they couldn't help the lad learn to control what lived inside him, no one could.

But Tarian couldn't help being afraid, either. Would Ashur Dal take Phelan completely under his wing, teach the lad as he had done Cynric, make Phelan into someone who wasn't human or Eyslken but rather some strange combination of both? If the enchantment on Phelan could not be removed, then Tarian wanted the boy to learn to live with the shadow wolf as best he could. But Tarian didn't want to lose Phelan in the process. He had already lost his wife; he didn't think he could bear to lose his son as well.

Saeth rode behind Ashur, Cynric and Phelan. The priestess usually preferred to avoid conversation, perhaps because she didn't want anyone to listen to the constant stream of invectives which she muttered to her horse as she struggled to remained upright in her saddle.

Tarian and Danya brought up the rear, sometimes chatting, sometimes riding along in companionable silence. Tarian told himself that he wasn't attracted to her, that he enjoyed her company simply because, as a Watcher, she possessed an outlook similar to that of a soldier. Being with her reminded him of the camaraderie he'd experienced with the men and women he'd served with during his years in the King's service—nothing more.

As they continued along the Southern Road, Tarian tried to unobtrusively keep an eye out for Lowri, peering closely at the trees they passed to see if she might be hidden in their branches. But if she were still following them, he saw no indication of it.

Near noon, a rider approached from the north, the first traveler they had encountered since leaving Pendara. People might be adjusting to the Change, Tarian thought, but traffic along the road hadn't returned to normal yet.

The woman wore a tabard emblazoned with the sun and crown, and as she drew closer, Tarian recognized her as the flame-haired rider who had passed Phelan and him on their way to the city. Cynric hailed her and she stopped. They all gathered close to listen, though Saeth's horse was skittish around the woman's blazing hair, as the woman—who had actually been dispatched by Cynric several days ago—told them what she had learned, which wasn't much. She had visited a half-dozen villages, all of which had been affected by the Change. She had also heard tell, though she hadn't witnessed it herself, of the mysterious energy globes which departed the bodies of the newly dead.

Cynric looked disappointed. "Do you have anything else to report? Even the most trivial bit of news might be of importance."

The woman thought for a moment, and Tarian tried not to stare at her eyes, which blazed like tiny furnaces.

"Half a day's ride back, I stopped to speak with a woodcutter. The man told me he'd heard a rumor that several people in a village called Bergron had gone missing, and that some of the residents claimed to have caught and killed a small demon."

Saeth sat upright in her saddle and gazed intently at the woman. "What manner of demon?"

The rider looked surprised. "Surely you don't believe such a tale, Priestess. If there's any truth to the story at all, this 'demon' was most likely some poor unfortunate—most likely a child—who had been deformed by the Change."

Tarian saw Danya give him a quick glance, then look away. He knew she was thinking about Lowri.

"I didn't ask for your opinion, Rider," Saeth snapped. "Did the woodcutter give you a description of this so-called demon?"

The flame-haired woman looked taken aback by Saeth's intense reaction to her story, and she hastened to recall more detail. "Let me think . . . I believe he said it was three feet tall or thereabouts, with shiny black skin and no facial features other than two white pupil-less eyes. Oh, and the creature had only three fingers per hand and two toes per foot." She frowned. "Or perhaps it was the other way around; I don't remember precisely."

"Thank you, Rider," Saeth said, her manner suddenly distant. "That was most helpful."

"Does it mean something, Ma'am?" the rider asked. "Is it a true demon?"

But Saeth gazed east, looking out over a dandelion-covered meadow, too lost in thought to respond.

Cynric thanked the rider and dismissed her, and the woman continued on her way back to Pendara. When the woman had departed, Saeth turned to her companions and said, "What she described is a Peccant, a minor demonoid, the least of Anghrist's servants."

"Are you sure?" Cynric asked. "Perhaps the rider was correct, and the Change merely transformed a child into something which resembled one of these Peccants."

Saeth shook her head. "I'm a priestess of Rudra. As such, I've been instructed in the hierarchies of both Girasa and Damaranth. What the woodcutter spoke of is clearly a Peccant. And I doubt the Change had anything to do with it, at least, not in the way you're all thinking. We have heard tell of no transformations which so clearly matched an existing creature. No one has been turned into a dragon, for an example, or," she glanced at Ashur Dal, "an Eyslk."

"No one that we know of," Danya pointed out. "But the Change has affected thousands of people, perhaps everyone in the entire land." She looked at Ashur. "Every human, that is. Who's to say someone couldn't have come to resemble a specific type of demon?"

"Are you thinking of Tarian's unfortunate wife?" Saeth asked. "The poor woman might fit a layperson's conception of what a demon looks like, but she doesn't match any of the seven types of dark servants discussed in the holy texts."

She paused then, and Tarian had the sense that she was trying to decide what more she should tell them.

"There is something else. Demons—and Glories, for that matter—can only rarely enter our world. The pact that Rudra and Anghrist made after the Sundering forbids it, save in the most . . . special of circumstances." She adjusted her rucksack before continuing. "Though of course Anghrist has been known to cheat. Still, I'd say the Final Battle would certainly qualify as a special circumstance."

Cynric looked at Ashur Dal. "I know nothing about demons," the Eyslk said, "save that the Eyslken have encountered them upon occasion in the past. I suppose it's possible this 'Peccant' in Bergron could be genuine."

"Even if it is, so what?" Phelan said. "The rider said the villagers killed it."

"In and of itself, a single Peccant isn't cause for alarm," Saeth said. "They're swifter than a full-grown human, but no stronger, and they haven't any special powers to speak of. The problem is twofold: firstly, if the Peccant is responsible for the abductions the woodcutter spoke of—"

Danya broke in. "If, is right. There's a chance the abductions could be completely separate from the demon."

"True," Saeth acknowledged, "but assuming the Peccant did have a hand in them, one of the demonoids would likely not be strong enough to abduct a single human, let alone several."

"Which means there would be others about," Tarian said, and Saeth nodded.

"You said the problem was twofold," Cynric reminded Saeth.

"Yes. Secondly, demons enter our plane through a rupture in the barrier between Damaranth and this world. Such ruptures are exceedingly rare, for the Gods made the divisions between the planes strong. When a breech does develop, it is usually a small one. The Peccants, because of their size, are the only demons who can come through the portal at first. Once they have entered our world, they begin immediately to carry out the orders of the more powerful demons."

"To do what?" Tarian asked.

"To make the rupture larger, of course," Saeth said, as if it were obvious to anyone with even a modicum of wit. "So that the bigger, stronger demons can come through."

"And how do the Peccants accomplish this feat?" Cynric asked.

"Human sacrifice," Saeth said

Phelan said what they were all thinking. "The abductions."

Saeth nodded. "The demons on the other side of the portal use the power granted them by the released lifeforce of the victims to widen the rupture. The holy texts say that such breeches between the planes are unstable and collapse after a time. But while they remain open . . ."

"Any number of demons could enter our world," Danya said.

"Yes," Saeth confirmed.

They fell quiet for several moments, as the implications of what Saeth had told them sank in. Finally, Ashur Dal sighed.

"I suppose the Silent Ones will just have to wait an extra day or two to speak with Tarian," he said.

"You're joking, right?" Danya said. "You undertook a Long Run in order to get Tarian to Vallanora as quickly as possible. That enchantment took weeks off your life. Now you're acting as if a detour to Bergron would be nothing more than a . . . a minor inconvenience! Do the Eyslken value their lives so little that they feel free to spend their life energy willy-nilly to fuel spells that they ultimately end up wasting?"

Ashur Dal bristled at the Watcher's words. "My life—what remains of it—is as valuable to me as yours is to you. But the lives of the residents of Bergron are worth far more."

Tarian couldn't believe what he was hearing. "Your people turned their backs on mankind five hundred years ago. What do you care what happens to a handful of villagers?"

Cynric opened his mouth, no doubt to defend his former mentor, but Ashur Dal cut him off with a gesture. "Thank you, Cynric, but I can speak for myself. After the Sundering, those Eyslken who survived the resulting cataclysm vowed that they would never again be pawns in the Gods' eternal conflict. But then Rudra created humanity—weaker and shorter-lived than the Eyslken, and thus more in need of a God to take care of them."

Saeth started to object, but Ashur Dal held up a hand to stop her. "Peace, Priestess. I know my words do not mesh with your own beliefs. For now, please hear me out."

Saeth pursed her lips in irritation, but she held her tongue.

"The Eyslken could easily have gone our own way and ignored these new, inferior beings which Rudra had decided to populate the land with. But we didn't view humanity in that fashion. Instead we saw humans as our younger siblings, and we chose to walk among them, to teach them to rely on themselves so they would not become dependent on Gods who would one day betray them.

"A dozen millennia passed, and by the time of the Blood Wars and the extinction of the dragons, we came to realize that our efforts were hurting your people more than they were helping. We saw clearly that despite our determination never to be used by the Gods again, we had been working to further Their plans all along. Far worse, not only hadn't we helped humanity become independent of the Gods, mankind had become too dependent on *us*.

"So we withdrew to *Selyv Nahele*, what you call the Greenmark, the last remainder of the great forest which had covered the entire world before the Sundering. We would stay in Vallanora, venturing out only to hunt our dark cousins, the Lukashen, to keep them from preying upon humanity."

Ashur Dal looked at Cynric and smiled. "We also occasionally took human pupils and taught them our ways so they might return to the outside world as our agents and work for the betterment of mankind in our stead."

Ashur looked into their eyes one at a time as he spoke his next words. "Since the birth of your race, the Eyslken have done everything we could to help you. Including isolating ourselves from the rest of Athymar when we thought our presence had become damaging to you. My people have done all of these things and more for your kind, and you think I'm going to quibble about the loss of *a few piddling weeks of my life?*"

None of them said anything after that. There was nothing they could say.

Ashur Dal nodded, satisfied, and turned to Saeth. "Do your holy texts say anything about how to close a rupture in the barrier between the planes?"

"Uh . . . as a matter of fact, they don't."

"I'm not surprised. Very well, I suppose we'll just have to figure it out for ourselves, then." Without another word, the Eyslk gently tapped his heels against his steed's flanks and the horse started forward.

"Looks like we're on our way to Bergron," Danya said softly, a hint of shame in her voice.

"Looks like," Tarian agreed in a similar voice, and the five humans followed the Eyslk northward.

CHAPTER TWENTY

As they traveled the next day, Tarian tried several times to draw Cynric out about why he had abandoned their camp, though he had no luck. That evening, the wizard snuck off again, this time bringing back several lifeless squirrels for breakfast. The next morning, when Danya jokingly commented on Cynric's hunting prowess, he murmured something about Eyslken snares. The others were content to leave it at that, though Tarian saw Ashur Dal looking thoughtfully at his *filmarr*.

Phelan participated in another early morning sparring session with Ashur Dal, this time alternating with Danya, who not only said she wanted to keep her swordarm from getting rusty, but that she needed the exercise after sitting all day on a saddle. Tarian had to admit that while Phelan had a long way to go, the boy showed promise.

The day's journey was uneventful for the most part. As they rode, Saeth engaged Ashur Dal in religious debate, almost as if she were trying to convert the Eyslk—or perhaps learn from him. Ashur managed to maintain his unflappable reserve during these conversations, though Saeth became quite animated at times, with unfortunate results for the others in the party. After accidentally afflicting the others with fever, headache and, in Cynric's case, a nasty attack of hiccups, Saeth agreed to let Ashur Dal teach her Eyslken meditation techniques which might help her better control her power.

That evening, Cynric remained with the others the entire

night, and the next morning they were forced to eat rations. Tarian wasn't surprised. Whatever Cynric was up to, he was too smart to continually arouse suspicion by sneaking off *every* night. Tarian decided to keep an eye on the wizard, and if he stole away during his watch one more time, he'd either confront the old man or tell Ashur Dal and seek the Eyslken's council. It should have felt odd, how quickly he'd come to trust Ashur Dal in so short a time, but so many things in Tarian's life—in *all* their lives—had changed so radically that trusting the Elysken so quickly seemed natural.

During their next sparring session, Ashur Dal let Phelan try out the mistblade, while he took Cathal. The lighter weapon made all the difference in the world for Phelan. Cathal was too heavy for the lad's build, and no matter how strong his muscles became, likely always would be. But with the mistblade, Phelan easily blocked Ashur Dal's blows— though Tarian knew the Eyslk, as fast and strong as his people were, was purposely holding back—and Phelan even managed to sneak past Ashur's guard once and accidentally nick the back of the Eyslk's hand. It was a small wound, one Tarian healed easily. It was thus he learned that while he couldn't heal animals, his power wasn't restricted solely to humans. That, or the Eyslken were close enough to human to make no difference.

This last thought gave Tarian something to ponder as they set out on the last leg of their journey to the village of Bergron.

In the drowsy heat of late afternoon, the six travelers finally drew near their destination. The village was situated on the Southern Road, about thirty miles north from the point where Tarian and Phelan had exited the Greenmark to take the road to Pendara. The country here, while techni-

231

cally not considered part of the Greenmark proper, was still lush with growth—the grass high and verdant, the trees tall and strong. It resembled the land surrounding Tarian's cabin, though of course these trees were sparser, and he felt a twinge of homesickness. It amused him, for as a soldier, he had grown used to being away from his home for months at a time. He knew, however, that what he longed for wasn't so much a place, but rather the *idea* of home. After what Lowri had said to him the night before last when she'd visited their campsite, Tarian felt as if she had destroyed their emotional "home" as surely as if she had taken a torch to its physical counterpart.

At least there hadn't been any sign of Lowri since. Tarian felt guilty at the thought, but he couldn't help it. He couldn't stand seeing her like that, couldn't endure her taunts. Better that she stay away, so he could try to forget what she had become and concentrate on doing what he had to do. He didn't know if it was still possible to help her—especially if she didn't want to be helped—but he was determined to try. What else could he do?

Finally, the village itself hove into sight. Bergron looked no different than a hundred others villages he had ridden or marched through during his time as a soldier. It was a simple collection of gray stone buildings with straw-thatched roofs, none higher than two stories. There was a square in the middle of Bergron, through which the Southern Road passed, though it was a bit too lopsided to truly deserve the designation. *The village trapezoid, more like,* Tarian thought wryly.

As they entered Bergron, they saw no one about. Perhaps they were all inside to escape the heat, or out working in the fields. Tarian thought of Gudrun, the deserted village Phelan and he had encountered on their way to Pendara.

He hoped Bergron hadn't suffered a similarly mysterious fate.

As they rode into the lopsided square, Saeth kept glancing about nervously, and she reached up to scratch the brown stubble which had begun to sprout on her head—stubble which found its match in her nascent eyebrows. Danya had teased her about the hair growth this morning, told her she needed a shave. Embarrassed, Saeth replied that since she had risen from petitioner to priestess and had been required to dispense with her hair and eyebrows, she had never actually shaved them herself. Acolytes had always done it. Not only wasn't she certain she could keep herself clean-shaven on her own, it hadn't occurred to her to bring along a razor.

Tarian had a somewhat similar problem. As a soldier, he had always shaved with a sharp dagger. But now he couldn't handle weapons. For all he knew, he wouldn't be able to touch a razor either. He now had a week's worth of black stubble on his face that was fast on its way to becoming a full-fledged beard. Danya had said it suited him, but he wasn't sure.

"It's not right," Saeth muttered.

"What's not right?" Cynric asked.

"My being here! This is a job for a High Priest, or even the Radiant herself!" She rubbed her stubbly head again. Her face had gone pale from nervousness, and Tarian feared she might lose the rations she had consumed when they'd stopped at noon.

"Do any of you know what my position in the Church was before the Change?" Saeth asked. "No? I was assistant to High Priest Kendahl. Although on occasion I helped him conduct various religious rites, my primary duty was to act as his scribe. I've read about demons, but I don't have any

233

actual experience with stopping them." Her voice grew soft. "I don't have experience with much more than taking Kendahl's dictation, really."

They all looked at Saeth, then at each other. None of them knew what to say.

Finally, Ashur Dal spoke. "I have never hunted demons either, and I am two hundred and ninety-three."

Danya grinned. "Which proves you're never too old to learn something new."

The Eyslk smiled. "Indeed." He turned to Saeth. "While I do not share your faith, I believe that you are sincere in your profession of it. Am I wrong?"

"No," Saeth whispered, and then, more loudly, "No, you are not."

"Then I suggest you draw strength from your belief, Saeth Fama."

The priestess hesitated, then nodded, and if she didn't look that much more sure of herself, at least she no longer appeared as if she might throw up at any moment.

They continued riding through Bergron. Every building they passed had its door closed, and it windows shuttered. Tarian had no doubt the doors and windows were barred as well.

"Where is everyone?" Phelan said, his voice hushed. Tarian knew the lad was thinking of Gudrun.

"They're here," Ashur Dal said, "hiding behind barred doors, frightened." When Phelan looked at him questioningly, the Eyslk said, "My ears may be small, but they work quite well. I can hear the villagers whispering to each other—about us, most likely," he smiled wryly. "I wouldn't be surprised if some of them took me for a demon."

Saeth snorted, but she didn't say anything.

"If I were a resident of Bergron," Cynric began, "and my

village was under assault by demons, I believe I'd gather with my friends and relatives at the local—"

"Church!" interrupted Danya.

"Precisely," Cynric said.

The church was difficult to find. It stood at the northwestern end of the village, a two-story stone and thatch building indistinguishable from all the others in Bergron, save for the relief of a blazing sun—the sign of Rudra—chiseled above the double wooden doors.

They dismounted and Cynric turned to Saeth.

"As the highest-ranking representative of the Church in our party, not to mention the *only* representative, I believe you should do the honors."

Saeth nodded, took a deep breath, then clasped the iron handle on one of the doors and pulled. The door refused to budge.

Saeth frowned, and tried again, but the door wouldn't open.

"It's probably barred," Tarian said.

"Nonsense," Saeth snapped, and Tarian's stomach gurgled. "The door to every church of Rudra—from the humblest one-room chapel to the Dawn Cathedral itself—is always open to any and all who seek the God of Light."

Saeth gave the door another sturdy but ineffective yank, this time letting out a most un-priestly curse word when the door balked her again.

Danya put a hand to her mouth to cover a smile. "It seems the villagers aren't particularly interested in sticking to Church doctrine right now."

"I don't suppose rules mean a lot when there are demons in your village," Phelan said.

"Rules are rules, no matter what," Saeth said. She pounded her fist on the door and shouted, "In the name of the most high God Rudra, open this bloody-damned DOOR!"

Nothing happened for a few moments, and from the look on Saeth's face, Tarian thought she was going to ask Cynric to blast the door open with a spell. But at last a timid voice came from within the church.

"Who—who's there?"

Tarian expected Cynric or Ashur Dal to answer and was surprised when Saeth did.

"I am Saeth Fama, priestess of Rudra, come from Pendara to investigate a report that this village has suffered demonic infestation."

That wasn't quite the whole truth, though it did streamline things a bit. Despite his decades of service in the King's army, Tarian wasn't an especially devout man, and he certainly wasn't an expert on Church dogma, but he was fairly certain Rudra frowned on lies. He doubted Saeth would appreciate his pointing this out right then, though.

They heard the sound of wood scraping against wood, and then, very tentatively, the door opened to reveal a bearded man in a simple brown tunic and trousers woven from coarse cloth. His face was haggard, and his large, watery eyes put Tarian in mind of those of a frightened dog.

He looked them over, his gaze lingering longest on Ashur Dal, those watery eyes of his widening even further at the sight of an Eyslk, then he turned and called back over his shoulder, "It's all right, everyone! They're human!" He turned back to them and looked at Ashur once more. "Or near enough, anyway." He opened the door wider and stepped back so they could enter.

As they walked into the small church, Tarian saw two wooden planks lying on the floor—no doubt they had been braced against the door to serve in place of a lock. Despite the fact that Rudra was a God of Light, the inside of the church was dim, and it took a few moments for his eyes to adjust. He saw the church was filled to capacity, every pew was jammed tight, every spot where someone could stand was taken. Men, women and children—some of whom bore obvious signs of the Change—did their best to draw away from the aisle and make room for the newcomers; that, or they didn't want to get too close to them. Many of the villagers were armed with knives, hand scythes, rakes, even simple homemade spears. Even inside their church, they refused to release their grip upon their weapons. The aura of fear was so strong that Tarian felt he could almost reach out and touch the villager's fright.

The church had thick beams overhead and windows that normally would have been open to the air and sunshine this time of year, but which were now shuttered. The floor was bare dirt, worn smooth and hard from years of use. The pews had been built from sturdy oak, as had the altar at the front of the church. On the wall behind the altar hung a faded tapestry depicting the sun rising over a sylvan paradise: Rudra looking down upon Girasa.

As they made their way up the aisle and toward the altar, Tarian became aware of a dull ache in his side. As they drew closer, the ache intensified to the point of fiery pain, and Tarian found himself pushing past Saeth and shoving villagers out of his way, so that he might reach the altar more quickly.

There, he found an elderly woman sitting with her legs beneath her, cradling the head of a lad not much younger than Phelan in her lap. The boy's face dripped sweat, and his eyes were closed as if in sleep, though he moaned softly. His tunic was dirty and torn, and while he had a number of fresh scratches on his face and hands, the worst wound was

237

on his right side, covered by a blood-soaked cloth held in place by a coil of rope. The bandage wasn't very effective; blood had leaked out and pooled on the ground beneath the lad. Tarian sniffed the air. He didn't know if anyone else would be able to detect it—Ashur Dal might—but even though the wound hadn't been made that long ago, an hour or two at the most, Tarian judged, he could smell infection setting in. The boy wouldn't last long without help. Fortunately for him, that help had arrived.

Tarian knelt next to the boy and stretched a hand toward his forehead. The old woman scowled and lifted her own hand, as if to strike his away, and Tarian gave her a reassuring smile. "Peace, Mother. I'm a healer." It felt strange to name himself such, instead of saying, *I'm a King's man,* or *I'm Tarian.* But if felt right, too.

He placed his hand on the wounded boy's forehead and felt the now familiar healing power within him go to work. The lad's injuries were extensive, and his healing took a bit longer than others Tarian had done, but after several moments, it was finished, and Tarian withdrew his hand.

The boy's eyes fluttered opened. He looked up at Tarian and frowned. "Who are you?"

Tarian smiled. "I—" He looked back over his shoulder at his companions gathered around him, then turned back to the lad. "We've come to help."

"Nasty business, this," Danya said, speaking softly. "I've seen worse on the streets of Pendara, mind you, but not by much."

The six of them stood on the edge of a forest clearing about a mile west of Bergron. Blood was everywhere, on the grass, on the trees, and pieces of what had once been men were scattered throughout the clearing, a feast for the buzzing flies which flitted from body part to body part, like gluttons at a banquet who couldn't decide what to eat first and thus were determined to try everything.

Even though these men had died several hours ago, the pain of their deaths still hung heavy in the air, making Tarian feel light-headed and queasy. He tried to gauge how many men had perished here by counting body parts, but there were so many and they were so scattered, that in the end he gave up.

Tarian had viewed similar scenes before—as had Cynric and Ashur Dal, most likely. He'd come across entire villages slaughtered by Lukashen and Dretchen, though they didn't usually kill with such savagery. The Lukashen wanted to keep as many people alive as possible in order to devour them later, and the Dretchen tended to eat what they could on the spot. But this looked like killing solely for killing's sake. It had to be the work of a demon, and not something as small as a Peccant either.

He turned to Saeth to ask her what she thought had done this, but the priestess was busy vomiting behind a tree. Tarian thought no less of her; he'd done the same thing as a lad the first time he'd encountered violent death; in his case a cousin who had been attacked by a rogue plains wolf while out hunting. It was rare for wolves to go after humans, but it had been a hard winter and the wolf had most likely been starving. Tarian and his father had tracked down the wolf and killed it, and Tarian had thrown up again after that.

"Get it all out of your system now, Son," his father had said, not unkindly. "You'll likely see worse things than this before you take your first steps onto the fields of Girasa. Best get used to it."

Tarian turned away from Saeth to give her what privacy

he could. He looked at Phelan. He caught the boy's gaze, and asked an unspoken question: *Are you all right?* Tarian knew better than to ask it aloud; he didn't want to embarrass the lad in front of the others, Danya especially.

Phelan was pale, and his hands trembled a bit, but he nodded. *I'm handling it,* his expression said, though Tarian wondered if he was, really. Worse, was the sight of such savagery stirring the dark wolf which resided somewhere within his son?

The humid summer air was thick with the stench of blood, viscera, and meat that was beginning to spoil. Cynric stepped over to Phelan, maneuvering carefully around bloody chunks of flesh. He held a sprig of mint in his hand, and he held it out to the boy. "Here, break this and hold it under your nose. It'll help deaden the smell."

Phelan looked at Tarian, and even though he didn't need it, Tarian said in a hushed voice, so as not to alert any demons which might be lurking close by, "I'll take one of those if you have more, Wizard."

Phelan took the sprig, cracked it, and smeared the juice on his upper lip. Cynric had leaves for everyone, and they all took them, especially Saeth, who snatched hers as if she were grabbing onto a lifeline. Even Ashur Dal took a sprig, though all he did was wave it under his nose once. Tarian thought that, like himself, Ashur had taken it only to make Phelan feel better, and he felt a sudden sense of kinship with the Eyslk that surprised him, more because of how natural it felt than anything else.

Tarian examined the scene more closely, and tried to reconcile it with what the villager he'd healed in the church—a crofter named Bruni—told them. The Peccants (though of course, the villagers didn't know them by that name) had begun to harass the people of Bergron more openly, and the villagers had managed to slay three altogether. Saeth had wanted to examine the bodies, but the villagers had burned them immediately. From their descriptions, the priestess was certain the creatures had indeed been Peccants.

But then several farms near Bergron had been raided by a much larger demon—or demons. Not only were people missing, but livestock had been mutilated and the farmhouses themselves destroyed.

A hunting party was formed, with the village priest as the leader. The members were chosen not only for their strength and bravery, but also for whatever new abilities the Change had granted them. Such mystical talents might be the only weapons they possessed which stood a chance of harming larger demons.

The hunters had tracked the new demon—for they had only discerned signs of a single individual, thank Rudra—to this clearing. Bruni had been a bit vague on the description of the thing, perhaps because it had attacked immediately upon seeing the humans and in the confusion, Bruni hadn't been able to get a good look at it. More likely, Tarian thought, the man's terror had made his memory shaky. Tarian had seen it happen to men and women after battle many times before; it had happened to him on occasion.

Whatever the creature looked like, Bruni was certain that it was big, fast, and deadly. Bruni was sure it could have killed them all easily, if it chose, but the demon seemed to take pains to only wound them. That was how he had ended up with the gash in his side. The demon had raked Bruni with its wicked talons, then left the crofter where he lay while it attacked someone else. None of their weapons had much of an impact on the demon. Its hide was too tough, and if a strike did manage to wound it, the hurt healed quickly. Their mystic powers had had more effect, especially those of a cooper who could hurl daggers of light from his fingertips. Bruni's own ability was an enhanced sense of smell; useful for tracking the demon, but not much else. Certainly not for avoiding the demon's talons. The demon had been forced to slay the more powerful of the hunters, and it was during this slaughter that Bruni, terrified beyond the capacity for rational thought, staggered to his feet and fled.

He couldn't recall how he'd made it back to Bergron. His next clear memory was of being inside the church, while his grandmother tried to tend to his wounds as best she could.

After several moments of studying the scene, Tarian pointed to several streaks of blood on the far side of the clearing. "See those? I'd wager they were left when the demon dragged off a survivor or two."

"No doubt to use their lifeforces to stabilize and strengthen the portal to Damaranth," Cynric added.

Danya turned to Saeth. "What manner of demon do you think it was?"

The priestess had taken her sprig of mint, torn it in two, and jammed a piece into each nostril. The effect would have been comical in any other situation. Now, it merely seemed practical. "It's difficult to say. The crofter's description wasn't very specific. Still, from what I've read, it's not the size of the breach in the planes that's important, but how strong it is. The more powerful a demon is, the more its own dark energy can disrupt a portal as it tries to pass through, causing the breech too collapse. Minor demonoids such as Peccants possess little power, and thus can come through an unstable portal without affecting it. As a breech is strengthened through the use of human life energy, it is possible for stronger demons to come through. From least powerful to most, the demonic hierarchy begins with Peccants and continues with Viles, Blights, Rages, Banes, Furies, and finally the dread Iniquities. My guess would be that the creature who did this—" she waved a hand at the carnage that surrounded them "—would be the next highest in the demonic hierarchy after the Peccant: a Vile."

"What can you tell us about these Viles?" Ashur Dal asked.

"Not much," Saeth said. "As Bruni indicated, they are vicious, strong, resistant to injury. Extremely difficult to kill."

"And these things are only the *second* most powerful type of demon?" Phelan said. "It's hard to imagine much worse!"

"Be thankful your imagination has limits," Saeth said. "The highest-ranking demons are capable of atrocities that would make your worst nightmares seem like a child's daydreams." The priestess still wore her rucksack—she'd refused to leave it back in the village with their horses—and now she reached up with a hand to stroke one of the shoulder straps, as if she thought she might somehow gain strength and comfort from touching the leather.

"So what do we do next?" Danya asked.

Cynric smiled. "Why don't you consult your advisor?"

Danya frowned. "My . . . oh, you mean Jessex." She reached into her pocket, and tried to remove the mouse, but then she yelped and withdrew her hand quickly. "Ow! The little bugger bit me!" She smiled ruefully. "I guess he doesn't feel much like making an appearance right now."

"Perhaps the smell bothers him," Ashur Dal said.

"I don't know about the rodent," Saeth said, "but the stink definitely bothers *me*. If we're going to talk, couldn't

243

we at least do it somewhere else?"

And so they picked their way carefully across the clearing—Ashur, Phelan, and Danya with weapons drawn—and followed the streaks of blood left behind when the Vile dragged off the survivors of the hunting party.

Ashur suggested that Phelan switch swords with him, for the lad still didn't have the muscles to wield Cathal effectively in a fight. Tarian wanted to protest that Phelan shouldn't be here at all, that he should've remained behind in the village where he would have been safe, but as Tarian had when they left the church, he held his tongue. He told himself that Phelan was a man now, able to make a man's choices—whether his father liked it or not. Besides, Phelan was more effective at using the lighter mistblade, and if the lad had to fight, Tarian wanted him to have every advantage, and then some.

"Why do you need a sword at all?" Phelan asked the Eyslk. "You're a wizard like Cynric, right? I mean, you taught him and everything."

Ashur Dal's expression remained neutral, but his voice was tight as he answered. "I no longer gather *Paytah*. I forswore the practice two decades ago."

"But you used magic to perform your Long Run," Phelan said, his voice rising to its normal tone.

"Speak softly, Phelan, if you must speak at all," Ashur reminded him. "The Long Run was a special case. The Silent Ones themselves exempted me from my vow for that one occasion, and I agreed because the need was so great. But now my vow is in force once again, and I will not Shape even to save my own life. Or indeed, any of yours."

Phelan looked stricken by the Eyslk's words, but Tarian, while he might not have agreed with Ashur Dal's stance, understood. Since meeting the Eyslk, Tarian had come to understand, at least a little, how much honor meant to his people. Tarian glanced at Cynric, wondering what—if anything—the falling out between teacher and student had had to do with Ashur Dal's forswearing of magic. From the hurt expression on the wizard's face, quite a lot, Tarian guessed.

They continued moving through the trees, the ground sloping gradually uphill. Phelan started to ask Ashur Dal another question, but Cynric cut in and suggested they remain silent from here on out, in order not to alert the Vile. It was a reasonable precaution, but Tarian wondered if the wizard also wanted to keep the subject of Ashur Dal's vow from surfacing again.

After half a candlemark or so, they heard a guttural voice chanting in an unfamiliar tongue. The words were harsh, formed primarily from consonants and low, throaty sounds. It sounded like the sort of language beasts might employ if they possessed the capacity for speech.

Tarian looked at Saeth, and she nodded, though her eyes seemed filled with uncertainly. They pressed onward, hurrying as fast as they could without making too much noise. The inhuman chanting rose in volume and pitch, and then it was drowned out by a shrill scream of terror and pain. A human scream.

Danya suddenly dashed forward, sword held at the ready, brow furrowed in equal measures of concentration and determination.

"Foolish girl!" Saeth hissed. "What is she thinking?"

Tarian knew she wasn't thinking. As a Watcher on the streets of Pendara, Danya was trained to react to a call of distress by charging ahead and jumping right into the middle of a situation. If she didn't, the person uttering the cry of distress might well be dead by the time she got there.

"No use in holding back now," Tarian said, and despite

the fact that he wasn't carrying a weapon of any kind, and couldn't have used one if he had, he ran after Danya. He heard the others hurrying along behind him, and although he couldn't see them, he knew what order they were in: Ashur Dal first, due to his Eyslken reflexes; Phelan next; then Cynric, hobbling along, his movement restricted by the injuries he'd sustained stopping the Rendish fleet. And after the wizard, if she chose to follow instead of hanging back and hiding—which given her complete lack of battle experience and training would be the wisest course, Tarian thought—was Saeth.

Tarian broke into a clearing and nearly collided with Danya, who had stopped and was staring dumbfounded at the blasphemous scene before her.

CHAPTER TWENTY-ONE

The Vile stood before a collection of rocks which served as a makeshift altar. Upon the altar was the body of an elderly man in a white priest's robe, the cloth over his chest torn and stained bright crimson, the chest beneath a ragged ruin. The demon held the priest's dripping heart in one massive clawed hand, studied it for a moment, then dropped it to the ground, where a half dozen Peccants began fighting over it. Tarian didn't know what the demonoids wanted with the organ since they didn't have mouths. Perhaps merely to play with the grisly thing.

He was distantly aware of the others joining Danya and him in time to see an ebony globe of shadowy energy rise forth from the dead priest. But instead of vanishing, the sphere was sucked toward a shimmering disturbance in the air behind the altar and absorbed by it. The dark energy hit the distortion with a loud crackling sound that reminded Tarian of sizzling grease, and the shimmering grew more distinct. There was a definite outline to it now; a crude, misshapen oval about the size of a grown man, which enclosed a hazy scene, as if the distortion were a window to somewhere else.

Tarian felt a stab of fear as he saw that the landscape within the portal was a barren, frigid plain. He almost thought he could feel cold air emanating from the breech and hear the lonely whistling of desolate winds. As impossible as it was to believe, they were gazing through a window to the frozen hell that was Damaranth itself.

Tarian realized then that a second body lay at the Vile's feet, a brown-haired woman in a leather jerkin and pants whose skin had the color and texture of oak bark. Tarian looked closely to see if she was breathing, stretched out his senses to determine whether or not she was in pain. He felt a sympathetic throbbing in his head, and knew that the woman was still alive, though she doubtless wouldn't remain that way unless Tarian and his companions did something fast.

The Vile became aware of them then, or perhaps it had been aware of them all along and only chose to acknowledge their presence now. Whichever the case, the demon turned slowly to face them. It licked the priest's blood from its fingers with a long black tongue casually, almost as an afterthought, then it grinned, showing oversized yellowed teeth which looked deadlier than a direcat's fangs.

The Vile stood over six feet tall, though its heavily muscled body was so broad and bulky, the demon appeared shorter at first glance. Its face resembled the apes Tarian had seen in the Kjartan menagerie, save for the creature's oversized pointed ears. Its eyes were small, black and hard, like chips of flint. It had long ebon talons on its fingers and toes which were covered with blood, some old, some fresh. Its tough, pebbly hide was a light gray in hue, like that of the giant sandrunner lizards ridden by desert raiders of the Feroz tribe.

The Vile pointed a black-taloned finger at Tarian. "You got Godfire strong in you, human. You all do." The demon trained its piggy gaze on Ashur Dal and crinkled its ridged brow. "'Cept Eyslk. He got no Godfire. Him I kill just for fun." The Vile grinned again, and gestured toward the breech behind him. "Godfire better than human lifeforce. Make gate stronger much faster. Many come through soon.

248

More like me—and worse. Need to make gate stronger first, though. Much stronger. Need your Godfire."

And with that, the Vile stepped toward them.

Danya turned to Tarian, thrust something into his hand. "Hold him where I can see him," and then she dashed forward to meet the Vile. Tarian looked down, realized that Danya had given him Jessex, not for safekeeping, though perhaps that was part of it, but rather so that she might be able to more easily view the mouse's movements and employ her power of myomancy.

The demon laughed as Danya charged toward it, and before she could swing her sword, the Vile slashed out with its left hand, using its talons like a cutting weapon. Danya didn't need Jessex's aid to tell her to skip backward, and the demon's talons hissed through empty air, barely missing her chest. Tarian released a breath he hadn't known he was holding, and he mentally willed Danya to be careful as she fought.

Tarian heard an inarticulate battle cry, and then Phelan was running forward to join Danya in engaging the Vile. Tarian shouted for the boy to hold back, that he wasn't ready yet, but if Phelan heard his father, he ignored him. Ashur Dal was close behind, moving with a speed and grace of a cat. No, a cat would've seemed slow and clumsy in comparison to the Eyslk's fluid movements.

Phelan, wielding the light mistblade, was able to actually get in a blow before the Vile even realized the boy was attacking. The Eyslken sword cut off the Vile's right ear as if it were slicing through a sheet of vellum. The ear fell to the ground, and a gout of foul-smelling black blood gushed forth from the demon's wound.

Despite the fact that Phelan shouldn't have been here, should've been back in the village were he would be safe,

249

Tarian couldn't help but feel a surge of pride. His son had drawn first blood.

But his pride was soon replaced by alarm as the Vile roared in pain and lashed out with his left arm. Phelan stepped back to avoid the blow, but he wasn't fast enough, and the demon's fist grazed his side. Phelan was knocked down, the mistblade flying from his hand. The demon grinned as it lifted a foot, clearly intending to stomp on Phelan's head.

Crazily, Tarian felt the Vile's pain and experienced an urge to rush forward and try to heal the infernal beast, even as it prepared to crush his son's head into jelly. The urge wasn't especially strong, though, perhaps because the demon was more angered than pained by his wound, and Tarian was able to stay where he was and watch as the demon's foot came down, down . . .

And then Ashur Dal was there. He swung Cathal at the Vile's neck, and the blade of Tarian's sword—the finest he had ever owned—bit into the demon's flesh. The Vile howled as brackish demonblood gushed from the wound, and he staggered, off balance. His ponderous foot thudded to the ground, missing Phelan's head by inches.

Tarian turned to Saeth and thrust Jessex into the priestess's hands. "Hold him where Danya can see him. I have to get my son." He ignored Saeth's yelp as she suddenly found herself custodian of what she still saw as a filthy rodent, and he dashed forward to pull Phelan out of danger.

Danya and Ashur Dal circled the Vile, doing their best to remain out of the demon's reach as they struck at it. Cynric was off to the side, kneeling, running his hands through the grass. No doubt looking for a Chaos fragment, what Ashur called *Paytah*, to fuel a spell. Tarian hoped the wizard found one fast. The Vile might only be the second lowest demon in Damaranth's fell hierarchy, but Tarian feared it was more powerful than they could deal with.

He reached Phelan, bent down, gripped his son beneath the arms, and began hauling him backward. The mistblade lay in the grass four feet away. Tarian didn't even consider trying to retrieve it. Just the thought of touching the weapon made him queasy. He felt a wave of intense frustration then. He was a soldier, damn it all; he should be wielding Cathal instead of Ashur Dal, should be helping his companions to bring the demon down instead of merely observing. Even as he pulled Phelan to safety, his mind was frenetically calculating battle strategy—ways to approach the demon, possible vulnerable spots to strike, how to get inside the creature's guard without getting his guts spilled onto the ground in the process. But bereft of the ability to hold a sword, they were wasted thoughts. Tarian had had a lifetime of training in the art of killing, but it was all useless now. Worse than useless, for it was distracting him when his mind should be on other things. Like his son.

As Tarian continued to drag Phelan away from the melee, the Vile's head swiveled in his direction, its porcine eyes narrowed, and its upper lip curled back from its fangs. It took three distance-devouring steps and lashed out, lightning quick for something so large.

Tarian let go of Phelan and half rose, instinctively lifting his swordarm to block the blow, as if he still wielded Cathal.

The Vile's night-black talons sliced through Tarian's wrist like a farmer's hand scythe through a stalk of wheat. Tarian's hand went tumbling through the air, and a fount of blood sprayed from the newly created stump.

Through the white-hot blaze of pain, Tarian thought, *At least I didn't lose the whole arm this time.*

Danya shouted, "Over here, you bastard!" and slashed a wicked cut across the demon's back.

The Vile grunted, sounding more irritated than hurt, and turned away from Tarian, who after all wasn't much of a threat at the moment, to continue dealing with Danya and Ashur Dal.

Tarian struggled to focus past the pain. He wasn't overly concerned with his wound; he felt confident that his healing powers would take care of it soon enough. But he needed to get Phelan away from the Vile before the demon decided to finish the lad off, or just stepped on while it fought the others.

Tarian jammed his bleeding stump against his stomach to staunch the flow of blood as best he could, then he grabbed Phelan's wrist with his remaining hand and dragged his son away from the Vile. He didn't spare a thought for his severed hand; indeed, he hadn't even seen where it landed. All that mattered was getting Phelan to safety.

When the fighting first began, the Peccants scattered, reluctantly abandoning the priest's heart. But it was better to lose a plaything than to be stepped upon by a Vile in full battle fury.

They watched from a safe distance while the mortals assailed their larger brother. They weren't worried. The thought that a demon could be brought down by Rudra's get was so ridiculous as to be beyond consideration. Sooner or later, the Vile would vanquish the mortals, creating all sorts of fun wet toys for the Peccants in the process. The Vile would then return to the task of stabilizing the portal between the planes. The Godfire that now surged through the mortals was powerful stuff, more than strong enough to create the first potentially permanent portal between the mortal realm and Damaranth since before the Sundering. It was even possible that if the demons could collect and harness enough Godfire, they might be able to completely destroy the barrier between their home and the mortal world.

The Peccants shivered with pleasure at the thought. To be free at last, to run rampant and fulfill every dark whim and debased desire . . . it would be glorious beyond measure.

When the Vile lopped off the healer's hand, the Peccants tensed, eager to get at this delightful new toy. They waited, watching the combatants, gauging when they'd have the best chance to . . . *move!*

The Peccants rushed forward, darting and dodging between mortal and demon legs, streaking toward their prize. The first Peccant to reach the hand snatched it up and kept running, unwilling to share it with the others. It ran for the trees, wove around the trunks, plunged through undergrowth, all the while exulting in the meaty-wet feel of the grisly trophy it had claimed.

But then the Peccant stopped cold as dagger-sharp claws plunged into its shiny ebon skin. If it had possessed a mouth, it would have squealed in agony.

The creature that had caught the demonoid lifted it to eye level. The Peccant struggled in the creature's grasp, holding tight to the healer's severed hand, refusing to relinquish its play-pretty, even in its death throes.

Its assailant—a winged, lizard-like being with scaled skin and wild yellow eyes—smiled. "I'll take that, if you don't mind." She plucked the hand from the Peccant's grip, then squeezed the demonoid, sinking her claws even deeper into its flesh.

As death rushed in to claim the Peccant, the last thing it

heard was the lizard creature's voice.

"I'm sure the hand's previous owner wouldn't mind. After all, he used to be my husband."

Phelan groaned and tried to get to his feet. He wasn't sure what had happened. The last thing he clearly remembered was charging the Vile—which looked like something straight out of the adventure chronicles he loved to read—and slicing its ear off with Ashur's mistblade. The Eyslken sword was a wonder, light as air, its edge sharper than any sword made by human hands. With it, Phelan felt as if he could do anything, as if he could equal the accomplishments of the heroes that he read about. Heroes like Cynric, Ashur Dal . . . and his father. Especially his father.

"Easy, son. You took a hard blow."

Phelan could barely hear his father above the sound of combat—the demon's enraged roaring, the sound of steel thunking into heavy flesh, the harsh breathing and grunting as Danya and Ashur swung their weapons. Phelan looked at Danya and despite the fact that she was a much more skilled and experienced warrior than he was, Phelan felt an urge to rush forward and protect her. He couldn't stand the thought of anything happening to her. If it did—

"Son? Can you hear me?"

His father's worried tone caught Phelan's attention. Not that there was anything special about it. His father always seemed to be worrying about one thing or another, especially where Phelan was concerned.

"I'm fine," he said, trying to keep the irritation out of his voice. He knew his father was worried because he loved him, but Phelan was a man now, and he didn't need Tarian fretting over him like a mother hen. Still, he did feel a bit shaky, so he allowed his father to help him to his feet. After all, even a man needed a little help now and then, right?

Phelan then saw the blood covering his father' tunic, noted the way Tarian held his arm pressed against his body.

"Father! Are you—"

"Already healing," Tarian said. He pulled the stump away from his stomach, and Phelan could see the wound— caused by the Vile's talons, he guessed—had already sealed over, and five tiny finger-buds were already visible.

Phelan realized that his father had risked his life to drag him out of harm's way, and it had cost him a hand. Sure, his hand would grow back, but even still . . . Phelan wanted to thank Tarian, but he wasn't quite sure how. He'd always had trouble talking to him, especially when it concerned something important. Maybe because Tarian had been away so much while Phelan was growing up.

But before he could even make the attempt, Phelan remembered the mistblade. "Where's Ashur's sword? I have to . . ." He had been about to say *help the others,* but then he felt something stirring deep within, and he realized that the wolf was struggling to get out.

No! Phelan concentrated on holding the animal at bay, using the meditation techniques Ashur Dal had taught him. He closed his eyes and pictured a cage of light surrounding the wolf, with bars made of pure thought—solid and absolutely unbreakable. Ever since the shadow wolf had killed the two bandits, Phelan had struggled to keep it from emerging again. The beast was wild, unpredictable, and Phelan feared it would turn on his friends just as easily as it attacked his foes. He sensed that it would never seek to do him harm; after all, he was its home, wasn't he? But who knew what else the wolf was capable of? Phelan certainly didn't, and however much use the shadow beast might be in a fight, he didn't want to risk the lives of his friends or his father. So he concentrated on making the bars of his mental cage stronger, thicker . . .

Then he heard a cry of pain shouted in a woman's voice.

His eyes snapped open, and he saw Danya lying on the ground before the Vile, blood streaming from a slash on her forehead.

Fear and fury welled within him, and the psychic cage he had been constructing fell away as if had been made of paper and sticks, and the wolf was free at last.

Stupid, stupid, stupid! Danya knew better than to get too close to the damn thing —its arms were too long and it moved faster than anything that big had a right to. But after what it did to Tarian, she wanted nothing more than to see the Vile dead at her feet.

Now here she was, lying on the ground, blood running into her eyes from where the demon had slashed her forehead, unable to see clearly. She was a Pendaran Watcher; she knew better than to let her feelings override her training. Yet she had done exactly that, and now it looked as if she would pay for her foolishness with her life.

The Vile stepped toward her, ignoring the wounds Ashur Dal inflicted upon it with Tarian's—Phelan's—whoever's sword. Cathal was an impressive weapon, if not in the mistblade's league; but no matter how much damage Ashur Dal did, the Vile just shrugged it off and kept coming toward her. The demon could afford to ignore its hurts. While it didn't heal at Tarian's rate, its body still repaired wounds at supernatural speed. Already the spot where Phelan had cut off the Vile's ear had healed over and formed pink scar tissue, though the demon showed no signs of sprouting a new ear. Short of taking an instantaneously fatal blow, which given the Vile's thick hide seemed unlikely, it appeared nothing could keep the demon from slaying Danya.

She turned her head, desperately searching for Jessex, hoping the little mouse might give her some indication of what—if anything—she could do to survive. She knew Tarian couldn't have him anymore, since he was taking care of Phelan. So that left Saeth. She found the priestess standing a dozen yards from the battle, her face pale, In her cupped hands was Jessex. The mouse was going through a series of frantic gyrations, but Danya couldn't see well enough through the blood to decipher them easily. She hurriedly wiped her eyes, and the action helped clear her vision a bit. As near as she could determine, Jessex was telling her to lie still, which didn't make any sense.

Then she heard a dangerous, rumbling growl, and a black streak launched itself through the air and slammed into the Vile's right side. The demon teetered and went down, hitting the earth with a sound like that of a felled tree. The wolf didn't pause; it leaped onto the demon and began savaging its neck with ebon fangs.

As Danya scrambled to her feet, she realized she was looking at Phelan's shadow wolf. She had never seen the animal before, had only heard Tarian describe it when he told Cynric the story of how Phelan and he had come to Pendara. At the time, she hadn't been able to reconcile the image of the sweet kid Phelan was with the notion of a wild bestial force lurking within him. But here it was now, and there was no denying its reality. She suddenly felt sorry for Phelan. It must have been devilishly hard to live with the knowledge that you carried a thing like *that* inside you.

Black demon blood flowed freely as the shadow wolf worried the Vile's neck. The demon shrieked with as much anger and pain, and struggled to throw the wolf off. Danya hesitated, unsure what to do. Should she attack the Vile

257

while it was down and risk getting caught between it and the wolf? Or should she hang back and wait to see how much damage the shadow beast could inflict? Ashur Dal was standing to the side as well, evidently trying to decide the same thing. But Danya didn't have to try to decide; she had a friend to help her.

She drew a sleeve across her forehead to mop up the worst of the blood, then drew the other across her eyes to clear them. She looked at Jessex, and squinted as the mouse performed an acrobatic routine. When he was finished, she frowned.

"Saeth has a *what?*"

Danya started toward the priestess.

CHAPTER TWENTY-TWO

Cynric had kept one eye on the battle the entire time while he swept the clearing for *Paytah*. Most places had at least a scattering of Chaos fragments, although often they were too small and weak to be of much worth. But this clearing had absolutely none that the wizard had been able to locate. It was completely barren, in a mystical sense.

Cynric knew little about breaches in the barriers between the planes, but he guessed that somehow, the disruption in the air that marked the opening between Athymar and Damaranth had somehow drawn all the *Paytah* from the surrounding area. Perhaps the breech had begun life as a mere pinprick, which then drew on the Chaos fragments around it to grow strong enough to permit a Peccant or three to come through. Once the *Paytah* was depleted, the Peccants had to find an alternate power source, lest the portal weaken and collapse. So they used the lifeforces of humans—at least, that's what they normally would've used. But from what the Vile had said, this particular portal had grown much stronger, much faster, thanks to some energy the demon had called *Godfire*.

Cynric was certain he had never encountered the term before, though for some strange reason it seemed familiar, as if he had known it once and forgotten it. Whatever this Godfire was, the wizard felt fairly confident that it was a result of the Change, and that the energy spheres which rose from the bodies of the dead were the physical manifestation of this power. Though as to why they winked out of existence so soon after departing the dead, he had no idea.

Cynric paused in his search to watch as the Vile knocked down Phelan, then took off Tarian's hand. Danya was the next to fall, and she surely would have been killed if Phelan's shadow wolf hadn't chosen to manifest itself. He watched the fascinating creature attack the Vile for a few moments—the wolf truly did seem to be formed of some shadowy substance—but then he forced himself to look away. He would be no good to his companions unless he could find and harvest *Paytah*. In his youth, he would have been able to give a good account of himself with the mistblade, but now he was old and slow. Worse, he was a wizard currently without magic.

That last wasn't *entirely* true. He had the power granted to him by the Change, though he was reluctant to use it against the Vile. So far, he had only employed it to nourish himself, as he no longer seemed able to derive sustenance from food and drink. And if a few small animals died so that he might live, what of it? It was no different than putting an arrow through them, cooking them and devouring their meat. Cynric now merely subsisted on a less . . . tangible aspect of the animals.

He knew he needed to tell the others soon. He could scarcely keep it a secret forever, and he was certain Tarian suspected, and most probably Ashur as well. But he wasn't ready to tell them, not yet. How could he admit what he had become? That he was now, in a sense, no better than a Lukash, for in order to live, he must feed on the life energy of others.

He continued searching for *Paytah*, and prayed that the shadow wolf would finish off the Vile so that he might be able to keep his shameful secret for at least a little while longer.

★ ★ ★ ★ ★

Ashur Dal had been about to interpose himself between the Vile and Danya when the shadow wolf attacked the demon. He watched for a moment, overwhelmed by the sheer fury of the dark lupine. Phelan and he had talked at some length about the shadow wolf, and what it felt like for the lad to constantly struggle to keep the creature contained within his body. Ashur had understood in an abstract sense; after all, gathering and Shaping *Paytah* demanded a high degree of mental control. But now that he actually saw the shadow wolf in action, Ashur realized he hadn't understood at all what Phelan had been going through, and he was impressed that the boy had managed to contain the beast this long.

The Eyslk debated whether or not to join the shadow wolf's attack on the Vile. They knew little about the wolf's nature; there was a chance it might turn on anyone who came too near. Ashur didn't want to end up fighting the shadow wolf. Not only because it would might give the Vile time to recover and renew its assault, but also because Ashur didn't want to risk harming Phelan. The wolf was part of the lad, somehow, and it was possible that any injury done to it might affect the boy. He decided to wait a few moments and see what success the shadow wolf had against the demon.

Out of the corner of his eye, he noted Danya walking over to speak with the priestess. He had no idea what that was about, but he didn't have time to find out. There was other work that needed to be done. Cathal wouldn't fit in the mistblade's narrow sheath, so he was forced to carry it as he stepped to the side of the second sacrifice the Vile had brought to its makeshift altar. He knelt and pressed his fingers to the woman's neck, searching for a pulse. But her

261

tree-bark skin was too rough for him to tell if her heart was beating or not. Eyslken hearing was much sharper than human, and normally he might have been able to listen closely and detect a heartbeat, but the battling shadow wolf and Vile made too much noise. He decided to assume the woman was alive and get her out of harm's way as quickly as possible.

He stuck Cathal point first into the ground, lifted the woman over his shoulder as if she weighed nothing, plucked the sword from the earth and kept a wary eye on the wolf and demon as he made his way over to where Tarian stood with Phelan. This woman might well be in need of a healer's ministrations.

Phelan stood, watching the shadow wolf fight. Ashur wondered why the lad didn't take advantage of the demon's distraction to retrieve the mistblade. Perhaps the lad became weakened when the wolf was free, or perhaps he was merely horrified at the sight of the unleashed fury which dealt within him.

"Phelan," Ashur said, and when the boy refused to acknowledge his presence, he said his name again, more loudly this time.

Phelan's head snapped around, and his eyes focused on the Eyslk. He looked as if he had just awakened from a dream.

Ashur nodded to where the mistblade lay in the grass. "Are you capable of fetching the sword?"

Phelan looked at the blade, hesitated, then nodded.

"Then go to it, lad, while I see if there's anything your father can do for this woman."

Phelan headed for the mistblade, keeping his gaze trained on the wolf and demon the entire way.

Ashur stuck Cathal in the soil again and gently lowered

the woman to the ground before Tarian. Tiny fingers already sprouted from the end of the healer's wrist, and Ashur gauged that he'd have the whole hand back within a candlemark or two. The Eyslk was astonished at the speed with which Tarian was healing. The Silent One who had summoned him said little of the Change that had affected the humans of Athymar, but Ashur marveled anew at its power.

"Are you all right?" Ashur asked.

"I'm doing as well as a man who just lost a hand can," Tarian said, smiling. He nodded toward the woman. "I assume you brought her to me to heal. My body is concentrating its resources on regrowing my hand, and until my own healing is complete, there's nothing I can do for her. I can sense she's not too badly off, though. I wager she'll come out of this just fine."

"That is, if we can stop the demon," Ashur said.

Phelan returned with the mistblade in hand. "We have a worse problem than the Vile!" He pointed the Eyslken sword at the portal, and Ashur and Tarian turned to look. There, visible through the waves of distortion, three hulking figures came stomping across Damaranth's barren plain. Two more Viles, and something else, a hideous creature that resembled a cross between a crustacean and a bipedal porcupine. The next highest demon in the hierarchy, Ashur presumed. He struggled to recall the list Saeth had given them. That would be a . . . Blight, he believed.

If the Vile's sacrifice of the village priest had strengthened the portal sufficiently, then there was a chance than any or all of the approaching demons would be able to enter this plane. And if they did, then the battle would surely be lost, for Ashur doubted their ability to handle one demon, let alone four.

"What are we going to do?" Phelan asked.

Ashur Dal looked at the trio of demons drawing nearer to the edge of the portal.

"That is a very good question," he said.

"I don't know what you're talking about." Saeth looked down at Jessex; she felt like squashing the tattletale mouse between her two hands.

"Don't deny it," Danya said. "Jessex says you have a weapon which can stop the demon. If you do, then for Rudra's sake, use it!"

Ever since they had set out to find the Vile, Saeth had been thinking of the silver dagger in her rucksack, wondering if this situation was the reason the Glory had given her the blade. The Glory had said the dagger itself would tell her when it was time to use it, and she had been waiting for some indication that the time was now. But so far, she hadn't received any signal one way or the other. How would a dagger communicate, anyway? Would it vibrate? Sound a metallic tone? Would it suddenly leap out of the rucksack and into her hand, shouting, "This is it!"?

This was the first combat Saeth had ever experienced, and it sickened her. The violence, the blood . . . and it was all so *confusing*. Things were happening so fast that she didn't have time to think. As powerful as the Vile was, she had thought the others could handle it. Now Tarian had lost a hand, Phelan had given birth to a black wolf, Ashur Dal was busy tending to a woman with skin that resembled tree bark, Cynric was scrounging around the clearing, looking for Rudra knew what, and Danya was standing here demanding she give up the silver dagger.

Far worse, Saeth could see other demons on the other side of the portal, coming closer. If they came through—

"Oh, all right." She handed Jessex to Danya, glad to be rid of the little rat, and slipped off her rucksack. She set it on the ground and withdrew the dagger. It was now housed in a sheath that Saeth had . . . borrowed from one of the displays in the Dawn Cathedral, the same one where she had acquired her helm and armor that the others had convinced her to leave behind. At least this sheath had proved more practical.

Danya reached for the blade, but Saeth drew it back. There was no question that she would give it to the Watcher; Saeth had no training in the art of warfare and would likely just get herself killed trying to wield it. Still, she had two conditions to go over before she would give up the dagger.

"You alone must wield the blade," Saeth told her. "I know the Eyslken is faster and stronger than you, but this is a holy object, and not for the likes of him to profane with his touch. Do you understand?"

Danya nodded, though Saeth could tell she wasn't happy about it.

"When you are finished—" *assuming we all live through this,* she mentally added "—you must return the dagger to me immediately."

Danya nodded.

"Very well then." She handed the sheath to Danya, and took Jessex from her, not pleased at all to once again have custody of the rodent, but recognizing that Danya could hardly take him into combat. "Use extreme caution. This blade deals wounds which cannot be healed, even by Tarian's power." Saeth wasn't certain this last was true, but it *felt* right. Perhaps the dagger was talking to her in its own way after all. "The slightest nick to your own skin could prove deadly." Saeth had been very careful the few times she had handled the blade. Even a simple cut could lead to infection and death, if it didn't heal. "I'd keep it sheathed until you're ready to use it."

Danya accepted the dagger, her face full of awe. "Should you say a blessing over it or something?"

With everything that was happening, the only blessing Saeth could think of at the moment was one to keep insects from ravaging a garden. "Just go kill the damned thing," she snapped.

Danya nodded, and hurried over to Tarian, Ashur Dal, and Phelan, leaving Saeth alone with Jessex. The priestess looked down at the little rat, and the rodent wrinkled its nose at her.

"Blabbermouse," she muttered.

Jessex made a snuffling sound, and while Saeth knew it was impossible, she would have sworn that vermin was laughing at her.

Danya approached them, her sword in one hand, and the sheathed dagger she had gotten from Saeth in the other. Tarian had been too preoccupied with other matters to listen to the two women, so he had no idea what they had argued about.

She quickly told them, though, and Tarian suddenly understood why the priestess had been so protective of her rucksack ever since they had departed Pendara.

Ashur Dal spoke without taking his gaze off the struggle between the shadow wolf and the Vile. "Is this dagger more effective against a demon than an ordinary weapon? Will it do more damage to the Vile because it is a 'holy' blade?"

"I don't believe so," Danya answered. "It just creates wounds that will never heal."

Just, Tarian thought. As if that wasn't enough.

"The wounds that we've struck, and which Phelan's wolf continues to inflict, do not seem to be slowing the demon down a great deal," Ashur said. "It not only has a thick hide, but unbelievable resistance to pain. Any injuries caused by a dagger would be superficial, and it would take a great many of them to wear the demon down, let alone slay it."

"We need to strike a mortal blow, then," Tarian said, "and fast, before those other demons—" He nodded to the portal. "—come through."

"If I move fast enough, I might be able to thrust the dagger into the Vile's heart," Ashur said.

"Uh, I promised Saeth that no one else would wield it but me," Danya said.

She didn't say why Saeth had extracted such a vow, but Tarian could guess. The priestess didn't want an Eyslk touching an artifact of the holy Church.

"Go for the eyes, then," Phelan suggested. "That's how Borysko killed the river serpent in *The Lay of Borysko the Bloodletter*. He thrust a spear through one of the serpent's eyes and into its brain."

Tarian hadn't thought he'd live long enough to see one of the foolish tales Phelan liked to read actually come in handy, but it was a good suggestion.

Ashur Dal thought so, too, for the Eyslk clapped Phelan on the shoulder. "Good idea, lad."

Phelan grinned as if Borysko himself had just paid him a compliment.

"Now here's what we'll do," Ashur began, but before he could finish, the Vile finally managed to grab hold of the shadow wolf. The demon sank its talons into the beast's ebon substance and heaved the creature through the air.

The shadow wolf howled as it flew toward a tree. It collided soundlessly with the trunk, its body splattering apart as it were made of tar. Thick gobs of shadowy substance smeared the tree, while others fell to the grass, again making no sound as they hit.

Phelan moaned and collapsed, dropping the mistblade to the grass. Tarian caught the boy before he could fall, and he gently set him down next to the woman Ashur had rescued.

"Son? Can you hear me? Are you all right?"

But Phelan didn't answer. His eyes had rolled back white in his head, and his eyelids fluttered rapidly. Tarian had seen such symptoms before in soldiers who had taken blows to the head. But he could sense no pain emanating from his son.

The Vile rose to its feet and grinned with satisfaction at the wolf's messy dissolution. Then it turned and began stalking toward them. They had no more time for making plans, and Danya and Ashur Dal charged forward to engage the Vile. They fought like demons themselves, Ashur wielding Cathal as if it were light as a feather, Danya fighting with both sword and holy dagger, each doing their best to inflict as much damage as possible while staying out of the Vile's reach. But Tarian knew they were fighting a losing battle. All they were doing was slowing the demon down, and while Danya might get an opening so she could make an attempt to stab the creature in the eye, she might not. Meanwhile, the three demons on the Damaranth side of the portal had almost reached the wavering distortion that hung in the air. A few moments more, and they would be through, and all would be lost.

They had no choice; either they stopped the Vile and somehow collapsed the portal, or they died.

Tarian searched for Cynric. The wizard was on the far side of the clearing, still rummaging through the grass.

"Cynric! We don't have any more time for games!" Tarian shouted. "I know what you can do! Use your power on the demon!"

In truth, Tarian only suspected what the Change had done to Cynric, and he was gambling that his suspicion was correct. The wizard hesitated, and Tarian thought the old man would refuse, but then he nodded. He stood and came running toward the Vile, a look of determination on his face.

Tarian couldn't help smiling. Now *that* was the Cynric Fenfallow he had seen stop a Deathmage ten years ago! Tarian turned to Saeth. "Priestess, use your magic to strike at the Vile!"

Saeth looked at him as if he were mad. "What am I supposed to do, make the damned thing *thirsty?*"

"I don't know!" Tarian yelled. "Use your imagination! Give it a headache or a fever! Just do something!"

Tarian forgot about the priestess then, and turned his attention to the problem of closing the gateway between the planes. Saeth's dagger was a holy weapon. Might it counteract the demon's magic? From Danya's description of its capabilities, it didn't sound as if it would. Besides, Danya needed the holy blade to kill the Vile. If only they had another enchanted weapon . . . . Then Tarian remembered: the mistblade. Cynric had said that it was made of pure Chaos, Shaped into the form of a sword by an Eyslken artisan. What would happen, Tarian wondered, if one type of magic—the mistblade—was forced into contact with another type—the portal?

There was only one way to find out.

Saeth struggled to come up with an idea. She was by no means comfortable with the notion that she possessed magic—especially when she didn't know precisely what that power was or where it originated. Once she had realized that she, too, had been affected by the Change, she had focused all her efforts on suppressing her magic so that it wouldn't cause her traveling companions unwarranted distress. It had never occurred to her that she might be able to use her power as a weapon.

Tarian's suggestions were good enough, she supposed, but she didn't think a headache or a fever would bother the Vile overmuch. It did have a physical body, that much was clear, else it wouldn't bleed from the wounds it took. But its body wasn't human, and the discomfort that might incapacitate a man or woman could well mean little or nothing to the Vile.

What could she tell about the way the demon's body worked by observing it? The Vile had a heart, else it wouldn't bleed. She could hear its bellows-like breathing, which meant it had lungs. It moved, so it had muscles . . .

Saeth had her idea. She focused her gaze upon the demon and concentrated with all her might upon a single word: *Cramp.*

Cynric approached the Vile from the rear, hoping the demon wouldn't see him. But before he could reach the fell thing, the Vile let out a bellow of pain and doubled over, contracting as if it had taken a severe blow to the abdomen, though as near as he had been able to determine, neither Ashur nor Danya had struck it.

Whatever the cause, Cynric decided to take advantage of the situation. He rushed forward and placed his hands on the Vile's pebbly back, and began to feed.

Tarian tried to rouse Phelan, but the boy remained in a

state of semi-consciousness. He glanced at the portal. The three demons had arrived, and they were pushing at the wavering distortion, as if some sort of membrane was blocking their way and they had to break through it. Saeth had said that breeches between the planes were difficult to maintain, and that the barriers worked to repair themselves. Still, Tarian knew he couldn't count on the portal collapsing of its own accord before the new demons were able to get through. And once they were through, they would have plenty of sacrifices available to strengthen the breach once more.

Very well, then. If Phelan couldn't wield the mistblade, then he would have to.

Tarian gritted his teeth and bent to pick up the Eyslken sword. As his hand closed around the hilt, he was assaulted by wave after wave of pain. Not his, but rather that of all the beings the blade had dispatched in its long life. Lukashen, mostly, but there were some humans among those whose lives the mistblade had taken, a few mages as well. Tarian nearly passed out from the psychic bombardment, but he forced himself to hold on to consciousness through sheer stubborn willpower.

He turned toward the portal, saw that one of the demons had managed to thrust a clawed hand through the membrane and was now pushing its whole arm into Athymar's plane. Tarian didn't have time to think; he stagger-ran toward the breech, and swung the mistblade at the portal. He was close to blacking out, and the swing was clumsy, but the portal was a large target and the Eyslken sword connected.

There was a bright, soundless flash of light, and then Tarian knew only darkness.

CHAPTER TWENTY-THREE

Tarian sipped spiced wine from a clay mug. "I got the idea from a tactic we used in the King's army. When a squad of soldiers encountered a Lukashen raiding party that had made camp, one of the ways to take the bastards by surprise was to sneak up on them, and then toss a jug of wine—" He held up his drink for emphasis. "—into their fire. The jug would break, splattering flaming liquid everywhere. The soldiers would then attack in the confusion."

"Hence the old phrase, 'fuel to the fire,' eh?" Cynric said. "I have to admit, I've used that trick myself once or twice."

"I certainly hoped you had the good sense to use cheap wine," Saeth said to the wizard.

Cynric looked offended. "Of course. Do you think I'd waste good drink just to set a Lukash's breeches aflame?"

Tarian smiled. The six of them sat around a table in the common room of Bergron's only inn, the Fox and Swan. A cheerful fire blazed in the hearth, the warmth welcome to the party, as they were all dressed in light robes. Their traveling clothes had become rather soiled during the battle with the Vile, and as soon as the innkeeper's wife had gotten a look at them, she insisted on laundering their apparel at once. Their outfits were now out back, draped across tree branches to dry overnight. They had been just as dirty as their clothing, and each had taken a warm bath. Now they sat close to the fire, sipping wine, content and drowsy.

The other tables had earlier been full of villagers eager to get a look at the "heroes" who had rid them of the demons, especially Ashur Dal, for none of Bergron's citizens had ever seen a member of his race before. But the tables were empty now. The innkeeper had shooed the local patrons off, in order to give his honored guests some privacy. In fact, it was getting rather late, and the innkeeper's family had gone off to bed, leaving only the man himself to see to their needs.

"You go right ahead and take all the time you want. No rush, no rush at all," the innkeeper had assured them. So even though they all should have been in bed by now—especially if they wanted to get an early start for Vallanora in the morning—they still sat, drank, and talked.

Tarian sat closest to the fire, Danya next to him. He'd noticed that Phelan, who was on the other side of the table, next to Ashur Dal, had given him a dirty look once or twice, no doubt wishing it were *he* next to Danya. But it wasn't Tarian's job to tell the Watcher where to sit, was it? Besides, he wasn't certain it was a good idea to encourage Phelan's interest in Danya. He didn't think they were . . . right for each other.

Cynric sat on the other side of Phelan, and Saeth sat at the end of the table, almost as if she had called all of them to a meeting. The priestess had kept them all at a distance after they'd vanquished the Vile and destroyed the portal to Damaranth. She had been especially thoughtful ever since they had brought the priest's body back to his small church, and she had performed a funeral ceremony—the first she had ever done on her own—with most of Bergron's residents in attendance. The priest himself would be buried on the morrow.

"How's the hand?" Cynric asked Tarian.

Tarian held up his right hand and wiggled the fingers. "Good as new." And the flash burns he'd suffered from the energy discharge when the portal collapsed had been replaced with fresh pink skin. Tarian had been ravenous when they gotten back to Bergron. His body had needed to replenish itself after all the healing it had done. He'd eaten five bowls of the mutton stew the innkeeper had brought them after their baths, and he was still a trifle hungry.

"It's a shame about the mistblade," Danya said. When the Eyslken sword had come in contact with the portal, the resultant energy emission had not only knocked down Tarian and rendered him unconscious, but it had destroyed the mistblade. Only the hilt was left.

Phelan scowled at his father, and Tarian understood how the lad felt. Phelan had come to think of the mistblade as his sword, his first as a man, and he had been good with it, although he still had a lot to learn. And now it was gone.

Tarian started to speak, but Ashur Dal held up a hand to stop him. "There's no need to apologize again, Tarian. I cannot think of a nobler purpose to which a mistblade may be put." He paused to take a sip of wine. "Were you Eyslken, your actions this day would have earned you an Honor Braid."

Before setting forth on this journey, Ashur's words would have meant less than nothing to Tarian, for he had only felt resentment at the way the Eyslken had absented themselves from the day-to-day life of the land. But now he inclined his head at the compliment. "We had a saying in the King's army," Tarian said. "'Many arms, but only one sword.' We defeated the Vile and closed the portal because we worked as a team. I'd say everyone sitting at this table is deserving of an Honor Braid."

Phelan especially looked pleased at that, and Tarian

wouldn't have been surprised if the lad asked Ashur Dal to begin braiding his hair this instant. Ashur and Cynric looked a bit uncomfortable, though. Tarian wondered if it had something to do with the fact that the wizard wore Honor Braids while the Eyslk did not.

The destruction of the portal and slaying of the Vile truly had been a team effort. While Tarian may have dealt with the portal, it was the combined efforts of Ashur Dal and Danya—not to mention Phelan's shadow wolf—which had kept the Vile busy long enough for him to do it. Saeth and Cynric's powers had weakened the demon to the point where Danya was able to get close enough to jam the priestess's dagger into the Vile's eye and into its brain, thus killing the foul creature.

Tarian had regained consciousness soon after that, and he tended to Phelan and the wood-skinned woman while the others swept the area for the Peccants. They had no trouble locating and dispatching the diminutive demonoids, for Ashur Dal's Eyslken nose was easily able to detect what he called, "their rather distinctive scent." They hadn't been able to find Tarian's severed hand, though. Not that Tarian cared overmuch. After all, what use was it to him now?

While the others were off hunting Peccants, the shadow wolf's scattered substance coalesced and reformed, and the ebon wolf trotted weakly over to Phelan, completely ignoring Tarian, and rejoined with his host. As soon as they were one again, Phelan's eyes opened and he sat up. Other than a headache, he felt fine. Tarian tried to relieve the boy's pain, but was unsuccessful. Whether that was due to Tarian's magic being solely focused on regrowing his hand or whether because Phelan's pain wasn't a physical ailment, Tarian didn't know. He decided to wait a bit before trying to heal the wood-skinned woman, in order to give his power a chance to restore itself.

When the others returned with the bodies of the Peccants, they piled them atop the corpse of the Vile, along with severed the arm of the second Vile that had reached through the portal just before its collapse, and burnt the unholy remains. Tarian then healed the wood-skinned woman successfully, and she returned to consciousness. She introduced herself as Wirke and said she had been selected to join the hunting party because she could understand the whispers of the trees.

Before the Change, Tarian would have thought the woman mad. Now he took her claim in stride. Wirke was grateful for their help, but devastated by the loss of so many of her party. Ashur Dal shouldered the dead priest, and together they all returned to Bergron. It was nightfall by the time they arrived, too late to do anything about the remains of the rest of Wirke's party. She vowed that as soon as the sun colored the eastern sky, she would gather together a group of villagers and return to the clearing where the Vile had slain her companions and make sure they received a decent burial—if wolves and such didn't make off with the bits and pieces during the night.

Still, they were able to hold a service for the priest, which Saeth presided over rather uncomfortably, and then they retired to the inn. Tarian reflected that the six of them seemed much more comfortable with each other now that they had gone through battle together. He had experienced such bonding numerous times during his career as a soldier, though familiarity with the process didn't make it any less affecting. The only one who didn't seem to feel it was Saeth. Ever since the service for the priest, she had been quiet and moody.

"Tell me, Priestess," Cynric began, "where did you

come across that dagger of yours? It's a fascinating weapon."

The dagger in question lay sheathed within the rucksack between Saeth's feet. From what Danya had told Tarian, the priestess had kept the rucksack near even during her bath. As protective as she was of the blade, Tarian wouldn't have been surprised if Saeth had taken it into the water with her.

"I . . . borrowed it from the Dawn Cathedral," Saeth said. "There are a number of holy relics preserved in a—a secret chamber. I would've asked permission, but . . ." She shrugged.

"But with all the higher-ranking priests gone," Cynric said, "there was no one to ask permission from."

Saeth nodded.

From the hesitation as Saeth spoke and the way the priestess refused to meet any of their gazes, Tarian suspected the woman was lying. More, she seemed slightly afraid, though of precisely what, he had no idea.

The others exchanged looks, and it was clear none of them thought Saeth was telling the whole story of how she had come by the silver dagger. But a silence fell over the party then, and Tarian knew none of them was going to challenge the priestess's explanation. In truth, what did it matter how she had gotten the blade? The fact was she had it, and the dagger had helped them defeat the Vile. What else was important?

Saeth looked at Cynric. "It appears neither of us escaped the Change, as we first thought." Her tone was neutral, but Tarian had the impression she was attempting to turn the conversation away from the holy dagger.

The priestess was successful. The others turned toward the wizard, who looked suddenly uncomfortable.

"It's true." He told them how he had first suspected he had been affected by the Change when his appetite for food and drink suffered. Then he spoke of draining the lifeforce from one of Enar's spiders, and how he had snuck off during his assigned watch to procure animals to feed his new hunger.

Saeth looked somewhat queasy at the realization she had breakfasted on food that Cynric had first drained of its life energy, and Danya didn't look too happy about it, either. It didn't bother Tarian overmuch. As far as he was concerned, it was just another way of killing an animal, and actually far more humane than most.

"I didn't say anything at first because I was ashamed." Cynric gave Ashur Dal a sideways glance. "I felt like I had become no different than a Lukash who feasts on the blood and flesh of others in order to gain strength and vitality."

"There is no need for shame, *Filmarr*," Ashur Dal said.

Tarian noticed the Eyslk didn't add the word *g'tanu* this time.

"You had no say in what the Change did to you," Ashur continued. "None of you did. But you do have a choice in how you use your newfound powers. When your companions needed you, Cynric, you pushed aside your feelings of shame and came to their aid, and you employed your new magic to help weaken the Vile. Such an action is cause for pride, not shame."

Danya lifted her mug. "Hear, hear!" she said, and they all toasted Cynric, even Saeth.

Cynric smiled and nodded his thanks at their tribute. But there was something in the wizard's gaze, Tarian thought, a not-quite-hidden slyness, which bothered him. Then it was gone, and Tarian wondered if he hadn't merely imagined it.

Cynric turned to Saeth. "The Vile spoke of something called 'Godfire' several times. Have you any knowledge of the term, Priestess?"

She shook her head. "There are no references to it in any holy text with which I'm familiar."

"The chronicles of the Eyslken contain no mention of 'Godfire' either," Ashur Dal said. "And my people's history goes back to the dawn of creation."

"Might it be a demonic term for lifeforce?" Danya asked.

"I don't think so," Phelan said. "Do you remember what the Vile told us when we first got to the portal? It said something about how Godfire was *better* than human lifeforce, that it helped make the portal stronger, faster."

Ashur Dal nodded. "Which clearly indicates that this Godfire is an altogether separate phenomenon."

"At least now we know what to call those energy spheres which rise forth from people after they die," Tarian said. "They're Godfire."

"But that still doesn't tell us what Godfire *is*," Danya added.

"True," Tarian agreed. "But they obviously have something to do with the Change, for the energy spheres were never seen before it occurred."

"I wouldn't be surprised if this Godfire in a sense *is* the Change," Cynric said. "I suspect Godfire, whatever its true nature, supplies the mystical energy which allows Tarian to heal, Phelan to summon his shadow wolf, Danya to communicate with Jessex, and so on."

"Two types of spheres have been seen," Danya said. "Light and Dark."

Cynric nodded. "And though we have had no official confirmation yet, it certainly seems as if the Change came on the heels of the battle at Heart's Wound. All of this raises some extremely disturbing questions."

"Indeed," Saeth said. "For if we all possess this Godfire, how do we know whether we harbor Light within us . . . or Darkness?"

No one spoke for a time after that as they pondered the implications of Saeth's words.

Finally, Tarian put his mug down. "I say we get some sleep and set out for Vallanora first thing in the morning. Perhaps the Silent Ones will be able to tell us more about the Godfire."

They all agreed and headed upstairs for their rooms, the humans wondering just what manner of power now dwelt within them.

Saeth and Danya shared a room, as did Tarian and Phelan, and Cynric and Ashur Dal. Saeth wasn't exactly thrilled with the arrangement. Although she didn't like sleeping outdoors at all—too many singing birds and chirping crickets—at least she could position her bedroll so it wasn't too close to the others. She'd slept alone on a small straw-filled pallet since she had entered Rudra's service at twelve. And even though over the years she had risen to the rank of assistant to a High Priest, she still slept on a similar pallet, only now instead of sleeping in the acolytes' dormitory, she had her own cramped quarters in the Dawn Cathedral.

It wasn't that Saeth disliked Danya. Although the woman was somewhat common and coarse, she had a cheerful disposition that the usually dour Saeth, instead of being put off by, responded to. Perhaps because opposite personalities sometimes complemented one another, she thought. Or perhaps it was because the Watcher never seemed to doubt herself. Saeth wished she possessed half of

Danya's self-assurance. She thought the Watcher would have done well in the Church. Her confidence would have served her well in negotiating the sometimes turbulent waters of Church politics. Saeth herself had never had much tolerance for such strife; she preferred to be left alone to do her work and contemplate her faith. Which was why at her age she was only an assistant to a High Priest and not a High Priest herself, she supposed.

There was only one bed. Danya asked Saeth which side she preferred, and the priestess left the choice up to her. Danya settled into bed, and asked Saeth if she was coming. The priestess declined, saying she wished to pray for a bit, though Danya was welcome to extinguish the candle that burned on the nightstand. She preferred to pray in the dark, anyway.

Danya seemed to find this last bit odd, but she nodded, bid Saeth good night, then blew out the candle. Saeth lowered herself to the floor and sat cross-legged, her rucksack in her lap, and waited for sleep to claim Danya. It didn't take long; soon the Watcher's breathing deepened and she began snoring softly.

Saeth waited a bit longer, just to be certain Danya was asleep, before rising and going to the window. She cracked open the shutters to allow a thin beam of moonlight to penetrate into the room. She breathed in the fresh night air, missing the tang of salt she was used to in Pendara. This was the furthest from the Shashida she had ever been in her life, and while she had found the countryside they had passed through to be pleasant enough in its own way, she missed the ocean.

As she stood at the window, her thoughts turned toward the funeral service for Bergron's priest that she had conducted earlier that evening. The villagers' sorrow at the loss of their spiritual leader had been almost overwhelming to her, so much so that she had almost had to stop the service at several points. Afterward, a number of people came up to thank her for not only helping to rid their village of the demons, but also for conducting the funeral rites for their priest. Their simple gratitude had touched her in a way nothing had before. She had spent her entire life of service to Rudra within the Dawn Cathedral, assisting other priests in their duties, and she had been happy enough, she supposed.

But decades of taking dictation and filing sheets of vellum couldn't compare to a single one of the grateful smiles she had received tonight from the villagers of Bergron.

You did well, Saeth Fama. In conducting the service, at least.

Saeth jumped. She recognized the voice that echoed within her head. It was the Glory that had given her the silver dagger. And it sounded disapproving.

You let the others know about the dagger. You let another wield it, even though the time for its use has not yet arrived.

Saeth knew that the Glory's voice was for her alone to hear, yet she still glanced back to make certain Danya still slept soundly.

Forget the Watcher. She will not awaken unless I will it. Explain yourself: why did you allow the holy dagger to be used?

Saeth felt like cowering in a corner of the room. But then she asked herself how Danya would reply, and then she answered.

"How could I not?" she breathed, so softly she barely made a sound. "Demons had penetrated the mortal plane. As a priestess of Rudra, it was my duty to stop them. Which I did, with the help of my . . . friends." Friends. The word was almost foreign to Saeth. She was friendly enough with certain other priests and priestesses in the Dawn Cathedral, but not to the point where she would have claimed any as her *friends*. Yet somehow the word seemed appropriate now.

Even the Eyslk? The Glory's previous anger was replaced by amusement.

Saeth smiled. "Perhaps, after a fashion. But I'll deny I ever admitted it."

She had the sense the Glory chuckled, and then its thought-voice grew stern once more. *Very well. But the silver dagger was given to you for one purpose and one purpose only. See that you do not use it again until the proper moment.*

There was no "or else" added to the Glory's mental words, but Saeth thought the implication was clear enough.

"The Vile spoke of Godfire, holy one," Saeth whispered. "What did the demon mean?"

But the Glory didn't answer. It had withdrawn its mental presence, leaving Saeth alone in the sliver of moonlight to contemplate the Glory's latest message—and why it had fallen silent rather than discuss the matter of Godfire.

Cynric lay awake, staring upward into the darkness. Ashur Dal sat cross-legged on the floor, breathing evenly as he meditated. Cynric, not for the first time, envied Ashur's ability to reach the deepest levels of Eyslken meditation so effortlessly. Despite his many attempts, Cynric had never mastered the more complex nuances of meditation. Ashur said it was because his mind refused to relax: it always needed to be busy, to have a problem to worry at. Cynric supposed that was true enough. He certainly had enough problems now.

He was relieved that he no longer had to hide the transformation the Change had wrought in him, but he hadn't told the others the complete truth, either. Yes, he needed to drain the lifeforce of other living beings in order to feed, but there was more to it than that. Much more.

First off, the taking of lifeforce felt like nothing he had ever experienced before. Shaping could be a dangerous pursuit, and those who followed its ways took a vow not to marry as long as they continued to work with *Paytah*. Cynric had made such a vow when he'd finished his training, and he had stuck by it ever since, though in truth he had been so busy working to safeguard Athymar that he hadn't had time for marriage. Which is not to say that he hadn't enjoy a few dalliances over the years. But even the pleasure a man and woman could find in each other's arms was nothing compared to the sensation of absorbing another's lifeforce.

And it seemed to be addictive. He was certain he only needed a small portion of lifeforce a day to sustain himself. The animals he had managed to ensnare and then drain since they'd left Pendara had been enough to feed his new hunger. But it wasn't a question of *need*; it was a question of *want*. The more lifeforce Cynric took, the more he wanted. If the Lukashen experienced anything remotely like he did when they drew strength from the flesh and blood of their victims, he could almost understand—

He squashed the thought, ashamed of himself for having it. Such dark notions had become increasingly more common since he'd absorbed the Vile's lifeforce, and he was afraid that in some fashion he had become tainted by it. He suspected that he took more than merely life energy from his . . . donors. Although he didn't think he could heal himself as Tarian did, his body had become stronger, his limp less pronounced. His senses of smell and hearing had become sharper, too, more like an animal's than a man's. Now, after draining merely a portion of the Vile's lifeforce, he felt stronger than ever, as if he could snap a sword blade in two with his bare hands. He also felt a cruel cunning dwelling deep within him, a cunning that seemed to speak to his darker needs.

If taking the life energy of a mere animal sparked such ecstasy, what might draining a human—

He bit down hard on the inside of his cheek, hoping the sudden pain would drive the thought away. He felt blood fill his mouth, and he swallowed its bitter, coppery tang. He couldn't become like the Lukashen, he wouldn't!

There were many temptations that came along with the ability to Shape *Paytah*. To guard against them, Eyslken wizards were taught to control their baser desires through various meditation techniques of the sort Ashur Dal was practicing now.

Cynric closed his eyes, focused on the regular sound of Ashur's breathing, and slowly, gently relaxed every muscle in his body. Before long, his breathing eased until it precisely matched the rhythms of his former teacher. Cynric allowed his mind to empty of all thought, and concentrated solely on the beating of his heart and the working of his lungs.

But deep inside him, darkness continued to stir.

Lowri's wings were growing tired. She had taken to the air as soon as she had snatched Tarian's hand from the little demon, and she hadn't paused for rest since. She had no clear notion why she had taken the hand, nor where she was flying to now. All she knew was that the Voice inside her required it. The Voice had made her strong, had granted her freedom. For that, she would do whatever it asked of her— and more.

The Dragon moon and the Wolf moon, both close to half-full now, were edging toward the horizon by the time her wings refused to carry her any further. She sensed there was more to her ability to fly than just her wings; her mind had something to do with it as well. But she needed both her mind and her wings working in concert to remain aloft, and she was so tired . . .

She clutched the hand to her scaled bosom as she glided toward the ground in wide spirals, searching for a suitable place to land. Moonslight glistened off a narrow river, and she caught site of a dark building on the bank that could only be a mill. She had no desire to go near the haunts of humans, not in her weakened state, but the Voice told her the mill was her destination. Surprised and more than a little curious, she descended toward the mill and lighted soundlessly upon its roof.

She cocked her head and listened for signs of life below, but she heard nothing save the river flowing gently by and the slow, regular creak of the waterwheel. She sensed the Voice wished her to go inside, so she placed the hand in her mouth, careful not to bite down too hard lest her sharp teeth puncture the skin, and crawled to the edge of the roof and swung over the side. She continued downward, clawed fingers and toes finding purchase in the mill's stone wall, until she came to a shuttered window. She pushed on the shutters, found them barred. She scuttled around to get her feet into position, and then gave the shutters three swift, hard kicks. The bar broke and the shutters burst inward. Lowri thrust herself through the now open window and landed lightly on the floor. She removed the hand from her mouth and looked around.

Her eyesight was far better than when she had been merely human, and she could see the millstone, hear it turning. She sniffed the air, but she scented no grain, only dust and rotting wood. Though the river's current kept the waterwheel turning, this mill hadn't been in use for some time.

Why had the Voice led her to this place?

She detected movement in one shadowy corner, turned to face it, fangs barred, claws raised. A swatch of darkness detached from the gloom and came gliding toward her. It was vaguely man-shaped, but otherwise it possessed no visible features. It was as if a shadow had forsaken its caster and could now move about of its own volition.

Even though she had never seen one before, Lowri knew what she was looking at: a Ghast, the earthbound spirit of a dead Lukash. Those humans who served Anghrist in life, whether knowingly or not, upon their deaths became the raw material from which the Dark One fashioned His demons. But Lukashen served their fell master in a different way after they died. Their spirits remained on the mortal place, seeking to inhabit and possess the bodies of unwary humans so the Ghasts might do Anghrist's work once more.

Unfortunately, Ghasts were bound to the place of their deaths, and they had no choice but to wait for a victim to come near enough before they could act. This one had probably died during a Lukashen raid on the mill, which was doubtless why it was deserted. The surviving Lukashen had most likely taken the humans that had worked here to feed their unholy appetite. Evidently Lowri had come within this Ghast's range, for it was approaching rapidly.

When she had been human, Lowri had been terrified of Ghasts. Her mother used to tell her stories about them in order to get her to behave, and she had done the same with Phelan a time or two herself. The worst part of living on the edge of the Greenmark for her was the fear that Ghasts might be lurking in the woods. Now that she had become a creature of darkness herself, the Ghast held no special horror for her, but she had no desire to be possessed by it either. She started to turn back toward the window, intending to leap through it to safety, when the Voice spoke once again. Lowri listened.

She turned to face the Ghast, knelt, and placed the severed hand onto the dirt floor. The Ghast hesitated, then it darted toward the hand, like a fish going for bait. It dwindled in size as it sank into the flesh, and within seconds, it was gone.

Nothing happened for several moments, then Tarian's hand twitched and the fingers began to scratch at the dirt beneath them. After all the hours Lowri had been flying, the hand displayed no signs of rot; it contained enough residue of Tarian's Godfire to keep the flesh preserved. Now the Ghast connected with that residue, and the ragged wrist began to sprout new growth.

Lowri grinned and squatted down on her haunches to wait. She had the feeling this was going to take awhile.

CHAPTER TWENTY-FOUR

"Doesn't this bloody forest ever end?"

No one answered Saeth. They were too busy picking their way through the thick underbrush of the Greenmark. They walked, leading their horses by the reins, and it was slow going. This was their second day in the great forest, and while Ashur Dal assured them they would reach Vallanora before sunset, Tarian saw no sign of it. The Greenmark was just as wild and untamed here as it had been where they'd first entered it, which made no sense. The trees here were ancient, their trunks so thick around it would take four or more men holding hands to encircle the circumference of the smallest. They stretched so high their branches and leaves intertwined in a canopy of green that allowed little sunlight to filter down through the forest floor. While this made the atmosphere within the Greenmark cool—which was a relief from the humid summer air they had endured since leaving Pendara—it should have resulted in an absence of ground cover. They should have been able to walk their horses through this section of the forest with ease. But if anything, the going here was slower than when they'd first entered the Greenmark.

Tarian suspected the Eyslken had designed it this way. Cynric had spoken of Vallanora as a *Hidden Place*, and Tarian had no doubt this lush undergrowth helped keep it that way. Not that the Eyslken likely needed it. The Greenmark was one of the most formidable barriers in Athymar. It stretched for hundreds of miles in every direction, from the western shore of the Urial Sea, down south to meet the edge of the Kjartan desert, then east toward the fishing villages between the Black and Golden Coasts. The forest didn't quite reach the eastern shoreline, though; it fell short by a bit less than a hundred miles. Thousands of years ago, in order to increase trade between the northern and southern halves of Athymar, the King requested the Dragon Mages to burn down a section of the thinnest portion of the forest so that a great road might be built linking the two halves of Athymar for all time. The Dragon Mages did as the King bade, and the road was built, stretching from Garanhon to Pendara, and although it was sometimes referred to as King's Way, most often it was known more simply as just the Southern Road.

Tarian would've have given a great deal for a road right then, or even a footpath. The going might have been a bit easier if they could've hacked away the underbrush with their swords, but Ashur Dal had forbidden them to purposefully harm so much as a single plant.

"The Eyslken are the caretakers of *Selyv Nahele*," he'd said. "It is a sacred duty which we take very seriously."

And so they made their way step by tortuous step through the tangle of green, and Tarian hoped that whatever reason the Silent Ones wished to speak with him, it would turn out to be worth all this effort.

"I've read that there are dragons still living in the forest," Phelan said. He sounded eager, as if he hoped to encounter one before long.

"Sorry, lad," Ashur Dal said. "While dragons may yet live in other parts of the Nine Known Lands, none remain in Athymar. My people were unable to save even a single drake, and believe me, we tried."

The sadness in the Eyslk's voice was palpable, as if he

spoke of a personal failure, though the last dragon had died two hundred years before his birth. As Tarian was beginning to learn, the Eyslken race possessed a long memory, and what happened to their forebears was still very much a going concern for them today. With the Eyslken, Tarian suspected, there was no such thing as *ancient* history.

"There *are* werms scattered about the Greenmark," Ashur said, "though not many. They tend to prefer swampy or mountainous areas. Still, one of the Eyslken's missions is to preserve as many of the land's plants and animals as we can within *Selyv Nahele*, for at its core, the forest itself is a remnant of the way Athymar was before the Sundering. In Vallanora, you can find creatures that haven't been seen elsewhere in the land for thousands upon thousands of years: stoneswimmers, woodbrothers . . ." Ashur lay a hand on Phelan's shoulder and smiled. "Perhaps even a small wyvern or two, if you're lucky."

"Really?" The expression of awe on Phelan's face made him look like a child again, and Tarian was filled with equal measures of pride and sadness. Pride at the man his son was becoming, sadness that the little boy he had once been was gone forever.

Tarian found it difficult to believe that all of the wonders of which Ashur Dal spoke lay within the same forest where Lowri, Phelan and he had made their home for so many years. True, this section of the Greenmark was nearly a hundred miles northwest of where their cabin lay, but even so. If Tarian had known at the time that Eyslken made their home within the forest, he might well have chosen another site upon which to build his cabin. Such a thought seemed almost alien to him now, and he was actually looking forward to seeing Vallanora.

It was difficult to judge the time of day this deep inside

the Greenmark, but Tarian guessed it to be mid-afternoon. Ashur Dal would probably have known more precisely—he seemed to know everything precisely—but Tarian didn't feel like asking. After a bit more time spent struggling with the thick undergrowth, they came to a part of the forest that was . . . different. Tarian wasn't certain what made it so, exactly. After all, it appeared to be the same sort of greenery they had contended with all day. Yet there was something about it that made Tarian want to avert his gaze, perhaps turn around and go back the way he'd come. Yes, he could see it now; this section of the Greenmark was far too thick and tangled for passage, better to head off and search for a less dense area that they would be able to negotiate more effectively. He started to turn, Danya, Phelan and Saeth doing the same, when Cynric bid them stop.

"What you're all experiencing is an aversion spell laid upon an Eyslken path," the wizard explained. "It's designed to subtly alter the perceptions of anyone who is persistent enough to make it this far into the Greenmark, to make them believe they cannot proceed any further and that they should turn back."

"If you remain in the presence of the spell much longer," Ashur Dal added, "you will begin to feel fear which will mount until you are forced to flee this area in terror. But Cynric and I shall hopefully get you past the spell's influence before that occurs. The spell is a visual one, in the main, so if you two will take my hands and close your eyes, I'll lead you through. Cynric shall guide the other two."

Danya and Phelan took the Eyslk's hands, and he led them forward—the humans pulling their mounts behind. The undergrowth seemed almost to part before them of its own volition. Tarian and Saeth each had hold of the reins of their horses.

"What about Ashur's and your steeds?" Tarian asked. "And the pack horses?"

"The aversion spell isn't designed for animals, though sometimes it does have a mild effect on them," the wizard said. "If the other horses don't follow us through, I'll come back and get them." He paused. "It might be best if neither of you actually came in contact with my flesh. I have yet to master the new ability granted me by the Change, and I would hate to accidentally drain a portion of your lifeforces."

"*You* would hate it?" Saeth said. She lay her hand on Cynric's right shoulder, and Tarian took the left. They closed their eyes and the wizard led them forward. Tarian felt a slight dizziness and roil to his stomach as they walked, but he didn't know if that was due to the Eyslken aversion spell or to Saeth's power to affect the body. In the three days since they had left Bergron, the priestess had gained a degree of control over her magic, though it still had a tendency to spill over, in somewhat milder form, onto those in her vicinity, especially when she was distressed.

The sensation passed, and Cynric told them they could open their eyes.

Tarian did so, and beheld a forest floor clear of undergrowth, as it should have been. More, they stood upon a hard-dirt path that was free of trees. It didn't appear as if any trees had been chopped down in order to make the path; rather, it seemed as if the forest had grown up *around* it.

The other horses hadn't followed them through, and Cynric was forced to return for them, plunging through a thick wall of greenery that emitted no aversion magic from this side. He returned with their other steeds, and since the path was more than wide enough, they mounted up so they could ride the rest of the way.

"It won't be long now," Ashur replied as he took the lead. "Less than a candlemark from this point."

They rode in silence, save for the clopping of iron-shod hooves on the hard earthen path, the jingle of tack, and the occasional snort of a steed as they continued on to Vallanora.

Tarian couldn't have said precisely where Vallanora began and the forest ended, for indeed, one blended with the other so intimately that as near as he could tell, there was no difference. One moment they were riding amongst trees with only the sounds of birdsong and cicada thrum for company, and the next they were amongst wooden dwellings that didn't appear to have been constructed so much as grown. Their shapes were rounded and somewhat irregular, as if no two were exactly alike, and leaves, moss, vines and oftentimes berries covered the outside walls. Indeed, if it hadn't been for the obvious doors and windows in the dwellings, Tarian wouldn't have recognized them as such.

Eyslken, garbed in simple one-piece tunics of varying colors, though by far the most common hues were variations on green, waved greetings as they passed. After all the trouble they had gone to in order to make their home a Hidden Place, the residents of Vallanora seemed not especially surprised to see a group of humans on horseback in their midst. If anything, the Eyslken actually seemed glad to see them.

Some Eyslken sat cross-legged in front of their dwellings, working on various crafts—whittling, carving stone, weaving—while others walked along the sides of the path, carrying baskets of vegetables or tending small herds of goats or sheep. If not for the setting, and the fact that its residents were Eyslken and not human, of course, the scene would've put Tarian in mind of any number of villages he had visited during his tenure as a soldier.

They continued onward, and while the dwellings became no larger or more elaborate, they did become more numerous and were clustered closer together, and Tarian had the sense that they were nearing the center of Vallanora. Here, there were less Eyslken doing chores and more engaged in what looked like good-natured debates. Groups of two, three, four and more Eyslken stood in clusters, listening with intense concentration, or with slight smiles and skeptical expressions, as one of their fellows went on at great length about one point or another. Tarian caught snatches of conversation as they passed, but he wasn't able to make head nor tails out of any of them.

"Now I understand where Ashur and Cynric get it," Danya whispered to him.

"Get what?" he asked.

"Their tendency to lecture."

Tarian grinned.

The farther they rode, the more animals they saw. Squirrels, chipmunks, rabbits, raccoons, opossum, foxes and even wolves and bear moved among the residents of Vallanora as if they too held citizenship, and aside from occasionally reaching down to give one a pat or a scratch between the ears, no one gave them a second glance.

The trees were filled with birds of every type—robins, jays, cardinals, orioles, sparrows, finches, hawks and falcons, and even an eagle or two—all living together in seeming harmony, filling the forest air with their combined song. Tarian saw one odd bird that appeared to have features somewhat akin to those of a lizard, with small claws protruding from its wings, patches of scale, and tiny sharp teeth. Phelan asked Ashur Dal if the bird was a relative of the dragons, but the Eyslk smiled and said, "Not quite; though in its own way, that creature is even more wondrous."

As they drew nearer to the heart of Vallanora, Tarian noticed that the trees, which up to this point had been primarily oak, elm and other types native to this portion of Athymar, became more varied. He noted chestnut, alder, cyprus, weeping willow, maple, birch, cedar, pine, spruce, fire, beechwood, dogwood, hawthorn, yew, ash, maple, poplar, bay, and dozens more. There were flowering trees, fruit trees, and species that Tarian had never encountered before in all his travels across the length and breadth of Athymar, strange plants with large green fronds, some of which were smooth and others of which were fringed.

It made no sense! He was a soldier by trade, not a greenskeeper, yet he knew that these trees shouldn't be able to co-exist here, that they needed different soil and weather conditions to flourish. The pine and fir were found primarily in northern climes, while the cyprus belonged to the warmer environment of the far south. Yet here they all were, together, hale and strong. It was the trees, more than anything else, which brought home to Tarian just how ancient the Eyslken race was and how wondrous was the lore they possessed.

Saeth seemed unaware of the multitude of different tree species surrounding them, but then she had spent her entire life in Pendara. Phelan surely had some notion that so many different types of trees wouldn't normally co-exist, though he didn't possess his father's knowledge of the land. But Danya had grown up in a country village, and she recognized the strangeness of this section of the Greenmark.

She made a sweeping gesture. "This . . ." She hesitated,

searching for words. "Isn't right," she finished lamely.

Fortunately, Ashur Dal understood what she meant. "The trees? So many different species thrive here due to the presence of Arboralis, the First Tree. We will reach it in a few moments, and you shall understand then."

Saeth had gone pale. "Surely you jest. You can't mean *the* Arboralis, the first living thing which Rudra brought forth upon the face of the world!"

"Rudra *and* Anghrist," Ashur corrected. "The Gods still cooperated back then, you know. And yes, I speak of that Arboralis." He smiled gently. "Do you know of another?"

"But Arboralis was destroyed during the Gods' battle at Heart's Wound! I mean, their *first* battle," Saeth amended, "the one which resulted in the Sundering!"

"Arboralis was close to death, true, as was nearly the whole world after what the Gods did to it." The normally reserved Eyslk didn't bother to disguise the bitterness in his voice. "When the Gods finished their fighting, the soil of Heart's Wound was dead and barren, no longer capable of supporting life of any sort. Rather than let Arboralis perish, my people brought it here to Vallanora—a small remnant of the way the world was at the dawn of creation—where they planted the tree in rich soil and worked for centuries to nurse it back to health." Ashur Dal reined his horse to a stop. "You may see the results for yourselves."

The tree Ashur pointed out seemed like nothing special to Tarian. It was a river birch, somewhat on the smallish side, its bark still a youthful red. Pleasant enough, Tarian supposed, but certainly nowhere near as impressive as the other trees which grew around it. Strange . . . there was something almost familiar about it—and then he remembered. It resembled the birch on the bank of the river Iphus, where Lowri and he had camped during the early days of their marriage, on their way back after spending several weeks visiting her parents. Although Tarian wasn't certain, he'd always suspected that they had conceived Phelan beneath the boughs of that tree.

What would a river birch be doing here, though? There wasn't enough moisture to keep it alive.

"Now it's my turn to accuse you of joking," Danya said. "This can't be Arboralis; it's nothing but a simple apple tree, just like the kind that grew near my grandparents' home."

Phelan shook his head. "No, it's not. It's an elm. It looks a lot like the one near our cabin that was struck by lightning two summers ago. Look, you can see where the bolt split the trunk."

"You've both been in this forest too long," Saeth said. "All this green isn't healthy; it's starting to addle your brains. That isn't an apple or an elm tree; it's naught but a single scraggly shrub which would barely come up to my knee if I were standing next to it." She paused. "It puts me in mind of one of the shrubs that grow out back of the little church in Bergron."

Tarian turned to Cynric for an explanation, for obviously magic of some sort was involved here. He found the wizard and Ashur Dal looking at each other and grinning.

"Each of us sees a different tree, don't we?" Danya guessed. "One that holds special meaning to us."

"Yes," Cynric confirmed. "All trees in the world are descended from Arboralis, but the First Tree itself exudes such powerful magic that it overwhelms mortal senses, and the only way we can perceive it is through the prism of memory. I, for example, see Arboralis as a white spruce which grew in the seaside village where I was born."

"And the Arboralis appears to me in different guises at different times," Ashur Dal said. "Perhaps because I have so many more memories to draw on than do you. This day, the First Tree seems to my senses to be a poplar, one that I also saw near Cynric's village, on the day I found him."

The Eyslk and the wizard looked at each other for a moment, their expressions unreadable, and then they looked away.

"What kind of tree did you see, Father?" Phelan asked Tarian.

"A birch." But more than this, Tarian refused to say.

"Here you are, Ashur, just as I predicted. I'm absolutely delighted to see you."

They turned to behold an Eyslka approaching. She was smaller and more graceful than Ashur Dal, though until he saw her moving, Tarian would have thought the latter impossible. She came toward them as if she were lighter than the air itself, flowing forward silently, her delicate sandaled feet barely seeming to touch the ground. Her lustrous white hair was fashioned into a multitude of Honor Braids interwoven with intricate, multi-colored beadwork. She wore some of the braids forward, some back, but all fell to her waist. Her pale features were so fine and beautiful, she might have almost been a Glory that had left Girasa to go slumming with mere mortals. She was garbed in a white robe that seemed to have been formed from mist rather than fabric, and its surface swayed and rolled gently as she walked, almost as if it were liquid.

Ashur Dal raised an eyebrow. "Oh? I was unaware you held any special fondness for me."

The Eyslka's laugh was a marriage between windchimes and bells. "I like you well enough, Ashur. But I wagered Reyana Mak that Arboralis would be the first place you brought our guests, and I was right. She owes me a blackberry pie."

"I'm curious," Ashur said. "What would you have owed her had you been wrong?"

"I would've had to watch her twins for two nights," the Eyslka said.

Ashur smiled. "Tend those boys? I wouldn't make that wager for all the blackberry pies in the Nine Known Lands." Then he frowned. "I don't suppose you had some . . . advice?"

She grinned. "Let's just say that I felt confident in wagering as I did."

Ashur shook his head. "My friends, allow me to present Entoria Taj, she who is Prime Cultivator of *Aiyana*, the Orchard of Dreams." Ashur introduced each of the members of his party in turn, with the exception of Cynric. Tarian wondered if that was because the wizard was already known to Entoria Taj, or if there were another reason. He noticed that the Eyslka didn't look in Cynric's direction, and in fact she seemed to be purposely ignoring him.

When Ashur finished, Entoria inclined her head. "Well met, all of you." She looked at Tarian. "Especially you, Healer. The Silent Ones have been awaiting your arrival most anxiously. If you will dismount, I shall take you to them at once."

The last two days of struggling through forest undergrowth had left Tarian's clothing a bit on the aromatic side, and he was reluctant to go with the Eyslka until he had had a chance to cleanse himself somewhat. And to be honest, the thought of meeting with a bunch of Eyslken spirits wasn't something he was exactly looking forward to.

Evidently, Cynric guessed what he was thinking, but the wizard said, "Preceptor, we have had a long, hot journey. If we could have a bit of time to rest . . ."

Entoria Taj didn't respond to Cynric's words, didn't

even flick a glance in his direction to acknowledge them. "There is no need to feel self-conscious, Tarian. The dead do not care what you look like." She smiled. "Or smell like, for that matter. They care only that you've come."

Tarian looked to Cynric, and the wizard nodded. Tarian tried to think of another reason to put off going with the Eyslka, but he couldn't. Besides, this was what he had come here for, right? He handed the reins of his horse to Phelan, gave the lad a reassuring smile, then dismounted.

Entoria Taj came forward and took Tarian by the arm, and Danya scowled.

"Ashur Dal shall take you to a place where your horses will be tended to, and then you may rest for a bit. Tonight, we shall hold a feast in your honor at the Glade of Revelry. Tarian and I shall rejoin you then."

And with that, she led Tarian away from his companions and toward his appointment with the dead.

CHAPTER TWENTY-FIVE

As they walked, Tarian asked Entoria Taj if the path they were on had a name. The Eyslka laughed and said there was no need to name the paths in Vallanora, for all Eyslken knew them too well. "Names aren't necessary for old friends," she said.

Eyslken nodded or smiled greetings to them as they passed, and Tarian had the sense that these greetings were as much for him as for Entoria, if not more so.

"I'm surprised by the welcome your people have shown us," he said. Then when he realized how that sounded, he hastened to add, "Not that I had any reason to think you would be less than hospitable. But your folk withdrew from the life of the land five hundred years ago . . ."

"And you thought it was because we had come to dislike humans for some reason," Entoria finished. "Nothing could be further from the truth. We consider you our brothers and sisters. And in one sense, you are our children."

"I do not understand."

"Rudra and Anghrist formed the world and all the creatures in it from Chaos. That includes the Eyslken. But when Rudra decided to bring forth a new race into the world, the race of Men, there was little Chaos left. Only fragments remained, scattered about the world. So He decided to use an existing race to serve as the vessel for the birth of the new."

"You mean . . . the Eyslken actually bore humanity?"

Entoria nodded. "Though it wasn't long before there

were enough human men and women to begin breeding on their own, and when that happened, no more humans were born unto my people. While we were not happy to be used by Rudra in such a fashion, we loved our human children as much as we did our Eyslken, and we strived to take care of them as best we could over the millennia. Finally, five hundred years ago, we came to believe that the best way to take care of humanity was to leave it alone for a time, to give it a chance to mature without our influence."

Tarian's mind reeled with the notion that in a sense he was blood kin to the Eyslken. "I understand your rationale, but to stand by while an evil like Baron Cavillor ravaged the land . . ."

Entoria Taj cast her gaze downward. "I know. When the Baron of Skulls rose to power, we debated long and hard over whether to reverse our decision and join with you humans in casting him down. We Eyslken have no kings or queens as you do. We agree to abide by whatever the majority chooses. We took a vote, and though it was a near thing, it was decided that our self-imposed exile would stand so that humanity would learn to fight its own battles." She looked at Tarian once more and smiled. "Still, some of us managed to find a way to, ah, work around the majority's decision. We increased the number and frequency of the parties sent forth to track down and deal with the Lukashen. And if a few of Baron Cavillor's human warriors happened to get in the way . . . well, it couldn't be helped, could it?"

"I wasn't aware of that." Although now that he thought of it, that explained a few things. There had been several times toward the end of his service in the King's army when he would receive intelligence that a squad of Cavillor's men was nearby, but when he took his own men to check into the report, they found nothing but abandoned campsites.

Entoria laughed. "You weren't supposed to be; that was the whole point."

Tarian grinned. "I must say, you're a great deal more merry than Ashur Dal"

Entoria's eyes sparkled with mischief. "Did you think all Eyslken were alike?"

"Of course not," he hurried to say, but he realized that had been thinking exactly that.

"It is true that we aren't as varied individually as you humans," Entoria said. "We were the Gods' first attempt at creating a race, and they made us somewhat . . . basic. Your people have far more complex hearts and minds than do mine."

Tarian was surprised. While he had resented the Eyslken for seeming to no longer care what happened to the humans they had helped for so long, he had always believed them to be the superior race—stronger, longer-lived, skilled at magic. That was a big part of why he had resented them so much, but now to hear an Eyslka speak of her race as if it were inferior to humans, at least in part, was mind-boggling.

"Given all that, I must admit we can be somewhat emotionally restrained at times. After seeing the Gods' passions get the better of them during the great battle that resulted in the Sundering, we realized the dangers of unchecked emotion. While we do not deny our feelings, we refuse to be ruled by them, either." She grinned. "Still, the Dal tends to be one of the most reserved clans, and mine, the Taj, one of the least."

They continued walking in companionable silence for a bit, and even though Tarian had only met Entoria Taj a little while before, he found he already liked the Eyslka a great deal.

"What of Cynric?" Tarian asked. "It appears as if he's less than welcome in Vallanora."

All traces of Entoria Taj's merriment fell away at mention of the wizard's name. "The one of which you speak has become what we call *nominari eraderix*. It means 'no name.'" She became silent, and Tarian thought that was all she would say on the matter. They came to a fork in the path, and after a moment's hesitation, Entoria steered him to take the right branch. As they walked, they slowly left behind the homes of the Eyslken until all around them was nothing but forest.

"Twenty years ago, the . . . human wizard was faced with a choice. A fleet of Rendish ships drew near Athymar, carrying an invasion force. The wizard could either have destroyed the fleet or allowed it to make landfall and let the King's army deal with the Rendish raiders. He chose the former."

From the coldness of the Eyslka's tone, it was obvious she thought Cyrnic had made the wrong choice. "He saved hundreds of lives, perhaps more, by choosing as he did."

"After seeing the world nearly destroyed by Gods who refused to keep covenant with the people They created, the Eyslken came to value honor above all else. Shapers take certain vows upon completion of their training. Chief among these vows is to never employ their powers in direct battle against foe who cannot defend themselves. When the wizard drowned the Rendish fleet, he broke that vow. Shapers also swear to never pass on the mystic knowledge they have acquired unless and until their teachers grant them permission. Shaping is a dangerous pursuit, both for those who take it up and for those who might be affected by its results. And it can easily be misused. Thus, we must ever guard against the irresponsible spreading of such potentially hazardous knowledge. The human wizard, against his teacher's wishes, chose to instruct others in the ways of Shaping."

Tarian guessed the Eyslka referred to the other mages that Cynric had trained and who had all accompanied King Rufin into battle against the forces of Baron Cavillor.

"You would doubtless argue that he had good cause to do so, and perhaps you are ultimately right. But the fact of the matter remains that the wizard broke two of the most fundamental vows a Shaper must take. And for that, he can never be forgiven."

Tarian thought of how Ashur had called Cynric *filmarr g'tanu*: apprentice-son who regretfully once was.

"Normally, a Shaper who breaks his vows is executed. But Ashur Dal argued for the human wizard. Even though he did not agree with the wizard's choices, he nevertheless understood them, and worked to make the rest of us share his understanding. In the end, we voted to spare the human wizard's life. But on one condition: Ashur Dal would have to shoulder a share of his student's disgrace. He readily agreed, and cut off all his Honor Braids and vowed never to practice Shaping again or to teach it to another. The human wizard became *nominari eraderix*. No Eyslken other than Ashur Dal shall ever utter either his human or Eyslken name again. And while we will not bar him from Vallanora, neither will we acknowledge his presence, either."

"It all seems . . ."

"Harsh? Perhaps so, but it is our way."

Entoria Taj didn't seem all that happy with the way things had worked out for Cynric and Ashur Dal, but Tarian decided not to press the point. Instead, he asked, "Have the Silent Ones ever asked to speak with a human before?"

She shook her head. "They rarely ask to speak with anyone other than the Cultivators." She smiled. "Why do you think they are called *Silent?*" Her smile fell away. "The last summons came well before I was born. That one should come now, and that it should involve a human . . ." She shook her head. "I fear it can only mean that Athymar is in dire need."

"But of all the humans they could speak to, why me?" Tarian asked.

Entoria shrugged. "Why not you? I'm sure the Silent Ones will address your question. But whether you can understand their answer is another matter entirely."

"I don't know what you mean."

"After the Sundering, the Eyslken turned away from worshipping the Gods, either of them, because we had come to believe They cared more about Their own quarrel than the world They had created. We did it at first as a form of protest too, in the hope that our action might catch the Gods' attention and make Them realize what They had done. We thought They might repent and things could return to the way they had been before the Sundering. It was a foolish notion. Instead, the Gods hardened their hearts toward us, and denied us entrance to either Girasa or Damaranth upon our deaths. With nowhere to go, our spirits were left to wander the world. But my ancestors resolved that if the Gods wouldn't accept the Eyslken dead into the afterlife, then they would create their own.

"They searched Athymar for a suitable place, and chose *Selyv Nahele*, for it possessed much *Paytah*. Then they sent forth Shapers to scour the land and gather as many Chaos fragments as they could find. It took several centuries, but eventually they were ready. The Shapers worked for six years with barely a pause for rest to work the greatest enchantment the world had ever seen, and when they were finished, *Aiyana* was born—a place where the spirits of my people might dwell until the end of time."

Tarian tried to imagine the determination of a people driven to create their own afterlife, but it was beyond him.

"But the Orchard of Dreams requires a great deal of tending to, and that's where Cultivators such as myself come in. The Orchard is a plane of existence separate from our own, like Girasa and Damaranth, though on a much more modest scale. But unlike those other planes, the Orchard is not natural, and if left alone its artificial reality would begin to crumble and eventually collapse. We Cultivators constantly work to maintain the Orchard's reality, to keep it from lapsing back into the Chaos it was created from. We have kept the Orchard whole for thousands upon thousands of years, and we shall continue to do so until the world itself grinds to a halt and the sun becomes naught but a burnt-out cinder hanging in a dead sky."

"What is the Orchard like?" Tarian asked. If anything, Entoria Taj's explanation had made him more nervous about speaking with the Silent Ones that he had been before. "What can I expect?"

"There is no way to know."

"Haven't you been inside?"

"Of course, though I am only one of a handful of Cultivators who have been. Most work from outside the Orchard. But I cannot answer your question because of the nature of *Aiyana* itself. It is a place outside of our normal space and time. Indeed, such concepts hold no meaning within the Orchard. It is as if *Aiyana* is a combination of the minds of all the Eyslken who have ever lived or will live, and it is as wild and changeable as thought itself. In a sense, the Orchard is like Arboralis. Your experience of it depends on your individual perception. But in this case, your perceptions are also affected by those of the Silent Ones, and since they are no longer mortal, their minds do not think as ours do, and they do not share the same concerns. You will most likely find the Orchard to be a very . . . confusing place, to put it mildly. But fear not: no matter what occurs or what you *seem* to experience, you shall not be harmed. While the Silent Ones may think differently than we do, they harbor no malice toward the living."

That at least was a relief. "Did I hear you right? Did you say the Orchard is a combination of the thoughts of *all* the spirits of the Eyslken, past *and* future?"

"That I did. Remember, within *Aiyana*, time has no meaning. The instant the Orchard was created, it was full of my people's spirits. All my people. Every Eyslken who lived and died since the Sundering—including those who have yet to live and die—dwells within the Orchard, even the Eyslken who make their homes elsewhere in the Nine Known Lands. We are all there, and we have been since the beginning."

Tarian struggled to grasp this concept. "You mean your spirit is inside the Orchard right now, even though you yet live?"

Entoria nodded. "As is Ashur Dal's, as is that of everyone who lives within Vallanora as this moment."

"Does that mean you've . . . met your own ghost?" Tarian asked.

Entoria smiled. "No. The Silent Ones tend to ignore the living, and since reality is malleable within *Aiyana*, I suppose I might not recognize my spirit even if we did encounter one another. But the Silent Ones make certain such encounters do not occur. If for no other reason than to keep the living from becoming . . . uncomfortable."

"I confess, I find the whole notion of speaking with spirits uncomfortable enough as it is."

The Eyslka laughed. "My people hold a different attitude about death than yours. It comes from having the reassuring presence of our own afterlife so near us, I suppose, and from not having to grow weak and sickly before we die. I know the precise moment when I shall depart this place of existence and take up residence within *Aiyana,* and I no more fear that moment than I fear my own birth. They are both merely passages from one state of being to another."

Tarian wondered just how much time Entoria Taj had yet to live; there was no way to tell simply by looking at her. But he didn't ask.

"I must admit that I took us by a longer route so we would have more time to talk," the Eyslka said. "But now we are here."

Tarian saw nothing to indicate they had reached the Orchard of Dreams. There were no gates, no markers of any sort, not even a path which continued on into the forest.

Entoria Taj must have read the confusion on his face, for she said, "The entrance to *Aiyana* is more mental than physical. You have only to walk past that white ash—" She nodded toward the tree in question. "—and you will be there." She smiled. "As simple as that."

"You're not coming with me?"

"I'm afraid not. The Silent Ones made it clear that they wished to speak with you and you alone. Be warned, though. As I said before, the Orchard can be quite confusing to mortal senses. It is possible to become lost within its twists and turns if one isn't careful. Whatever happens, remember the white ash. It is the only feature of the *Aiyana* which is unchanging and as long as you keep it in sight, you shall be able to find your way out. Do you have any final questions?"

Tarian looked past the ash, but all he could see was more trees. "Do I have to do this?"

The Eyslka laughed. "Only if you wish to discover why the Silent Ones summoned you."

Whatever their reason, the Eyslken spirits had thought it important enough to temporarily release Ashur Dal from his vow never to work magic again so that he might conduct the Long Run and reach Tarian in as short a time as possible—and lose weeks of his life in the process. If Tarian turned back now, Ashur's sacrifice would have been for nothing.

He took a deep breath and walked past the ash tree.

CHAPTER TWENTY-SIX

Tarian stood among a grove of trees which looked no different than any other in Vallanora. Moments passed as he waited for something to happen. A slight dizziness, perhaps, as he crossed over into *Aiyana's* plane, or mayhap a chill sliding down his spine at the approach of Eyslken specters. But he felt nothing. Had the Silent Ones changed their minds about talking with him? Had he done something wrong? He turned around to ask Entoria Taj—

—and found himself standing in a long hall with an earthen floor and thick tree roots criss-crossing overhead in place of ceiling beams. The walls were covered with rough bark upon which clung huge fireflies as long as a man's forearm. The glow from the insects' nether regions illuminated the hall with soft yellow-white light. The hall was filled with row after row of simple benches made from long lengths of split logs with tree-branch legs. At the far end of the room was a large mosaic constructed from small colored stones that depicted a stylized sun. But it was a design Tarian had never seen before: half was radiant yellow, while the other was baleful green.

"It's a symbol of the Gods."

Tarian whirled around to behold an Eyslken male. At first he thought it was Ashur Dal, for there was a definite resemblance, but this Eyslk was somewhat shorter, his features less fine, skin not quite as pale. Perhaps he belonged to a different clan, Tarian thought. The Eyslk wore three Honor Braids, two on the right, one on the left, and the rest of his ivory hair hung loose well past his shoulders. He was garbed in a robe the color of the clearest, bluest spring sky. As Tarian watched, tiny clouds seemed to drift slowly across the garment's fabric.

He took a step back, and the Eyslk chuckled. "*Aiyana* is amazingly responsive to thought, Tarian Ambrus. Indeed, in a very real sense, the Orchard of Dreams is naught *but* pure thought. I'd advise against indulging in idle fancies while you are here."

Tarian had to tear his gaze away from the clouds—they looked so real, as if he could almost reach into the robe and touch them—and he met the Eyslk's eyes. They were the same blue as his robe. "I'll be sure to keep that in mind. You have me at a disadvantage; you know my name, but I don't know yours."

"Names mean little to us. There is no need for such crude designations when we swim in each other's thoughts. But if it makes you more comfortable, you may call me Hastiin."

"Do you have a clan name?"

Hastiin smiled. "We are one clan here."

Tarian nodded toward the mosaic. "You say that is a symbol of the Gods, yet it is not one with which I'm familiar."

"That's because it hasn't been used since the Sundering," Hastiin said. "It's the combined symbol for Rudra and Anghrist, for once my people honored both."

"You worshipped the God of Evil?"

"Before the Sundering, Anghrist wasn't considered as such. My people believe the true wrong is when the Gods seek to manipulate mortals to further their own selfish ends. In this light, both Rudra and Anghrist are what you term 'evil.' And it is the reason why we have Summoned you."

Though Tarian had come to learn what the Silent Ones wanted with him, he found himself reluctant to get straight to the matter. Instead he asked, "What is this place?"

"A memory," Hastiin answered. "The Orchard of Dreams is nothing but memories." He touched his hand to his chest. "In a manner of speaking, that's all we are too. Memories kept alive by the efforts of the Cultivators who work ceaselessly to maintain *Aiyana*. To be more specific, though, this is Godshall, the place where our ancestors came to commune with the Gods, to praise them and seek their counsel."

"You speak as if They would communicate directly with you."

"Before the Sundering, They did. But after . . ." Hastiin trailed off. "This is an exact replica of Godshall. Save for that, of course." He gestured toward a rear corner of the hall where a white ash tree stood. It was the white ash which marked the entrance to the Orchard of Dreams, the tree which Entoria Taj had warned Tarian to keep in sight the entire time he was within *Aiyana*. In his wonder at actually being here, he had forgotten to look for it. He wouldn't forget again.

"Why are we here?"

Hastiin shrugged. "Why not here? We have to start someplace, and this is as good a place as any and better than most. Godshall was destroyed, as was nearly all of the great civilization the Eyslken had built, when the Sundering occurred. Godshall stood in the midst of verdant grasslands which later came to be called Heart's Wound."

Hastiin made no mystic gesture, spoke no magical word of command, but Godshall vanished abruptly, and Tarian found himself standing on a vast barren plain beneath a gray sky, the craggy shapes of the Grimkell Mountains rising off in the distance. Cold, biting wind lashed at his skin, carrying with it the stench of death and decay. All around, for as far as the eye could see in any direction, the plain was strewn with corpses in battle gear. Men and women, Lukashen and Dretchen, lay scattered on the ground, clutching swords, pikes, staves, tulwars, battle axes, poleaxes, crossbows, shields, war hammers, morning-stars, flails, daggers . . . every weapon conceivable. Even a few battle werms lay upon the field, the great serpents' crimson coils drawn tight in death. Most of the humans wore tabards emblazoned with the Sun and Crown over their armor, though some had the Greensun design of Anghrist on theirs. Horses and charred battle wagons lay amid the carnage, and the only signs of life that Tarian saw were the crows and Dretchen which worried at the corpses—the latter even gnawing on the bodies of their own kind.

"This is Heart's Wound today," Hastiin said softly, his voice somehow clearly audible over the howling of the wind. "Keep in mind that this is but a recreation from the combined memories of the Silent Ones—for in *Aiyana* time holds no meaning, and thus we can recall what you would term the future. But for all intents and purposes, you are looking upon Heart's Wound as it appears this very moment."

Tarian barely heard Hastiin's words. Recreation or not, the battlefield looked real, smelled real, felt real. Tarian was no stranger to the wrack and ruin of war, but in his most fevered nightmares he had never imagined slaughter of this magnitude. It was like a scene from the lowest levels of Damaranth itself. King Rufin's army and Baron Cavillor's forces had met in battle, and from the looks of things, there were no victors save the eaters of carrion.

"Were there no survivors?" Tarian asked.

"None, aside from a handful of Dretchen that hung back because they were too timid to face the enemy, and who now find themselves with a grisly banquet laid out before them. But while many of Rufin's and Cavillor's people died at each other's hands, many more perished from a different cause. Come."

Hastiin began walking across the field, picking his way carefully among the dead. Tarian hesitated. He glanced over his shoulder and saw the white ash not more than a dozen yards behind him. The tree served as a reminder that even though he seemed to be standing upon Heart's Wound, in truth he was still within Vallanora, and as real as this might feel, it was in the end but an illusion. Thus reassured, Tarian started after his Eyslken guide.

They walked for a time, and Tarian periodically looked behind him, half expecting to see the ash tree keeping pace, as if it were marching along as well. But it didn't. It remained were he had first seen it, and it quickly began to recede in the distance. Tarian became concerned. Entoria Taj had warned him that he must keep the ash in sight at all times, for if he didn't, he might become lost in the Orchard of Dreams, and while Hastiin might be able to lead him back, or perhaps one of the Cultivators might find him, Tarian didn't want to take the chance that they couldn't.

He was about to say something to Hastiin, when the Eyslk stopped and pointed to a pair of corpses locked in a deadly embrace, gauntleted hands wrapped around one another's throats. Tarian recognized one of them as King Rufin, and he felt a reflexive urge to fall to one knee, even though the man was clearly dead. He wore polished plate armor and winged helm, his great broadsword Gunnolf lying on the ground next to him, the mighty blade broken in twain. Rufin's black beard held more gray than the last time Tarian had seen him, but even in death the King wore a look of determination on his face, as if the cessation of life was merely a minor inconvenience that would not keep him from battle.

Tarian felt a wave of deep sadness upon seeing the body of his monarch. He had attended the man's coronation as well as his wedding, had fought under his father's banner, and then later under Rufin's. Tarian had thought of himself as a King's man, and now here that king lay, dead.

Rufin's opponent could be no other than Baron Cavillor himself. Tarian had never seen the man before, and he was surprised at how nondescript the dread Baron of Skulls looked. Strip away his ebon armor, blood-red cape and the skull-shaped helm with black-painted ram's horns, and the Baron would've have seemed no different than any other man. He appeared to be in his mid-thirties—a bit younger than Tarian had expected, given the man's reputation as a brilliant military strategist—was clean-shaven, and had soft features that seemed more suited to a bard or a priest than a cruel, savage warlord. Cavillor's blacksteel battle-axe, Bloodshedder, supposedly a gift from Anghrist Himself, lay on the ground next to Rufin's sword, its handle broken.

"Look closely," Hastiin said. "You will see that neither man has a mark on him."

Tarian saw that it was true. Their armor displayed no signs of having been breached; no blood was visible. Their faces were not swollen purple, their necks not canted at awkward angles, so they had not strangled each other or broken their opponent's neck.

"How did they die, then?" Tarian asked.

Hastiin gazed upon the bodies of the two warriors for a moment before answering. "When the Gods first mani-

317

fested upon our plane—here, on this very spot on Heart's Wound—and fought one another, They nearly destroyed the world. They withdrew before their creation was laid waste, for if there was no world left to rule, then what good would victory be? They continued striving one against the other over the succeeding millennia, using mortal vessels to carry out their schemes and to do their fighting. Many were the battles fought in the Gods' names, but occasionally over the thousands upon thousands of years since the Sundering, did avatars of the Gods arise, mortal beings imbued with a portion of the Gods' essences. Lodura, the daughter of Rudra, and the Bloodlord Kalle were two such." Hastiin nodded toward Rufin and Cavillor. "When they met upon this ancient battlefield in what the Gods intended to be their Final Battle, they too became avatars. They were filled with the Gods' power and became unimaginably strong.

"But the Gods forgot Themselves in their battlefury and infused their latest avatars with too much of their strength, and Heart's Wound, fragile ever since the Sundering, threatened to tear apart, creating vast quakes throughout the Nine Known Lands, perhaps destroying the world once and for all.

"Again the Gods pulled back rather than wreck Their creation, but this time, They conceived of a plan. Which of Them came up with the idea first, or whether They hit upon the notion at the same time, no mortal can say. If their Godly might was too much for a pair of avatars to wield, perhaps if it were spread among more avatars, then the Gods could continue their conflict without risk of damage to creation.

"And in the instant they thought of Their notion, They agreed to the plan, and thus was it done. Using Rufin and Cavillor as conduits, they discorporated and spread their power throughout even human being in Athymar."

Tarian drew in a sharp intake of air. "The Change," he whispered.

Hastiin nodded. "Every human man, woman and child in the land fell unconscious for several moments as the Godfire entered them. And when they awoke, they found themselves possessed of Godly power. All so the Rudra and Anghrist might be able to continue their ancient feud more directly through the beings they created. The Eyslken, Lukashen and Dretchen were spared the Change. Whether because the Gods used two humans through which to spread their power or for some other unknown reason, I cannot say."

Tarian struggled to understand what the Silent One told him. Inside him was a portion of a God's lifeforce, and it was this power, this Godfire which allowed him to heal. "The energy spheres which rise forth from the newly dead. Some are light, some dark."

"They are the fragments of Godfire leaving one host in search of another. If you were to die this very moment, your Godfire would leave you, and search out the nearest human babe in the process of being born and enter the infant's body. The light-colored spheres are fragments of the power of Rudra, while the dark derive from Anghrist."

Tarian touched his hand to his chest. "Which do I have within me?" And which did his poor son—infused as he was with a shadow wolf—contain within him?

"No one can say. Healing power such as yours would seem to come from Rudra at first, but Anghrist's servants, such as the Lukashen and the demons, also possess supernatural healing abilities. Your Godfire could have come from either deity."

"If the Godfire within me is dark, then does that make

me . . . evil?" He thought of Lowri and of how the Change had warped her mind.

"Not necessarily," Hastiin said. "While Good or Evil may whisper in a man's ear, urging him down one path or another, it is, in end up, up to him to choose where he will walk. Though sometimes the whisper may be more like a shout and harder to ignore."

Tarian thought of how Lowri had said there was a Voice inside her now, inside all of them, and that she listened to hers while he ignored his.

"Why is there such a disparity in the abilities granted by the Change?" Tarian asked. "Why do I have such vast healing powers, while another man might possess only the ability to . . ." He thought of the gatekeeper who had granted Phelan and he access to Pendara. "To alter the color of his eyes?"

"Think of glass shattering. Some pieces are large, while others are medium-sized, and still other fragments are small. While the discorporation of the Gods was a planned act, the disbursement of their power was not. Indeed, the element of chance in this plan was the main attraction for Them. They are too evenly matched in strength for one to triumph over the other directly. But now chance plays a role in their struggle. They do not know which human shall receive what ability, nor what he or she will choose to do with it." Hastiin shook his head in disgust. "The Gods are like children who have invented a new game to play, with humans the gamepieces and Athymar the board."

As a soldier, Tarian could appreciate the cold logic of the Gods' strategy, but as a man, he was appalled that they would use their creation in so thoughtless a fashion. Anghrist he would've expected it from, but Rudra? He was beginning to think that the Eyslken had the right of it when they turned their backs upon the Gods after the Sundering.

"I thank you for the revelations you have given me, Hastiin, but you still haven't answered one question: why have you Summoned me?"

The Silent One gestured at Rufin and Cavillor. "Because of them. Do you see any signs of decay upon their bodies?"

Tarian shook his head.

"That's because there is none. They are perfectly preserved, for these corpses are the Gods' touchstone in this plane. Their power flows through these forms—Rudra's through the King, Anghrist's through the Baron of Skulls—and out into the land. Were anything to happen to either of these bodies, the flow of Godfire would be cut off."

"And the Change would be reversed," Tarian said.

"Perhaps. It is equally possible that someone with enough mystic knowledge could use one or both of these bodies to tap directly into the flow of Godfire and draw the lion's share into him or herself, becoming unimaginably powerful. Such a being could at the very least pose a great threat to the land, and at worst might set off a new disaster akin to the Sundering if they cannot control the mighty forces that rage within them while they stand upon Heart's Wound."

"That still doesn't tell me why I am here, nor why you have forsaken your silence to tell me all of this."

Hastiin's expression grew grim. His sky-blue robe darkened, and the clouds depicted upon its cloth became angry and black, as if a storm approached. "Because you, Tarian Ambrus, are the only man who can prevent the destruction of the world."

Tarian almost laughed. It sounded like something out of the ridiculously melodramatic lays that Phelan so enjoyed reading. "How did you ever come by such a foolish notion?"

Hastiin smiled. "Simple. You told us. Or rather, you will. Remember, all the Eyslken who have ever lived are here within the Orchard of Dreams, and while you cannot perceive the others, I speak for us all."

"All the Eyslken . . . does that mean Ashur Dal is here, and Entoria Taj?"

Hastiin nodded. "I speak for them as well. They might have met with you themselves, if it were not for the Silent Ones' preference for not appearing to their living acquaintances while their previous selves yet exist outside the bounds of *Aiyana*. We feel the Orchard can be confusing enough for the living without such added complications."

Tarian couldn't argue with that! "So you are telling me that I—or rather a future version of myself—told you to Summon me?"

"Not directly. But after we are done here, you will inform your companions, as well as Entoria Taj, of what we discussed. And when it is their time to pass over into *Aiyana*, we shall know what they know. We already do. We knew to Summon Ashur Dal, where to tell him to find you, and to temporarily release him from his vow to no longer gather *Paytah* so he might employ the magic of the Long Run to reach you as soon as possible."

Tarian's head was swimming. Since the Change, he had gotten somewhat used to dealing with strange events, but this was too much at once. He decided he would sort out all the whys and wherefores later. "You say only I can prevent the destruction of the world. How will I do this?"

"You might not. Despite the fact that we remember the future as easily as we do the past, we do not remember only *one* future. Some of us recall how you and your companions journeyed to Heart's Wound and after great hardship, restored the land to its former state. Others recall how you failed, allowing Anghrist to at last triumph over Rudra, ushering in the Dark God's reign over the world. There are memories of other outcomes as well. Presumably, the world itself may perish in one scenario, though since Vallanora and thus *Aiyana* would also be destroyed in that case, there are obviously no Silent Ones who remember such an event. Still, one can speculate, can't one?"

"Yes . . . of course." Tarian felt as if he might be ill. All those possible outcomes, all resting somehow on *his* shoulders . . . "Why me?"

Hastiin shrugged. "Chance. The Gods threw the bones and they spelled out your name. It's as simple as that."

Tarian wanted to deny everything that Hastiin had told him. He wanted to turn around and run back to the white ash, leave the Orchard of Dreams and forget he had ever heard of the place. But he had never been a man to shirk his duty, and he wouldn't do so now.

"What can I do?"

"It is your ability to heal which makes you the key figure in determining Athymar's destiny. There is a race going on, Tarian. A race to reach the bodies of Rufin and Cavillor, the conduits through which the Gods channel their power into the land. Others beside you and your companions have heard the Voices of the Godfire within them, urging them to travel northward to Heart's Wound. If they reach the conduits before you and seize the reins of power, all will be lost."

"Am I . . . to heal them?" Heal Rufin, at any rate. There was no way Tarian would heal the Baron of Skulls if he could avoid it.

Hastiin shook his head. "Though both Rufin and

Cavillor's bodies have been preserved, they are truly dead and thus beyond your power. However, there is another who has hovered in a state between life and death for two thousand years. One who once resurrected will possess the ability to draw Rudra's Godfire into herself and wield it for the preservation of the land."

Hastiin didn't move, but suddenly the grisly battlefield of Heart's Wound was gone, replaced by an underground chamber lit by burning torches. Upon a crude stone dais lay a comely young woman in a gossamer gown, long raven hair spilling over the edge of the rock. Her arms rested at her sides, and her chest was covered by a crimson smear of blood where, Tarian knew, the fell Bloodlord Kalle had once thrust his sword into her heart.

It was the daughter of Rudra Himself.

Lodura.

CHAPTER TWENTY-SEVEN

Entoria Taj was waiting for him when he left *Aiyana*. The Eyslka didn't inquire as to what he had learned within the Orchard, and Tarian didn't feel like volunteering any information. He needed to sort through everything Hastiin had revealed to him before he would be ready to discuss it with anyone else.

They walked in silence back to the heart of the Eyslken settlement, and Entoria led him to his companions, who were watching with more than a little amusement while Saeth debated religion with an Eyslken philosopher. A crowd of the First Folk had also gathered to watch the exchange.

"But the Gods cannot abrogate their responsibility to their Creation," said the philosopher, who was taller than most of his people and almost skeletally thin. "Just as mortal parents have a responsibility to protect and care for any children they bring into the world, so too are the Gods accountable to us."

"But that assumes the Gods can be compared to mortals, and they cannot," Saeth countered. "They are as far above us as we are above ants. We cannot apply our standards of behavior to them, and we cannot hope to ever fully grasp their reasoning."

The philosopher nodded, as if conceding a point. "You say our standards of behavior should not apply. Does this go as well for moral codes? And if so, are you saying that Anghrist is not, as the doctrine of your belief system makes clear, evil? And if He is not, does this mean that Rudra is not good?"

"While we can never hope to know why the Gods do what they do, we can certainly see the results of their actions here in the mortal realm. Since the Sundering, Anghrist has sought to overthrow His brother and establish dominion over all creation. Rudra has opposed Him, in order to allow us the continued freedom to choose our own destinies. Rudra forces His will upon no man or woman, yet He is open to any who wish to follow Him." She smiled. "If Rudra were like Anghrist, He would never have permitted the Eyslken to turn away from Him. At the very least, He would have sought retribution. But He has not. He has allowed your people the freedom to choose, even when it has taken you away from Him. Would Anghrist grant the same freedom to the Lukashen should they seek a similar freedom?"

"You spoke of the Sundering. How do you explain the fact that Rudra, by choosing to engage in battle with Anghrist, was partially responsible for the destruction of much of the world? Would it not have been better if Rudra had declined to fight, thereby preserving Creation?"

"Evil must be opposed," Saeth answered. "If Rudra had not fought, it is true that Eyslken lives might have been spared, and the Nine Known Lands might still be one vast continent. But what would existence be like under Anghrist's rule? Would your ancestors have wished to live under the Dark One's heel? Would you?"

"You speak of Rudra's part in the Sundering as if He chose to go to battle with His brother to protect Creation. How do you know that He did not fight instead because He no longer wished to share the world with His brother, but instead wished to rule it alone?"

Saeth looked at the Eyslk for several moments, brow furrowed in thought. At last, she said, "I have no proof; I have only my faith."

"Then it seems we have come to an impasse," the philosopher said. "I found our discussion most invigorating. You have honored me with your words." The Eyslk bowed from the waist, and then withdrew to the sound of the Fyslken onlookers rubbing their hands together vigorously.

Tarian gave Entoria Taj a questioning look, and she said, "It is our way of indicating appreciation."

Danya stepped over to Saeth and clapped the priestess on the back. "Well fought!"

Saeth looked around, as if she were just now realizing how many people had been watching, and her cheeks turned crimson. "Such discussions are commonplace in the Dawn Cathedral. They are usually entered into during meals. I've witnessed variations on this debate ever since I was a child. Though I must admit to a reluctance to enter into them myself."

"You certainly didn't seem reluctant today!" Cynric said, grinning.

"No, you didn't," Tarian agreed.

His companions turned at the sound of his words. Phelan, Danya, Saeth, Cynric, and Ashur Dal stared at Tarian for a moment, as if they couldn't quite believe he had returned from the Orchard of the Dreams so soon. Then they hurried over to him and began peppering him with questions.

He held up his hands for silence. "Please, I need to think upon what I have learned, if for no other reason than so that I can explain it clearly to you. I promise that I shall reveal everything in due time."

Danya frowned. "And just how *due* are we talking?"

He smiled. "After dinner should be due enough, I think."

"Speaking of which," Entoria Taj said, "we knew Ashur Dal was going to bring at least one guest back with him, although we weren't certain exactly when they would arrive. Nevertheless, we have made preparations for a welcoming feast, and now that you're all here, it shall be held tonight. Until then, we have quarters set aside where you can rest."

"And take a bath too, I hope," Danya said.

Entoria smiled. "Of course."

"Good, because I smell worse than a Pendaran canal at low tide."

They laughed and Entoria Taj led them to their quarters. Along the way, Tarian couldn't stop thinking about what Hastiin had told him. *There is a race on, Tarian. A race to reach the bodies of Rufin and Cavillor . . . . Others have heard the Voices of the Godfire within them . . . . If they reach the conduits before you and seize the reins of power, all will be lost.*

One thought rose above the rest: What others did Hastiin speak of?

He was finished.

Lowri looked upon the naked man lying curled on his side on the floor of the abandoned mill. Unlike Tarian's, his skin bore no scars, displayed no sign of the hardships of a soldier's life. But then, this wasn't Tarian, was it? It was someone brand new, almost like a babe, in a way.

Narrow shafts of afternoon sunlight filtered through holes in the roof's thatch, and outside, birds sang joyfully in the trees, almost as if to herald the new birth that was occurring in their midst.

If the annoying creatures had any notion precisely what was being born in here, they wouldn't sing quite so gaily,

Lowri thought. No, not so gaily at all.

His eyes opened for the first time. They were solid black—no pupil, no iris. Just moist darkness. He looked at Lowri, who crouched several feet away, her wings folded behind her. He displayed no reaction to her presence. He slowly sat up, then rose to his feet, and though it was the first time he had used his body, he moved with ease and grace.

Lowri examined the being standing in the dim light of the mill. Aside from the eyes and the lack of scars, he could have been Tarian's twin. *Could've been?* she thought. No, *was.*

"I am Lowri," she said.

His eyes narrowed slightly. "I remember you."

"You saw me when you were but a Ghast, when I brought you the hand from which your new body blossomed."

He shook his head. "I have other memories. Fragmented, indistinct, but they are there. I see a human woman, blonde, holding a toddler boy in her arms. She is laughing. It's you, isn't it? The way you were . . . before."

This was unexpected. "You possess the memories of the man from whose flesh you sprang."

"Some of them, yes." He fell into a fighting stance, held his arm out as if he gripped a sword. He made a couple passes through the air with his imaginary weapon. "My memories of battle are much clearer, however. I recall steel." His mouth twisted into a cruel smile. "And blood. I remember the blood *very* well."

"Tarian was engaged in battle with a demon when he lost the hand from which you grew. Perhaps that it why your memories of battle are stronger."

The man shrugged. "Perhaps. It doesn't matter. I am

who I am, and I remember what I remember." He frowned. "I need a name, don't I? I suppose I could call myself Tarian Ambrus, but I don't feel as if I am he. Besides, I would prefer a name of my own."

"As I watched you grow, I gave much thought to a name," Lowri said. "When I was human, I had a small garden behind the cabin where I lived. Sometimes, I would remove a twig or shoot from one plant in order to graft it onto another. Such a graft is called a *scion*. It is a word which also means *descendant*, with implications of *he who shall one day rule*."

The being with a human body and the soul of a Ghast considered for a moment. Then he smiled. "I like it. Scion, it is. I have a name; now I need a purpose."

Lowri grinned, displaying her sharp teeth. "Oh, you have a purpose, Scion. Believe me." Then she laughed. Scion regarded her quizzically for a moment before finally joining her.

The feast was held in a glade not far from Arboralis beginning at dusk. Tarian half expected the glade to be lit by huge fireflies, as in his vision of Godshall, but instead wooden poles were erected around the perimeter of the glade, upon which were set glass globes filled with some manner of luminous lichen. The fungus bathed the glade in a soft blue-green light that Tarian thought somewhat eerie at first, but after a time he grew used to it. Normal fireflies filled the surrounding trees, though for some reason they ventured not into the glade itself, and their cheerful blinking added greatly to the atmosphere. The animals that were normally so abundant throughout Vallanora also kept to the treeline, though a few who were obviously beloved pets accompanied their Eyslken companions into the glade.

The humans sat cross-legged on the grass with Ashur Dal, Entoria Taj and a half dozen Eyslken dignitaries whose names Tarian couldn't keep straight. But they were all Preceptors, the closest thing to leaders that the Eyslken seemed to have. As Cynric had explained just before the feast began, the First Folk had refused to follow a single leader ever since the Sundering. They believed no one, not even the Gods, could avoid being corrupted by the power inherent in such authority. Instead, although they looked to their Preceptors for guidance, each individual Eyslken could vote on decisions affecting their entire group.

While Tarian thought it a good notion in theory, it didn't seem very practical. If everyone could vote, and the votes of the youngest and most inexperienced weighed just as heavily as those of the more seasoned Preceptors, then decisions would be made based not on the wisdom of elders, but rather on which side could carry the most numbers when it came time to cast votes.

In a sense, though, wasn't that how things had worked in their party since leaving Pendara? Any number of them could have been leader: Ashur Dal, Cynric, Tarian. Danya too, most likely, though as a Watcher she was more used to working alone than with a group. Yet they functioned as individuals who listened to and respected one another. It wasn't an arrangement any of them had planned; it had just worked out that way. And so far it had worked out well enough. Still, Tarian thought, six people on a journey were quite different than an entire nation of Eyslken. Their system seemed to work for the First Folk, so who was he to question it?

They were served an astounding variety of fruits, vegetables, nuts and cheeses in bowls made of bread. No meat, though, for as Tarian learned, Eyslken had been strict vegetarians since the Sundering. They refused to devour the flesh of another living creature, even if it meant starvation. Tarian was surprised at the sheer amount of food available. He was no farmer, but he was certain that it was far too early in the season for so many different types of produce.

He asked Ashur Dal about the amazing bounty of his people, and the Eyslk explained that it was due to the presence of Arboralis within Vallanora. "Here, there is no end to the growing season, and it is always harvest time."

Along with food, the Eyslken served several types of drink, from a stout ale called woodnut to a light fruity wine called *yahto*. Tarian's favorite, though, was a fiery concoction named *tohopka*, which he learned meant *wild beast* in the Eyslken tongue. Wild was right; he was only able to sip it gingerly, for it burned all the way down his gullet. But what a pleasant burn it was!

There were some Eyslken children in attendance too, though less than Tarian had expected given the sheer number of adults they'd seen since entering Vallanora. When asked, Entoria Taj said the First Folk weren't as prolific as humans, and that the population of Vallanora had remained fairly steady over the thousands upon thousands of years since the Sundering.

Tarian kept an eye on Cynric as they ate. The rest of their party was clearly enjoying themselves—especially Phelan, who couldn't stop grinning at finding himself in a place not even the overly melodramatic poets he liked to read could have imagined. But while Cynric kept a smile firmly fixed to his face, the wizard couldn't mask the sadness in his eyes, for he was *hok'ee*: abandoned, shunned by his adopted people. Not a single Eyslken acknowledged his presence, not a man, woman or child—not even those members of the Leyati clan who were serving food and drink. No sustenance of any sort was offered to Cynric, which Tarian supposed didn't matter in a purely practical sense since the wizard no longer subsisted on food and drink. But Tarian could tell how much it hurt Cynric to be surrounded by such merriment and not truly be a part of it.

There was entertainment, too. Eyslken musicians played lively tunes on lute, fiddle, flute, tiompan, bells and drum while a group of dancers performed an intricate routine, their lithe, graceful bodies seeming at times to flow like water or mist. Ballads were then sung, some in Eyslken, some translated into Parthalan, the common tongue of Athymar. Some were songs tinged with sorrow, while others were comical tunes displaying a ribaldry that Tarian would never have expected from the First Folk.

Tarian tried his best to enjoy himself, but he couldn't stop thinking about what he had learned in the Orchard of Dreams. At last, the feast drew to a close, and the Eyslken began to depart for their homes.

"This is as good a place for you to talk as any," Entoria Taj said. She rose to her feet. "You may remain here as long as you like; Ashur Dal can show you the way back to your quarters when you are done."

"Please stay," Tarian bid the Eyslka. "As a Cultivator, perhaps you shall be able to shed some light on what I experienced within *Aiyana*."

Entoria nodded and sat once more. Tarian took a deep breath, then began his tale.

When he was finished, Saeth was the first to speak. "This is outrageous! Rudra would never be party to such a fell scheme!"

Cynric stroked his beard thoughtfully. "You must admit, my dear Priestess, it would explain a great deal."

Phelan touched his hand to his chest. "You mean I have part of a God inside me?"

Tarian nodded. "That's what Hastiin said."

Ashur Dal, who had up to that point been lost in thoughtful silence, looked at Tarian with an intense expression. "Who?"

"Didn't I mention it before? Hastiin was the name of the Silent One who served as my guide in the Orchard. Does the name mean anything to you?"

Ashur Dal looked at Cynric. Something passed between the two of them then, though just what, Tarian couldn't have said. The two looked to Entoria Taj, who shrugged.

"It is not an uncommon name among my people," she said.

"Can you describe the Silent One to me?" Ashur Dal asked. When Tarian was finished, he said, "That is the same spirit who spoke with me. I wonder why he did not give me his name."

Cynric smiled. "Perhaps because you did not ask."

Ashur Dal didn't smile back, though he did nod. "Perhaps."

"What does it matter what the Silent One called himself?" Danya said, Jessex sitting on her knee. "Didn't you listen to Tarian's story? The King is dead, the battle at Heart's Wound lost!"

"Believe me, Madame Watcher, I listened," Cynric said. "The Shapers I trained, the wizards who accompanied the King into battle, are likely all dead as well."

"As are those members of the priesthood who rode with the King," Saeth said softly.

"But the battle itself was not lost," Ashur Dal said. "For many of those who lie dead at Heart's Wound did not perish by sword, but rather at the hands of the Gods. When They chose to spread Their essence throughout the land, the resultant energy release must have been too much to bear for those mortals in proximity to the Gods' avatars, Rufin and Cavillor."

Cynric nodded. "The same thing can happen during a Shaping gone awry, though on a much smaller scale, of course. The energy backlash can be deadly both to the spellcaster and to those unfortunate enough to be near him."

"I find myself dumbfounded by the audacity of the Gods," Ashur Dal said. "Unable to bring Their full strength to bear in the mortal realm without risking the destruction of Creation, They have instead chosen to scatter Their power among you humans, employing you all as avatars to continue their ceaseless quarrel."

"Even if it's true," Saeth said, "and I am not granting that it is, the Gods have still given us a choice. Indeed, the element of chance is a main factor in Their plan, according to the Silent One. We can listen to the Godfire within us or ignore it, as we will."

"I'm sure that will be a comfort to those malformed by the Change," Cynric said bitterly. "Think of the King's daughter, with her transparent skin or—"

"My mother," Phelan put in.

They were all silent for several moments after that. At last, Tarian spoke.

"The question before us now, is what do we do about it? If the Silent One is right, then either Rufin or Cavillor can be used to tap into the Gods' power, and even now there are those traveling to Heart's Wound who intend to do just that. If they succeed, the Nine Known Lands might be laid to ruin."

"*If* they succeed," Saeth pointed out. "The Silent One said the Eyslken spirits 'remembered' several different outcomes."

Entoria Taj spoke for the first time since Tarian had begun his tale. "The Silent One spoke true. What we term the future is not fixed, and any of the outcomes the Silent One mentioned are possible. Which will prove to be the true future is entirely up to us and the choices we make."

"Ah, but which choices are the correct ones?" Cynric said. "Isn't that always the crux of the matter?"

"It doesn't seem that complicated to me," Phelan said. "We go to Heart's Wound, and we stop whoever it is that wants to claim the Gods' power for themselves."

Danya gave the lad a playful punch on the arm. "That's the spirit, Phelan!"

Phelan grinned and rubbed his arm as if he were silently vowing never to wash it again.

"That's far easier said than done, my boy," Cynric said. "According to what the Silent One told your father, the only way we can do that is to resurrect Lodura herself. And unless the Silent One was thoughtful enough to give him a map . . ."

Tarian shook his head. "Hastiin gave me no indication of where Lodura rests."

Cynric spread his hands. "Then we have no idea where to begin looking."

"I can't believe you're even willing to consider such blasphemy!" Saeth said.

"Why not?" Danya challenged. "Do not the holy texts speak of Lodura returning on the day when Athymar is in its greatest need? Seems to me that day has come. And perhaps Tarian is to be the instrument Rudra has chosen to accomplish his daughter's rebirth."

"I suppose it's possible . . ." Saeth grew thoughtful, and the others were silent for a bit to give her a chance to think. "The Bloodlord Kalle slew Lodura by plunging his unholy sword Torment into her heart. Lodura had already been greatly weakened in battle with Kalle, and was unable to marshal her strength to resist Torment's fell power."

"And so she died," Cynric said. "But I don't see how Tarian—even if we could locate Lodura's body—can help. His ability to heal, while extremely potent, doesn't extend to overcoming death itself. Especially when the subject in question has been dead for two thousand years."

Saeth said, "There are some indications in various texts that at the moment of her wounding, Lodura—while unable to heal the injury caused by Torment—used her powers to remove herself from the flow of time, thus staving off her death and preserving her body."

"So if we found her today," Danya said, "she would be as she was two thousand years ago, frozen in the process of dying from a sword wound."

Saeth nodded. "And if such were the case, then Tarian might well be able to heal her. If his power could overcome that of the Bloodlord's dread blade Torment."

"What happened to the Bloodlord?" Phelan asked.

"He kept Lodura's body as a grisly trophy for a time," Saeth said, her eyes flashing in anger at the thought. "Eventually, Kalle was defeated by an alliance between the Church, the King's Army, the Dragon Mages, and the Eyslken." She nodded to Ashur Dal and Entoria Taj, who both nodded back. "What happened to Lodura after that isn't clear, although I have read hints that the Church, wishing to prevent further desecration of her body, saw that she was laid to rest in a remote location where none might ever find her. And for two thousand years, no one has."

"Then how are we supposed to?" Phelan asked.

"I could consult my books and scrolls at Garanhon," Cynric said. "It's possible that a clue to Lodura's resting place might be contained somewhere within those tomes of lore."

"Ancient Church records are housed within the archives of the Parhelion," Saeth said. "One of the scholars there might be able to help us."

Tarian noted how Saeth said *us*, as if there were no question she would continue with the party, even though her stated quest—to learn the true nature of the Change—had been fulfilled.

"Then it sounds as if we are bound for Garanhon," Danya said.

Tarian looked at the others, and together they nodded. Even Ashur Dal.

"I have come this far with you, I might as well continue," the Eyslk said. "Perhaps I shall be of some help." He smiled at Phelan. "And the lad and I have not finished our lessons in swordcraft yet."

Phelan grinned.

Entoria Taj stood. "I shall go speak with the other Preceptors and inform them of what the Silent Ones have told you, Tarian. There are those among the Eyslken who are . . . uncomfortable with our decision to withdraw from the life of the land. It is possible that given the dire circumstances, they will choose to aid in your quest."

"And I shall go as well, to speak for our cause," Ashur Dal said. The two Eyslken departed, leaving the humans alone in the glade, awash in the blue-green glow of luminous lichen.

"I suggest we retire to our quarters and get a good night's sleep," Cynric said. "Whatever the Preceptors decide, it appears that the rest of us will embark for Garanhon on the morrow."

And with that the party rose and left the glade behind, their thoughts on the journey they would begin tomorrow—a journey to resurrect the daughter of a God.

About the Author

Tim Waggoner's most recent novels include *Thieves of Blood*, *Pandora Drive*, and *Like Death*. He's published close to eighty short stories, some of them collected in *All Too Surreal*. His articles on writing have appeared in *Writer's Digest*, *Writers' Journal*, and other publications. He teaches creative writing at Sinclair Community College in Dayton, Ohio. Visit him on the web at www.timwaggoner.com.